FINALLY FRANELLA

Cheryle Coapstick

Series:
MY MAMA'S MAMA

———————————————

Alaska's Firy

About Miss Ruth

Alaska's Mama

They Settled in Sitka

Heaven's Ray

Finally, Franella is for
Everyone who thinks
They don't fit!

First paperback edition July 2025

Paperback: ISBN 979-8-9988472-0-2
eBook: ISBN 979-8-9988472-1-9

Cover model, Emily Coapstick

Cover, interior design and all things artistic and technical by Andy Towler
aplusscreative.com

Published by Biorka Books
chercoaps@gmail.com

A Message to Readers

So much happens before you can read one of my books, whether you pick up a physical copy or click on a digital version. My team of faithful helpers and encouragers is so necessary in bringing you the stories that fill my mind and my heart. They know who they are, and I have thanked them often, both publicly and privately.

Your time, dear reader, is valuable, but limited, and I want to thank each one of you who has chosen to spend time with the characters and stories I love so much. You have given me a gift that is beyond measure.

I pray that my books will offer more than mere entertainment. I ask God to reveal whatever message He has for you in these stories. I am honored to write for Him, and for you.

Thank you for being a part of MY Mama's Mama.

PROLOGUE

Somerview Women's College Graduation
Oxford, England, 1950

The ornate, circular assembly room of the Sheldonian Theatre in the middle of Oxford's medieval city was packed. Students and their proud families squeezed close together on the uncomfortable, tiered wooden benches. The overcast sky outside the 17th-century building filtered the light through its ornate windows. The diffused light illuminated the cupola's superbly painted ceiling, aptly titled *Truth Descending on the Arts and Sciences.*

The culmination of many years of hard work and honest endeavor by these proud young men and a few women had been honored and rewarded. These prestigious students had matriculated some years ago and today received their awards and diplomas. Those who achieved the highest academic levels were recommended by their various proctors and tutors and had their names sent to the university's sole selection committee, where a few were chosen to speak. One by one, they rose, made their way to the speaker's box, introduced themselves, and read their prepared remarks.

Franella Feddersen, uncomfortable in her black robe with its wide bell-shaped sleeves, felt a trickle of sweat between her shoulder blades. As each honoree rose to speak, Franella became more agitated. Now, it was her turn. The Oxford University Doctor of Philosophy robe with its blue lining and red border rustled as she stood. Because Franella had reached the pinnacle of achievement, her gown was marked by broad velvet panels down the front and three chevrons on the sleeves. The tassel hanging from her academic mortarboard swayed with every bob of her head.

The last one to rise, Franella approached the speaker's box with leaden feet and a heavy heart. She felt the pain of the past, which overshadowed her present accomplishments—doctorates in literature and philosophy.

She looked around the horseshoe-shaped room but didn't see him. He said he'd be here, that they both would. Behind her, the row of Oxford's deans, proctors, and other dignitaries, in their solemn attire and frowning faces, sat stiff and unapproving. She was an American and a woman, and even though several of her papers had been published in prestigious journals, those who had voted against her showed their disdain by refusing to look her way.

She tapped the microphone, breathed deeply, and cleared her throat. She licked her dry lips and opened her mouth. No words came. She tried again. The audience, hushed and expectant, fed her anxiety. As she remained silent, their expressions, which had been merely curious, reflected her agitation and, as the minutes passed, became judgmental. It was the Windy City all over again. Franella felt the familiar shaking start in her fingertips. She fisted her hands on the podium, hoping her fellow students and many professors would not sense her fear. She drew in several gulps of air.

Out of the corner of her eye, she saw Dean Blythe-Smith. He whispered for her to begin through the gap in his front teeth. She gave him a slight shake of her head. Frantically, he motioned for her to continue. Franella stared at his long, thin fingers, flapping like a gull's wing. She bit the inside of her cheek until she tasted the metallic tinge of blood. She pictured herself screaming and tearing her speech into minute pieces and flinging it at the audience. She saw herself as a child, unable to sit still, study, or even read. What was that rambunctious child in tattered overalls doing here wearing this illustrious gown and mortarboard? She belonged in the wilderness of Alaska, not among the spires of Oxford.

She crumpled the pages of her speech and let them fall to the floor. Heart pounding, shoulders squared, and eyes staring straight ahead as if she were wearing blinders, Franella Feddersen marched out of the centuries-old building. She wove her way through the audience, unmindful of their stares and whispered comments. Once outside, she tore off the mortarboard and tossed it aside, then leaned against the entrance door, doubled over, and pressed her hands on her stomach, ignoring the misty drizzle. *Breathe, I just need to breathe.*

The two men seated center right in the twenty-second row had held their breaths as they willed her to continue, then looked at each other in horror when she left.

"I thought she could do it," the middle-aged man in the tweed jacket said.

"I know Tollers; I did too. The question is, what do we do now?"

"You're the better speaker. Take over for her. I'll find her and take her to the Baby. We'll meet you there."

"Shouldn't we let Blythe-Smith handle it?"

"I don't think Old Mud and Whiskers is up to it. He looks like one of your skinny marsh-wiggles crawling to the speaker's box, ashen face and bulging eyes. Poor man." Tollers gave his companion a slight shove. "Go on, Jack. Redeem the situation."

Jack laughed, "You're right. He's very marsh-wiggleish, all elbows and knees. I wonder if I was thinking of him when I created that character. But let's say no more. I haven't sent the manuscript to the publisher yet."

"Go on, put the poor man out of his misery."

Dean Blythe-Smith leaned into the microphone as he looked toward Franella's escape route. "Americans!" his voice shook as he searched for the words, "I'm sure we're all grateful for what they did during the war, but where's their couth, their civility?" His deep sigh whistled through the gap in his front teeth. "Can we expect anything different?" There were one or two titters from the audience and a few smiles. The rest did not respond.

He shook his handkerchief and wiped the sweat from his brow. His smile was a mix of confusion and gratitude as he watched the portly professor come forward.

Outside of the ornate building designed by Christopher Wren, the English air was chilly, the clouds low and gray, reminding Franella Feddersen of home. She should never have left Port Alexander; she knew that now. *Why did I think I could be somebody?* The old feelings of emptiness returned, and she saw the barrenness of her soul. Awash in a vacant sea, the images attacked. She hit her fists on the side of her head, but still, they taunted her. A few moments later, she felt someone pull her arms down.

"Sorry, I haven't done that in years," she mumbled.

He didn't answer but put his arm around her shoulder. She leaned against him and laid her head on his chest. "Who did I think I was?"

"Why, my dear, you are your own wonderful self."

"Herring Pete said it was the only way to solve the problem, but he just wanted to get rid of me."

He patted her shoulder and led her a few blocks to the taxi stand. She stumbled and would have fallen had he not kept his arm around her. He hailed a taxi and settled both of them in the back seat. "Who is Herring Pete?" He pulled a large white handkerchief from his vest pocket and mopped her face. She took it, blew her nose, and attempted to hand it back to him.

"I dismantled his still."

"What?"

Franella sniffed, hiccupped, and sniffed again. "He's a horrible, no-good man. Just terrible and rotten. He added to my misery."

"You'll tell me and Uncle Jack all about it, and we'll find a solution."

Franella turned wide eyes to him and said, "I could never call him—Uncle!"

He chuckled, held his pipe out, "May I?" At her nod, he lit it and chuckled again. "We will keep the uncle part between ourselves, but I know he has a deep affection for you."

"I'm nothing, nobody."

"Come, my dear, I will not hear such talk from you."

As the audience saw the professor rise and approach Dean Blythe-Smith, curious but tentative applause spread throughout the auditorium. Blythe-Smith breathed a sigh of relief, shoved his face into the microphone, and said, "This man needs no introduction." He hurried away, mumbling about classless, uncouth, undependable Americans.

Jack reached for the crumpled paper Franella had dropped. He smoothed and folded it, then put it in his vest pocket. "This is a graduation ceremony you won't soon forget, but not for the reason you think." Some in the audience laughed hesitantly, unsure of his meaning. "I am going to tell you a story, one that is true. It begins on an island on the other side of the globe. A cold world of the north, unfamiliar and strange to us, I'm sure."

ONE

Twelve years earlier, 1938
Southeast Alaska

Ade Bunderson, an experienced fisherman out of Sitka, Alaska, didn't like the flat calm. The day was exceptionally warm, deceptively so. The sky had turned a pale sepia, and the hair on Ade's arms stood on end. He looked to the sea's horizon, and an icy dread ran from his shoulder blades to the back of his neck. He not only sensed danger in the air, he smelled it.

A short time later, a solid wall of rain scudded toward him, and a sharp gust heeled the boat over. He spun the wheel and righted the vessel. The wind continued to pick up, and he struggled to keep the boat level and the compass steady. The storm tried to pull the windward stabilizer free whenever the boat was laid over. Visibility dropped as the strong gusts picked up massive amounts of water, and the clouds let loose.

Ade grabbed his marine radiophone and called Sitka's Coast Guard station. "The winds are erratic and unpredictable, blasting out of the northwest around 48 knots. I suspect a polar low."

"Fishermen ten miles north of you have reported winds as high as 70 knots. It's a big one."

"There's no way I can outrun it."

"Do you require assistance?"

"I'm about seven nautical miles south of Port Alexander. I think

I can plow through the chaos. Let Ollie know, will you, Chet?"

"Sure, Ade. Report when you reach Alexander."

"Will do. Out."

Ade reduced his speed until he had just enough power to maintain headway. His navigation lights didn't help with visibility as he maneuvered through the black churning water and darkened sky. The rain attacked in solid sheets, and the wind blew it sideways. Obsidian clouds swirled above and sometimes dipped into the vicious waves. He turned the Ollie B. into the wind at a 45-degree angle to reduce stress on his beloved vessel. He clenched his jaw, and the muscles in his arms knotted as he held the wheel. He planted his feet, but it took everything he had to stand steady and keep the boat on her compass course. He licked the salty moisture from his upper lip. Whether it was from the sea or a cold sweat, he didn't know. What he would give for a strong cup of coffee with some of Mike's secret ingredient. That wasn't going to happen anytime soon.

Ade set his radiophone to frequency 2638, which was the one most used for ship-to-ship communication in Southeast Alaska. He heard conversations between fishermen north of him who were enmeshed in the tempest. Everyone was trying to reach the nearest sheltered cove or inlet. Chances were, some weren't going to make it. There was nothing Ade could do for those who were fighting for their lives in this freak storm, just as they could not help him. He hated that it was every man for himself.

With one part of his mind, he concentrated on the volume of water washing over the bow. With another, he reviewed the many storms he had faced since coming to Alaska a decade and a half ago. None seemed as treacherous as today's tempest.

That wise old Tlingit from Sitka, Petroff Bravebird, had taken a teenage Ade on as a deckhand and taught him everything there was to know about these Alaskan waters. Together, they had come through many squalls and storms. The Alaska Native had an uncanny way of feeling the weather before he saw signs in the sky or sea. He shared that knowledge, and Ade absorbed it, although he could not match Bravebird in experience or innate wisdom. After a truly harrowing experience, Petrov Bravebird told him a good seaman weathers the storm he cannot avoid and avoids the storm he cannot weather. Ade was in the midst of this storm, and it remained to be seen if he would weather it.

His muscles ached and occasionally spasmed; his body was cold and spent. Ade ignored the pain and frozen exhaustion as he tried to keep the boat angled into the waves. He wondered if his wife, Ollyanna, was praying for him after hearing from Chet. Of course she was! He thought perhaps he should join her in this divine endeavor, but it wouldn't be right to ask the Almighty for help after ignoring Him for so many years. He left that sort of thing to her. She was much better at it.

A tall mass of water rose out of the tempest like a giant sea dragon looming and ready to strike. The green water was translucent but solid, eclipsing Ade and his small fishing trawler. He hung onto the wheel, and all thought was chased from his mind. The water sluiced his face and ripped his sou'wester from his head, leaving only his wool watchcap. Ade loved that oilskin hat with its gutter-front brim and longer back to protect his neck. Water now poured down his neck. He locked his knees and braced himself once more as wall after wall of water tried to submerge his boat. Ade's heart pounded as the swells rolled the vessel from side to side. His muscles felt like they were on fire, and he was bone-tired from wrenching the wheel—first one way, then the other. Wave after wave surged toward him until time and space had no meaning. There was only the wind and the water and his hands, frozen and locked on the wheel.

Energy sapped, Ade was relieved several hours later when the wind abated slightly and the temperature rose a few degrees. The Ollie B. steadied herself and kept on top of the waves. He increased speed and pushed forward, although the angry seas still impeded his progress.

He knew every inlet, bay, and cove on the perimeter of Baranof Island. Most were isolated and uninhabited. He had bypassed many that might have given him shelter. Because it was just a few more miles to Port Alexander, where Ade knew he could get a hot meal and an even hotter shower. Against his better judgment, he had let that thought propel him forward, and he hoped he wasn't a fool.

Once safely inside Alexander's harbor, the water was still vicious, but the waves did not attack. Although the Port Alexander harbor was considered a protected waterway, the seas were still choppy. The churning, white-topped waves moved in every direction, forcing Ade to continue to pay attention.

As he approached the inner harbor, the restless waves slowly let go of their angry energy. How long had Ade battled the sea? It seemed like days instead of hours. However, it was finally safe to let go of the wheel for a short moment. He pulled a Prince Albert tobacco tin from the large pocket of his oilskin slicker. The tin housed cigarettes he had previously rolled, as well as his matches. He pulled off his gloves and hunched over, trying to protect the flame as he struck match after match. No luck. He wrenched the soggy cigarette from his mouth and threw it overboard, then pulled another from the tin and tried again. Ade swore and threw the damp matches and cigarette case into the sea. He vowed he'd buy a pipe as soon as he was back in Sitka. Many fishermen preferred it because they could hold the pipe's bowl to warm their hands and clamp it between their teeth in stormy weather. Even if the pipe went out, they could suck on the spent tobacco. His fishermen friends said it gave them comfort.

Ade shivered and let his frozen body slump against the wheel. Why hadn't he bought a boat with a covered pilothouse? He knew why. Money. If the Depression ever ended and he caught enough fish, his next boat would have one.

Black clouds continued to blanket the sky, shutting out the weak sun's waning light and pressing down on the sea. Exhausted and craving nicotine, Ade maneuvered closer to the pier. Half-frozen rain plummeted in sheets as the boat bumped the dock. Between the wind, waves, and continued low visibility, it took several attempts to secure the mooring. As Ade jumped to the dock, mooring rope in hand, a gust of wind pulled off his watch cap and dropped it in the harbor. Pellets of sleet plastered his hair to his head, and icy water dripped into his ears. He shivered and cursed as he added an extra mooring line to secure the Ollie B.—storms this angry were supposed to restrict themselves to the winter months. After shaking his fist at the sky and swearing some more, Ade sighed and reminded himself this was Alaska, always unpredictable and often fierce.

He hoped all those other fishermen—men he had known for years had found a safe harbor from this monster storm. Just like him, they knew the risks of living in the Territory and choosing this occupation. Decades ago, the gold of the Klondike had seized the passion of thousands. Today, these rugged men of the North lusted after King Salmon.

Recently, the salmon stock had declined from overfishing, and the processing plant in Port Alexander, like so many others in Southeast Alaska, was no longer economically viable. Fish prices had dropped, and fuel prices increased. The Depression had definitely come to Alaska. Many seasonal fishermen had quit and returned to their homes in Washington state. Most of Port Alexander's buildings were boarded and abandoned.

Around seventy or so intrepid fishermen and their families remained in the ghosted town, determined to eke out a living. These fearless or perhaps foolish people were the permanent residents of this settlement at the tip of Baranof Island.

After double-checking the boat's moor lines, Ade returned to the Ollie B. and shucked off his oilskins. The wool jacket and fisherman's knit sweater he wore were damp and soggy, and so were his wool trousers. Water had seeped into his boots. He changed his wet socks and pulled on another pair of boots. He grabbed a change of clothes, stuffed them into his waterproof knapsack, and made his way to Torvald's Tavern and Bathhouse. He imagined hot water pouring over his half-frozen body and steam seeping into his lungs. He planned on using all of Torvald's hot water. At twenty-five cents a shower, he deserved it. His stomach rumbled, reminding him of how hungry he was.

He raised his eyes to the tiny town. Windows were shuttered, and no one was about. There were no lights on in Torvald's unpainted building. *If Torvald has left town since I was last here, I'll hunt him down and take off his head.* Ade rattled the doorknob.

Locked. More for protection from the wind than fear of intruders, he thought. He dropped the knapsack, cupped his hands around his eyes, and leaned on the glass. In the dimness, he saw a sign over the bar advertising a church supper. The Lutheran Ladies Missionary Society was putting on a pancake social complete with black bear bacon, reindeer sausage, pancakes, lingonberry syrup, coffee, and, of course, the ubiquitous lutefisk. All you can eat for twenty-five cents. *Darn that Torvald, he must be at the church.* Ade's stomach rumbled, and his mouth watered. Sighing, he grabbed the knapsack and headed down the muddy road. His soggy wool clothing scratched against his skin, and he cursed Torvald again. The wind pushed against him, and he bent over like an old man unable to walk without a cane.

TWO

———

Like most small towns in Southeast Alaska, Port Alexander's social life revolved around the bar and the church. People who filled the bars on Saturday night sat in the pews on Sunday morning. Ade favored the former and avoided the latter, much to his wife's dismay. He did enjoy all the church potlucks and shared dinners.

If Torvald wasn't at the church, it would be food first, even though the soggy clothes made him as uncomfortable as a hermit crab in an ill-fitting new home. His belly rumbled, and told him food would be welcome.

He turned the corner, and light cannonballed out of Lutheran windows. Ade was surprised it hadn't blown out the glass. He kept his eyes on the brightness and plodded on while he cursed the foul weather.

Herring Pete took his money and cleared a place for him in the crowded church hall. Ade surveyed the room while removing his wet jacket. His nose twitched, assaulted by the damp wool and fishy odor from wet coats hanging on the backs of the chairs. After-dinner cigarette and pipe smoke wafted toward the ceiling and clouded the room like early morning fog. It almost overpowered the smell of the sizzling bacon and hot coffee.

Practically everyone in Port Alexander was here. Ade returned greetings from several of the townspeople with a wave and a nod.

"A little storm can't keep us from helping the heathen, right Bunderson?"

Ade looked at Herring Pete's rheumy eyes, shaggy hair, mangy beard, and rotted teeth. The old man could pass for a heathen any day. Ade gave a slight nod, looked around the room, and asked, "Where's Torvald? I need a shower."

"What's that? Can't hear you."

Ade raised his voice over the room's cacophony: silverware clanking, chairs scraping, coffee cups rattling against saucers, people talking and laughing, excited children running around the perimeter of the room, squealing and screaming, and mothers shushing them. At the far end of the hall, the town's musicians, two old Swedes, played their accordions and sang. No one listened.

"He's flipping pancakes. I reckon that shower's going to have to wait an hour or two," Herring Pete cackled and set a platter of pancakes in front of the wet fisherman, then cringed at the loud profanity coming from Ade's mouth.

"I ain't no prude, and the good Lord knows my swearin' vocabulary is as good as the next man's, but darn it, you can't curse in here, not out loud, anyway," Herring Pete snapped, looking around.

Ade had the grace to blush. He forgot he was sitting in the church's fellowship hall. He kept his eyes downcast, avoiding the unholy stares of the nearby church women. "Get me the keys from Torvald, will ya, Pete? I'm soaked through and liable to catch my death."

Herring Pete leaned close to Ade's ear and said, "Speaking of death, did you hear about the Feddersens? Their boat's been missing for two months. They're presumed dead."

"They?"

"Feddersen and his misses."

"And the girl?"

Herring Pete frowned, "That devil girl's been staying with Pastor Nels. Her wild ways are driving his wife crazy. They got six kids of their own, ya know." He refilled Ade's empty coffee cup. "Say, didn't your girl Firy get along good with Franella a couple of summers ago? Maybe you could take her. Be nice for Firy to have a sister." Herring Pete cackled and bumped Ade with his elbow. "You'll have to smack her a time or two to settle her. She's a wicked one."

Ade shook his head at Herring Pete's attitude toward Franella. "Firy's my niece and has two sisters." Ade scratched the stubble on his chin and thought about that hot shower. "I don't need any more kids, but the Salvation Army has an orphanage in Sitka."

Herring Pete grinned and slapped Ade on the back, "I'll let the pastor know. I'm sure he'd like to see the last of Franella Feddersen."

Pastor Nels sat at a table near the kitchen with his wife, May, and their six blond-haired, blue-eyed daughters. There was no sign of Franella. Herring Pete leaned over and whispered in the pastor's ear.

"What did he say?" May asked.

Herring Pete stepped close, leaned over her shoulder, and said, "Sitka has an orphanage for the Feddersen girl, and Ade Bunderson said he'd take her."

"Good," May shrank from the unkempt man. His odor overpowered all the others in the room. She pressed her napkin to her nose.

"I'm not sure it's the best thing for the girl," Pastor Nels said, wiping his mouth with his napkin. "She's special."

"She's not special," May said, "She's annoying."

Herring Pete nodded, "You're right, Mrs. Pastor, that girl is really annoying." He tapped his fingers on his temple. "A bit off in the head, if you know what I mean."

May frowned and refused to acknowledge Herring Pete's statement. She put her hand on her husband's arm. "It's best for our family if she goes. Put your own first. Isn't that right, girls?"

"That's right! I agree!" Herring Pete spoke much louder than what was considered polite, even in the noisy church hall. May shot him a withering look and shivered at his rotten teeth.

The girls nodded and clapped their hands. The youngest said, "But I like Nella; she's funny." Her mother shushed her by shoving half a pancake in her mouth.

"I'll let Ade know," Herring Pete said, "You're doing the right thing, Pastor Nels. You don't want that little hellion around your sweet girls." He poured the pastor and his wife more coffee and brought the children more tinned milk.

"That man is an interfering busybody and the worst gossip in town while although he tells everyone what a good Christian he is," Pastor Nels said.

May wrinkled her nose. "He's no Christian, but he's right about the Feddersen girl. You have to admit that."

Pastor Nels stuffed his mouth full of reindeer sausage and didn't answer.

Franella had taken the empty lingonberry syrup container into the kitchen to be refilled. She felt the muscles in her face tense and become rigid as she placed the syrup in front of the pastor. He raised his face to thank her. Franella kept her eyes vacant. She didn't want him to know she had heard his wife's words and how they had hurt.

She took her seat next to the youngest Nels daughter, stabbed a pancake, and let it dance through the syrup puddled on her plate. Appetite gone, she twirled her fork and waltzed the fluffy pancake in a sticky circle. Franella bent her head and slid her eyes around the room. Families and friends sat together, talking and laughing like a pod of humpback whales bubble-feeding. The joyful trumpeting of whale song echoed throughout the church hall, but she sat silent and alone in the midst of Port Alexander's bubbling family pod. Franella Feddersen had known these people all her life, but she was adrift, like flotsam and jetsam, wreckage from a sinking ship, pushed and battered by the tide. How long until she went under?

Mrs. Nels scolded her for dawdling as the other children finished their meal. Franella pushed her plate away, grabbed her jacket, and silently followed. As they passed the table where Ade sat, May Nels patted him on the back and whispered in his ear. He lifted his head, and over May's shoulder, he saw dark-haired Franella Feddersen trailing the blond stair-step Nels sisters. Franella glared at him. He smiled, and the glare deepened. Flustered, Ade turned away and grabbed his coffee cup. The girl must be grieving her folks. He thought his smile had conveyed kindness and sympathy, but evidently, she didn't think so.

Later that night, when all the girls were asleep, Franella slipped out of bed and crept to the top of the stairs.

"She's too wild. She doesn't fit here." May sat on the arm of her husband's leather chair. "It will be good if Ade takes her away."

He closed the book he was reading and said, "I don't think she's wild at all."

"Unruly then, undisciplined."

"How so?"

"The girls and I spent the morning weeding and hoeing the garden. After ten minutes, I looked up, and Franella was gone. The other day, when we cleaned and canned the fish, she disappeared. Today, I washed and changed the bedding, but I couldn't find her."

"Is she lazy, then?"

"She flits from one thing to the next. The chores do not hold her. She cannot settle."

"Maybe her mother never taught her how to do those things." Pastor Nels opened his book. May took it and set it on the side table.

"Britta, may she rest in peace, did her best with that girl. She was often disappointed that her daughter would not pay attention. Franella caused her poor mother great shame."

Franella Feddersen swallowed hard and crept back to the loft bedroom all of the girls shared. Their quiet breathing and soft snores told her they still slept, all except for the youngest, who looked at Franella with wide eyes. Franella put her fingers to her lips in the universal sign for silence and sat next to her on the bed they had shared for the last two months. The child crawled to her and sat on Franella's lap. As she rocked the little girl, Franella imagined her mother filled with embarrassment when talking to the women of Port Alexander.

The tears fell down her face. A hard knot formed in her stomach. What kind of a daughter was she to bring such humiliation to her mother? She gently lowered the now-sleeping little girl and pulled the covers over her. Franella sat on the end of the bed, hugged her knees, and silently wept.

If only she had returned to the top of the stairs, she would have heard Pastor Nels, "Not paying attention? Franella sits in my study for hours. She pores over my books and asks intelligent questions. Her Hebrew and Greek are coming along nicely. It's almost as if she's in another world when her nose is in a book."

May frowned and stood, "The Hebrew and the Greek, and all the big books. It is not a world for women. Better she should learn to cook and clean. I tried to teach her. For two months, I have tried."

Pastor Nels patted his wife's hand and said, "I'm sure you did your best."

"You should not allow her near your books." May picked up a doily, shook it, and set it back on the side table. She moved the lamp two inches to the left.

"Would you make coffee, please?" He reached around her for his book, a signal the conversation was over.

"It is ready and hot on the back of the stove. I also have a plate of your favorite cookies." As she moved toward the kitchen, she turned and said, "I pity the poor fellow Franella marries. He will never have good home-cooked meals when he wants them. That girl is a disaster in the kitchen," May said as she fixed a tray for the two of them.

Pastor Nels gazed at the pages of his book without seeing the words. Franella's husband may never have homemade meals, but he would have a wife he could talk to beyond the mundane. He closed the book softly, laid it on the table, and leaned back in his chair. He sighed; perhaps it was good his six daughters were a carbon copy of their mother. The men of Port Alexander were not known for their intellect. "I loved your mind, Franella. You were a perfect student, and I shall miss our conversations," he whispered.

The storm that brought Ade Bunderson to Port Alexander raged within Franella Feddersen. It created a nervous agitation, and she could not sleep. Some hours later, she crept out of the pastor's house and headed to the woods north of town. The wind had flown away, and the storm drowned itself in the deep. The rain, more of a gray drizzle, veiled the night and covered her departure. Franella shivered and wished she had worn heavier clothing, but she would not return for a jacket or gloves. She turned her back on the harbor and followed the trail next to the creek and soon was enveloped by the Tongass.

Sometime later, the misty rain stopped, and moonlight flooded a meadow ringed with lupines. Raindrops glistened on the blossoms like diamonds. Franella paused, breathing deeply of their grape-like scent. She pictured the many times she had wandered through this place, edged with the tall, colorful flowers and filled with nagoonberries. She pictured herself taking a bucketful to her mother, who made the best nagoonberry pie. Franella turned away from the image and plunged into an area of old-growth hemlocks and cedar. Behind a waist-high wet fern, she found a hollowed-out tree trunk and wedged herself in. Damp from the drizzle, hungry and uncomfortable, she drifted into a restless sleep.

Several hours later, the eastern sky cracked, and the sun broke through, shattering the tenuous fog. It formed into panels of lacy curtains and then morphed into delicate spiderwebs as the sun continued to climb and illuminate the forest. Franella shivered in the morning's early light. Wet, cold, and hungry, she berated herself for poor planning. She should have brought food and a blanket. Nevertheless, Ade Bunderson would be on his way back to Sitka by now, and she was safe.

She saw herself walking back to town as if she had just taken a midnight stroll, but she knew there would be consequences. Perhaps if she hid out for the rest of the day, Pastor Nels and the others would worry for her safety and be grateful when she turned up unharmed. She stretched the kinks out of her cramped muscles and thought about how she could get away from herself, whether in these woods or back in town—away from the pain—away from the grief.

A raven perched on a fallen log at the edge of the trail. It followed her with its blackberry eye. The bird cocked its head and flew to a nearby bush, still gazing at her. Ravens had such significance among the Tlingits and other North Coast Natives. Had this raven been sent to her? What was he trying to say? With one eye on the bird, she slowly fluffed the fern to hide the entrance to her sleeping nest. She wouldn't leave any hints as to where she'd been. She dusted her hands on her overalls and followed the iridescent black raven deeper into the forest.

She had only traveled about a quarter of a mile when Herring Pete's dog snarled and snapped at her heels. As the raven squawked and flew away, Franella felt a stabbing so deep it left her soul bereft. "Come back, Raven."

The barking dog pushed against her. Franella stood still and whispered, "Shut up, you stupid dog."

The wolf-like animal wouldn't let her take a step in any direction. Herring Pete ambled up the path, whistling and twirling a six-foot length of rope.

"Call off your dog, Pete," Franella yelled.

"Not until I tie you tight, girl. The others think you're harmless, but I know better."

Franella took a half-step, and the dog snarled, its saliva dripping onto her feet. "I'm not going anywhere. Call off your dog."

"Never mind my dog."

"What are you doing out here anyway?"

His rheumy eyes looked her over, and he laughed as he wrapped the rope around her wrists.

"If your dog wasn't here, you'd never be able to tie me up."

"You're not like the rest of us, you devil girl," he snarled.

"You're just mad because I found your still in the woods and smashed it."

"If that's all you did, I could have rebuilt it, but you threw the copper tubing in the bay and broke all the glass bottles. I have half a mind to do the same to you."

Franella smiled, "If you do, Pastor Nels will curse you and send you straight to hell."

The color left Herring Pete's face, and he shivered. "I'm a good Christian."

"Ha!" Franella laughed in his face.

"I'm going to drag you back to town trussed up like a hunting trophy," he laughed and spat tobacco juice near her feet.

"You're a real big man, Pete."

"Yes, I am, so shut your yap." He tugged the rope tighter, pulled a flask out of his back pocket, and took a long drink. The dog snarled louder, and Herring Pete gave him a not-too-gentle kick.

Franella twisted her head, searching through the dappled green canopy. The silent black raven watched from a nearby cedar branch. He shook himself, and the sheen of his feathers glistened. Franella gasped when she saw a blue under-feather.

Some Natives thought a blue feather meant someone watched

you from the spirit world. Others said if you found a blue raven feather, it meant you were on the right path. The raven's loud caw, almost a shriek, told her to keep going. Hands tied, pulled along by Herring Pete, Franella knew this was not the right path.

According to Tlingit legend, Raven was sometimes deceitful, a trickster. Raven made friends but also enemies. "I'm your friend, Raven," she called over her shoulder.

The gentle wind sauntered through the treetops, and the creek gurgled and splashed over the rocks. Herring Pete took another swig from the silver flask he always carried, jerked on the rope, and Franella stumbled forward. "Nothing here but woods and water, you stupid girl."

Franella looked over her shoulder. Raven had made himself invisible. She was stupid, but there was no way she would admit that to Herring Pete or anyone else. As he dragged her through the woods, she looked daggers at his back, but when they entered the town, she kept her eyes on his feet. Much to her relief and his annoyance, no one was up and about to see his triumph and her humiliation. He drained his flask and pulled her toward the dock.

THREE

By mid-afternoon, Ade had refueled the Ollie B. and prepared to sail up the coast. Several uneasy townspeople were on the dock to see him off.

"It's just like that girl to run off," Mrs. Nels said, wringing her hands, "I tried."

Her husband put his arm around her, "Of course you did, my dear. No one could have done more."

"Stay a little longer, Ade," Torvald called, "Franella will turn up."

"If she does, let me know, and I'll fetch her," Ade replied.

"Eh, what's that?" Herring Pete scratched his head, "Where did she go? I put her in the galley."

"Ade's galley?"

Herring Pete nodded and grinned. His foul-smelling, tobacco-stained teeth caused the women in the crowd to turn away.

Torvald set a stern eye toward the old man and said, "You've been in my bar all day. What do you mean you put her in Ade's boat? When?"

Herring Pete spat tobacco juice on the dock, scratched his dog behind the ears, and said, "Don't know. Yesterday?"

"Think again, Pete," Pastor Nels said.

"Maybe it was last night." He pulled the flask out and shook it. Empty. The dog bumped his leg. Herring Pete pushed the animal away. "Just after dawn, I think. Tied her to the bunk."

"You tied her up?" Ade yelled.

"Just doing my Christian duty," Herring Pete whined.

Pastor Nels frowned and turned his back on the man. Ade rushed below deck and found a dejected and unwilling passenger huddled and silent, knees drawn up, head resting on them. Ade studied her as he gently untied her hands and ankles. She was a skinny thing with long dark pigtails. Bony, all elbows and knees. She was dressed in faded overalls and a plaid shirt. He didn't remember the color of Franella's eyes, and the miserable girl refused to meet his gaze. He set a mason jar of water next to her, then put a tin of peanut butter and a loaf of bread on the counter. "Sorry, Franella. I ate all the jelly."

"Bunderson, is the girl alright?" Pastor Nels yelled.

"She's not talking, probably thirsty, but she's okay," Ade called through the porthole.

"I did good." Herring Pete looked to the others for affirmation, his rheumy eyes begging for praise. Some nodded, others shook his hand. "Bunderson, see that you don't bring her back!" he yelled.

The townspeople shared Pete's sentiments but were reluctant to say so. They waved goodbye, returned to their lives, and put that troublesome Feddersen girl out of their minds. Pastor Nels hunched his shoulders and followed them. His wife grabbed his hand and described the dinner she would make to celebrate that the pesky girl was gone.

"I'm going to cast off now. It's a short trip with no detours, so less than a hundred miles up the coast. The weather's good. We'll be okay," Ade said, "Safe, I mean."

She sniffled and wiped her nose on her sleeve, still refusing to look at him. There was nowhere to run, nowhere to go.

"I'm sure Firy will be glad to see you, and the lady who runs the orphanage is nice."

Franella's head snapped up, and she glared at him, "I've read *Oliver Twist*. I know what orphanages are like!"

Her eyes were large and a bright blue, as beautiful as Alaska's forget-me-nots. Her long, thick lashes and brows were a smoky charcoal. Light freckles scattered across her cheeks. She was pretty now but would be absolutely stunning if she put a little meat on her bones. "I'm sorry, girl, but Torvald told me they found wreckage from your dad's boat. There's no doubt your parents are gone, and you are an orphan."

Franella's eyes widened, and she moaned.

"They didn't want to tell you. Didn't know how you'd take it. But you knew, didn't you? Sorry, kid."

Franella closed her eyes, shuddered, and drew in a ragged breath. The emptiness filled her once more. She pressed her face on her knees again and hid from this fisherman who was taking her away. Ade watched her for a moment, shook his head at the forlorn sight, and went topside to cast off.

The boat chugged up the coast, its engine a constant low thrum. Seabirds followed the boat's wake. They sang and hoped to entice the fish to rise within striking distance. Ade remained at the wheel, giving Franella time to think, not realizing that was the last thing she wanted.

As hard as she tried, she couldn't keep her imagination in check. In her mind, she saw giant waves slice the sea like her mother's biggest knife sliced white bread. A mountain of dark water poured over their boat, and her mother's mouth opened in a silent scream. Her father lunged but couldn't reach the terrified woman as the wave thrust her overboard. Agony distorted his face until he resembled a fierce sea monster. The hungry swells swallowed him as well, and together, her mother and father choked on the cold, salty water. Franella squeezed her eyes tight and hit the sides of her head with her fists. Still, the pictures flashed through her brain like a never-ending horror movie.

"Franella," Ade called, "Will you make me a sandwich? There might be some fireweed honey in the bottom cupboard."

She didn't respond so Ade called twice more. His voice finally penetrated the awful images, and they faded to a dull gray. Franella forced herself to focus on the sandwiches. She smeared peanut butter across the bread, and the sticky honey dripped onto her fingers and from there to the counter. She told herself to imagine the many times Ade Bunderson had sailed the Ollie B. into Port Alexander. She hoped imagining those scenes would keep the tormenting images of her parents from returning. She bit the inside of her cheek and forced the murderous sea to the outer edges of her mind.

In past years, each time Ade had offloaded his catch at the cannery, he stopped by for coffee or something more substantial with her father. Each year, Ade's fish stories grew larger and wilder. Her father's laughter grew to match. The one enjoyed the telling, the other delighted in listening. Pots of coffee were drunk, and plates of pastries were consumed. Ade praised her mother's baking, so the Scandinavian housewife enjoyed feeding him, especially the Danish pastries he favored. If Franella remembered correctly, Ade's wife was a Yupik and had not mastered baking the delicate Danish and Norwegian confections. Ade would never taste those baked goods again, and Franella vowed she would abstain from them forever. If she couldn't have her mama's pastries, she wouldn't have any at all.

Two years ago, Ade brought his niece to Port Alexander for the summer. She and Firy were supposed to become friends. But the girl's mother had recently passed away, and Firy was in no mood to be anyone's friend. *Now I know how she felt. I'm sorry, Firy.*

Firy's horrible, grief-stricken summer was a good one for twelve-year-old Franella. Once Firy discovered Franella's inability to read, she said, "Franella Feddersen, you are going to learn to read this summer, even if it kills me," Firy shoved her grief deep below the surface and refused to talk about her mother. Now Franella understood why.

With driftwood sticks, cartwheels, and sand on the beach, Firy unlocked reading for me when no one else could. I will be forever grateful to her for that. But I don't want to see her. How can I tell her I didn't understand how she felt when she lost her mother. Franella blew her nose, took a bite of the sandwich, and choked when she couldn't swallow around the lump in her throat. Firy *has a brother, two sisters, and a stepfather. She even has a dog. I have no one. I won't be an orphan; I won't!*

She licked the honey from her fingers, flipped her braids over her shoulders, and wiped her face, scraping the emotion away. She stiffened her expression. When she took the sandwiches to Ade, he gave her a long look. She met his eyes briefly, then looked away. He thanked her for including coffee and the last of the cookies.

The rogue storm had lasted a mere forty hours, and today was a rare day in Southeast Alaska. The clouds were gone, and the sky a clear cornflower blue. The storm had freshened the air, and there was no evidence of the recent foul weather.

The deep green forests of the islands and islets along the coast of Baranof Island embroidered the intense blue-green waters of Sitka Sound, and in the distance, a hazy Mt. Verstovia beckoned. The sun dazzled the mountain forests with a comforting warmth. A soft breeze ruffled the trees on the nearby shores. At any other time, Franella would have exalted in feeling the sun's rays on her skin. It always had an uplifting and cheerful effect on her. Not today.

Returning below, she threw herself on the bunk, tried to keep her body still, and refused to feel. But she couldn't settle. She rose to her knees, pressed her face into the open porthole, and gulped the crisp, briny breeze. The Ollie B. sailed parallel to the forested shore. The various greens were reflected in the tranquil waters. How peaceful it looked, but the sea could also bring treachery and misery. Franella looked to the horizon. Somewhere between here and China, her parents' bodies rested, and she was now forever alone.

Slicing through the deep water, the boat and the sea seemed to whisper, *You're just like Oliver.* She wrinkled her forehead and looked at the small alarm clock fastened to the wall above the bunk. Much to her dismay, the boat was making good time. She took one more salty gulp of air and plopped back on the bunk, pressing a pillow over her face so Ade wouldn't hear her cries. *What will happen when we dock in Sitka?*

FOUR

"I'll bring Firy to see you tomorrow," Ade said as he deposited Franella at the Salvation Army Orphanage.

"Absolutely no visitors for the first six weeks," Major Bernice said, "Franella Feddersen needs time to become accustomed to the schedule and the rules."

"But, ma'am, she's all alone."

"So are all the little wretches, er, poor dears, that come to us." Major Bernice looked at Franella and frowned, "Lift up your head, girl, and don't slouch."

Ade shuffled his feet and sighed, "Maybe I should take her home for a few days until she, well, until she..."

"Certainly not." At six-foot-two, Major Bernice loomed over Ade until he mumbled in agreement. The stern woman turned her attention to Franella. "Do you have something in your satchel that you can wear other than those disgusting dungarees?"

"Overalls. Not disgusting." Franella lifted her red-rimmed eyes to Major Bernice. "I have another pair. Patched. Clean. And I'm not an orphan!"

Major Bernice stiffened, and her words, although quiet, were slowly pushed through clenched teeth. She drew out each syllable until it had a head and tail, "Since you're new here, I will forgive your disrespectful tone. It makes your face ugly. I can't abide ugly children. Watch what you say and how you say it. I will be respected!"

Each word smacked Franella in the face like a beaver's tail slapping the water when it sensed danger. Her head dropped lower with each word. She put her hands in her overall pockets and felt the two items that were her life. A faded photograph of her parents and her diploma from the Calvert Correspondence Secondary School. Major Bernice continued her harangue until Franella whispered. "Sorry."

Ade watched as Major Bernice turned her back on the miserable girl and clapped her hands. A mousy-looking young woman came running. "Sophie, take this girl to the supply closet on the second-floor landing. Here's the key. Find her a skirt and blouse. Burn those awful boy clothes and her satchel; it's stained, patched, and dirty."

"Yes, ma'am." Sophie took a reluctant Franella by the hand and dragged her toward the staircase.

"I won't stay here," Franella shrieked.

Ade took a step forward, but Major Bernice held up her hand. He stopped, looked at the ceiling, and shoved his hands in his pockets to keep himself from doing something he'd regret.

Major Bernice narrowed her eyes. Her crow's feet produced deep crevices in her full face. Her voice was deceptively gentle, her lips parted, and her teeth bared. "Franella dear, our Chief of Police, Stormy Durand, will drag you back by your ears before you've gone as far as you can spit."

Franella looked over her shoulder at Ade, fear and a cry for help in her eyes.

"Miss Ruth is due back in Sitka next week. She'll come to see you, Franella. You'll be fine." Ade called after her. Shoulders slumped, he turned and made his way to the Sitka Café.

"Has anyone seen Stormy?" Ade called as he let the restaurant door slam behind him. Foul thoughts toward Major Bernice filled his mind.

The big round table in the back dining area overlooking Sitka Sound was filled with his cronies: Jake Steiner, shoreboat pilot; Ivan Mishkin, boat builder and, according to Ivan, the last genuine Russian in Sitka; and finally, Bill Wall, millworker and Firy's stepfather. Mike Evans, the owner of the café, stood at the table, coffee pot in hand.

"Chief not here. Why you want?" Ivan stroked his mustache.

"I just dropped a gal, Franella Feddersen's the name, off at the Salvation Army Orphanage, parents lost at sea, and I don't know," Ade shook his head, "Something didn't sit right. That Major Bernice is something else, a regular drill sergeant."

"She is babay." Ivan hunched his shoulders and stared into his coffee.

"A baby?" Jake asked, "You mean a babe? I don't think so."

Mike laughed, "Anyone who's seen Major Bernice knows there is no way she could be called a babe!"

Ivan laughed, but it didn't sound cheerful. "Not babe. Not baby. Babay. Russian troll." He scratched his head and pulled on his mustache. "Er, like American boogerman."

"You mean boogeyman," Jake laughed.

"What I said is," Ivan replied.

"What do you want Stormy for?" Bill asked.

Ade rubbed his chin. "I wonder who has legal jurisdiction over the gal. Pastor Nels says he thinks she's got family in Denmark or Norway. That would be better than the orphanage."

"How old is she?"

"Around twelve or thirteen, maybe fourteen." He shrugged and reached for his coffee.

"I was on my own at fourteen," Jake said, "Some of you were too."

"It's different for girls," Bill sighed.

"Five girls I have," Ivan's mustache wilted into his coffee.

"Did you ask her about her relatives? Does she know how to get in touch with them?" Jake asked.

"She didn't say much on the trip from Port Alexander," Ade sighed, "When Miss Ruth gets back, she can talk to the girl."

"I thought you said no visitors," Bill Wall said, "I know our Firy would want to see her. Remember, she spent the summer with her a couple of years ago."

"Miss Ruth will see. Rule not matter." Ivan lifted his cup, Mike filled it, and raised the pot along with his left eyebrow as he looked at each man at the table. They all nodded, and he poured another round.

Each skirt and blouse Sophie pulled from the jumbled stack in the supply closet was rejected by Franella.

Sophie leaned close and whispered, "It will be easier if you do what you're told. In two weeks, I'll be eighteen, and I can leave. I was six when my parents died, and it took me a long time to learn the rules. It's not so bad if you go along to get along."

"I am not an orphan," Franella said through gritted teeth.

Sophie nodded. "I know. For the first two years, I expected my parents to come for me. I wouldn't believe they were dead. My advice is to find a friend among the others. It will help with the loneliness."

Franella lowered her gaze and sniffed. The kids in Port Alexander thought she was odd, and their parents agreed. Franella knew she would make no friends here. She didn't know how.

Sophie reached into the pile of donated, used clothing and pulled out a pair of culottes. She held them to her nose. "These don't smell too bad. It's a divided skirt, almost like overalls. The pleats will disguise that fact, and Major Bernice will be happy. And Franella, I won't burn your clothes." She looked up and down the empty hallway and whispered, "Come."

They tiptoed down the basement steps. Sophia led her to the massive oil furnace in the corner. There was a two-foot space between the back of the furnace and the cement block wall.

"This is my hideaway. We'll stuff your bag with old newspapers, and I'll burn that."

Franella managed to smile a little, but it did not reach her eyes. "Thank you." She looked around the cluttered basement. "Are there any books around here?"

"Major Bernice is not in favor of books, but I have some hidden. The high school has a small library. School starts in a few days."

"Done with school."

"You have to go to school."

Franella folded her arms and leaned against the basement wall. "Completed all grades."

Sophie's eyebrows rose. "You don't look that old."

"Fourteen. Finished. Two years." Franella paused, took a deep breath, and said, "I mean, I'm fourteen, and during the last two years, I've completed all the Calvert School correspondence courses through 12th grade and also several electives."

While staying with Pastor Nels, Franella worked diligently to correct her staccato speech pattern. He told her the short, choppy sentences she used were off-putting to most people and were not considered good communication. It was difficult to continually be aware of how she sounded, and in times of stress, she had a tendency to become anxious and return to her former way of speaking.

Sophie whispered, "Don't say anything to anybody. Just go to school. Trust me, you don't want to be here all day. Major Bernice is a mean old witch. You'll do nothing but wash dishes and make beds, take care of that rotten little—never mind." Sophie counted five blocks up and seven blocks over from the corner. She wiggled out two large cement blocks. "Nobody knows about this but me. All my treasures are here. There's room for your things."

Sophie stuffed Franella's meager wardrobe deep in the wall's cache. She took Franella's hand, squeezed it, and said, "For some reason, I think I can trust you."

"You don't know me."

"I remember what it was like. You have that same lost look I saw in the mirror every morning when I brushed my teeth."

Franella shrugged. She had no idea what her face looked like. But she knew what loss was about. Even when her parents were alive, she felt oddly bereft. To the folks in Port Alexander, she was that addlepated, undisciplined brat who ran all over the place, wild and illiterate. They shook their heads, sighed, and turned away. To her mother, she was like a puffin that flapped its wings four hundred times a minute just to get off the ground. More often than not, the puffin's flight was jerky and its landings, bumpy. Awkward. Ungraceful. No one would ever look at Franella Feddersen and think swan. Her father, a gentle and quiet man, did not know how to stand up to his wife's constant barrage of negative comments about their only child. He was a simple man; fishing and food, that's what life was about, and a good cup of coffee. Try as he might, he couldn't see past his erratic daughter's quirks.

Franella chewed on the end of her pigtail and wondered if they had ever loved her. Even in the midst of her family, she had been alone. Franella shoved her hands in her pockets and felt the two pieces of paper she kept close. She could no longer picture the past. There were no images. Without the photograph and her diploma Franella did not exist.

She clutched the ugly, divided skirt and equally horrible blouse and followed Sophie upstairs to the large room with multiple bunks. It hadn't been easy sleeping with Paster Nels' daughters. How could she sleep in a room filled with strangers? Across the hall was another large room for the boys. Twenty-seven orphans in all.

"This bottom bunk near the window is free. Now it's yours." Sophie pulled a cardboard box from under the bunk. "There are sheets and a blanket in here. Major Bernice doesn't believe in pillows."

"That's strange."

Sophie rolled her eyes and nodded. "There's a lot to get used to in this place." She pulled a paperback book from a deep pocket in her skirt. "I'll tell Major Bernice you were worn out and needed to rest. I'll come and get you for supper. I need to find some matches and finish my job," She winked and picked up Franella's battered satchel.

"Better change your clothes now. I'll hide them later."

Franella found the donated culottes were too big around the waist. She tugged the ribbons from her pigtails. Tied together, the ribbons were just long enough to use as a belt. She left her old clothes in a heap on the floor and pulled the sheets out of the cardboard box.

Franella was never very good at household chores. At least, she never performed up to her mother's standards or Mrs. Nels's either. She threw the sheets on the bed and haphazardly tucked them. The blanket she rolled up for a pillow. She raised the window blind to let in the afternoon sun and settled in for a good hour's read before supper. She turned the book over—Jack London's *White Fang*.

Franella read the first few pages and let the book fall from her hands. She curled into the fetal position. What was to become of her?

A small boy crept into the girls' room. "What's your name? Mine's Tommy, and I'm five."

"Franella and I'm fourteen." She almost smiled at the small for his age, brown-haired boy.

"That's a funny name, and you're a funny-looking girl. You have spots on your face."

"They're called freckles."

"I don't care. They're funny. What's that?" He pointed to the heap on the floor.

"Just my old clothes."

Tommy grabbed them and held them high. "Overalls? That's for boys. Big dumb girl. And what's that on the bed? Do you have a book? I'm telling!"

He ran out of the room with Franella on his heels. She grabbed him by the arm and pressed her face into his, "Don't tell, or you will be very, very sorry."

Tommy jerked his arm from her grasp, still clutching her clothes. He stomped on her foot and ran. Foot throbbing, Franella stood, undecided. Should she run after him or return the book so she and Sophie wouldn't suffer for having the forbidden item. *This is a horrible place, and I am not an orphan!*

After he gave the clothes to Major Bernice and tattled, Tommy was sent on a mission to find the rule-breakers. He saw the two girls open the door to the basement. No one was allowed down there! He spun around and ran back to tattle again. This should earn him a huge reward.

Major Bernice crept silently down the cellar stairs with Tommy close behind. When Sophie pulled out a cement block and replaced the book, Major Bernice shrieked, "What kind of rebellion is this? What have you hidden in there?"

Sophie sighed and pulled out a Bible, six books, two magazines, a candy bar, and a pair of jeans. She left Franella's things in the hideaway.

Major Bernice yelled up the basement stairs, "Tommy, come here!"

She jumped when Tommy tugged on the back of her dress and said, "I'm here already. I did good."

She smiled and ruffled his hair, "You did very good. Take these things to the burn barrel."

"I'm sorry, Major Bernice. I'll help Tommy. He shouldn't use matches," Sophie said.

"I like fire." Tommy yelled and stamped his feet, "I can do it by myself."

Spittle formed in the corner of the Major's mouth, and she spoke angrily, "Be quiet, Tommy! Sophie, I want to know if there is anything else in that hidey-hole." The guilt on Sophie's face told her there was. "Empty it now!"

Sophie pulled out Franella's other pair of overalls, a shirt, several pairs of underwear, and a well-worn nightgown.

Major Bernice turned to Franella, "Sit on your bunk and think about how you're going to get on here. You better obey the rules or there will be trouble. Sophie, burn everything. And you should have read that Bible; it might have improved your behavior." The sour-faced woman left, pushing Franella in front of her.

Sophie watched them go and whispered. "I'm sorry, Franella, I think we might have been friends."

Franella was halfway up the stairs and didn't hear Sophie's soft-spoken words or see the sadness in her eyes.

"Let's go, Sophie. I'm going to poke the fire with a stick. I like fire." Tommy jumped up and down and pulled on Sophie's sleeve.

They stood before the burn barrel where Sophie had left Franella's satchel. She knelt before the little boy. "Tommy, I'll give you this candy bar if you don't tell I'm not going to burn my things."

He snatched the candy bar from her hand and ran toward the door. "Major Bernice! Major Bernice! Sophie's bad. She's not obeying."

Sophie, grateful that Major Bernice had not inspected the hidden treasures, sighed and took the small envelope from the hollowed-out Bible. It contained the dimes and nickels she had saved over the years, almost four dollars. Primarily obtained from empty soda bottles she'd found along the side of the road and returned to the grocery store, she jingled the coins and slipped them into her pocket.

The director of the Pioneer's Home had promised her a job when she turned eighteen. She'd have to lie about her birthday, but it was a small price to pay. Fortunately, the job, although the wages were small, included room and board. Sophie looked up and saw Franella's face pressed against the window. She lifted her hand.

"Goodbye, Franella," Sophie whispered. She picked up her belongings, left the Bible, climbed over the orphanage fence, and didn't look back.

Franella raced down the stairs and out the back door when she saw the Major and Tommy standing at the burn barrel.

"Please, my things," Franella cried.

"Get back upstairs, disobedient little wretch." Major Bernice had thrown everything into the barrel and tossed in a match.

Franella fell to her knees. "A photograph of my mama and papa and my school certificate are in the pocket. You had no right." She pulled on Major Bernice's arm.

"I have every right!" Major Bernice jerked her arm free, and she raised her hand to strike Franella.

Little Tommy's excited cries of "Hit her! Hit her!" seemed to bring the Major to her senses.

She lowered her hand, gritted her teeth, and said, "Get to your bunk before I give you what you deserve."

Franella ran.

FIVE
September, 1938

Three orphan boys she hadn't spoken to yet, Arthur, Albert, and Anthony, and a girl named Ruby, accompanied Franella to the front door of the high school's rectangular cement building. It was a short walk from the orphanage. The boys, all seniors, entered without a word. The girl turned to Franella and said, "I'm a junior, an upperclassman. I can't be seen talking to a lowly freshman. If we pass in the hall, do not speak to me or acknowledge me in any way."

"But Ruby, I thought we were friends."

"I mean it, Franella, don't talk to me." She left Franella bereft in the hallway near the front door.

The sound of a shrill bell ring made Franella jump. Ninety-seven students that had filled the main hall disappeared into several classrooms. Franella stood uncertain, then looked for the office. She found it on the second floor.

"I'm sorry, we have no record that you are a student here," the secretary said.

"I've already graduated," Franella said, "But Major Bernice said I have to attend here anyway."

The secretary shuffled her papers, sharpened her pencil, and said, "How old are you?"

"Fourteen, what's that got to do with anything?"

"Don't be impertinent."

"I just asked a question."

"Sit on that bench over there while I talk to Mr. Hendricks." The secretary knocked on the principal's door and went in. As soon as the door closed, Franella left the bench and knelt in front of the door. She looked through the keyhole and strained her ears.

"She said she's already graduated. She's one of Major Bernice's waifs from the orphanage. Sassy thing."

"Just put her in the freshman class. She'll be fine," Mr. Hendricks said.

"I don't have any transfer papers or any information about her."

"It doesn't matter; just get her to class. We can figure everything out later."

Franella hurried to the bench. The secretary glared at her and said, "Follow me."

The class was already in session. The secretary pointed to a chair in the back row as Miss Benson, the history teacher, droned on, and the students feigned attention. Two minutes later, Franella raised her hand, "Excuse me, but slavery was only one cause of the Civil War. The politics at the time were complicated."

Heads turned, a few kids snickered, but most stared silently.

Miss Benson's eyes flashed, "Who are you, and why are you questioning me?"

"Nullification versus secession, Northern and Southern nationalism, expansionism, economics, the debate over whether slavery was sanctioned by Scripture, and more."

The teacher pulled a handkerchief from the sleeve of her sweater and blew her nose.

"Name's Franella Feddersen, and I wrote my senior research paper on the various causes of the Civil War."

"This is Freshman history. There's no way you wrote a senior research paper." Miss Benson strode across the room and stood before Franella.

"I'm not a liar," Franella said.

"Are you saying I am?" Miss Benson's face mottled.

Franella shriveled inside but met the teacher's gaze. "I'm saying I know what I wrote, and I am not a liar."

There was more snickering and several whispers among the students.

"Who is she?"

"That's my old sweater. Mom gave some of my things to the orphanage last year."

"Well, then, I guess she must be Little Orphan Annie."

"I think I've seen her on the beach. Odd girl."

"Quiet!" Miss Benson snapped at the class then opened the door and said, "I think, Franella Feddersen, you had better pay a visit to Mr. Hendricks."

Mr. Hendricks took off his glasses and said, "Why are you here?"

Franella lifted her puzzled eyes to his. "I think it's because Miss Benson doesn't know what caused the Civil War."

"What? I don't understand." Mr. Henderson held his glasses to the light, saw the smudges, and frowned.

"She didn't either. She thinks it's only slavery. She's wrong."

Mr. Hendricks licked his lips and said, "And you felt the need to correct her?"

"Teachers should know what they are talking about if they are going to teach it to others. Don't you think so?"

"Are you sure you know what you are talking about?" The principal pulled his handkerchief out of his vest pocket and methodically cleaned his glasses. He squinted at Franella.

"Like I told Miss Benson, I wrote my senior paper on the causes of the Civil War."

"You mustn't spread stories, my dear. You are not a senior."

"Volcanoes. Erupting." Franella felt her thoughts scatter.

"What?"

Franella pressed her hands to her temples. "Sorry. My mind jumps around when I'm agitated. I was seeing the volcano erupt." At Mr. Hendricks' raised eyebrow and grimace, she added, "In the photo behind you."

Franella felt her agitation increase as Mr. Hendricks continued to ask questions about her schooling. She could tell he didn't believe her. Finally, the bell rang, signaling the next class period.

"Freshman history is over. You may go to Room 2. Algebra with Mr. Paulson. Try not to question him, okay?"

"My math classes included calculus and college-level trigonometry," Franella said as she left, "I'll know if he's right or not."

Mr. Hendricks sighed and called his secretary, "Keep your eye on that girl. She's going to be trouble and it's going to be a long year." He put his glasses on, ripped them off, and attacked the stubborn smudges.

At the end of the school day, Franella hovered outside of the school's entrance, hoping to walk home with Ruby. A gaggle of girls swirled out of the double doors, laughing and chatting. Franella stepped forward, "Hi, Ruby, I..."

Ruby ignored her, and the girls kept walking. One of the senior girls turned, stared at Franella, and said, "Ruby, what is she like?"

"I don't know." Ruby averted her eyes.

"Oh, but you must find out. It will be delicious to know all about her."

"Please, Blanche, I really don't know."

Blanche put her arm through Ruby's and looked over her shoulder to Franella who still stood outside the school's entrance. "I took you under my wing out of the goodness of my heart, Ruby dear. You're not like those other unfortunates, are you? You're willing to do what I say, or do I need to go with my other friends."

"Come on, Blanche, we don't need any of those orphan girls, not even Ruby."

"Shut up, Shirley." Blanche snapped and then leaned close, whispering in Ruby's ear, "Remember when I had my mother order my new school clothes from the Sears catalog? I chose two outfits I knew would look good on you. After they arrived, I told my mom they didn't fit, and I would take them to the orphanage."

Ruby looked at her shoes and nodded.

"We both knew Major Bernice wouldn't let you keep anything nice, so I hid them in the back of my closet and let you sneak in through my window early in the morning to change and then again before you have to go back to that dismal prison."

"I'm ever so grateful, Blanche."

"Then do what I say with no hesitation, or I will drop you. I can do it in the blink of an eye."

Ruby's eyes widened, and her breath quickened, "Please don't do that. All I know is that Franella is from Port Alexander, and Major Bernice hates her. Says she's too smart for her own good. Doesn't know her place."

"From what I heard today, she certainly isn't afraid to take on the teachers," Blanche rubbed her hands together and laughed. "So delicious."

Ruby gulped, "She is really awkward, knows a lot of facts and stuff, but doesn't know anything about being a teenage girl if you know what I mean."

"Is she a tomboy?"

"Maybe. I think it's that she's never gone to school, never made friends, and doesn't know how to act around kids her own age. She doesn't know a thing about movie stars, clothes or make-up. She's strange, that's all."

"Thanks, Ruby. I'll let you know if I want more." Blanche looked over her shoulder again at the forlorn Franella Feddersen. "This could be a deliciously entertaining school year."

That first day set the tone for Franella's sojourn at Sitka High School. Franella kept her eyes down and hugged the hallway walls when going from one class to another. She didn't speak to anyone and so far, no one had spoken to her.

In both the grammar school and the high school, the orphans were looked down on by most students and some of the teachers. The boys fared better, especially if they were good baseball players, which the three high school orphan boys were.

Several days later, Franella's culottes and too-small sweater were denigrated by Blanche, the leader of the school's elite clique, and Ruby laughed along with the others.

"You're just her slave, Ruby. She doesn't really like you," Franella said.

"She's just jealous," Blanche said, glaring at Franella and then patting Ruby's shoulder.

"That's right! You're just jealous, Franella!" Ruby snarled.

"Et tu, Brute?"

"Huh?"

"Read your Shakespeare." Franella stomped off.

Ruby laughed, shrugged her shoulders, held out her hands palms up, and said, "Like I told you, she doesn't know how to act around normal people."

After correcting her teachers for the fifth time in two weeks, Franella was suspended for three days. She left for school in the mornings as usual so Major Bernice wouldn't find out about her punishment. She wandered around town and then asked for Sophie in the foyer of the Pioneer's home.

Sophie came at a trot, out of breath, "I don't have time for you, Franella. When I'm done with my shift I just collapse on my bed. But the people here are nice. It's much better than the orphanage. The food's good, too. Maybe I can see you on my next day off."

She met Ade on the docks. "I'd like to take you home for lunch, Franella, but my wife is expecting, and she's nauseous all the time. Maybe after the baby is born."

At a loss, Franella continued to wander. She stood outside Mr. Akervik's general store, ignoring the Native women sitting on the wooden sidewalk selling their baskets and mukluks. She admired a wooden crate full of Japanese glass globes—fishing floats.

A boy Franella didn't know and who must be skipping school like she was, yelled as he rode past on his bicycle, "Hey, that's my sister's sweater. Are you a thief or just one of those raggedy orphans?"

Franella picked up a glass float and let it fly. It landed on the gravel road several feet away from him but didn't break. "What a lousy throw. We'll never let you play baseball with us. Ratty orphan!" He laughed and sped away, yelling over his shoulder, "That sweater looked better on my sister. On you, it's just ugly."

Mr. Akervik ran out of the store, shaking his fist and yelling. Franella stood with her head hanging. Mr. Akervik gave her a lecture on civilized behavior and added, "Don't come around my store again, understand?"

Franella wandered past the Russian Bishop's house and onto Crescent Beach. She found a dry spot near a large driftwood log and used it as a backrest. The fog rolled across the bay, closing over the tiny islands that dotted the sound. One after another, the tiny uninhabited islands were enveloped in the hazy gray. It was as if they no longer existed. Franella wiped the wetness from her face as the murky mist of rejection, loneliness, and grief enveloped her. Like the nearby islets, she was in danger of disappearing.

SIX

The following week, Miss Ruth returned to Sitka. As soon as she came into the Sitka Café, her nose was assaulted with the odor of frying onions, sizzling reindeer hamburger, and fragrant bear bacon. Her ears were likewise assaulted. Everyone spoke at once.

"Dead. They are dead!" Ivan yelled across the room, waving his cigar above his head.

"Did you hear about the accident, Miss Ruth?" Jake asked.

"The girl is miserable. Anyone can see that," a grandmotherly-looking woman sitting at the counter, lingering over her coffee, said. Others in the café did not agree. The comments came fast and furious. There was no use trying to decipher who said what.

"She causes trouble wherever she goes," a bored housewife said. Her lunch companions nodded.

"Poor thing. It's not her fault."

"She needs to learn some self-control," a grizzled fisherman spat the words.

"She's just a child."

"Old enough to know better, I say."

"If she was mine, I'd give her a good paddling," a retired logger yelled.

"Leave her alone. It's not your business."

"Somebody's got to do something!"

Agrafena left the kitchen and sidled up to Miss Ruth. "They

are at it again. I hope you can do something for the poor girl." Miss Ruth nodded as Agrafena hustled back to the grill.

Miss Ruth held up her hand, and the buzz throughout the room slowly dissipated. "Mike, coffee."

She looked toward the round table. Chairs scraped the floor, and the men scooted close together. Ade spun an empty chair from a nearby table. Miss Ruth sat and breathed in the fragrance of the strong coffee Mike set before her. The other diners, hoping for more details, leaned toward the round table to hear Ade tell the story once more. Ade finished by saying, "She's a good girl. I've known her since she was a wee thing. Just a bit odd, that's all."

"Very odd," Jake said.

Miss Ruth listened intently as the men around the table dissected and then stitched Ade's story together again. Miss Ruth tapped her foot and prayed for patience. When they finally finished, she turned to the rest of Mike's customers and asked, "Does anyone else have grievances against Franella Feddersen or anything nice to say?"

Some in Sitka had had run-ins with the unpredictable girl and were eager to share. Rumors about her behavior at the high school continued to fall from the sky like unwanted bird droppings from gulls flying over Sitka.

"My boy says she corrects the teachers. I say the teacher's right even if the teacher's wrong. It's about respect." One customer slapped the table with his palm. Others murmured their agreement. Some shook their heads.

"It ain't respectable for the teacher not to teach stuff right. I say, good for the girl."

"Half the time, she don't go to school, just walks the beaches or runs around town. That ain't legal."

"You've seen her, haven't you, Stormy. You need to drag her back to school or lock her up."

"Yeah, Stormy, do your job."

The lawman drained his coffee cup, stood, and threw some change on the table, "I can't say I'm up on the Territory's truancy laws, and I won't say I've noticed her anywhere." He tipped his hat to the diners, winked at Miss Ruth, and left. His large mastiff, Bull, the only dog allowed in the café, padded after him.

Miss Ruth was grateful to see the café's conversation shift from Franella's errant ways to Stormy's inability to notice goings on in Sitka. She quietly slipped out after him. He leaned against the telephone pole, rolling a cigarette. He grinned when he saw her. "I figured you'd be along."

Tommy opened the door and asked, "Who are you?"

"I'm Miss Ruth. I haven't seen you before. What's your name?"

"Everybody's in school." Tommy slammed the door.

Miss Ruth knocked again and opened the door. "I came to see Major Bernice. Will you fetch her for me?"

"I don't want to. I'm playing."

Miss Ruth pulled her spectacles off and stared at Tommy. She pulled her long black skirt up so the tips of her boots showed as she stepped inside.

"Are those cowboy boots? Real ones?"

Miss Ruth put her fingers to her lips and said, "Shhh. Nobody is supposed to know. If you're good, the next time I come, I'll tell you about the ranch in Texas where I grew up."

46

"With cowboys and Indians and horses and everything?" Tommy slapped his thigh, pranced around the room, and yelled, "Giddy up!"

"And cows, you can't be a real cowboy without cows. Now bring Major Bernice to me."

A few minutes later, Major Bernice was pulled into the room by an excited little boy. "Here she is. Now tell me about the cowboys."

"Next time, if you're a good boy."

Tommy stamped his foot and opened his mouth. Major Bernice whispered in his ear, took him by the shoulder, and pushed him toward the door.

"I'm always a good boy, and I'm gonna take two cookies, not one," he yelled as the major closed the door in his face.

Major Bernice shrugged her shoulders and turned to Miss Ruth. Her eyes flattened as she sagged into the upholstered chair. She did not invite Miss Ruth to sit. "So, we meet again. What is it this time?"

Miss Ruth moved across the room until she towered over the overstuffed woman in the overstuffed chair. Major Bernice wiggled in the chair, looking everywhere except at the woman standing before her. "Oh, good grief, sit down."

Miss Ruth sat and said, "Franella Feddersen."

Major Bernice looked away. Her brow furrowed like a newly plowed field. "Such a wretched child."

"I want to see her."

"I can't allow it. I pride myself on following the rules."

"What rules would those be?"

"You know the Salvation Army motto. Soap, soup, and salvation." The Major straightened her shoulders. "I save all the children who come here."

"You?"

"Do not insult me, Miss Ruth. You are not in charge."

"Nevertheless, I am going to take Franella for the day."

Major Bernice stood and smoothed the wrinkles over her ample midsection. "Absolutely not!" she hissed.

Miss Ruth removed her spectacles, pulled a handkerchief from her pocketbook, and took her time cleaning the lenses. She kept her gaze on Major Bernice. "May I remind you that since the last board meeting, we have been watching you closely. I'm sure you do not want this matter brought before the entire board. You realize we always send a copy of the minutes to district headquarters."

"Rules are rules." Major Bernice's voice had lost some of its force, "Your board has no authority over me."

Tommy sat right outside the living room door. He had just finished his cookies. He jumped up, marched into the room, and hollered, "Rules are rules!"

"That's right, Tommy," Major Bernice rumpled his hair, "Good boy."

Miss Ruth crooked her finger, and Tommy crossed to her. She crouched before him, looked him in the eye, "Every cowboy follows the rules."

The boy nodded, and Major Bernice smirked.

Miss Ruth continued, "Cowboys know rules are made to protect the cows. When they are in danger, the cowboy takes care of them because the cows are more important than the rules." She looked over Tommy's head. "I'll be here Saturday morning at nine. See that Franella is ready. I'll return her at five."

Major Bernice glowered as Tommy galloped around the room and yelled, "Cows are more important than rules. Cows are more important. Moo-oo-oo! Giddy up."

Miss Ruth turned in the doorway and returned Major Bernice's glower, "And Major, I will know if you are in any way unkind to the girl. She won't have to say a thing. I will know."

Sitka's soggy weather continued. The gulls and ravens squawked and begged the few tourists and many locals for breakfast. Most hurried on their way—the tourists to the shops and the locals to work or to the Sitka Café.

The following Saturday, before Miss Ruth was halfway up the wooden sidewalk, Franella burst out of the orphanage straight into Miss Ruth's embrace. "I thought you'd never get here."

Miss Ruth hugged the girl tight and let her cry. Then she pulled the scarf from her head and tied it over Franella's unruly attempt at braids. They walked through Sitka to the cafe and bought a bag of Agrafena's French crullers since Franella had vowed to never have Danish pastries again.

They continued down the entire length of Lincoln Street and into the woods to Miss Ruth's cabin near Indian River. Almost everyone in town hailed Miss Ruth, some with questions, some with rumors, and others who just wanted to chat. Most stared but didn't speak to the impatient girl standing next to Miss Ruth. As the soft drizzle turned to a more insistent rain, the people melted off the sidewalks like snow on a hot day.

The small cabin was cozy and almost warm. Miss Ruth took

the fireplace poker and stirred the embers back to life. Homespun quilts and soft pillows were thrown over the bed in the corner, and muslin curtains filtered the sunlight on the days the sun decided to visit the inhabitants of Sitka.

"Why can't I live here?"

"I wish you could, dear one. The law says since I'm unmarried and past a good mothering age, I'm not suitable." Miss Ruth put the teakettle on. When it boiled, she added the fragrant leaves.

"That's stupid!" Franella sniffed and wiped her nose on her sleeve. She was silent, then, in a small voice, said, "Do you think God let my parents drown because I wished you were my mother that summer you and Firy came to Port Alexander?"

"Never! Bozhe is never vindictive, never cruel." Miss Ruth's tone was sharp, and Franella cowered. "I'm sorry, Franella. I didn't mean to snap. Bozhe is loving and merciful. I want you to know that."

"I do. It's just that I feel so guilty. I should have gone fishing with my father that day, but I had a touch of the flu, and so my mama went instead." Franella blew her nose and turned away from the painful subject. "Can't you change the law? What if I tell the judge I think you are suitable?"

"The law is the law, and the judge doesn't care what you think. More's the pity."

"Sophie said the orphanage owns me until I'm eighteen."

Miss Ruth handed her a handkerchief and reached for the honeypot. She put a spoonful of fireweed honey in Franella's cup, added the hot tea, and stirred it slowly, then pushed the cup across the table. She opened the bag of crullers and put one on a plate for the girl. "I often travel to the other islands, but whenever I am in Sitka, I will take you for the day. I'll see you as often as I can."

Franella drank her tea and then asked, "Do you think I will have a happy ending like Oliver Twist?" she shivered, "He suffered a lot before the end. Do you think I will suffer?"

"There are no easy answers, dear one. I do know life has a way of surprising us. We think we know who we are and what we want, and so we chase it. We are often wrong."

The young teenager looked at the woman who was old enough to be her grandmother. "That's not very helpful."

Miss Ruth pursed her lips and said, "No, I suppose not."

"I know I'm smart, but I can't figure this out."

"We are going to leave the future alone and focus on the day-to-day, at least for now."

Franella paced the small cabin and said, "I don't want to say anything bad about Major Bernice, but she's rotten."

"If you don't want to say anything bad, dear one, then don't."

"But she…"

"I understand. Many of the townspeople are aware of the situation and are working on it. It will be challenging to make any changes, but we are trying."

"I don't know how to act around the other orphans."

"Don't act, dear one. Just be yourself."

"I don't know myself," Franella plopped down in the middle of Miss Ruth's bed. "The people in Port Alexander thought they knew me." Franella hugged the pillow. "They didn't like me. It won't be any different here."

"I wish everyone saw you as I do, as Bozhe does," Miss Ruth said.

"I'm fourteen and all alone in a new place. I'm smart. I can make myself different if only someone tells me how." She looked at Miss Ruth, despair in her eyes. "Will you?"

"Dear one—"

"That's the trouble, Miss Ruth. Nobody thinks of me as their dear one. They never have." A tear hovered at the corner of her eye, and she batted it away. "What shall I do?" Franella asked.

"Pick nagoonberries in Totem Park. I have your mother's pie recipe. Do you think between the two of us, we can make a decent pie?"

"You know I'm a terrible pie maker," Franella said, hiccupping, then wiping away another tear.

"You know I'm worse," Miss Ruth chuckled and hugged the girl.

"But what about my life?"

Miss Ruth reached deep into her outside storage cupboard and retrieved two berry buckets. She handed one to Franella. "I need some time to think and pray. Bozhe knows."

Franella had forgotten Miss Ruth talked over all things with her God, whom she called Bozhe. Franella's mother always said a little religion went a long way. For Miss Ruth, it seemed a lot of religion went a little way since she had to return to it again and again.

SEVEN

The low October sun slanted into the principal's office. He shuffled the papers on his desk, shook his head, and said, "I'm flummoxed. I don't know what to do."

"You're a fine educator and administrator, Mr. Hendricks. Surely there is something," Doc Brown said.

"And you're the head of the school board, Doc. I'll take any suggestions you have."

"The girl is smart, no doubt about that. She just won't shut up. Keeps correcting all her teachers," Mr. Paulson, the math teacher and staff representative, said.

"I heard from my son that Franella forces you teachers to admit when you're wrong," Doc Brown chuckled.

"It undermines our authority." Mr. Paulson crossed his arms and frowned, "She pointed out a simple math mistake in front of the whole class and didn't listen to a single explanation I tried to give." The man seemed to pout.

"I heard she took a piece of chalk and filled the blackboard with an equation no one could understand. What did you do, Paulson?" Doc Brown grinned.

"What any self-respecting teacher would do. I forced her to erase the offensive calculations. It was way beyond my students."

"Was it beyond you?" Doc was clearly enjoying himself.

"That's neither here nor there," Mr. Paulson's face reddened, "I warned her that if she wanted to get on well in life, she needed to get on well in school. I told her it would be impossible if she kept disrespecting and interfering with her teachers. She dared to, well, she said..."

"Einstein! She said the word Einstein and walked out of the room." Miss Benson, the history teacher, patted Mr. Paulson's arm, "That's what I heard, anyway. So disrespectful."

"That girl dared to compare herself to Einstein. The audacity!" Mr. Paulson folded his arms, glared at everyone in the room, and said, "Something has to be done!"

"It's been almost two months, and all the teachers, myself included, are complaining that the students have not settled. They're always wondering which teacher Franella will correct next. Some of the senior boys are making bets," Mousey Miss Benson added.

"I've had reports that some students even turn to Franella during class and ask if the teacher's right," Mr. Hendricks shook his head. "I agree she's disruptive, and something must be done, but what? I wanted your suggestions before we take this matter to the entire school board."

They looked at one another and shrugged. "Anyone?" Mr. Hendricks asked.

"Didn't the girl claim she's already finished school through Calvert Correspondence?" Doc asked.

"She's just fourteen, and it's a rigorous program." Mr. Hendricks pushed his glasses back on his nose. "I don't think she's capable of doing the work."

"Have you checked?" Doc asked.

Mr. Hendricks cleared his throat, shuffled papers on his desk, and ignored the question.

Miss Ruth sat in the back corner of the room, her spectacles perched on the end of her nose. Her long black skirt and jacket were relics from a bygone era, but they suited the tall, thin, sixty-something woman. The well-worn cowboy boots peeking from her hem seemed out of place. She had not spoken as the meeting dragged on for the better part of two hours. She assumed the men had forgotten she was there, although Miss Benson kept glancing her way. Miss Ruth looked at the large clock on the wall. She'd give them another forty-five minutes and then present her case. They'd be fatigued and frustrated enough to agree to anything.

"...and so, you see. It's the perfect solution. At least for the short term," Miss Ruth said.

"I don't like it. There's no precedent for it. I'm not sure what the authorities will say," Mr. Hendricks shuffled the papers on his desk, picked up the paperweight, and put it down again. He tapped his fingers on the edge of the desk.

"You're the authority, Mr. Hendricks. It's for you to say." Miss Ruth looked at him over her spectacles.

"I don't know that I want the responsibility." He took a white handkerchief from his back pocket, shook it out, and ran it over his bald head.

Miss Ruth sighed, held on to her rising temper, and said, "Then delegate the authority to me. I will be happy to take it."

"Excuse me, but you're not a teacher," Mr. Paulson said.

Mr. Hendricks smiled, and Doc Brown laughed, "Mr. Paulson, you're new to the Territory, so you can be forgiven for not knowing. Miss Ruth was a teacher here in Sitka and on Afognak Island long before you were born."

"Well, she mostly taught Indians, the Native children, I mean. I don't think that counts for much," Miss Benson said.

"Miss Benson, I'm shocked you would say such a thing," Doc snapped.

Miss Benson ducked her head and blushed, "Sorry, I didn't mean anything by it."

Miss Ruth bit the inside of her lip, kept her expression serene, and did not respond.

"She's not part of our staff. She's not official," Mr. Paulson huffed.

Doc laughed again, "A lot of things in the Territory are not official."

Mr. Hendricks leaned over the desk. "Now, Doc, you know I try to follow the rules, and Mr. Paulson's right. Miss Ruth is not employed by the local school district. My hands are tied."

"Untie your hands and hire Miss Ruth for a dollar a year. Franella Feddersen will be her only student and no longer your problem. I'm sure you can do some fancy paperwork to make it seem official," Doc answered.

"We don't have any space available for classes with only one student," Mr. Hendricks said.

"I will conduct her classes elsewhere. She won't need to come anywhere near the school."

Miss Benson and Mr. Paulson glanced at each other. "That would be lovely," she whispered.

"I agree," he mouthed.

Mr. Hendricks' face brightened the room like the aurora borealis brightened the night sky. "Excellent! If you need books or other supplies, see my secretary."

"I believe we should keep this little plan as quiet as possible," Mr. Paulson said, "It's unorthodox."

"This is Alaska. Believe me, no one will care," Doc said.

Mr. Hendricks wiped his head again, relieved that Miss Ruth had taken over. Then he stood and held out his right hand. Miss Ruth gathered her papers and stood. Everyone shook hands with everyone else.

When Miss Ruth shook Mr. Paulson's hand, she looked over her spectacles and said, "Don't forget Einstein didn't get on well in school either."

"In fact, they sent him home, didn't they? I guess his teachers weren't smart enough," Doc laughed and winked at Miss Ruth while Mr. Paulson cleared his throat, sputtered, and found he had nothing to say. Miss Benson consoled him as they left the building.

As Miss Ruth left and turned onto Lincoln Street and walked toward Totem Park, she wondered why the school officials couldn't see what a fine mind was hidden by Franella's awkward behavior and scrawny body? Couldn't they see the value she possessed? The town's educational system had improved since Miss Ruth arrived in 1890, and the quality of academic personnel had increased, but there was still a long way to go. It wasn't always easy to persuade highly qualified teachers to trek to the still-wild Territory of Alaska.

Miss Ruth muttered to herself, "I'll do the best I can for you, Franella, but your mind is much sharper than mine. It won't take long before you surpass me. Indeed, you will surpass everyone on this island. Then what?"

She was surprised that Sean Conner came to mind. What did her long-time friend have to do with Franella Feddersen? A raven flew overhead and landed on her shoulder. "Is that you, Jimmy? I have a lot on my mind today, no time for you." The raven screeched as if its feelings were hurt and flew off. "Where was I, Lord? Oh, yes, what are we going to do about Franella's future?"

EIGHT

Miss Ruth wrote to the Calvert Correspondence School. While waiting for a copy of Franella's transcript and diploma, she tested the girl in a variety of ways. Franella's general knowledge seemed far beyond someone who had completed high school, and her ear for languages was uncanny. Franella's childhood lack of attention seemed to be a thing of the past, at least when it came to learning. Everyday tasks continued to be difficult for the girl to focus on. The fact that Franella didn't care about housework or sports and was still uncomfortable in large groups aggravated her lack of attention.

Miss Ruth decided to play to Franella's strengths in outlining her educational program. The problem was going to be Major Bernice. Franella knew it, and Miss Ruth knew it.

Miss Ruth said, "We need to let Major Bernice think she is in charge of your schooling."

"Don't do that, Miss Ruth. She doesn't like me. I'll be miserable." Franella sucked on her lower lip, "Please."

Miss Ruth hugged the girl. "Don't worry, I'm only going to let her think she's in charge."

"The girl is not special. Why does she need her own program? That's what schools are for. She needs to settle down and do what she's told."

"Major Bernice, I'm sure with your ability to look into the lives of the precious children in your charge, you can see each one's strengths and weaknesses, each one's potential," Miss Ruth kept her expression placid.

Major Bernice sat a little straighter, "Well, yes. I pride myself on what I do here."

Miss Ruth leaned a little closer, spread a dozen closely typed sheets of paper in front of Major Bernice, and said, "To tell you the truth, the school doesn't know what to do with her. They just want to be rid of her. Poor girl."

"Humph," Major Bernice nearly choked.

"I'm sure you have some ideas about Franella."

"It's the teacher's job to take care of that girl."

"If only they did their job as well as you do yours." Miss Ruth's voice dripped honey, and Major Bernice slurped it like a black bear at his favorite honey tree. Miss Ruth adjusted her glasses and continued. "In spite of how Franella looks to others, I think she has a delicate constitution. I don't want to overwhelm her."

Major Bernice's eyes narrowed, and she opened her mouth to speak.

Miss Ruth hurried on, "As you can see, Major, I've written up several class outlines for the child. I was hoping you would give me your advice. What do you think is right for her? Remember, we don't want to give her too much."

In truth, Miss Ruth planned to teach Franella everything outlined, but it wouldn't hurt to let Major Bernice think she was in control.

Miss Ruth handed Major Bernice a sheet of paper, "What about this class in Russian language and history. I think it might be too difficult. We don't want to discourage the girl."

Major Bernice looked through each paper, and her eyes gleamed like ice-blue splinters off an iceberg. She reached for a paper at the edge of the table. "Hmmm, Tlingit. I think you should also make her learn Tlingit."

Miss Ruth shook her head, "That's one of the most difficult languages around. I don't know any non-native who's really learned it. No, it's too much. I fear Franella would be miserable." She gathered up the papers and put them in her old battered briefcase.

"I do believe Franella is a remarkable child, and I don't think it would burden her." Major Bernice tried to smile, but her eyes were hard.

Miss Ruth was not surprised to see the maliciousness in the Major's eyes. "But the alphabet has over fifty letters!"

"She can do it if she studies hard enough," Major Bernice pursed her lips and narrowed her eyes, "It would be good for her, teach her a little discipline."

Miss Ruth hid her smile and tried to look concerned, "I don't want to be contrary, but I'm afraid the task would be too much for her. She's still grieving the loss of her parents. Are you sure?"

Again, Major Bernice simpered, "I'm sure she's up to it. Such a delightful child." She couldn't keep the malice from her voice.

"As long as you're certain." Miss Ruth snapped the clasp of her briefcase and said, "I'm grateful to you, Major."

"Why can't I just sit in the library all day and read? I've finished high school already."

"As wonderful as that would be, dear one, Sitka's library is small, and although it has some excellent books, I want you to challenge yourself and stretch your mind."

"That sounds like a lot of work."

"It will be. I am going to have several people tutor you, and I've sent away for some college prep courses."

"I've never let myself dream of college."

"Bozhe willing, it will happen. He's given you a beautiful mind, and I'm sure He wants you to develop it as much as you can."

Franella smiled, "What am I going to study?"

Miss Ruth handed Franella a neatly typed sheet of paper that said Russian history and language with Father Alexi, Tlingit language and myth with Petrov Bravebird, reading at the library, books chosen by Miss Drake. Hebrew and Greek.

"There's no teacher for Hebrew and Greek," Franella said.

"I'm working on it."

"What are you going to teach me, Miss Ruth."

Miss Ruth tucked an errant wisp of hair behind her ear and said, "We are going to spend as much time together as possible, dear one, and together we are going to learn to be."

"Be what?"

"To be whatever it is, Bozhe wants us to be, of course." Miss Ruth saw the confusion on Franella's young face and pulled her into a comforting hug.

NINE

As Firy left the Russian Bishop's house after school one drizzly day, she saw Franella striding up the wooden sidewalk. The two girls stopped and looked at each other, unsure of what to say. A raven flew overhead, screeched, and landed on Firy's shoulder. Franella took a step back.

"That's just Jimmy. He won't hurt you," Firy said, "But don't leave your jewelry or any little shiny thing lying around." Firy turned to the bird, puckered her lips, and made kissy noises, and the raven put his beak to her lips, "You're just a thief, aren't you, Jimmy?"

"I've never seen a raven land on anyone. Is he yours?"

Firy shook her head, and Jimmy flew away, "He lives at the ballpark, and he belongs to himself. All of us kids have searched the bleachers, but we've never found his cache of stolen items or his nest. He's the smartest raven around. But, like I said, he's a thief. Candy wrappers, keys, a metal chain, hair barrettes. If you are nice to him and share your snacks, he might just bring you one of his trinkets," Firy laughed, her eyes following the bird. "Of course, it might be a bracelet or something he stole from someone else."

"I don't have any jewelry or money to buy candy, so he won't mind me."

The girls looked at each other for a moment. Franella bit her lip, and Firy scuffed her feet on the wooden sidewalk.

"I heard about your folks. Sorry." Firy said.

"Yeah, me too. About your mama, I mean, it was two years ago, but I bet you still miss her." Franella put her hand over her stomach and tried to control the rumbling. She didn't know what to say to Firy, how to express her sympathy and her grief.

Firy avoided looking at the other girl. She sniffed, wiped her nose on her sleeve, and said, "Sorry, Frannie, I have a lot of chores. It's my turn to take care of Anna Marie and Great-gram. Maybe we can visit next week."

Franella was disappointed in the conversation but knew it was her own fault. She never knew what to say. "You're the only one who's ever called me Frannie. Friends." Franella shivered in the chilly, misty rain. "I've been here for months and haven't seen you. Missed you."

"Major Bernice won't let town kids in the orphanage. She says we're a bad influence on her charges."

"Don't get me started on the old bag," Franella said.

"Maybe Uncle Ade can take us out on his boat, that is if you're not afraid," Firy bit her lip and dropped her eyes, "I mean—sorry. Your folks and all—I forgot."

"It's okay," Franella said, but it wasn't. Firy's comment threw violent images into Franella's mind. Images of fomenting waves, a capsized fishing vessel, and her parent's bodies tossed about by the deadly sea. "I have to go, Firy. I'll see you around." Franella clutched her stomach and turned away.

"Maybe we can have a tea party with Miss Ruth," Firy called to Franella's back as the girl rushed away, "I'll bring Anna Marie. You'll like my little sister. She's so sweet."

Franella tried to outrun the pain in her belly. She stumbled toward the water. She had lived near and on the water her whole life. She had always loved the sound of the surf, the froth and foam of the breaking waves as the tide came in, the many moods of the ocean, and the animals it contained. Now, it was the evil entity that took her parents. Despite that, she was drawn to the sea's mysterious depths and the wonder of its constant tides, the eternal ebb and flow of its waters.

She clambered over the barnacle-covered rocks on Crescent Beach and let the rain mingle with her tears as she stared into the tide pools. The seaweed left on the beach by the receding tide typically had a salty, fishy odor. Today, the aged kelp gave a putrid sulfuric rotten egg smell that didn't help her stomach.

Franella stood at the water's edge, letting the incoming waves spill over her shoes. She saw several Pacific white-sided dolphins. Their joyful frolicking in the harbor did not elevate her mood, nor did the mama otter floating on her back with her young one sitting on her chest. Being here in Firy's hometown caused Franella to think of that summer two years ago when she met the so-called Russian princess.

TEN

Two years earlier, 1936
Port Alexander

"Franella Feddersen, have you got yourself up that tree again?"

"No, ma'am," she pictured herself in the chicken coop gathering eggs.

"Franella Feddersen, did you sneak a book up there with you?"

"No, ma'am." She thrust the picture book under the bib of her overalls.

"Franella Feddersen!" the harsh voice carried through the neighborhood, "Are those berry buckets full?"

"Yes, ma'am." She saw them full of huckleberries, or maybe she'd picked sweet nagoonberries.

"Franella Feddersen, come here now." Her mother flapped her apron and stamped her foot. Franella dropped out of the tree, and the picture book and empty buckets fell at her feet.

"Franella Feddersen, the Good Book says, let your yes be yes, and your no be no."

"Huh?"

"I declare, girl, you wouldn't know the truth if it up and slapped you in the face, doncha know?"

Franella cupped her cheeks with her hands and wondered how it would feel to be slapped by truth. Mama tugged on her daughter's braid, re-tying the ribbon. "Get that wild look out of your eyes. The truth won't really slap you."

"No, ma'am. I mean, yes, ma'am."

"Take these buckets, and don't come back until they're full." Franella opened her mouth to protest. Her mother pulled a cookie from her apron pocket and slipped it between her daughter's lips. "No more yes ma'aming and no ma'aming me, or we'll never get the pies made."

The girl groaned. Mama stamped her foot again. "Don't be groaning and complaining like the Israelites did in the desert. It brought the wrath of God, doncha know?"

Franella tried to picture what that would look like. She knew God sent the Bible people manna bread and quail birds to eat. Maybe wrath was some kind of dessert. Wrath pie. Probably just as good as manna bread.

Her mother pushed her through the gate, looked upward, and chastised the Almighty. "I declare, Lord, I don't know why you saddled me with that girl. Goodness knows she ain't a bad child, just off somewhere in her own head. I declare it doesn't get the chores done, doncha know?"

Franella lumbered across the meadow, then sat on an upturned bucket and played the other like a drum. The warm sun enticed her, and soon, she lay next to the huckleberry bushes and went to sleep. When she awoke, she wondered why she was there. She didn't even like huckleberries. Nagoonberries, now that's a berry.

"Franella," called her father from the back door, "come to supper." Her folks were almost done eating when she arrived with a berry-stained face and one bucket half full.

Her mother ladled fish chowder into a bowl, knowing she, herself, would have to find the missing bucket in the morning and finish picking the nagoons. "Tomorrow, we bake pies." She set the bowl on the table. "Come. Eat."

"Aww..."

"You must learn. You will bake pie, and tomorrow at supper, you will present it to Miss Ruth."

Franella jumped up. Over went the bowl of chowder. She threw out her arms. "She's coming. Hooray!" The glass of milk crashed to the floor. "Sorry, Mama. Sorry, Papa."

"Franella," her papa said in his soft voice, "Get a mop and rag. Clean up the mess." He patted his wife's hand, "It's okay, Britta. Miss Ruth will be in Port Alexander all summer."

"All summer?" The mop stabbed her father in the eye as Franella turned and squealed in delight. Günter Feddersen rubbed his eyes and saw his tired wife reach for another biscuit. She slathered it with butter and jam. Sometimes, biscuits and jam got them through the day. Pies. Cakes. Doughnuts. He pictured all the sweet things they liked to eat in the wake of their daughter's many mishaps.

Early the following morning, Franella finished her oatmeal and asked permission to meet Miss Ruth at the dock. They didn't know what hour she would arrive, but Franella wanted to be there anyway. She grabbed an extra biscuit, and the jam toppled to the floor as she raced out the door.

Britta sighed and wiped up the mess. Günter lit his pipe. "Did you tell the girl that Miss Ruth is bringing her a friend?"

Britta shook her head and let the dishes clatter into the sink. "I don't know if I can have an Indian in my house."

"Miss Ruth says she is Creole, which is Russian and Native."

"Even so," Britta shuddered, "everyone knows they're dirty and...and heathenish, uncivilized."

"Britta, anyone Miss Ruth brings into our home will be welcome. You will be kind."

Britta frowned and wiped the table.

"Our Franella has no friends. We do this for her, eh, Britta?"

She grabbed the broom. Her husband took it from her and forced her to meet his eyes. "People are people. Dear Britta, you remember how you felt when my mother would not accept you, my little Danish..."

"Just because I wasn't Norwegian..."

"So, you look at this girl who is also not Norwegian, and you remember how you felt."

"But Günter, a Native."

"All people are loved by God, is it not so?"

Britta nodded, but as Günter left the house, she muttered, "Some He loves more than others, and I don't see how He can care about those dirty..."

Britta attacked her already clean house with a dust cloth and a broom. She realized their daughter did not fit. No matter how much Britta squeezed and pushed, Franella would not be molded. Now, Miss Ruth was bringing a Native child, who also would not fit, not in this town, not in this house.

Before noon, Britta's racing thoughts settled into a plan. Not a good plan, to be sure, but a plan, none the less. Britta stripped off her apron and grabbed her pocketbook. Like a seiner carefully setting out his net to capture a particular species of salmon, Britta set out by innuendo and rumor to do the same. First stop: the Lutheran Women's Society for the Propagation of the Gospel, next the Women's Auxiliary of the Sons of Norway, then the Port Alexander Ladies' Sewing Circle. Of course, she admonished everyone to be discreet and swore them all to secrecy.

By the time Britta reached home, everyone in the bustling fishing village knew Miss Ruth was bringing a Russian to spend the summer with Franella. Britta cautioned them not to treat Firy Oskolkoff like the aristocrat she was, the great-great-granddaughter of Princess Maria Maksoutoff, the wife of Alaska's last Russian governor. After all, they were all Americans now, and royalty was of no consequence.

At the beginning of the fishing season, Port Alexander swarmed with boats and barges arriving. Supplies had been ordered by Anderson's Bakery, Finn's General Store, and Torvald's Tavern and Bathhouse. Businesses during spawning season flourished as the population increased more than tenfold over winter's permanent residents.

Uncle Al's boat carried Miss Ruth's supplies for the summer. Clothing: minimal. Foodstuffs: adequate. Her Sunday school and Bible study materials were abundant, as were her medical supplies. She even had a box of what she called fripperies for the Ladies' Sewing Circle.

The docks flooded with townsfolk who came to welcome the fishing fleet and pick up mail and supplies. A skinny, dark-haired girl ran up and down the dock, pigtails flying. She waved and screeched, "Miss Ruth, did you bring them?"

Miss Ruth waved from the bow. "I brought you the biggest hug in Alaska. Just wait till I get ashore."

Franella laughed. "What else?"

"I brought you a friend."

Firy hunched behind Miss Ruth. Franella frowned, standing on one foot, then the other, "Nobody wants me for a friend. I'd rather have picture books."

Firy tugged on the edge of Miss Ruth's jacket, "Now, can I go home?"

"You have a job to do this summer, my girl."

"She doesn't want me for a friend, and I don't like her either."

When Miss Ruth wasn't looking, Firy stuck out her tongue. Franella was waving to the mail carrier two boats over and didn't see.

Miss Ruth knelt and held Firy's hands. "I know your mama's death makes you sad all the time, and that makes you mad. But I need you to help me with Franella Feddersen."

"I can't do anything, don't want to," Firy growled, wishing Miss Ruth couldn't see the sad and mad that was in her.

"She needs you."

"What's the matter with her?"

Miss Ruth lifted the last box of books and looked at Franella, who leaned over and scraped at the barnacles on the pilings. "I say nothing's wrong with her, but the people here in Port Alexander will say everything."

"Is it nothing or everything?" Firy put her hand on her head, which had started to hurt.

Franella watched Ade Bunderson tie up the boat. She'd heard bits of the conversation. "They say I'm addled." She yelled across the dock.

"What?"

"Addlepated. Most people say I'm half-witted, but Miss Ruth says I'm not, so I must be full-witted."

"I never heard of anybody being full-witted," Firy called.

"Pelican," Franella said.

"What?" Firy looked around.

"Gone now. You like pelicans? Beds, blue coverlets."

"What?"

"You and Miss Ruth are staying with us. They like fish you know, all kinds."

"Who? What?" Firy scratched her head.

"The pelicans, silly, what did you think I was talking about?"

"Grab a box, girls." Herring Peter ordered and spat tobacco juice, barely missing his mongrel dog. He stacked Miss Ruth's boxes and Firy's salt sack in his cart and turned to Franella. "Lead the way."

"You know where I live."

"Don't sass me, girl." Herring Pete's rheumy eyes leaked into his scruffy beard. His mongrel dog loped alongside him.

Franella led them to her home on the outskirts of Port Alexander, jabbering to Miss Ruth all the way. Firy frowned and looked over her shoulder. Uncle Ade waved and gave her a thumbs-up.

Firy turned away and kicked at a rock in the dirt road. Why couldn't she stay home or spend the summer on the Ollie B? Why must she stay with this strange girl who wouldn't shut up?

72

ELEVEN

"Firy, your heart is like a sunflower, bent over and droopy." Franella dug into the wet sand with a stick.

"Is not..."

"I can see it." Another hole poked.

"Cannot." Firy put her hands over her heart just in case.

Franella frowned and looked over the water. She sighed and threw away the stick, and said, "My mama's a teakettle, always boiling, steaming, and whistling. The stopper blows if I don't answer right."

Firy rubbed her chest, glad that Franella's attention had moved on. "Do you know the right answers?"

"Most of the time, I see them on her face."

Firy shook her head. "I never met anybody like you, Frannie."

"They always call me Franella. Never Frannie, Fran, or Ella. Just Franella Feddersen."

"Well, I'll call you Frannie."

Franella Feddersen smiled. "I like you, Firy Wall. We can be best friends."

"Uh, okay." Firy felt sorry for Franella, whose mother was nothing like her own mama had been.

Franella frowned again, "Mama's always asking me how I got into our family. She says I'm not like the rest of them." Franella bit her lip to stop its quiver.

Firy looked away. "What picture do you have of your papa?"

Franella Feddersen laughed, "He's an old tabby cat sleeping in front of the stove."

Firy tucked her hair behind her ear and picked up the stick. "I wish I was like you, Frannie, seeing pictures and all."

"Tell you a secret since we're best friends. Promise not to tell?"

Firy nodded.

"Even though I'm twelve years old, I only look at picture books. I can't read, can't figure out the words." She dug at the sand with her bare foot.

Firy had outgrown her fondness for reading when Uncle Ade taught her to fish. Boats rather than books called to her. Still, whenever she wanted, she could pick up a book and read. "I'll teach you."

"Teachers in Wrangell said I was hopeless. Papa read my lessons to me and asked me the test questions. He wrote down my answers. Finally, he said I did not have to go to school anymore. Then Mama signed me up for correspondence school."

"Was that better?"

"Papa still read the lessons. It was easier to listen when I was mending the fishing nets. Still couldn't read."

Firy whispered, "The words are made of little letters."

"I know that. I just can't remember their names."

"You don't have to. You can put pictures of the sounds in your head."

"Too hard, I don't know what the sounds look like."

Firy put her hands on her hips. She stamped her foot and stared at the other girl. "Franella Feddersen! Frannie! Miss Ruth said I'm stuck here all summer to do a job, and that job is you. Now lay down on the sand."

The low tide had left the sand damp, but Franella did as she was told. Firy used the stick to draw a line the length of Franella's body.

"Squirrels..."

"What?"

"There are squirrels in the clouds searching for nuts."

Firy gripped her stick tighter and sighed. This was going to be a long summer. "Close your eyes."

"Doesn't matter, I still see them."

"You tell those squirrels to go back to their tree clouds, then pull the curtains over your eyes so you don't see anything until I tell you. Now stretch out your right hand like you were going to reach that kelp." Firy drew another line, pulled Franella to her feet, and pointed, "See, that's almost you."

"What?"

"The long up-and-down line is your body. The half line across the top is your arm."

Firy handed a wary Franella Feddersen the stick. "Poke the sand where your belly button would be and draw a short line across."

Again, Franella did as she was told, barely seeing the squirrels in the tree clouds.

Firy made the F sound, "Hear that? That is the sound of F-F-F-F-Franella Feddersen."

Franella made the sound again and again as she drew F's up and down the beach. "I am Franella Feddersen, and you are my friend Firy. F-F-F."

"That's right," Firy yelled, then muttered so the other girl wouldn't hear. "My name starts with F, and this is going to be a long, long summer."

The beach became their classroom. The sand their paper. Sticks their pencils. Franella worked hard, but the pictures of the letters wouldn't stay in her head.

"I'll never learn. I quit."

"Frannie, look at me. You are the smartest girl I know."

"Everyone knows I can't sit still enough to pay attention."

"You are going to learn to read if it kills me. Now, let me think." Firy snapped her fingers. "It's because your brain is too full. It spills over and runs through your body and gets your muscles riled up. That's why you move about so." Firy sat on a log and stared at the sun glistening silver on the water. "Miss Ruth says when we have problems or troubles, we can ask Bozhe. That's the secret."

"Did you ask Him why your mama died? What did He say?""

Hands on her hips, Firy Oskolkoff Wall looked Franella Feddersen in the eye and growled, "Don't talk about my mama. Ever!"

Franella held her hands behind her back to stop their shaking. She rocked toe to heel and took a shallow breath. "I'm sorry, Firy."

"Just shut up."

Franella cried. Seeing her body shake, Firy, although still mad, came close and patted her shoulder. "Sorry. Pay attention."

Franella hiccupped twice and wiped her nose on her sleeve.

"You're going to learn to read this summer. I promise."

"But what if it does?"

"Does what?"

"Kill you?"

Firy waved Franella away and watched her run up and down the beach doing somersaults and cartwheels. She lay in the sand above the tide line and made a sand angel. "I feel better now. I'm ready to write the letters again."

"That's it, Frannie. You're a genius."

"What?"

"You have to keep moving. Do jumping jacks or somersaults or wave your arms or something before and after your lesson."

Franella laughed out loud. She picked up the writing stick and waved it above her head. "And in the middle, too."

"That's the secret."

And so, it proved to be.

TWELVE

American women during the Depression used and reused whatever resources were available, and so, too, did the women of Southeast Alaska. They favored the 100-pound salt sacks used to mild cure salmon on the fish scows. After washing and bleaching, the material softened and proved useful for dishtowels, tablecloths, and children's clothing.

Miss Ruth brought yards of embroidery floss, ribbons, and rickrack to the weekly Ladies' Sewing Circle to use as embellishments. Neither Firy nor Franella was interested in Hardanger or Huck embroidery.

They sat among these Scandinavian housewives when forced but stabbed their fingers several times. After staining the bleached fabric with blood, Britta banished them to the backyard. Miss Ruth gave them paper and crayons to design the embellishments.

Several weeks later, the sewing circle examined the girls' efforts and found their designs worthy of adorning the aprons and dishtowels.

"Franella should grow up to be a fashion lady for the movies. There is a movie ship somewhere in the Alexander Archipelago, doncha know?" Britta said.

"Yes, it's called the Neptune. Daniel Salzman is documenting the lives of Southeast Alaska's fishermen." Miss Ruth said.

"My husband will find the boat. They will take her designs to movie people in Hollywood, America."

"I think, dear Britta, the good Lord has a different path for Franella."

"He should only tell us. She is all the time looking at picture books and now drawing squiggles and swirls and making with the letters, doncha know?"

Miss Ruth moved to the open window. "Bring me the white coverlet from the clothesline, girls."

Miss Ruth spread the coverlet in the middle of the sewing circle. All the women agreed that the white-on-white embroidery was lovely.

"Yes, it is pretty," Britta said, "It took me two weeks to finish stitching the design."

"But what is it?" asked Miss Ruth.

Britta wrinkled her brow, "Wiggles and swirls."

Miss Ruth laughed and held up the coverlet, "You are right, of course, but if you look closer, you will see..."

"Psst. Miss Ruth," Franella motioned from the open doorway, "Mama can't read. She doesn't know I hid words in the design."

Miss Ruth hugged Franella, "Your Mama has embroidered all the names of God on that coverlet. Please think about telling her. I think it would make her happy."

Franella shook her head. "Don't make me. She doesn't know why God put me in her family." Franella put her hands on her hips, looked heavenward, and used her mother's critical voice. "You couldn't bless me with a dozen children like all my friends. You only gave one, and such a one! She is like no one else, doncha know? What am I to do with her?" Franella's eyes misted, and she sniffed.

Miss Ruth dropped to her knees and held the young girl. Franella wiped her face on Miss Ruth's new black vest, unaware of what she had left behind. Miss Ruth looked heavenward as Franella had done. *See Bozhe; she has baptized my vest.* "You know your mama loves you."

"I wish you were my mama."

"Why do you say that?"

"Mama is too heavy for me."

Miss Ruth raised her eyebrows. "How so?"

"Most of the time, when I mess things up, she wails and wonders what's to become of me. If I manage to do something even a little bit right, she brags to her friends and wants to show me off to the whole world. It's too much for me, heavy."

"The Lord has chosen you to be Britta's child. He has His reasons. You're twelve now, so I'm going to share with you woman to woman."

Miss Ruth and Franella sat in the grass in the backyard. Franella straightened her skirt and folded her legs under her. She looked into Miss Ruth's eyes and heard Miss Ruth clear her throat and whisper, "My mama died the day I was born."

Franella sniffed, hiccupped, and leaned against Miss Ruth's shoulder. She heard the thump of the older woman's heart.

"I was raised by my grandpa and his sister, my great Aunt Elvira. Like your mama, she excelled at cooking, cleaning, canning, and sewing."

Franella Feddersen's face scrunched up. She knew Miss Ruth would tell her she needed to excel also.

"It is important to do all those things and do them well. Some women give their lives to this because God has called them. Others, he calls to a different path."

"Mama doesn't know that."

"Aunt Ellie didn't know either. Although she loved me, I didn't feel it because she didn't understand the way I was made here or here," Miss Ruth said, tapping her heart and temple.

Franella sighed and again wished Miss Ruth was her mama. She was sure Firy did, too.

"The Lord told me to be gentle with Aunt Ellie, to let her teach me womanly things when all I wanted to do was work the ranch with my grandfather. I remember Aunt Ellie wanted me to bake the best pie crust in the territory."

"Did you, Miss Ruth?"

Miss Ruth threw her head back and laughed, "No, and I haven't made a pie since I left the ranch when I was twenty."

"But you're so old..."

Miss Ruth reached into the pocket of her long black skirt. "Have a lemon drop, and let me tell you about the women the Lord brought into my life to give me what Aunt Ellie couldn't."

Franella settled in the grass. She could see Firy peeking around the corner of the house but did not motion her over.

"Their names were Maureen, Iolana, and Sister Agnes."

Franella didn't move a muscle. The picture in her head of a young Miss Ruth and the women who filled up the lonely places captured her attention and focused her. She forced herself to remain still as Miss Ruth finished. "I think your mama could use some help serving the coffee and pie."

"I will be the best coffee and pie server in the territory." She scrambled up, and the screen door banged behind her. Miss Ruth prayed Franella would not drop the pie or slosh the coffee.

Firy tiptoed around the corner of the house, then ran into the woman's open arms. Miss Ruth began again. "My mother died the day I was born..."

"Oh, Firy, I'm going to miss you. I wish summer was just starting, not ending."

"Yeah, me too." Firy, distracted, watched the horizon. The Ollie B. should be here soon. Home. Family. Anna Marie. She feared her baby sister wouldn't remember her.

"Firy, will you write to me?"

"Sure."

"I can read now. You were a good teacher."

"Uh-huh." Firy kept her gaze on the harbor.

"I mean it. No one else figured it out. You are a genius. Firy, look at me." Franella blew her nose and rubbed her eyes. "You're the only friend I've ever had, and I'll be lonely without you." She scrubbed her eyes again with the now soggy handkerchief.

Firy looked at her, perhaps for the first time that summer. "Frannie, I wish you had sisters or a cousin to live with you, even a brother or a dog. Then you wouldn't be lonely."

Franella said, "When you talked about your mama, it made me happy. I wish your mama wasn't dead. I wish my mama was like her."

"You wish a lot of impossible things," Firy didn't know what to say about Franella's mama or all the sad things inside. She shut her ears to Franella and turned her attention to the Ollie B. sliding into the mooring slip. Uncle Ade threw her the mooring rope.

"Firy?"

"I'll write to you, Frannie. Really, I will."

Families prepared to leave until the next season; goodbyes, farewells, and promises to keep in touch were offered and received. The end of the salmon season in Port Alexander mirrored its beginning.

Uncle Al loaded Miss Ruth's bags and boxes as she said her goodbyes. The women from the Ladies' Sewing Circle hugged her and then turned to Firy.

"Pleasure to make your acquaintance," one bobbed.

"So nice to have you here for the summer."

"So sweet of you to befriend that addlepated Franella Feddersen."

Firy's stiff posture relaxed once the pleasantries ceased. The crowd faded away until only the Feddersen family remained. Günter shook Firy's hand, and Britta enveloped her in a suffocating hug, "I knew you were a royal from the first moment I saw you. Come back anytime, little princess."

Firy, anxious to board her uncle's boat, turned to Franella. Awkward. Silent. Uncle Ade shouted, "Time to shove off."

Firy whispered, "I'm almost glad I came."

Miss Ruth hugged Franella and handed her two books, Little Women and Nancy Drew.

THIRTEEN

The yellow warmth of the sun hovered over the cold water of Sitka Sound. A lot had happened in the two years since Firy had visited Port Alexander and unlocked the secret of reading for Franella. Since then, Franella had consumed almost every book in the village, most more than once. The port's hard-working families had few books and little time to read. They thought Franella even odder as she went door to door begging for reading material. Books, old newspapers, she'd take anything. Most houses at least had a family Bible, but they were not shared.

Now, she was in Sitka, which had a library. It was perhaps the only good thing about her current situation. When she could, she escaped to the library and lost herself in books. Franella laughed out loud when she remembered the first time she hid behind the bookshelves. Miss Drake, the librarian, caught her doing jumping jacks.

"It helps me learn, ma'am."

The librarian raised an eyebrow, "Are you sure it's necessary?"

"Yes, ma'am, and sometimes I do squats. There's not enough room to do cartwheels."

"I should think not."

"I'm not bothering anyone, and it helps me concentrate."

The librarian looked at the awkward girl in the ugly clothes who waited almost daily for the library to open. She smiled when she remembered the first time Franella came. She had run her hand over a row of books and murmured, "I love you. I really do. I'll come to you every day."

Miss Drake's face softened, and she said, "I think you read more than anyone in Sitka. Do what you need to do. Just remember to do it quietly."

"Yes, ma'am. Could you help me? I'd like a book about the Russians in Alaska, one about Napoleon, and maybe one about how tea is made. Crocodiles, do you have a book about crocodiles? Oh, and I desperately want a book about how the English language came to be, you know, its history."

Miss Drake took a deep breath, "That's quite a list. I'll see what I can do, my dear."

Several weeks ago, Franella had started lessons with Father Alexi. The rest of her tutoring sessions began shortly after that. The long hours of intense study kept her mind occupied. It helped free her from the images that came unbidden and tormented her.

Today, Franella felt the ebb and flow as the wind stirred up whitecaps on the incoming tide. The tide came in and went out. Would her emotions ever flow like that? They seemed to plunge downward, and she couldn't force her feelings to move in an upward direction. Loneliness and aloneness haunted her. She turned away from the water and, with a determined step, headed to St. Michael's Russian Orthodox Church.

"May I borrow one of your Russian history books?"

"You want the one written in English?" Father Alexi asked.

"I want to try to translate the one written in Russian."

Father Alexi stroked his beard, "I'm not sure you are ready for such a difficult task, my dear."

"Please, I need to lose myself," Franella looked at the tip of her shoes, then felt the Father's hand patting her shoulder.

"I understand, my dear." He motioned for his cleric, Father Mikail, to bring the history books in both English and Russian. "I know what it's like to lose and be lost."

Franella took the books, looked into his sad eyes, and mumbled her thanks. The two priests stood in the doorway and watched her cross the gravel road. "I think it would help the girl if you shared with her how you lost your firstborn son and baby girl in Russia and then the rest of your family in the shipwreck off Kodiak," Father Mikail said.

Father Alexi turned away. The young cleric sighed and gently murmured to the priest's retreating back, "It would help you also, Father."

Franella stumbled toward the library, where she sat in silence. *Father Alexi can't see my loneliness or notice the hollowness inside me, so why does he know I lose myself in books? But when I finish reading, the emptiness returns. I'm sure he doesn't understand how I struggle to face each day and dread the years ahead.*

FOURTEEN

For a short while, those who lived in Southeast Alaska, especially the children, enjoyed the explosion of fall foliage—gold, red, and orange, which vied with the ubiquitous vibrant evergreens. Just as quickly as those intense colors came, they dropped, and the ground was covered with dry, brittle leaves. Sitka's children loved the crackly crunch they sounded when piled, and the kids rushed to wade through them on Sitka's rare, crisp fall days, knowing that all too soon, those leaves would be soddened and soggy.

The temperature decreased, and the rain increased in both volume and intensity. The shorter, wet, chilly days prodded the inhabitants to make sure their preparations for winter were adequate. Johnny, the Bear Boy, made efforts to relieve the citizens of Sitka of any foodstuffs they left unattended. Like everyone else, he needed to resupply his cache for winter. This usually meant he bothered the townspeople by begging and thieving. Johnny liked to supplement his forest foraging with white man's food.

Major Bernice warned the orphans to be aware of the large, unkempt Tlingit and to run away if he came near. Her warning made Franella curious.

One Saturday, Franella visited her only friend, who lived on the corner of Biorka and Baranof streets. "Firy, who is this Johnny, the Bear Boy that Major Bernice warned us about?"

"He was a friend of my mother's. Nobody else liked him. He doesn't speak English."

"I want to meet him."

"No, you don't. He's just a crazy old Tlingit."

"I'm going to meet him."

"You're nuts," Firy scowled.

"Help me."

"He won't come until spring. I hope you forget."

"I won't. Tell me about him."

Firy sighed, "My mother always filled a knapsack with food and stuff and hung it on our back porch for him. She put an old tin washtub out for him so he could bathe. Nobody else in town was nice to him."

At the beginning of spring, a soft yellow sun hung over Sitka Sound and glistened on the water. Eagles and ravens competed with seabirds for scraps from the seiners and trawlers as they unloaded their catch at the fish canneries—a typical fishy day during king and silver salmon season.

Franella showed up at Firy's bright and early on the first day of spring. "Where's Johnny?"

"Can you come next Saturday? We'll put out the food, and Johnny will come."

"How will he know?" Franella asked.

Firy shrugged, "He knows."

Franella held little Anna Marie while Firy filled an old knapsack with Pilot bread, a package of Velveeta Cheese, two cans of peaches, and a Sugar Daddy.

"Where is everybody?" Franella asked.

"My cousin Masha is back in Ninilchik for a while. Elizaveeta is with her stupid friends, and Henry is playing baseball. Papa Bill is at the mill."

"I don't think your papa likes me," Franella sighed.

"He doesn't like anybody since Mama died, just Anna Marie."

"Sometimes, I'm like that. I don't like anybody, just you and Miss Ruth," Franella said.

Firy turned away from the sadness in Franella's voice. "Papa will be mad if he finds out Johnny, the Bear Boy, was here. I hope Johnny comes and goes before Henry gets home. He'll tell on me."

"What about Elizaveeta?" Franella asked as she handed Anna Marie to Firy.

"Thanks for getting her to sleep. I hope I can lay her in her crib without waking her."

As Firy came back into the room, Franella said, "Your sister?"

"I can make her not tell. Big sisters have their ways."

"I wouldn't know."

"Mama was always good to Johnny, so he likes us. I'll sit on the porch and wait. You stay in the house with Anna Marie, and I'll get you when he's ready."

"How long before he shows up?"

Firy looked out of the kitchen window. "Those yellow flowers were buds yesterday. Now, they're blossoms. Johnny will be along soon." Firy bit her lip, "Darn it! Sven and the Jensen twins are playing ball on the road."

"Everybody plays on the road."

Firy threw up the sash and leaned out the window. Popeye, Papa Bill's mutt, rested his front legs on the windowsill, wagged his tail, and barked as Firy yelled. "Sven! Take the twins and get off my road!"

"It ain't your road," he answered.

Firy slammed the window shut and turned to Franella. "This is bad. I saw Johnny turn the corner. He's coming this way."

"I thought that's what we wanted," Franella said.

"Johnny's a big man, but Mama says he's like a little boy, and those guys out there are mean to him. It scares him."

As Franella raced out the door, she looked over her shoulder and shouted, "You tend to the boys. I'll take care of Johnny."

Firy looked toward the mongrel dog she had come to love, "Anna Marie is asleep in her crib. Stay with her, Popeye."

Popeye wagged his tail and barked.

Firy shook her finger, "No barking! If Anna Marie is still asleep when I get back, I'll make you a baloney sandwich."

Popeye's ears perked up, and he drooled but did not bark. He trotted to the bedroom and lay in the doorway.

Johnny, the Bear Boy, lumbered down the road and stopped when he saw Franella running toward him. Franella noticed the confused look on his face and slowed. She tiptoed toward him, smiled, and tried to remember the Tlingit greeting Petrov Bravebird had taught her. She couldn't picture the word, so she pointed to herself and said the Tlingit word for girl, "*Shaatk'atsk'u.*"

Johnny nodded as if to say I knew that. Franella shrugged, pointed to him, and said, *"Sh yaa.awudaneiyi."*

Johnny, the Bear Boy, grinned, put his hand on his heart, and repeated the word several times. Apparently, he liked being called a respected person.

Firy stood toe to toe with Sven and ordered him to take his friends and leave.

"Who's going to make me? You're just a girl."

90

Firy grabbed the bat out of his hands and held it over his head. "Get going, Sven."

"Alright! You don't have to get nasty! I'm supposed to be on my way to the post office anyway." Sven ordered the twins not to be stupid and ran down the street.

"Dirty rotten coward!" The Jensen boys yelled after him and then strutted toward Johnny. Franella felt the old Native stiffen and saw fear come into his eyes. She stepped in front of him. The twins took their slingshots out of their back pockets and scooped up a handful of pebbles.

"I wouldn't do that if I were you," Franella growled.

"Yeah, who's going to stop us?" the older by-two-minutes twin said.

"That old Native is good for nothing—shouldn't even be breathing," the younger by-two-minutes twin tried to sound tough.

Firy raced over and stood next to Franella, "You boys better watch out. Franella speaks Tlingit, and she can tell Johnny it's okay to beat you—practically to death."

Franella cupped her hand around Firy's ear and whispered, "I just started my lessons. I only know a few words, none of which will be useful."

"What did she say?"

"She said Johnny knows many Tlingit curses. His mother was a spirit woman."

"So what?"

"That's like a witch."

Wide-eyed, the twins looked at each other, then Johnny and the girls. "We're not afraid," they said in unison, but their voices quivered.

Jimmy the Raven, circling overhead, dived, and the Jensen

twins threw their hands up to protect their heads. Jimmy cawed, circled in an upward spiral, shrieked, and flew away.

"Franella, tell Johnny to curse the boys before he beats them up."

"How'd you like a raven to peck your nose off when you're sleeping." Franella, older than the others, stood tall and, in her most mature voice, said, "Without a nose, you'll have difficulty breathing, and you will die."

"I think Jimmy the Raven would like the job," Firy said.

Franella turned to Johnny and slowly recited the days of the week in Tlingit. Johnny looked puzzled and raised his hand as if to stop her.

"That's his cursing hand," Firy cried, "Run! Run fast so the curse misses you!"

The younger-by-two-minutes twin dropped his slingshot and pebbles. Both boys ran. Johnny, the Bear Boy, asked Franella why she listed the days of the week, but of course, she didn't understand him. Firy made signs for Johnny to follow them to her house. She picked several of the yellow flowers near the porch and gave them to Johnny. He put them in his shirt pocket and said, "Mama."

Firy sniffed, not wanting to remember how her mother had taken care of Johnny. She settled him at the kitchen table, unhooked the knapsack from the cache hook on the back porch, and brought it to him.

Anna Marie still napped. Popeye came into the kitchen and settled at Johnny's feet, but his eyes followed Firy as she sliced the baloney, and Franella slapped it between slices of white bread. The girls made six sandwiches. Johnny, the Bear Boy, ate four and put two in his pockets. Popeye nuzzled the old man, sniffing at his pockets. Johnny pushed the dog away and said his goodbyes. Popeye followed him to the door, whined, and looked at Firy.

"I didn't forget you, Popeye. Do you want your sandwich with bread or without?" He danced around the kitchen and barked. A wail from the bedroom told Firy Anna Marie was awake.

Franella sat with her elbows on the kitchen table. "That does it," she said, reaching for a lemon drop from the small dish near the salt and pepper shakers. "I'm going to have Petro Bravebird step up my lessons. Tlingit is the hardest language I've ever tried to learn."

"Why do you want to learn it anyway?" Firy asked as she held Anna Marie on her hip.

"Because it's there, and I don't know it."

"Just how many languages do you know?" Firy asked.

"Danish from my mama, Norwegian from my papa. I picked up some Swedish from the people in Port Alexander. There were some Chinese workers at the cannery, but I never met them. I'd like to learn Chinese, it's such a pretty sing-song language. Paster Nels taught me a little Hebrew and Greek. He didn't really speak it but studied the meanings of Bible words. It was interesting. Miss Ruth said the new Lutheran pastor is willing to teach me the Bible languages as soon as his wife and children arrive and get settled." Franella shrugged, "He's uncomfortable meeting with me alone. Isn't that weird? Anyway, Father Alexi is teaching me Russian. None of them are like Tlingit."

"When I first met you, Frannie, I told you how smart you are. I can barely manage English. I'm so dumb. I hate school."

"Miss Ruth told me there are all kinds of wisdom. Someday, you will realize the kind of smarts you have." Franella smiled at her young friend.

Firy shook her head. "My mama was smart. Kind, too. Everybody loved her."

"I think you must be like your mama. I've heard people in town call you Our Firy, like the 'our' was part of your name. That must mean they love you."

Again, Firy shook her head.

Franella rattled on, "Johnny, the Bear Boy is interesting to me. You said your mama liked Johnny, and I do, too. He's going to be my friend,"

Firy slammed Anna Marie's cup of tinned milk on the table. "You can't. People will think you are as crazy as he is. Nobody likes him, not even me!"

Franella shrugged and chomped the lemon drop between her back teeth. "Nobody likes me, and almost everybody thinks I'm strange, and you know what, Firy? I don't care." Franella grabbed another lemon drop and pushed away that niggling thought deep inside that said she did care.

FIFTEEN

"Mr. Bravebird, can we double my Tlingit lessons? I need to learn faster. Maybe triple them."

"Why do you wish this?"

"I want to talk to Johnny, the Bear Boy."

"Johnny is his own self, not like others. Are you sure?"

Franella nodded. She felt an affinity with the unkempt old Native but would not articulate it. Petrof Bravebird looked at Franella for a long minute. She met his gaze and resisted the urge to lower her eyes. Finally, he said, "I will talk to Johnny and if he is agreeable, he will join you for lessons. I will act as interpreter, and you will have many conversations about Raven and Eagle and the time before time. This will increase the pace of your learning. But only if Johnny, the Bear Boy, finds you acceptable. You understand this?"

"He will agree."

"How do you know this?"

Franella squirmed. She had learned not to let too many people know that she thought and perceived in pictures and images. Somehow, she felt this elder of the Raven moiety would understand. She took a deep breath and said, "Johnny's heart is an abandoned eagle's nest. There are no eggs, no eaglets. It is barren. Johnny feels the emptiness."

Again, Petrov Bravebird stared at Franella for a long moment. She felt his eyes penetrate her soul. He stroked his chin and said,

"You see this?"

"I do."

"You know this pain as well, I think."

Franella looked over the water and let silence be her answer.

"Someday, you will see baby eagles in the nest." Petrov Brave-bird prophesied.

An image of Johnny's heart and hers filled with baby birds flashed in front of Franella's eyes. She blinked rapidly and caught her breath. She saw herself and Johnny, the Bear Boy, linked, then lightning exploded around them and they were forever separated. She pressed her hand to her eyes to stop the painful image.

The following week, and three times a week thereafter, Johnny, the Bear Boy, joined Franella and Petrov Bravebird for lessons. Petrov insisted that all their lessons take place at the Russian Bishop's house or Sitka's small library. Johnny was uncomfortable in the library, and although Miss Drake welcomed whites and Natives alike, she turned up her nose at the unkempt and rather smelly Johnny.

Father Alexi was more accommodating and provided a small room where they could meet. If the weather cooperated, they sat outside the back door of the large building. The private yard kept prying eyes away from the white girl with the two Native men.

Johnny could not push his tongue around English syllables, but this proved to be a motivation for Franella. Soon, she and Johnny were able to have simple conversations in Tlingit, which usually ended in laughter.

Johnny, the Bear Boy, spent more time in town than in past seasons. The townspeople of Sitka were ready to see him go and blamed Franella for his lack of departure. She had proved herself to be just as strange as the old Tlingit, although she was not a thief like Johnny.

Franella and Johnny could be seen almost daily on Crescent Beach, in Totem Park, or sitting on the seawall across from the post office. They were engrossed in their own conversations and ignored the townspeople who came for their morning mail. It looked innocent enough, but it was unseemly for a white teenage girl to be seen with an older Tlingit male. The odd couple often disappeared into the trails on Harbor Mountain or Mt. Verstovia. They frequently walked up the hill behind the new Pioneer's Home to the Russian Cemetery.

Franella read the names on the gravestones aloud. Many were young children. Johnny remained stoic and silent, refusing to answer her questions, although, to be fair, he probably didn't understand her fractured Tlingit. "This is a holy place," he said.

Franella often stood near Firy's mother's grave and wished her own mother had a gravesite she could visit.

"Is not right," Ivan blew on his too-hot coffee.

"You boys know I don't usually agree with Ivan, but this time he's right. A white woman and a Native man, it doesn't look good," Bill Wall said.

"But Bill, you were a white man with a Native woman, Ade said, "and so am I."

Bill slammed his cup on the table. "You know that's different."

Ade shook his head and reached for his coffee. "Franella comes from good stock. I visited her old man every time I was in Port Alexander. I admit she's an odd duck, but she's a good girl."

"Not to good if she's fooling around with a Tlingit," Bill groused.

"You better hope Agrafena's not within earshot. She's the best cook in the Territory, Native or white. You don't want to be banned from the café for bad-mouthing Natives and whites intermingling," Stormy Durand spoke quietly as he paid for his meal and left.

Bill chewed his bacon carefully, "All I'm saying is that Feddersen girl is having an influence on our Firy. I don't like it. She brings that old Tlingit to my house. I've had to chase him off several times. Dirty Native. It's not right, and I have to protect my daughters."

"That's quite a speech, Bill. You must be seriously bothered," Jake said. No one mentioned Bill's wife had cared for Johnny until the year she died.

Carrying the steaming plates, Agrafena weaved through the tables. "Let them be. They are harming no one."

"Looks not right," Ivan said.

"You don't look right!" She slammed the plate of black bear bacon and eggs in front of him. "Eat. Don't talk, old man."

After she had delivered Ivan's food and Bill watched her retreat to the kitchen, he said softly, "You guys know I got nothing against the Indians..."

Jake laughed, "It would be pretty bad if you did, considering your wife was a Yupik. I mean—" Jake shoved more eggs in his mouth.

Bill glowered at him and picked up his coffee cup. "As I was saying, I got nothing against the Natives, but Ivan's right. It doesn't look good for a young white woman..."

"You already said that," Mike reached over, grabbed Ivan's cup, and drank his coffee, "Can't you talk about something else?"

Ivan scowled, and Mike poured him another cup from the pot he continually carried.

"She's a scrawny little girl, hardly a woman, and that Tlingit is old enough to be her grandfather," Ade said. "Nothing is going on with the old man and the girl. Franella is an innocent."

"It doesn't matter. The rumors are flying, and I fear no good will come of it," Bill said. "Something has to be done, and soon."

Franella sat at the orphanage's dining table. The meal, as usual, looked bland and unappetizing. She was almost relieved when Major Bernice crooked her finger. Franella followed the major into her private sitting room.

"It's come to my attention that you are acting in an unladylike way, although I expected nothing more from you. Still, it is my duty to see that you exhibit proper decorum and refined ways. After all, when not within these walls, you are representing this fine institution, and everything you do reflects on me."

"That's ridiculous."

"Don't be impertinent!" The spittle that gathered in the corner of Major Bernice's mouth whenever she lost control was beginning to form.

Franella looked past Major Bernice's shoulders and said nothing.

"What do you have to say for yourself?"

"I say I don't know what you are talking about."

"I've had reports you are running around town with a Tlingit man. A heathen Indian! I won't have it!" Major Bernice's voice cracked and rose. "You are shaming me!"

"Seagulls."

"What?"

Before she thought about the consequences, Franella said, "Your soul looks like the town's garbage dump, full of seagulls picking through the refuse. Rotten. Putrid."

Major Bernice crossed over to Franella. "Stand up, you wicked, wretched child."

Franella stood. Major Bernice slapped her across the face, and Franella fell back into the chair.

"I may have to keep you until you are eighteen, but I won't have you infecting the other children with your evil ways. You are not to come to the dining table until everyone has eaten and the dishes are done. If there are any scraps left, you can have them alone in the kitchen. And don't think anyone will believe you if you say anything. Miss Ruth is off-island at the moment. If you run to her when she returns, it will be the worse for you. Now get out of my sight!"

Several weeks later, Johnny, the Bear Boy, asked Franella why she had become so thin. Since he still didn't speak to anyone in town, she thought it safe to tell him about her punishment from Major Bernice, although she did not reveal it was her association with him that infuriated the good Major.

Johnny sat in silence, then held out his hand. She slipped her hand into his, and he pulled her from the driftwood log they had been sitting on. "I will show you how my grandfather's grandfather lived in this good land of Shee."

Franella laughed, "I don't see how that will fill my belly."

"It will. This beach and the forest will be your kitchen. But you are hungry now, so we go to the woods, which is filled with food that does not need cooking."

The twenty-minute walk towards Indian River only increased Franella's hunger. As they entered the woods, she didn't see anything that looked edible. Like most people in the town, if it wasn't a berry or honey, it wasn't food. She said as much to Johnny.

He chuckled and gripped a young shoot about half an inch above the woody stem of a Devil's Club plant, avoiding its vicious thorns. He twisted it and pulled it upwards, then offered it to her.

Gingerly, she began to eat it, then broke into a wide grin, "Carrots! A spicy carrot with a hint of pine. It's good."

Franella reached for the plant's berries. Johnny knocked her hand away. "Not good. Make sick."

Franella sat back on her heels, "The shoots are good, but the berries are not?"

"Good for bears, not humans."

"What about the leaves?" Franella asked.

"Good, and roots good for tea, medicine. Sacred to Tlingits. Come, we must go further into the woods."

Franella looked at the sun falling lower into the western sky. "It's getting late. I better head back."

"Come." Johnny, the Bear Boy, headed deeper into the forest, past mossy, lichen-covered tree trunks. He did not look back as he pushed aside the underbrush, thick with ferns and berry bushes.

She pictured another wretched evening at the orphanage, listening to Major Bernice elaborate on Franella's many failings, trying to stay out of Tommy's sight so he wouldn't snitch, and facing more rejection from Ruby. The thought did not appeal. She scampered after Johnny. She refused to think about the consequences that would surely come tomorrow.

They trekked through the underbrush for a while then Johnny turned toward the east fork of Kaasda Heen—Indian River. They passed a second growth of Sitka spruce, western hemlock, and Alaska yellow cedar, then crossed several minute streams that eventually fed into Indian River. Their banks were etched with moss, grass, and many wildflowers—daisies, larkspurs, forget-me-nots, and others Franella didn't recognize. They skirted a small muskeg meadow with a view of the Three Sisters mountains.

The last portion of the hike had Franella out of breath. The upward grade was more than she expected. They climbed over a large tree that had fallen across the trail. Franella yearned to ask where they were going and how long it would take to get there, but she had learned it was not the Native way.

Johnny marched in silence. Occasionally, he pointed, and Franella saw deer, a porcupine, and a beaver dam. She hoped to see a beaver but did not. She followed Johnny without speaking.

She caught her breath when she heard a faint rumbling; it became louder, and then she saw the 70-foot Indian River Falls. The last few hundred feet to reach the cascading water, they were forced to scamper over boulders protruding from the creek.

The aged Tlingit and young woman stood side by side in awe of the tumbling water.

Johnny, the Bear Boy, led her to a thicket, and they picked fiddlehead ferns and nettles. Johnny showed her how to clean them.

He brushed away as much of the ferns' brown husk as possible, then washed them in the creek several times. He set them aside to be sauteed later.

They picked saltbush, spruce tips, and burnet, which Johnny said was for a salad. Puffball mushrooms, chocolate lily, cattails, white clover blossoms, and a plant Johnny called Eskimo potatoes, and wild mint completed the day's foraging.

Alaska's extra-long twilight approached as Johnny led her to a secluded meadow. Hidden at its far edge in the underbrush was a crude cabin covered with vines and brush. Johnny made her vow to never reveal its location.

"I give you my word, Johnny. I probably couldn't find my way back here if I tried." Franella said as they entered. She saw animal pelts nailed to the wall and a bearskin rug that had seen better days covered the floor in front of the fireplace. Baskets hung from the low rafters. She assumed they were filled with dried berries and smoked salmon. The two small windows on either side of the door were filthy and allowed little light to enter.

He nodded briefly and lit a kerosene lamp that hung on a large, rusty nail next to the fireplace and another that rested on a rough wooden table. The only other furniture was an old metal army cot in the corner and two small benches under the table. Johnny made a fire in the fireplace of the one-room cabin. The cabin smelled of woodsmoke.

Johnny placed a pot of water on the grate and waited for it to boil. When boiling, he added the fiddlehead ferns. "Boil fifteen minutes, or you will become sick."

"What's in them to make a person sick?"

Johnny shrugged, "It has always been so."

He tore the saltbush and burnet leaves into a bowl and added the mushroom and spruce tips. "Salad," he said.

"Weeds." She smiled, and after taking a bite, she said, "Good."

After eating, Johnny steeped the mint leaves, and they drank the refreshing tea.

"Time to sleep," Johnny said.

Startled, Franella went outside and looked at the sky. The sun slanted low on the horizon, splashing gold, crimson, and purple across the heavens. She watched the sun drop behind the tips of the western mountains on Kruzof Island, and darkness fell. Franella shivered but did not let Johnny, the Bear Boy, know of her concern. Major Bernice would have her hide when she returned to the orphanage.

She closed the door behind her and said, "Where will I sleep?"

Johnny pointed to the cot in the corner.

"And you?"

He wrapped himself in a Hudson's Bay blanket, went to the opposite corner, and settled himself on the floor. Franella watched him for a moment. She removed her shoes and snuggled under the black and red Chilkat blanket embellished with Johnny's clan's regalia. His gentle snores lulled her to sleep.

Johnny, the Bear Boy, woke her before dawn. They drank water from the creek and trekked the four or so miles back to town as the sun broke through the misty clouds covering Mount Verstovia. "We will forage on the beach. Much good food."

Franella had grown up in a fishing family and was used to eating many varieties of fish, as well as mussels, clams, crabs, and other shellfish. Johnny introduced her to bull kelp, black seaweed, ribbon seaweed, and sea lettuce. They were free on Sitka's many beaches.

She tried not to make a face but was unsuccessful. Johnny laughed and said, "The more you eat, the better you will like them."

She coughed, nodded, and took another bite. "I don't think so," she said.

Johnny knew nothing of the government's rules and regulations controlling the forests and waters of the Territory of Alaska. Chief of Police Stormy Durand halted his early morning patrol when he saw the young girl and the old man foraging on the beach. They were harvesting out of season. Clams, crabs, and other shellfish were regulated by the Commission of Fisheries of the United States. Stormy stuck his thumbs in his belt buckle and watched them for several minutes. His mastiff, Bull, nudged his thigh. "Right, Bull, it's time to continue our patrol. Besides, the dang government is too intrusive, and we are not game wardens."

Franella held her shoes in her hands and tip-toed through the front door of the orphanage.

"Pssst, Franella," Ruby whispered as she came down the stairs, "Where were you all night?"

"Nowhere."

"You spent the night with that old Tlingit, didn't you?" Ruby took her by the arm and pulled her back through the door, down the porch steps, onto the wooden sidewalk, and around the corner where they could speak without being heard. "I covered for you with Major Bernice."

"What?"

"When she asked where you were, I told her you were visiting the outhouse. I told her Tommy's hogging the indoor bathroom again. It earned me a lecture on not picking on poor little Tommy." Ruby laughed, "At least it distracted her."

"Thanks, Ruby. Does that mean we're friends?"

"Good gosh, no!" Ruby put her hands on her hips and glared. "It means I do for you, and you do for me."

Franella's face fell, and that old pain in the pit of her stomach started to rumble. "I was hoping we could be friends." There was no response from Ruby. Franella's shoulders slumped. "What do you want me to do for you?"

Ruby's smile merely lifted the corners of her mouth, it did not infuse her eyes, "I'm glad you asked. The American Legion dances are starting soon—every Friday and Saturday night. I'm going with Blanche and Shirley."

"But the curfew, Major Bernice won't like it."

"Why she set that ridiculous curfew is beyond me. But that's where you come in, Franella, dear. I'll muss my bed, make it look like I was sleeping. If she checks, you tell her I'm helping one of the little boys who's puking his guts out."

Franella wrung her hands, "But you won't be."

Ruby rolled her eyes and sighed, "You know our dear Major can't abide illness, especially vomit."

"What if she wants to call the doctor?"

"Just say it was something he ate."

"But Ruby, it's all lies. I'm not a liar."

Ruby grabbed Franella by the arm. "That's how it works. You cover for me, or I'll tell her you've been sneaking out and staying overnight with men."

"That's a lie!" Franella slammed her foot on the floor. At Ruby's arched eyebrow, she admitted, "It was only one night and one man, and he's ancient."

Ruby laughed, "Do you think that will make a difference to the major? She's already got it in for you and that old Indian."

Franella shook her head and looked at her feet.

"Besides, I know you leave the orphanage around dawn most mornings. I've been protecting you, and now you are going to protect me."

Franella's tongue stuck to the roof of her mouth, and she fisted her hands.

"You better go. The young ones are already awake and dressing."

"But I just got back."

"Your clothes are dirty, and your hair is messy. You don't want that rotten little Tommy to see you and tattle. Go." Ruby pushed her, and not too gently.

Franella turned and ran the several blocks to the beach. A raven swirled about her head, screeched, and followed her. "It's not the right path, Jimmy. Lying is not the right path. I'm trapped. What would you do?"

Jimmy the Raven screeched, circled her once more, and flew back toward the orphanage. Franella followed, crouching and staying close to shrubs and trees. She stood across the street, hiding. The school-aged orphans left, and soon, Major Bernice appeared with her shopping basket and little Tommy in tow. When they were safely out of sight, Franella raced inside, changed her clothes, and stuffed the dirty ones under her bed. She'd deal with them later; she was already late for her tutoring session with Father Alexi.

Franella kept leaving the orphanage every morning before the others were awake. Ruby continued to make excuses for Franella on those rare occasions when Major Bernice asked about her.

"Birch bark tea and spruce tip syrup are my favorite things. Thank you, Johnny. You have taught me so much. I confess I'm not fond of seaweed, but I like the Eskimo potatoes."

"I am no cook. I will take you to Agrafena at the Sitka Café. She will teach you many ways to prepare what we find in the forest and the sea."

Franella laughed, "I have no interest in learning to cook. Just pull it out of the ground and eat. That's my motto."

Johnny, the Bear Boy, placed his hand on her arm and said, "Soon, I will take you to Agrafena. You may not enjoy the cooking, but in a few years, you will be a woman."

"So?"

"So, you must cook."

"Are you sure you want to go to the dance, Ruby?" Franella asked the following Friday night.

"I'm sure."

The girls were all asleep in the large room. Franella stood at the window looking for Blanche and Shirley. She turned to the older girl and said, "You look pretty, Ruby."

"Thanks. Blanche gave me this dress. I hid it under my mattress. It's a little wrinkled, but I can't help that. I hope Blanche doesn't notice."

"Your lipstick is pretty. Did Blanche give you that, too?"

Ruby blushed, "No, I got it myself at Wortman's drugstore."

"But Ruby, where did you get the money?"

"Never mind. Keep looking out the window."

Franella turned her attention to the road and saw the girls. "They're coming."

Ruby tiptoed down the stairs and out the door after Franella made sure Major Bernice was in her private sitting room at the back of the orphanage. Tommy was in the backyard poking a stick in the burn barrel. The trio ignored Franella, who stood in the doorway and watched them.

Blanche linked arms with Ruby. "So, what's going on at the orphanage?"

"Nothing much," Ruby said.

"Come on, Ruby dish. Tell me something naughty about Franella."

"You're just jealous, Blanche, because Franella is so pretty," Shirley said.

"You're much prettier, Blanche," Ruby lied.

"What? Are you blind?" Shirley asked.

"Shut up, Shirley." Blanche turned toward Ruby, "Tell me again that I'm prettier than that awful Franella."

Shirley snorted, "Even in those ugly orphan clothes, with no make-up or jewelry, she's the prettiest girl in town."

Franella stood in the shadow of the orphanage's entryway. She looked into the oval mirror next to the hall tree. *Am I prettier than Blanche? Am I pretty at all? Since coming to Sitka, my freckles have faded, and even though I'm still thin, I have curves in the right places. I guess I look okay.*

Blanche turned to the other girl. "How many times do I have

to tell you to shut up?"

Shirley curled her lip but remained silent.

"You better watch it, or else Ruby will be my new best friend."

"I've always been your best friend," Shirley gasped, "I always will be."

"I don't like you very much right now. You can go to the dance by yourself. Ruby and I are going to stop at Wortman's Drugs on our way and have a soda."

Ruby edged closer to Blanche and whispered, "I might know something."

"Spill," Blanche squealed.

Ruby hurried to the corner, and the two girls followed. "You have to promise not to tell," Ruby still whispered, checking to see that they were far enough away so Franella couldn't hear.

"Cross my heart," Shirley said.

"I thought I told you to leave," Blanche growled.

Shirley looked daggers at Ruby, then turned away. Head bowed and sniffing, she shuffled down the sidewalk. Ruby didn't notice that Blanche had made no promises. Ruby told her how Franella had spent the night with a Native man.

Blanche licked her lips, and her eyes gleamed, "Delicious! It's hard to believe. Are you sure?"

"Oh, yes. I caught her just after dawn, trying to sneak back in."

They sat on the stools at Wortman's soda fountain and Blanche prodded Ruby for more details.

"That's all I know, honest." Ruby quivered.

"There must be more, best friend."

Ruby licked her lips and thought. She didn't want to say it was Johnny, the Bear Boy, since he was just an old man. She began to give Blanche all the details she could think of. It didn't matter that none of them were true.

"Don't say anything to anybody else. Promise? I'm going to save this information for just the right time."

Arm in arm, Ruby and Blanche approached the American Legion Hall and heard the music wafting out the doors. They forgot all about Franella.

SIXTEEN

Johnny, the Bear Boy and Franella sat on the steps outside of the Sitka Café's back door.

"It smells so good it makes me hungry, even though we just ate," Franella said.

"Seal oil."

"What?"

"Agrafena still cooks with seal oil."

"Seal oil?"

"Forget I said it."

"Why?"

"Just forget."

A moment later, Agrafena appeared at the door, wiping her hands on the salt-sack apron tied around her waist. "I understand you want to learn to cook," she said to Franella.

"Well, I..."

Johnny, the Bear Boy, stood and spoke rapidly to Agrafena in Tlingit. She answered loudly and just as rapidly. Soon, they were nose to nose, arms flailing, and faces flushed. Franella only caught a word or two. "Please, you are talking too fast, and I can't follow. What are you saying?"

Agrafena turned, looked at Franella, and sighed," Can you be trusted?"

"I don't understand," Franella stammered.

Johnny, the Bear Boy, nodded, and Agrafena looked intently at Franella. She must have seen something she liked, for she said, "Be here tomorrow morning at four in the morning."

"That early?"

"I will teach you before I prep the kitchen. We open at six in the morning."

The following morning, a reluctant Franella knocked on the back door of the Sitka Café.

She pointed to the sink. "Wash your hands. We start with fry bread; it is easy enough."

They stood side by side at the large prep table in the crowded kitchen. Franella mimicked Agrafena's every move.

Later, a frazzled Franella pulled a dark, almost burnt mess out of the hot oil. "It doesn't look very good."

Agrafena took the bread, "Hmmn. You taste."

Franella leaned over and sniffed, "It smells burnt. I don't understand. I followed your instructions accurately."

"Taste."

Franella took a bite and made a face, "It's horrible. The outside is burnt, and the inside is doughy."

"You must eat your mistakes."

"I don't think I can."

"Make another batch. Do not overmix. The oil should be hot, but not too hot. Watch for bubbles around the tip of a wooden spoon in the hot oil. Cook long enough, but not too long. Make sure the bread is golden brown, not too dark, not too light."

"Is that seal oil?"

Agrafena sighed, "Johnny spoke of seal oil, didn't he? He should not have done that."

"Why"

"In my grandmother's time, one of the ways you proved to the whites in a court of law that you were civilized was to swear that you never used seal oil."

Franella tilted her head and stared at the Native woman. She scrunched her face in thought, and after a moment or two, she said, "That is the stupidest thing I've ever heard."

Agrafena laughed, "Here in Alaska, the white man has often proved himself stupid. Those in power impose their stupidity on others. However, I use seal oil whenever I can get it. But I tell no one."

"It's your secret ingredient, isn't it? Mike has his under the counter, and you have yours here in the kitchen? I won't tell."

Agrafena laughed and turned to her kitchen prep. Franella tugged on her apron. "What if someone asks me if you use seal oil? I am not a liar."

"You do not have to answer every question directly. You can say it's none of their business, or you can tell them to ask me. Now, tend to your fry bread. I have things to do."

Franella watched the pot of hot oil carefully, but her mind was on the stupidity of the white men who thought seal oil was uncivilized. Her mind went to all the things she observed and considered stupid. It was not limited to one race. She imagined other races and cultures had their own forms of stupidity. Her reading of history and biography proved it.

"Help!" Franella yelled.

Mike and Agrafena ran into the kitchen and saw that the pot of hot oil had burst into flame. Mike dealt with the fire, covering the pot with a large cookie sheet while Agrafena grabbed Franella, dragged her to the sink, and ran her arm under cold water. "Where's the pot lid? We always keep it close just in case," he snapped.

"It was in my way. I put it in the cupboard by the refrigerator," Franella stammered, "I'm sorry."

"Keep it close next time." Mike glared at his wife and returned to his morning ritual of making the coffee and filling the salt and pepper shakers.

Franella saw the look that passed between the married couple, "I hope there isn't going to be a next time," Franella muttered to herself.

Agrafena heard and smiled, "Be here tomorrow morning for your next lesson."

Franella didn't fare any better the following morning. She stood at the massive grill filled with bacon and sausage. "This looks like a whole pig's worth," she said.

Agrafena laughed and handed Franella a spatula. "A large group of hunters is coming in this morning before Jake Steiner guides them up Harbor Mountain. I'll give you a cooking lesson later. For now, watch the meat. It's black bear bacon and reindeer sausage—much better than pig."

Agrafena bustled around the kitchen, making several batches of fry bread, mixing pancake batter, cracking eggs, and chopping onions. Once that was done, she filled a cart with the café's crockery and went into the dining room.

"Fena!" Mike yelled.

Agrafena's head jerked up. She stared in horror as she saw smoke wafting out of the kitchen. The acrid smell of burnt bacon followed. They raced into the kitchen. The pile of shriveled, charred bacon and burnt sausage filled the grill. Franella turned to them, spatula in hand, "I don't know how that happened! One minute, everything looked crisp and delicious, and the next—this!"

Agrafena grabbed the spatula. "Franella, bring the garbage can over here. Mike, open all the windows and doors. We need to get the smoke out of here."

"Those hunters will be here soon," Mike complained, "This won't do the café's reputation any good."

"Our reputation will survive," Agrafena snapped as she filled the trash can with burnt meat and cleaned the grill. "Franella, bring me more bacon and sausage. The bottom shelf of the big refrigerator."

"I'm sorry," Franella whimpered.

"There's no time for that now. Hurry!"

Ten weeks later, Franella's cooking had not improved, and no matter how she analyzed the situation, she did not know why. "I'm ready to give up."

"You must cook with your hands and your heart. The salmon, the venison, the berries, the eggs, they know you do not respect them."

"It's just food; it can't know how I feel."

Agrafena banged a large fry pan on the stove and dashed some seal oil into it. "Your heart and, I dare say, your mind are elsewhere. You have no reverence for what the Creator has provided."

"I like to eat it, especially when you cook it," Franella said, "It looks so easy and tastes good when you do it."

The café was not yet open, so Agrafena took Franella by the hand and led her to a vacant table. She motioned to Mike, and frowning, he poured them each a mug of coffee. She pushed the basket of French crullers toward Franella. "I see the beauty and the art in preparing food. It is my offering to the people who come here. It is not just fuel for the body. It is sustenance for the soul. It is a gift from the Creator."

Franella sniffed and said, "Well, you are the best cook I've ever known."

Agrafena patted her hand and sighed, "I will tell Johnny, the Bear Boy your lessons are over." The Native woman looked out the window as gulls flew over Sitka Sound. She turned back to Franella and her mouth turned up in a slight smile. "Do not ever cook for him."

Relieved, Franella nodded.

Agrafena shuddered and added, "Do not cook for anyone."

SEVENTEEN

The day came when Johnny, the Bear Boy, disappeared from the streets of Sitka. It was time for him to hunker down until next spring. The townspeople were relieved, but Franella missed him.

Her lessons with Father Alexi, Petro Bravebird, and Miss Ruth continued.

"I'm getting bored, Miss Ruth. I've read all the books in Sitka's library. I've also read all of Father Alexi's Russian books twice. I've made a notebook of all the Tlingit words I know. I've written down all the myths and legends Johnny, the Bear Boy and Petro Bravebird have taught me." She wrung her hands, "I feel myself becoming anxious. I need something to focus on."

"Come with me, my dear."

"Where?"

"We are going to the Sitka Sentinel. You'll like Sam Mitchell. He's a crusty old newspaperman. Don't let him intimidate you."

"Is he smart?"

"Very."

Miss Ruth introduced the teenager to the editor.

"So, you're the mysterious Franella Feddersen I keep hearing about?" Sam Mitchell's eyes twinkled, but he sounded gruff.

"What do you hear? Never mind. I'm sure it's all negative." Franella looked around the noisy room. She waved to the lady at the linotype machine.

Sam coughed and looked for a cigar. "Yes, well, er, what can I do for you?"

Miss Ruth leaned forward, put her elbows on Sam's desk, and cupped her chin in her hands. "My friend Franella is bored. I think it's time she learned what's going on in the lower forty-eight and beyond. World affairs are becoming complicated and dangerous."

"And how can I help with that?"

Margaret Mary slapped several back issues of the Seattle Times on the worktable and motioned Franella over. "Start with these, my girl. When you are finished, I'll give you issues of the Anchorage Daily News and the Vancouver Sun. You'll find the Sun interesting. It has a decided British slant."

Franella barely heard. She was already deep into the first issue of the Times. Sam lit his cigar, blew the smoke toward the ceiling, and eyed Miss Ruth. "What am I supposed to do with her?"

Miss Ruth laughed, "Just let her come when she's finished her studies for the day. Give her several papers and ask her if she has any questions or opinions about what she's read. You won't be disappointed, Sam."

"She's just a young girl, and the good folk in Sitka are decidedly divided about her. Most think she's odd."

"She's more than that, Sam. And since when have you let other people's opinions influence you?" Miss Ruth asked.

"Mr. Mitchell, sir. There is going to be a world war, isn't there?" Franella lifted her head from the newspaper.

"Don't worry your pretty little head about it," Sam said.

Franella rolled her eyes. "Chamberlain's a coward. Hitler's a bully, and bullies are never satisfied."

"Have you finished those papers already?" He asked.

"I read very fast."

"Well, Franella, what do you think's going to happen next?" Sam rolled his cigar between his fingers and looked at the girl over the glasses that had slid down his nose.

Franella held up the newspaper. "Look at this map, and you'll know."

Sam puffed on his cigar and chuckled, "Why don't you tell me."

"I think Hitler is going to gobble up Poland, and the world is going to blow up. England says it's committed to Poland. They are allies, you know. But Chamberlain is such a weak man, I bet he doesn't do anything."

Sam's eyebrows rose to his balding head. "I agree the British Prime Minister is weak, but President Roosevelt promised America would remain neutral. He will keep his word."

"Sure, just like all the promises to the American Indians were kept by all the past presidents. I thought you were smart, Mr. Mitchell."

Miss Ruth cleared her throat and glared at Franella.

"What did I say?" the girl asked.

"You said exactly what you thought, young lady. I can respect that." Sam laughed, "I can see we are going to have some good conversations."

Miss Ruth turned to Sam and whispered, "I think Franella and I need to have a conversation about tact and diplomacy."

Sam shook his head. "No need on my account. I heard about her math prowess. I thought it was some kind of savant thing."

"It's across the board, Sam. Her mind is something else."

"You know I can hear you," Franella laughed as she folded the newspaper. "This is going to be fun. I can be here tomorrow at two in the afternoon. Will you have your work done by then, Mr.

Mitchell so that we can talk? I can come every day."

Miss Ruth laughed and said, "Sam, you're always complaining there's no one in town for you to talk to about international events. Let this girl read the papers, and you will be amazed at her questions and insights."

Sam chewed on his cigar and thought. "I don't know about every day. I do have a newspaper to run, but yes, come tomorrow."

Franella stacked the papers nicely, "I just saw Sophie, Miss Ruth. It looks like she's heading to the post office. I'll wait for you there."

Sam took off his glasses, wiped them with his shirt tail, replaced them, and spoke quietly, "I've heard some rumors about her and Johnny, the Bear Boy. Nothing good."

Miss Ruth's mouth fell open. "They are just two lonely lost souls."

"I fear what will happen to the girl should Major Bernice hear about her and the old Tlingit."

"Speaking of our good Major, have you heard anything from the National Headquarters of the Salvation Army? They haven't answered my letters."

Sam pushed the stacks of papers around on his desk and pulled a letter from under a thick file. He scanned the page and said, "So far, they haven't found anyone with the necessary qualifications who's willing to come to Alaska."

"I've missed the last couple of board meetings. Anything new?"

"We're making more surprise visits, which seem to irritate Major Bernice, although she is syrupy sweet to our faces. We're all sorry for the orphans and feel powerless to do anything."

"I don't know how much longer we can wait. We may have to take matters into our own hands."

Sam Mitchell placed his cigar in the overflowing ashtray, clasped his hands, and leaned toward Miss Ruth. "I assume you have something in mind."

"I have a few more details to work out with your wife, actually," Miss Ruth smiled.

"I have my life arranged just the way I like it. Don't disrupt it. Her job is to take care of me, not a bunch of orphans, poor mites."

Miss Ruth reached across the messy desk and patted Sam's hand, "Now that Sam Jr. is at the university, she's bored. I'm going to give her something meaningful to do. But don't worry, she'll still take care of you."

"How are you going to get rid of the Major?"

"That's the part I haven't figured out yet."

"Let me know if you need my help."

"Thanks, Sam." Miss Ruth stood and reached for her pocket-book.

EIGHTEEN

The high school boys from the orphanage, Arthur, Albert, and Anthony, had all tried to engage Franella in conversations over the past few months. They were almost as awkward as she was and soon gave up their attempts.

A tall, athletic boy named Lester spied Franella on the beach.

"Say, you're from the orphanage, right? Do you know Albert? He's a friend of mine."

"I know him," Franella kept her eyes on her feet.

"Swell," Lester said, "Can I walk you to wherever you're going?"

"I'm not going anywhere."

"Oh," Lester was momentarily without words but soon recovered. "Do you like this beach? The sawmill down the way is sometimes smoky and smelly. I'm partial to Sandy Beach on the other side of Sitka. It has a great view of Mt. Edgecombe. Have you been there?"

Franella nodded.

"What about Swan Lake? Most girls think the lily pads are pretty, do you?"

Again, Franella nodded while she continued to study the tips of her shoes.

"Maybe we could have a picnic there someday." Lester grinned.

Franella raised her head, and her blue forget-me-not eyes stared at him. "I, that is, I...did you know the Russians used to cut big blocks of ice out of Swan Lake, pack it in sawdust, load it on clipper ships, and sell it in San Francisco?"

Lester's grin faltered, "Picnic?"

Franella studied her shoes again.

Lester's face fell and he sighed, "Well, I guess I better go. Maybe we can talk again soon."

Franella felt a flutter in her stomach but forced herself not to move a muscle even though she felt like running.

Lester shoved his hands in his pockets, defeated. "Goodbye, Franella. Maybe I'll see you again sometime."

Franella watched him go, then took off running toward Miss Ruth's cabin near Indian River. Her heart thumped erratically. She felt something, but what? She hoped her Miss Ruth was home, and that the old woman knew something about boys.

"It's the same boy who sits in the library and stares at me while pretending to read. I don't know what he wants."

"Maybe he wants to get to know you."

"Why would he want to do that?" Franella grabbed a handful of lemon drops that Miss Ruth kept in a jar next to the salt and pepper shakers. She placed them in a line on the kitchen table and ate them one by one.

"You are a very interesting person, Franella," Miss Ruth said.

"He doesn't know that."

Miss Ruth sighed, "I think it's time for the next phase of your education. You are not going to like it, but it is necessary, and I know you can do it."

"What's that?"

"You are going back to high school."

"The school year is nearly over. I hated it; the kids didn't like me, and the teachers didn't want me there."

"I will speak to Mr. Hendricks."

"NO!"

Miss Ruth took off her spectacles and leaned toward Franella, "Listen carefully and picture yourself doing this. Take a few minutes to think, and then if you have anything to say, you may speak. Understand?"

Franella gulped and nodded.

"You are not going to learn from the teachers. In fact, I do not want you to listen to them or speak in class. Take a notebook and some pencils, and work on your languages while they give their lectures."

"Don't make me do this." Franella pleaded.

"As you walk the halls from one classroom to another, I want you to make eye contact with three or four girls. Look at them and smile. A day or two later, say hi or tell them you like their sweater or the way they fixed their hair."

"What if I don't like anything? I won't lie."

"Find something to like, even a little." Miss Ruth's face betrayed her frustration.

Franella shook her head. "I get nervous just thinking about it. I don't know if I can do it."

"Think about it while you are in the classroom. Write down some ideas. Use that brain of yours."

"I'll try," Franella knew she wouldn't try very hard, but Miss Ruth wasn't going to give up.

Miss Ruth nodded. "Now, I'm off to St. Peter's church for a rather dull board meeting. We'll talk some more on Thursday after your tutoring session with Father Alexi, and I'll arrange for you to start school on the following Monday."

Thursday came all too soon for Franella, and she dutifully knocked on Miss Ruth's door.

"Miss Drake and I have discussed your wardrobe, or rather your lack of one. The few clothes I bought you when you first arrived in Sitka didn't last long."

"Rotten old Major Bernice."

"Let's not talk about her. Miss Drake has a few things that she thinks might fit you. Her niece visited two years ago and outgrew them while she was here. We've also sent for two skirts and three blouses from the Sears and Roebuck Catalog. They should be here soon."

"That's nice of you and Miss Drake, but you know Major Bernice will just take them away again."

"We thought of that, too. Miss Drake lives on Etolin Street near the high school. The clothes will be kept in a cupboard in her backroom. Like everyone else in Sitka, she never locks her doors."

"So, I can go there whenever I want?"

"Just don't forget to change back into your old clothes before you return to the orphanage."

"What if someone tells Major Bernice, and she asks about them? I'm not a liar."

"Bite your tongue and don't answer."

"She will be so mad," Franella grinned, "It will be worth it."

Franella rose from the table and hugged Miss Ruth, "I didn't know how much I hated these old rags. Thank you and Miss Drake, too."

Miss Ruth poured more cups of tea. "Now, what about this boy?"

"Lester! His attention is embarrassing." Franella refused to meet her eyes.

Miss Ruth added fireweed honey to the tea and quietly looked at Franella, who squirmed in the hard-backed chair.

"To be honest, I guess it's my response that's embarrassing. I don't know what to say or how to act. I've never been around boys."

"But it's kind of nice that someone is interested," Miss Ruth smiled.

Franella felt that peculiar flutter in her stomach. She ducked her head and whispered, "He seemed nice."

Franella peered into the cupboard at Miss Drake's and felt like she had said, "*Open Sesame.*" Ali Baba would have been pleased. The saddle shoes on the bottom shelf were a tiny bit large, but Franella pulled on two pairs of thick socks, and they felt comfortable. A navy-blue pleated skirt and matching sweater completed her outfit.

"You look lovely, Franella," Miss Drake said, taking a sip of tea from a delicate china cup as she stood in the doorway leading from the kitchen to the back room. "Have you always worn your hair in braids?"

"Day and night since I was little."

"Wait here," Miss Drake soon returned with a brush and two silver barrettes. She unloosed Franella's braids, brushed them, and clipped her hair back at the temples with the ornate barrettes. "Your braids have made your dark hair cascade in lovely ripples down your back."

"Wow, Miss Drake, you sound like a poet."

Miss Drake laughed, "Go into the living room. There's a mirror over the davenport. Take a look and tell me what you see."

Franella looked, squinted, and looked again. "I look like me, but not me."

Miss Ruth knocked and then came into the living room, "Who have we here? I almost didn't recognize you."

Franella blushed and said, "I'm nervous."

"We need to practice," Miss Ruth said; at Franella's look of confusion, she added, "Miss Drake is going to be Blanche, and I am going to be you."

"What?" Franella wrung her hands.

"Everyone is going to be shocked you're back in school, and they will be amazed at the beautiful butterfly that's come out of her cocoon. You are no longer skin and bones and all awkward angles. You are a lovely young woman."

"So pretty," Miss Drake said, "Wait, let me get my camera."

Franella blushed.

"We'll pretend you're walking down the hallway, and Blanche is coming toward you." Miss Ruth turned to the librarian and ordered, "Stand there, Miss Drake."

Miss Drake, as Blanche, took her position, screwed up her face, and frowned, "What are you doing in school, Franella, and where did you get those clothes?"

Miss Ruth looked past Miss Drake, "Good morning, Shirley. Your hair looks nice."

Miss Drake stamped her foot. "I asked you a question."

"Oh, hi, Ruby. I didn't see you there," Miss Ruth said.

Miss Drake raised her voice, "No one ignores me! Answer

my questions!"

Miss Ruth turned her head and said, "Hi, Lester, I'm going to be at Crescent Bay after school. Maybe I'll see you there."

"You want me to talk to Lester," Franella gasped.

"Sure, if he's around, it will make Blanche livid," Miss Ruth smiled, "If he's not there, say goodbye to Ruby and Shirley and tell them you need to hurry to class."

"Do not look Blanche in the eye," Miss Drake said, "Do not acknowledge her existence."

Franella smoothed her skirt and looked the two elderly spinsters in the eyes. "You two could be on the stage. You're something else." She shook her head. "I'm not sure what."

"We'll be waiting for you after school," Miss Drake said.

"We'll want a full report," Miss Ruth added.

"Be careful that Ruby doesn't follow you. I wouldn't be surprised if Blanche puts her on your trail," Miss Ruth said and handed Franella a small packet of lemon drops.

They pulled back the curtains and watched as Franella rounded the corner. "The boys are going to hover around her like bears around a honey tree," Miss Ruth said.

"We may be sorry for encouraging this," Miss Drake frowned.

"It had to be done. She needs to learn to live in the world, even if that learning is awkward and painful."

"The coffee pot is on, and I want to hear your ideas about the orphanage. I'll help however I can."

"Good, I am going to need you."

NINETEEN

"We have to do something about Franella." Blanche sat between Ruby and Shirley at the soda fountain in Wortman's Drugstore.

"Aw, Blanche, leave it alone. Franella's not hurting anybody," Shirley said, "In fact, I think she's nice. A bit odd, but nice."

Blanche turned to Ruby, "What do you think?"

"I guess she's okay." Ruby wrung her hands and refused to look Blanche in the eye.

"I don't like the way the boys are starting to pay attention to her," Blanche snapped.

"Especially Lester," Shirley said.

"Some of the girls are sitting with her at lunch. I don't like it."

"Franella this and Franella that! What did we use to talk about before Franella came back to school?" Shirley asked.

Blanche ignored Shirley and asked Ruby, "Where did she get those clothes? I told you to find out."

Ruby shrugged, "She leaves the orphanage in her old clothes and returns the same way. When I ask about the new ones, she looks through me and doesn't answer."

"Did you tell Major Bernice Franella is a thief?"

"I don't have any proof," Ruby stammered.

"Give up, Blanche. You're just mad because Franella's prettier than you, smarter than you, and Lester likes her," Shirley bent her head over her straw.

"Shut up, Shirley," Blanche ordered, "Ruby, come out to the sidewalk with me. We need to speak privately."

"Do I have to, Blanche?" Ruby looked to Shirley for help.

Shirley slurped the last of her soda, slipped off the stool, and faced Blanche. "I might just have to make friends with Franella. She's a lot nicer than you."

"You wouldn't dare!" Blanche screeched.

Shirley blew her bangs out of her eyes, "I'm getting really tired of you, Blanche. You don't know what I would dare." She waltzed out of Wortman's.

Blanche frowned and hissed, "I'll deal with you later."

Shirley shuddered and covered her ears with her hands, but she did not turn around. Blanche grabbed Ruby by the arm and dragged her to the corner of Wortman's next to a display of movie magazines. "Okay, Ruby, what was that delicious story of Franella and the Tlingit man. I think it's time we let the good people of Sitka know what that horrible Franella Feddersen has been up to."

"That was so long ago," Ruby whined.

"I remember every detail you told me, and we are going to spread it around. The first thing you're going to do is tell Major Bernice."

"Please, Blanche, don't make me do that. I told you it's old news. Nobody remembers, and if they did, they don't care."

"We're going to make them care." Blanche gave the unwilling Ruby a shove. "Don't talk to me until you've done what I said."

"Please..."

Blanche leaned over and whispered in Ruby's ear, "This is what you are going to say...tomorrow we'll add a little more and then more. Soon, that wretched Franella Feddersen is going to be in a heap of trouble. Now go."

Halfway to the orphanage, Blanche caught up with Ruby. "I changed my mind."

"Thank you, Blanche. I was dreading facing Major Bernice. You don't know what she's like."

Blanche spat out her chewing gum and gnawed on the end of her thumb. "Let me think. This campaign requires subtlety."

"Campaign? Subtlety?" Ruby faced the fuming teenager and said, "I don't want any part of this. Please, Blanche."

Blanche put her arm around Ruby, "Why, my dearest dearie dear, this was all your idea. Remember? Now, we're going to put your plan into action, but slowly. I'm going to tell Miss Benson I'm worried about Franella. All I'm going to say is that she is too trusting, that she doesn't really know what boys or men are like. When she presses me for more information, I'll tell her I promised you I wouldn't say anything. Dollars to donuts, she'll want to hear the truth from you."

Ruby wrung her hands and stammered, "I'm too nervous, I can't do this."

Blanche patted Ruby on the shoulder and grinned, "Good. If you're nervous, it will come across that you don't want to get Franella in trouble. In fact, you can say that. Make Miss Benson pull the information out of you."

Ruby hung her head, knowing Franella was right. She was nothing more than Blanche's slave. "What do you think will happen after that?"

"She'll probably tell Mr. Hendricks. They might have a meeting with the teachers, or they might talk to Franella or Major Bernice. They will do something, I'm sure. I'm going to let a few things slip to my mother, and she'll carry it to the Lutheran Ladies Sewing Circle, and they will spread it throughout the town. They might even write a letter to Major Bernice." Blanche shivered in delight, "When Major Bernice hears about Franella from multiple people, she'll question you. Answer the same way you will for Miss Benson."

"I'm afraid I might cry."

"Even better."

TWENTY

This particular winter found the good people of Sitka soggier than usual. Dark clouds had hovered over the town for weeks, letting loose with all the water they held. Partnering the clouds—a white, patchy fog constantly swirled around Mt Verstovia and, behind it, the Three Sisters.

Boats sat in the harbor, bobbing on the waves. Fishing season, dismal as it was, had closed weeks ago, and so had hunting. The mountains were full of snow and ice, and the local logging operations had shut down until spring. No logs meant no lumber for the sawmill. The men of Sitka were bored. They sat around the American Legion Hall, the town's bars, or the Sitka Café.

With nothing to keep them occupied, they were primed to discuss whatever news, rumor, or innuendo came their way. Blanche and Ruby fed everyone's insatiable curiosity bit by bit, and the plan had the desired results. The awful news about that Feddersen girl trickled from the high school girls to their mothers and from there to the men of the town.

Who was this man, and what had he done to that sweet Feddersen girl? Most said he was a Native. The majority of the townspeople felt that although she was odd, she was an innocent and had been ruthlessly taken advantage of. Sitka's fathers became suspicious as well as protective. Others thought the girl was truly wild and had obviously come to no good through her own actions.

"If that girl has put my position in jeopardy or ruined my good name, she will pay," Major Bernice vowed as she scribbled several pages. She threw her pen down, stuffed the notes into envelopes, and sealed them. "Take one of these to the Sentinel and give it to Sam Mitchell."

"What if he's not there?"

"Wait for him. Under no circumstances are you to give it to that busybody Margaret Mary. The other is for Miss Ruth."

"And the third note?" Ruby asked.

"For my personal file, if it's any of your business, which it's not." Major Bernice scowled.

The murky sky above Sitka mirrored Ruby's heart. The clouds were as dark and thick as her overcast soul. Dread and guilt followed her on Sitka's sidewalks. The envelopes felt heavy in her coat pocket. She slipped her hand in and pulled one out. She tapped the envelope on her chin, then waved it like a fan. Mr. Mitchell would never know the message came in an envelope, would he? She could easily slit it open and see what Major Bernice was plotting, couldn't she? No one would blame her, would they?

Ruby took the long way around, dipped out of sight behind the Pioneer's Home, and read:

Dear Mr. Mitchell,

I'm sure you have heard the talk about Franella Feddersen. That girl has been in trouble from the first day she came to me. I have done my best to be an example of a virtuous and good woman, but to no avail. I have talked and talked to her, but it's done no good. I think corporal punishment is in order, and I'm not afraid to institute it. The girl is a bad seed. I fear her influence on the other children in my charge.

Franella must go! Out of my orphanage, out of Sitka, and preferably, out of Alaska! I will find a way, and I expect you and the other members of your so-called board to support me in this.

I write this in all sincerity and with the best interest of all the orphans of Sitka.

Sincerely,

Major Bernice

Ruby entered the Sentinel office, handed the note to the editor, then turned and left without a word.

After reading the message, Sam reached for the telephone. "I hope your plan is ready to put into place, Miss Ruth. I'm afraid the Major is going overboard."

Ruby walked through Sitka to Miss Ruth's with her head down and her hands shoved in her pockets. The misty drizzle chilled her. There was smoke coming out of the chimney and a light in the window, but Ruby did not want to talk to Miss Ruth. She tiptoed to the porch and slipped the message under the door.

On her way back to the orphanage, Ruby saw Franella leave the library. "Franella, wait up," she called.

Franella spoke without enthusiasm, "Hi, Ruby."

Ruby bit her lip and squeezed her eyes tight, then blinked several times.

"Are you okay?" Franella asked.

"No. I've done something awful, and I don't know how to fix it."

"What did you do?"

"I can't tell you."

"Okay. See you later."

"Wait. I need to tell."

"You need to tell me, but you can't? You seem confused, Ruby."

With several stops and starts, gulps and tears, Ruby explained Blanche's plan to destroy Franella. "She made me do it! I didn't have a choice."

"How could you be so stupid?" Franella snapped, "A person always has a choice. And you made the wrong one!"

"Don't tell Blanche I told you." Ruby pleaded.

"You have no idea what you've done!" Franella stomped away.

"Johnny, the Bear Boy did this evil thing," Ivan said. His World War I relic, an old rifle he called Katerina, lay across his knee. "I am ready."

Bill snorted, "Much as I dislike that old Tlingit, it couldn't have been him. He's been holed up in the woods for months, just like he is every year."

"I heard he was seen near Indian River last week," Jake said, "Spring is late this year, and it's past time for Johnny to arrive."

The others nodded. Everyone at the Sitka Cafe was prepared to believe the worst about Johnny, the Bear Boy. They always had.

Stormy Durand stopped by their table and clapped Ivan on the shoulder. "Don't be too eager to use Katerina."

"I use," Ivan snarled and shook his fist.

"He'd have to use that old gun as a club. He hasn't been able to find the proper ammo," Jake said.

"Not for years," Ade added.

Ivan glared at the others and retreated into a dignified silence.

"Seriously, Stormy," Bill said, "What are we going to do about this situation?"

Ade glared across the table, but Bill kept his eyes fixed on Stormy.

"Bill!" Ade growled, "I told you there is no situation. She's a nice kid."

Those from several nearby tables disagreed, and rumors were repeated throughout the café. Ade frowned and raised his eyes to Stormy's.

Stormy hooked his thumbs into his belt loops and rocked on his heels. "All I've heard is a bit of gossip. No crimes have been reported."

"Do you think any girl or woman would report such a thing?" Bill asked.

The men at the table shook their heads. Mike came with his ever-present coffee pot and poured another round. "Agrafena says the elders in Indiantown are getting nervous. They don't want any trouble. She assures me none of their young men are involved, but some of the town's high school boys have been hanging around the Sheldon Jackson school and harassing the Native boys when they come out of their classes."

"I've heard a few of the cannery workers make threats while I piloted the shore boat," Jake said. "Everyone is sure someone did something to the Feddersen girl."

"People want to know if it was with or without her cooperation," Jake said.

Stormy snagged a nearby chair and sat down. "Exactly who are these cannery workers, and who has been making threats? I don't want anyone in this town taking the law into their own hands. I'm the only one on this island who wears a badge."

"Don't get riled, Stormy. People are concerned that this, whatever it is, doesn't spread. We can't have wild Native men coming after white girls," Bill growled.

Stormy's tone matched Bill's, "Right now, the only wild things I see are rumors and gossip, and none of you are helping!"

Bill pulled his tobacco pouch out of his pocket and then put it back. He tapped his fingers on the table. "I don't mean to tell you how to do your job, but..."

"Then don't," Stormy said through a clenched jaw.

"...you need to investigate this!" Bill finished and reached for his tobacco pouch again.

Stormy smashed his hat on his head and stomped out of the café, slamming the door behind him. A minute later, the door opened, and he yelled, "Bull!"

The large dog, lying at Ivan's feet, growled and refused to move. "Dog, he stay," Ivan said and rubbed Bull between his ears. The men at the table hid their grins. It wasn't often that Bull defied his master. Stormy ambled to the table, his eyes never leaving the dog. "What are you trying to say, fella?"

Bull whined, circled the table, and put his paw on each man's thigh, then lay down next to Stormy.

Ivan opened his mouth but, at Stormy Durand's glare, promptly shut it. Stormy sighed, threw his hat on the table, and sat down. He took a deep breath, rubbed his mustache, and said, "Bull seems to think you louts are good men, but you've got this situation upside down. As far as I've been able to tell, a couple of disgruntled high school girls have been spreading rumors. I don't know why. What are the facts? Where is the evidence? What does the alleged victim say?"

The men hung their heads and grabbed their forks or coffee mugs to cover their embarrassment. Ivan hefted Katerina onto his lap, rubbed the gun's well-polished stock, and said, "I think..."

"Shut up, Ivan!" the others yelled.

<hr />

Early the following Saturday morning, Franella heard a tapping on her window. She looked out and saw Firy about to throw another handful of pebbles.

"I'll be right down," Franella softly called.

The girls hurried away from the orphanage toward Swan Lake. They sat close to the edge and dangled their feet among the lily pads. The mountain streams that fed the lake chilled the water. Soon, their teeth chattered, and they pulled their frozen feet out, drying them with their sweaters. "Still too cold," Franella said.

Firy told Franella everything her brother Henry said was going on at the high school. Henry was only a freshman, but everyone liked him, and he moved freely among the various cliques. He was privy to all the gossip from all the high school groups.

"Ruby told me Blanche had a plan to spread horrible stories about me. Now that I think of it, some of the kids have been looking at me strangely. What did Henry say again?" Franella shivered and told herself it was from the cold water.

Firy sniffed, "He said almost everybody believes you've been sneaking out and spending your nights with a Tlingit man. The girls are appalled, and the boys are outraged."

"But I never," Franella said and then remembered the night she had spent in Johnny, the Bear Boy's cabin. "Well, only once."

"Franella!" Firy shrieked.

"It was Johnny the Bear Boy." Franella heard a noise behind her. She turned and saw Tommy running toward the orphanage as fast as his rotten little legs could take him. She sighed, knowing he had heard her confession. There was nothing to be done. Major Bernice would be waiting for her with some torturous punishment. She turned back to Firy and kept the fear out of her voice. She forced herself to speak calmly, "A while ago, when Johnny and I were hiking, he showed me which plants along the creek were edible. By the time we reached his cabin and made our supper, it was late. I knew I should have hurried back to the orphanage, but I just couldn't face it."

"Couldn't face what?"

Franella stared at Firy, "Tommy is a little rat, always making trouble. Ruby is so influenced by Blanche that she is mean to me, and Major Bernice is, well, I can't say!" Franella plunged her feet back into the water and shivered. She just couldn't tell Firy that she wasn't allowed to eat with the other orphans and that she was hungry all the time.

Firy bit her lip, scratched the back of her neck, and reached for her shoes. Without looking at Franella, she asked, "How did anyone find out about that? Did you tell?"

"Of course not, Ruby caught me sneaking back in and guessed, but she promised not to tell."

Firy frowned and shook her head, "It's obvious she told Blanche, but why would Blanche spread that around now, and why would she make up all those nasty lies that you...that you?" Firy bit her tongue. She couldn't voice the horrible details.

Franella looked toward the horizon, her heart as empty as always. "I don't belong. I never have."

The only good thing about going to school the following day was that it kept her away from Major Berniece. Franella couldn't stand the looks and whispers that followed her through the hallways. No one sat with her in the cafeteria, and even Lester turned his face away. She caught up with him after school.

"Let me tell you what actually happened." She pleaded.

He couldn't meet her eyes. "You don't have to."

Franella breathed deeply and forced herself to tell Lester everything about the night she spent in Johnny, the Bear Boy's cabin.

"So, you admit you spent the night with him. An old man, and what's worse, he's an Indian! I can't believe you would do such a thing."

"Please, Lester. It was all perfectly innocent, and he was a gentleman."

Lester fisted his hands, and the cords in his neck stood at a rigid attention. "He's a filthy siwash, and if I see him in town, well, he'll wish I hadn't."

Franella felt the heat in her face. Her eyes flashed, and she spoke quietly but forcefully. "You obviously believe there was more to the story than what I said."

He looked at her, and his face matched hers in color. "I just know white girls don't spend the night with Indians, especially not Tlingits. It's disgusting! He's old enough to be your grandfather!"

"What are you saying?" Franella felt hot tears threaten.

Lester studied the toes of his shoes. "I'm saying I can't be friends with a girl like you. Don't speak to me at school or if you see me in town." He shoved his hands in his pockets and turned away.

School was even more difficult the following morning. Franella received poisonous looks, and she believed Lester had told the others about her night with Johnny the Bear Boy. The girls let their disdain and disgust show on their faces, and the boys refused to look at her.

The suspicious tension surrounding her was overwhelming, and she slipped out of the building and ran to Miss Ruth.

"Look at the sky, Miss Ruth. It's whalebone white."

"That's a lovely way to describe an overcast sky."

"I meant it looks skeletal, dead. The smooth clouds are so dense, so the sun's rays can't penetrate. It's what I look like inside. Bleached bones."

Miss Ruth gathered the teenage girl into a fierce hug and said, "Tell me everything."

Franella described how she felt when she was first told her parents' boat was missing, and continued until her conversation with Lester. She spent over an hour explaining the events and feelings of her life to the older woman. Her eyes often filled with tears, but she sniffed and refused to let them spill over. "My heart is an orphan, and I am painfully alone."

Miss Ruth sighed and prayed for wisdom, "I'm not going to offer you any platitudes. Your life is difficult. Only Bozhe knows why."

"He allowed my parents to die. He let Blanche spread those horrible rumors, and now people think I'm a...a...a woman of ill-repute." Franella choked on the word.

"Where did you hear that phrase?" Miss Ruth asked.

"I read it in a book. I know what it means. It's hurtful that everybody thinks that."

"Not everybody, dear one."

"It's not fair."

"No, it's not. But pain is never wasted."

"That's not logical. Nothing good can come of my misery."

"It's not something you can reason out in your mind. You can only understand with your spirit."

Franella frowned, "I don't know how to do that."

"Bozhe has his hand on you."

"I know there is something out there, but what or who, I'm not sure. I sort of believe. I mean, I kind of believe all you've told me about Bozhe is true, but I can't picture it. I can't see it, don't feel it. I can't put all the pieces together."

"You can't force it. In time, Bozhe will reveal himself to you. He will give you understanding."

"I pray that's true," Franella whispered.

"That's the word, pray. Continue to pray."

"I wish He would hurry up," Franella said, sounding like the impatient teenager she was. With a heavy heart, she shrugged, tried to smile, and held up the dainty china cup. "I don't know what I would do without you."

"You would do just fine." Miss Ruth said, pouring more tea, "I know Sitka is uncomfortable for you with all these vile rumors. I'm working on a plan for you for next fall. How would you like to go to the University of Washington?"

"Leave Alaska? Leave you? No."

"Just think about it."

"What do you think, Stormy?" Miss Ruth had come to the lawman's office early the following morning.

144

"A few folks in town have a vigilante spirit just now, and now you say Major Berniece knows the man was Johnny, the Bear Boy?"

Miss Ruth frowned and bit her lip. "Courtesy of little Tommy. For the sake of Johnny the Bear Boy, it might be best for Franella to leave town for a bit."

Stormy Durand scratched Bull behind the ears and said, "I assume you have a plan."

Franella lay her head on the table and wept. Miss Ruth rubbed her back and spoke softly, "We'll go to Seattle and check out the University. It's your decision whether you return to Sitka after that."

"What about Johnny?" Franella lifted her head, and her eyes still glistened.

"I'll take care of Johnny. We'll be gone for several weeks. I think things will have calmed down by then. As much as you love Alaska, I think you are destined to go out into the world."

"The world is too big, and I feel so small."

"Never forget Bozhe goes with you."

"Alone. Always alone." Franella shuddered.

"Sam Mitchell's son is attending the University of Washington, and I'm sure he'd show you around."

"Not a boy, especially not a college boy."

Miss Ruth laughed, "Okay. I have very good friends who live in Ballard. Fisherfolk. Norwegians. Their daughter started at the university last fall. I thought you could board with them, and you two girls could attend the college together."

"Aren't there hundreds of students there. I'm just a village girl. I'd be lost."

Miss Ruth rubbed Franella's back. "It will be a new world for you. Of course, nothing is settled yet. You will be their first sixteen-year-old student."

"Sixteen at the end of August and starting college in September? I can't do it." Franella shook her head.

"I'm sure there will be hoops to jump through to obtain permission." Miss Ruth continued.

Franella shook her head.

"School will be out next week, and we're booked on the Star of Alaska the week after that."

"School is awful. I can't go back, not with everybody looking and whispering."

"You are strong, Franella. You can bear it."

Franella nodded, but she knew Miss Ruth was wrong. Every disgusted look and every poisonous whisper put another dent in the armor she put around her heart.

"We'll stay with my friends in Ballard and visit the campus. We can go every day, and you'll learn where the buildings are. There will only be a few summer students there. Once you see the library, you will be eager to enroll."

Franella tried to picture herself in the big city of Seattle, but no images came to mind. Finally, she lifted her eyes to Miss Ruth's, "I've never been on a big steamship."

"We'll pack our bags and get out of Dodge, as they say in the West," Miss Ruth laughed.

TWENTY-ONE

"I'm nervous, Miss Ruth. What if they don't like me?" Franella bit her fingernails as she and Miss Ruth walked west on Market Street to the home of Oskar and Freja Aaby. The sizable Victorian farmhouse covered two city lots and had a large garden in the back.

Miss Ruth patted the girl's arm. "They are fisherfolk from the old country. Just like your family, the husband is Norwegian, and the wife is Danish."

"What is their daughter like?"

"Nora is nineteen. She's determined and a bit shy."

"What does she look like?"

"Tall and slender like you. But fair, with pale blond hair and light green eyes. Very Nordic."

"A real Viking, huh?" Franella guessed, smoothing her own hair, which Miss Drake often called burnt umber and Miss Ruth said was brown.

"She wants to be a doctor."

"I wish I knew what I wanted to be."

"It will come, my dear. When Nora was younger, she loved to read and spent all of her time on frivolous romance novels."

Franella laughed, "Did you tell her that?"

"Certainly not! And I shouldn't have mentioned it to you either. It's just the opinion of an old lady not minding her business." Miss Ruth tucked her arm through Franella's and continued,

"Please don't mention my remarks to her. Look. There's Nora's mother, Freja."

The short, plump figure on the large porch that wrapped three sides of the house flapped her apron, hailed them, raced down the steps, and enveloped Miss Ruth in a fierce hug. She turned to Franella and did the same. Franella stiffened and looked over the woman's shoulder to Miss Ruth, who merely smiled and gave her head a slight shake.

"So, you are not one to hug." Freja took a step back, shrugged, and then smiled, "I will not remember, and soon you will enjoy."

Franella stared.

"Pardon the English. Is not so good."

Franella nodded and greeted Freja in Danish, thanking her for the opportunity to board with them during the school year. Freja's smile nearly broke her face. "You speak the Danish so well. Your mama, bless her, must have been a wonderful teacher. We will have many conversations. You will help with the English, yes?"

Again, Franella nodded, and as the three women entered the house, she noticed the fisherman's boots and oilskins lying over a wooden trunk next to the door. A sight that made her slightly homesick.

"My Nora, she is not so good with the language." Freja laughed, "Perhaps I am not a good teacher like your mama. Nora says she must spend all her time learning the medical words. She has no time for her mama's Danish or her papa's Norwegian."

"I speak Norwegian also."

"Oh, Oskar will be so pleased," Freja told them Nora would be home soon as she led them to the kitchen at the back of the house. Two sizable free-standing cupboards filled one wall. If Franella remembered correctly, they were called Kitchen Queens or Hoosier cabinets, just like the one her mother had in Port Alexander. Another stab of homesickness. Freja set the coffee pot back on the stove and enveloped Franella once more before she settled the girl and Miss Ruth at the large oak table that filled the center of the kitchen. "Franella, you shall be another daughter to us. The good Lord took my boy a few years ago. The others did not live past their first year. Now, our good God has brought you to me! I am blessed."

Franella quietly translated all of this to Miss Ruth as Freja poured coffee and pulled pastries from the oven, all the while chatting in Danish. The smell reminded Franella of her mother's kitchen. She breathed deeply as tears pricked her eyelids, and she blinked them away. She looked around the homey room and saw a myriad of Scandinavian baked goods piled on the counter. Her childhood vow to abstain was forgotten as Freja handed her a plate. Franella leaned over and inhaled, then complimented Freja, who blushed and said, "Ya, these are good. But they will not be so good as the memory of your mama's, doncha know?"

Franella looked to Miss Ruth, who smiled and said, "Eat up, dear one."

The University of Washington campus, with its stately buildings, was impressive. The landscaped lawns and shrubs were immaculate in the sunshine. Miss Ruth knew the brilliant greenery was due in part to the region's abundant soft rain.

As she entered the administration building and made her way to the appropriate office, she rehearsed the reasons they should do her bidding. Mentally, she prepared for battle and asked Bozhe to arm her with the proper weapons.

"I'm sorry. This application has been denied," the Director of Admissions, Mr. Parker, scanned the paperwork and laid it on his desk.

"That's why I am here," Miss Ruth said, calm and serene.

"The Admissions Committee has made its decision, and I don't have time..."

Miss Ruth bristled but kept her tone civil, "I'm asking you to reverse it. We have fulfilled every requirement. You have Franella's certificate of completion from the Calvert Correspondence School and letters of recommendation from her tutors in Alaska."

"Really, Miss Ruth? An Indian and a priest?"

Miss Ruth squared her shoulders and bit her tongue. She was glad she had left Franella in Ballard. "You have the results of her medical tests and the university's general intelligence examination, which I assure you are exemplary."

Mr. Parker sorted through the papers in front of him. "She appears to be healthy, and her scores on the intelligence exam are the highest we've ever recorded. That's beside the point." He also squared his shoulders as he leaned over his desk, "She is simply too young."

"Can you show me the university's written policy that states the age restrictions for this fine institution?"

"It's a matter of common sense."

"Sir, your sense is not common at all. How does it make sense to deprive this young woman..."

"Child!" he interrupted.

"We grow them up fast in Alaska."

"That may be, but we are not in the wilderness. Seattle is an up-and-coming city. We even had a woman mayor a few years ago."

Miss Ruth relaxed, leaned back in her chair, and smiled. She could work with this. "You mean Bertie?"

"Excuse me?"

Miss Ruth's smile grew wider. "Bertie. Bertha Landes, who, with her husband, took many of your university students to the Far East on research tours. Bertie, who was a leader in the Women's University Club. Bertie, whose husband was a professor here and a one-time dean. Need I go on?"

"How do you know her?" Mr. Parker gulped and stuttered.

"I've been a school teacher and women's advocate in the North since the 1890s. Bertie and her husband brought teachers to Alaska on tour. Let's call her and see what she thinks about your refusing admission to a perfectly fine young woman."

Mr. Parker shook his head, "I'm only thinking of the girl. She's young, and you know boys will be boys."

"Miss Ruth laughed, "Franella is from the Territory of Alaska. I assure you, she can take care of herself. At age thirteen, she destroyed a still belonging to Herring Pete, Port Alexander's official town drunk. She befriended an old Tlingit who most of Sitka thought was dangerous and crazy. Believe me, all she wants to do is study and learn, but if need be, she can take care of herself." Miss Ruth refrained from telling the man that Franella was awkward in social situations and tended to speak whatever was on her mind without discerning the consequences.

"Even if we were to admit her, I doubt your little orphan could afford our out-of-state tuition. It's fifty dollars a quarter." Mr. Parker crossed his arms, leaned back in his chair, and smirked.

Miss Ruth ignored the man's sarcasm and silently thanked Bozhe for her good friend Sean Conner. She reached into the large handbag at her feet, pulled out a battered cigar box secured with a rubber band, and placed it on the desk. She removed the rubber band and grinned as she imagined herself shooting the piece of rubber in his direction. Mr. Parker gasped as she raised the lid.

"Are you aware, Mr. Parker, that the price of gold is thirty-five dollars an ounce?"

Slowly, he reached for the box's contents: "There must be several pounds of nuggets here."

"Not quite, but enough, I'd say, for Franella's entire education."

"And some left over for a nice donation to the school."

Miss Ruth closed the cigar box, wrapped the rubber band around it, and put it back in her pocketbook. "Are you rethinking the Admissions Committee's decision about Franella?"

Mr. Parker licked the sweat from his upper lip and forced the avarice from his eyes. "Where did that gold come from? Are you sure it's wise to keep it in a cigar box in your bag?"

Miss Ruth laughed, "The largest nuggets are from the Klondike, others are from the Chichagof mines north of Sitka, and the rest are from the hills above Juneau. It doesn't really matter where they are from. What matters is their value." She patted her handbag and gestured to his office door. "And just outside your office, I have two burly fishermen from Ballard who will escort me to the First National Bank in downtown Seattle, where this little cigar box will join the others."

"There's more?"

"Hmmm." Miss Ruth sat back and watched the battle play out on Mr. Parker's face. She waited in silence, and as much as she didn't like it, she had to respect that his avarice lost the conflict.

"I can't take the responsibility of admitting a child to this adult institution," Mr. Parker rubbed his eyes, and his mouth settled into a resigned frown.

Feigning defeat, Miss Ruth rose and said, "Why don't you have dinner with Franella and me this evening? I'd like you to meet her before making your final decision."

"I don't see the point. It won't change my mind."

"I know," Miss Ruth smiled, "But I think you'd find her an interesting—" she paused and then said, "—child." She stood and held out her hand.

"I don't think…" Mr. Parker wrung his hands while Miss Ruth kept her hand outstretched and her gaze firmly on his eyes.

It could have been a staring match, but the man wavered, shook her hand without meeting her eyes, and said, "Fine. I'll come. But don't expect anything from me."

Miss Ruth gave him the details about where to meet. She turned at the door, smiled, and said, "By the way, don't be late. You know Bertie is a stickler that everyone be on time."

Miss Ruth's satisfied smile and the sound of her cowboy boots on the tile floor left Mr. Parker aghast. He hurried to the door to say he couldn't possibly have dinner, but she was nowhere in sight. He leaned his head on the doorframe and said, "That Miss Ruth is just as forceful and cunning as Mrs. Landes. I have a feeling that come fall, Franella Feddersen is going to be a student here."

TWENTY-TWO

The rain came down in solid gray sheets, but the interior of Aabys' house was warm and cozy. The large dining room table was set with a crisp white cloth, delicate china dishes, and damask napkins. Place settings for ten rimmed the large oval table. Freja issued orders to Nora and Franella. "Put the farikal next to Oskar's place at the head of the table. He will serve."

"Psst. Miss Ruth, that's lamb stew," Franella whispered.

"Nora, put the fenalar next to it," Freja ordered.

"Fenalar is a salted and dried leg of lamb. See how thinly it is sliced," Franella said.

"Remember, Mama, I can't help clean up. I have to study."

Franella saw the disappointment in Freja's eyes, although the woman did not rebuke her daughter. Franella determined she would help. She whispered to Miss Ruth. "You know I can't cook a lick, but I can help clean up."

Miss Ruth nodded and said, "Good girl," as she put a bowl of boiled potatoes and another of caramelized browned potatoes on the table. Nora was right behind her with a platter of buttered rye bread topped with cold sliced potatoes. "It's a good thing we all like potatoes," she said.

"I'm so glad your mama has that large potato patch in the backyard," Miss Ruth said, "It's a blessing during these hard times."

"And I'm the one that gets to hoe it when I should be studying," Nora added as she set a bowl of meatballs and one of pickled herring on the table.

Freja placed a large platter of kogttarsk—poached cod with a creamy mustard sauce—in the center of the table. "Come, everyone, it's time to eat."

Oskar was in charge of saying the blessing before and reading Scripture after the meal. Freja made sure everyone ate, constantly enticing them to take another helping. Oskar's brother, Lars, and his family filled the five extra places at the table.

"So, Miss Feddersen, where is your father's family from in the old country?"

"I think just north of Tonsberg."

"So, we are from a little village just south of there. Perhaps our families knew each other."

Franella frowned, "My father was an only child. He never spoke of his family or Norway."

"I heard of a Feddersen family. Their boy, Günter, was orphaned as a teenager, and he soon left for America."

"My father's name was Günter," Franella stammered.

"Perhaps the Günter I knew back in Norway was your father. Would you like me to write to my cousins and find out?"

Franella could only nod. She filled her mouth with the hearty lamb stew and kept her eyes downcast. What if that Günter was her papa, an orphan? Suddenly, Franella felt closer to her father than she ever had before.

Olga, Lars' wife, elbowed her husband. "Let the girl eat. No more questions."

"I was only..."

She elbowed him again. "No more." Olga turned to Miss Ruth

and said, "When do you return to Alaska?"

Miss Ruth patted her mouth with her napkin and replaced it on her lap. "I have a meeting with the Salvation Army in Seattle the day after tomorrow. After that, I'll be heading north."

Olga elbowed her husband again and raised her eyebrows. He nodded. She turned to Miss Ruth and said, "Our boat is outfitted, and we will be heading to Petersburg early next week. We can take you that far. From there, it will be easy to get a ride to Sitka."

"Thank you, but I have matters to attend to in Sitka as soon as possible." Miss Ruth turned to Franella and said, "Would you like to stay and then head north with Lars and Olga? I am sure Ade Bunderson could fetch you from Petersburg."

Before Franella could formulate an answer, Freja wrung her hands and said, "Oh, I was hoping the girl could stay altogether. Summer is a busy time for me. I make pastries for several of the fine hotels in Seattle. With Nora in summer school, I have no one to help."

Franella looked toward Miss Ruth with panic in her eyes, and the color drained from her face. She said, "I don't, that is, I can't..."

Miss Ruth patted Franella's arm while she addressed Freja, "Franella has many areas of expertise. The kitchen isn't one of them. No shame in that."

Freja smiled and said, "I am expert in kitchen. I am not expert in the money."

"No shame in that," her husband winked and helped himself to more rye bread.

"The English, you know," Freja said as if her husband had not spoken.

"I'm sorry, Freja," Franella gulped, "I'm not good with people either."

"Only I need you to stand next to me and say what I say and tell what they say. The neighbor girl I will hire to work in the kitchen. You will stay the summer and help with the money, yes?"

Franella looked toward Miss Ruth, who said, "You don't need my permission."

Franella's face reddened. She leaned toward Miss Ruth and whispered in Russian so the others wouldn't know, "What about the Major. Doesn't she own me for another two years?"

Miss Ruth grimaced, "She thinks she does, but you let me take care of her. This is a better place for you. That is if you want to stay."

"Alaska is all I have left of home. My heart hurts when I think of leaving." Franella swallowed around the lump in her throat. She took a deep breath, sighed, and said, "Life is so hard."

"Will you stay?" Freja asked.

"I guess."

Miss Ruth said, "We can write often. In fact, I will go to the post office today and purchase a supply of stamps for each of us."

TWENTY-THREE

The run-down building that housed the Salvation Army Soup Kitchen with offices on the third floor was not in the best part of town. Located near Pier One on Seattle's shabby waterfront with its cheap hotels and flophouses, bars, and bathhouses, the area drew the worst of the worst. Nevertheless, Miss Ruth made her way through the grimy streets with a grim determination. There were some catcalls from derelicts sprawled on the sidewalk. Miss Ruth lifted her skirts a few inches and marched on. Her long black dress, fashionable around the turn of the century nearly forty years ago, had seen better days. To the men in the gutter, she appeared nun like, except for her cowboy boots and the large pocketbook draped over her arm.

Miss Ruth had no time to focus on her surroundings or the people who inhabited them. She was on a mission. Major Bernice must be ousted, one way or another. The orphans of Sitka deserved better.

Miss Ruth crossed the street and entered the soup kitchen. The stench of unwashed bodies, stale tobacco, and cheap wine emanating from the restless men sitting at the long tables nearly knocked her over. Although they had been forced to wash their hands and faces with strong lye soap, the grime of living on the streets clung to their bodies as tight as barnacles.

The metallic clatter of pots and pans from the kitchen echoed the sound of the men banging their silverware on the table.

Frowning, the Major General brought the men to order. He nodded at his wife, who sat at the piano in the corner. He led the men in a hymn and frowned again as they sang half-heartedly. Their minds and stomachs focused on the yeasty smell coming from the kitchen as the cook pushed open the swinging door, bringing huge platters of rolls and setting them on the tables. The men knew the rules—three hymns, a short sermon, and a prayer before they were allowed to eat. The Major General, not an unkind man, cut his sermon short and invited the men to eat sooner rather than later.

Miss Ruth whispered to the piano player, who directed her to the staircase. "Third door on the right. Make yourself comfortable. The Major General will be with you shortly."

Miss Ruth smiled her thanks.

The door opened, and the smell of good, strong coffee preceded the man who carried two large mugs of the comforting brew. He placed one near Miss Ruth and settled himself behind his desk. He took a large swallow and said, "What can I do for you, Miss Ruth?"

"I'm sure you have received my letters about the orphanage in Sitka!"

The Major General crossed to a large wooden filing cabinet in the corner of the room. He pulled out a relatively thick file. "I admit yours are not the only complaints I've received about Major Bernice."

"And yet no action has been taken, Major General."

"I'm not sure what the solution is. Call me Walter." He spread the file across the desk. "It's not as easy as you think. Major Bernice's brother is a General at National Headquarters. To be honest, I think he likes the fact that she is far and away in the Territory of Alaska."

"That may be, but it's the children I worry about. All of our efforts to monitor Major Bernice and hold her accountable have been in vain. She believes she has total control over these children. I wrote about how the townspeople have formed a board to try to reform the way she runs the orphanage. It has not been successful."

"As I explained in my letters, your board is not authorized by the Salvation Army. Major Bernice knows the only power you have is that of public opinion, and she seems to care little for that. She prides herself on being a strict and disciplined officer." He furrowed his brow and rubbed his thin mustache. "I realize there is a problem, but I haven't found anyone willing to transfer to Alaska."

"What about National Headquarters?"

"As the head of the Western District, which includes Alaska, I have jurisdiction over Sitka's orphanage. It's up to me to find someone. Besides, I don't want any undue attention from Major Bernice's brother."

"The women of Sitka's various churches have banded together. They believe they could run the orphanage without Major Bernice."

"That may be, but I could face a court-martial if I pulled her out of Alaska and allowed civilians to take over the institution."

"Really?" Miss Ruth's eyebrows rose, and she stared at the Major General.

He sighed and said, "Her brother is very powerful."

Miss Ruth leaned back in the chair, placed her chin in her hands, and thought. She sent a quick prayer heavenward and sighed, "As I understand it, the army has an orphanage in Valdez and another near Palmer. I would hate for you to force the Major on anyone, but I think General Caruthers could keep her in line."

"I have the authority to transfer any officer in the Western District to where I think they are needed, and I'm familiar with Caruthers, a good man," the Major General said. "You know him well?"

"We've worked together in the past. If you have any doubts about me, you can ask him for a reference."

"No need, I'm sure."

"What would be the process of transferring Major Bernice?" Miss Ruth asked.

"A mountain of paperwork for me, and then I would issue Major Bernice her orders, along with a steamship ticket to Anchorage and instructions on how to travel to Palmer or Valdez."

"Could she refuse?"

"She would probably be upset. She might write to her brother and ask him to intervene, but that would take time."

"The orphans in Sitka are miserable. Can I count on you, Major General?"

"I will have to pray on it," he said.

"Then I have no doubt you will make this happen. I have been praying for nearly a year. Bozhe has assured me the time is now."

"Bozhe?" the Major General inquired.

Miss Ruth smiled, "The Russian name for God. Don't worry, Major General, we will give Major Bernice a proper send-off." Miss Ruth rose.

"Sit down, Miss Ruth. This will require a fair amount of paperwork. I will need a liaison in Sitka. If Major Bernice doesn't want to leave Sitka, she will likely stall, and there is a slight chance she would ignore my orders. It would be necessary to have someone there to enforce them—someone who could stand up to the major.

Unfortunately, I don't have anyone in Southeast Alaska that I can send to Sitka, even temporarily." He leaned forward, one eyebrow raised, and looked intently at Miss Ruth.

Miss Ruth smiled and said, "Walter, I believe I can be even more determined than Major Bernice. If you give me a copy of her orders and a letter of authority, I will make sure she's on the steamship."

"If only it were that easy. But you are not a part of the Salvation Army, and Major Bernice is not required to take orders from civilian personnel." He reached into his lower desk drawer and handed her several pieces of paper. "These are enlistment forms. I'm afraid you would need to disaffiliate from any other religious organization you might belong to. Fill out these forms and return them as soon as possible. Even then, I make no guarantees she'll go."

Miss Ruth caught her breath and chewed on her bottom lip. Join the Salvation Army? Could she? For the miserable orphans of Sitka, she could. "Why wouldn't she go once she's given the order?"

"The longer you are in the Army, the higher your rank. She will not like taking orders from you."

"They are not my orders; they are yours. I will merely be the enforcer." Miss Ruth sat ramrod straight in the wooden chair, steel laced her voice.

The Major General smiled grimly. "I do believe you are a match for Major Bernice. I'll notify General Caruthers and the staff in Palmer, it's a little more, shall we say, primitive than Valdez. I think that's where we should send her. The mail between here and central Alaska is even slower and more erratic than to the Southeast. That will work in our favor in case the Major wants to communicate with her brother."

"If you take care of the paperwork, I will take care of Major Bernice," Miss Ruth declared.

"I doubt she will go quietly," he sighed.

TWENTY-FOUR

"I wish I were returning to Sitka with you now that you are getting rid of that awful Major Bernice," Franella stood on the dock as Miss Ruth prepared to board the Star of Alaska steamship.

"I'm glad you won't be there. I'm not looking forward to our showdown," Miss Ruth said.

"She's a mean old witch, and I hate her!" Franella said and then gulped, "Don't you?"

Miss Ruth looked at the young woman who stood before her. Franella Feddersen had a brilliant and mature mind, but her emotions were as young as her teenage body. "I don't know what kind of life or childhood Major Bernice had. I don't know what circumstances she lived through. I have no idea why she is so contentious. We must always pray that the things we suffer make us better, not bitter."

"That didn't happen in the Major's case, did it? She's bitter and miserable and tries to make everyone around her the same," Franella squeezed Miss Ruth's hand. "I guess I'm glad I won't be there to see all the ruckus."

"I'm praying it won't come to a ruckus."

"Miss Ruth, can I ask you a favor? Will you ask Sophie if she wants to work at the orphanage after the major is gone? She's so good with the little kids, except for Tommy, of course."

"That's a brilliant idea. I do have a plan for Tommy. I'm going to send him with Major Bernice, but I will let her think it's her idea."

"Tommy's a little monster, but even I wouldn't foist him on Major Bernice."

Miss Ruth laughed and winked at Franella, "Tommy needs a strong father figure in his life. General Caruthers is just the man for the job. Soon, little Tommy will transfer his attachment from Major Bernice to the General."

"I do admire you, Miss Ruth, but you are a devious woman. Gloriously devious," Franella laughed.

"Surely not!" Miss Ruth winked again. "It's time we say our goodbyes."

Franella choked back tears and forced a smile. Miss Ruth was her last connection to Alaska and home. The elderly woman had known her since she was a baby. As soon as the ship sailed, Franella would be truly alone.

Oskar, Freja, and Nora hugged Miss Ruth in turn. Freja, of course, took two turns and then hugged Franella and thanked her for staying. The Star of Alaska's horn blasted, the engines thrummed, as Miss Ruth walked up the gangway.

Franella held back her sobs.

Freja took the girl by the arm as Oskar led them to his nearly decade-old Model A Ford. "She is like a mama to you. You will miss her, yes? You love her, no? It is good to cry. Come, we will go home and eat. You will feel better. You can write her every day, and Oskar will take your letters to the post office. We will be your family for as long as you want. It is good, yes?"

Franella nodded, and that seemed to satisfy Freja. As they approached Ballard, Freja, who was sitting in the back seat with Franella, tapped Oskar on the shoulder. "You will stop at the Sons of Norway Lodge. I will show the ladies my new daughter. Franella will say hello."

Nora, who sat next to her father, turned and looked at her mother. "Do we have to? I need to study."

"We go." Freja slapped Oskar on the shoulder, ignoring her daughter.

You are a nice woman, but you are not my mama. Oskar is not my papa, and Nora is not my sister. I am an orphan. There, I admit it! I'm an orphan, alone in the world. Hundreds of miles away from my Alaska. God, how could you have let this happen to me? Franella folded her arms around her stomach, pressing them tightly, but it did not alleviate the pain. She leaned her head back as the Model A bounced over Ballard's dirt roads.

Stoically, she followed Freja into the lodge. She smiled and said all the right things as Freja showed her off and bragged that she now had two brilliant daughters. Modern women! College-bound and out to change the world.

Nora rolled her eyes and winked at Franella, "Pay her no mind. The other ladies will forget about us as soon as we are out of the door. All they want their daughters to do is marry and have babies."

"Doesn't your mama want that?"

Nora smiled, but when she spoke, there was a bitter edge to her voice. "Don't get me started. Mama and I have had conversations about that for most of my growing-up years. I think she has given up on me and so pretends she's proud of me."

"I think she is truly proud of you. How could she not be?" Franella said as she eyed these Scandinavian women, so reminiscent of the ones she had known in Port Alexander. Their conversations were full of new marriages, recipes, cleaning techniques, and those of those newly blessed with children.

166

Nora took Franella by the arm and said, "Mama, we'll be at the table in the corner. Franella is thirsty, and they are serving fresh lemonade."

"But I'm not..."

"Shhh." They took their glasses and made their way to the small table with the bright yellow oilcloth cover. They sank into the wooden chairs in the out-of-the-way corner. Nora said, "Let me tell you some of my mama's not-very-subtle ways of extolling the virtues of wifery and motherhood to the exclusion of anything else a female can do. She will soon bombard you with such talk."

Franella gulped and said, "What shall I say?"

"Just smile and tell her that she's right."

"Is that what you do?"

Nora drained her glass of the pale-yellow liquid and carefully set it back on the table. She spoke without meeting Franella's eyes: "I am going to be a doctor no matter who stands in my way, even if it's my own mother."

"But Nora..."

"Keep your ears open because you are going to hear her say..." Nora's voice was low and controlled, and she spoke at length.

"Oh, my." Franella's face flamed, and she rested the cold glass on her cheek.

TWENTY-FIVE

University of Washington, Seattle

Dear Miss Ruth,

Freja said I could write to you every day, but Oskar said it's wasteful to spend money on daily stamps. After all, they cost six cents for air mail and three cents for regular mail. He is a practical man and a dear one.

He is a quiet man like my papa. He is a businessman, a fisherman, and the owner of several boats. He's a good boss, and people like working for him. During good years, he invests his profits, mainly in land.

I know that you left Oskar the money for my room and board for the year. He said since I am helping Freja with her pastry business, there is no need for me to pay rent. I told him to return the money to you, but he had already spent it!

My mouth fell open, and he chuckled. "Come, we will take a ride," he said.

Just a little north of Ballard, he pulled over and stopped the car. "See this land covered in wildflowers? It is yours. By the time you leave the university, the edge of Ballard will be here, and your land can be sold for much more than its purchase price."

I gulped and nodded. If this is not all right with you and Mr.

Conner, please let me know, and I will tell Oskar he must sell the land now and return the money to you. Otherwise, I will bring it with me after I graduate. Me, a landowner! I'm just a girl.

I don't see much of Nora. When she's not attending her summer classes or studying in the library, she is holed up in her bedroom memorizing body parts and medical terms. She says when the fall quarter starts, we can visit on the way to and from the university. Nora is quiet and somewhat aloof, but there is a tension in her. Sometimes, it spills over at the family dinner table. I keep my head down and force myself to remain silent. It's not easy.

Freja irritates me. She means well, but she wants to mother me. She continually grabs me and hugs me. "Poor little orphan! You are a daughter to me. Your mama would wish it so, doncha know."

I don't know how to respond, so I just nod. I don't think she realizes how unsettled I have become around her, and I think it would hurt her feelings if she did. I will be glad when classes start.

I miss you and my Alaska.

Franella

Dear Miss Ruth,

The university is immense and overwhelming. Nora showed me how to fix my hair, so I look as old as the other girls. No one knows I'm just sixteen. I plan to keep quiet so no one will guess.

Recently, the literature professor asked me to stay after class to discuss one of my papers. Apparently, he liked my perspective on Faust. I told him about my correspondence school and my rath-

er unorthodox tutoring in Alaska. He offered to compile a list of books that would give me a broader knowledge of the world. These are books to read outside of my regular assignments. I'm excited about that. Oh, he also told me I should keep my unique perspective. I was afraid to ask what he meant.

There are a fair number of social activities available. Nora is not involved in any, and although I have been asked to join a few student groups, I have declined. Freja frets about this, and I have promised her that after I've learned to balance my homework, outside reading, and translating for her, I will be ready to do something social. As you know, I am more comfortable alone with my books, but it's challenging to tell Freja no. She made me promise to drag Nora along when I become a social butterfly.

I must say, going to the fine hotels and restaurants in Seattle and translating for Freja has been eye-opening. Seattle is such a large city that I can't get my bearings. If left on my own, I'm sure I'd be lost in a few minutes. I feel more at home on the sea and in the woods.

Freja is outgoing and friendly to all the staff, from the bosses down to the dishwashers. She treats everyone as if they were her best friend. She was indeed being cheated by two managers of the better restaurants. Seeing how she stood up for herself without anger amazed me. I tried to match her tone as I translated, and I'm happy to say things were resolved without rancor. The managers, red-faced and stuttering, blamed the error on their accountants, and Freja accepted the explanations, even though I proved that was not the case.

I didn't have to speak unless I was translating, and I believe my observations of her interactions will help me as I encounter *uncomfortable situations of my own.*

I found a book in the library by Emily Post. It's about etiquette and manners in polite society. I'm anxious to see what she has to say. I am determined to become comfortable wherever I find myself.

*If the university had a class on how to behave in different social circumstances, I would take it. I am reading **How to Win Friends and Influence People**, which is interesting. However, I'm not certain I care about influencing people, and I'm not sure what having a friend is like—one that isn't old like you, I mean.*

I miss you and my Alaska.

Franella

Dear Miss Ruth,

I know I told you I wanted to get to know Nora better. Now I'm not so sure. There is much friction between Nora and her parents. They are gentle, traditional, and loving. She is determined and forceful. It is as if she has blinders on and can only see her goal of becoming a doctor. Nothing else seems to matter to her.

You know how easy learning is for me. It's not for Nora. She spends hours trying to memorize terms and meanings. I suggested we study together. It was a disaster. I read a chapter while walking around the kitchen table. You know I have to move unless I am in a state of deep focus. She quizzed me, and of course, I knew all the answers. She threw the book across the room and refused to study with me again. I know I haven't done anything wrong, so why does it feel that way?

Dale Carnegie and Emily Post do not have the answers I need.

I miss you and my Alaska,

Franella

Dear Miss Ruth,

Freja is starting to depend on me for the things Nora refuses to do. I am willing to help in every way that I can, but Nora resents me for it. I feel each of them is pulling me in a different direction.

I'm happiest when Oskar takes me to his boat. I help him repair the nets, and he tells stories of his life in Norway. It makes me think of my papa. I don't understand how being with Oskar can make me happy and sad at the same time.

I still haven't joined any clubs or attended any social activities. There is a history club I would enjoy, but Freja will want me to take Nora, and Nora will refuse, and there will be more tension. It's not worth it. I was much happier in the woods with Johnny, the Bear Boy. How is he? You haven't mentioned him in any of your letters.

You would be proud that once in a while, I arrive at class early and linger after so I can chat with the other students and, occasionally, the Professors. This is not easy for me, and no matter how often I force myself to engage with others, my palms sweat, and I stammer. It's almost impossible not to blurt out what I'm thinking, especially if the others are incorrect in what they say. I'm trying to politely ask where they did their research or if they have a reference they could cite. It seems people become offended if you correct them. I don't get it, but I'm trying. Can you hear me sigh?

As always, I miss you and my Alaska,

Franella

Dear Miss Ruth,

Please keep Firy informed about me. I am so grateful to her for the reading thing, but we are so different. Her life is chores and taking care of her great-grandmother and little sister. She hates school and would rather be fishing with her Uncle Ade.

I love school and hate Seattle! Too many people. The mountains are too far away, and I can't really smell the sea.

Professor Good teaches a fantastic literature class based on the Bible. For our final test, he had us sign in at the library. When we did, we were given a blue exam book and a folded piece of paper with a few words on it. We had three hours to find where the phrase was in the Bible, to explain it within the context, and its meaning and relevance in history, literature, and within society as a whole. It took me forty-five minutes to find the reference. I scoured the card catalog and found about twelve different reference books. I stacked them around me, read, researched, sifted, and collated the information. I wrote furiously until the librarian tapped me on the shoulder to let me know my time had expired. Many students refuse to take Professor Good's classes because of the way he tests. It was exciting, but I know Firy wouldn't be interested. I don't know what to write to her. Tell her I am well. Just to let you know, I was graded the highest in the class, not bragging, just a fact.

I miss you and my Alaska.

Franella

Dear Miss Ruth,

The psychology professor is keen to have us analyze ourselves.

When he found out I had lost both of my parents and was sent to an orphanage, he seemed almost excited. The other kids had peaceful growing-up years, nothing out of the ordinary, he said. He asked to meet with me, and he shared a lot of his insights with me, even though I shared as little as possible. He said it was like pulling hen's teeth.

He says I not only lost my only family, but by leaving Alaska under such adverse circumstances, I have lost my sense of place. So I am without family and without—home. He believes I bury my emotions by reading and direct all my energy toward learning. I let knowledge and facts fill me, but when I am not studying, that feeling of fullness drains away, and I am once again empty. He says I must find something to fill and sustain me, or I will learn and learn and never come to myself.

I suppose he is right. I thought about when you talked of Bozhe and how He is the filling agent. I tried to make myself believe, but as you said, it can't be forced. My mind is open, but my heart holds me back.

But enough of this introspection. I'm going for a walk. Time to shake off these feelings.

I miss you and my Alaska.

Franella

Dear Miss Ruth,

Freja continues to include me in all the family activities, even when I would rather stay in my room to study. I feel bad because

Nora does stay in her room. I attend each activity yet continue to feel like an outsider. Don't get me wrong, they are wonderful people. They have taken me into their home, but they are not my family! And this is not Alaska. I am forever alone, forever outside.

I miss you and my Alaska.

Franella

Dear Miss Ruth,

It has been a month since the surprise attack on Pearl Harbor, a place I had never heard of. Everyone here is frantic and unsure of the future and their role in it. Several of Oskar's deckhands have enlisted in the Navy, and he expects more will do so in the coming weeks. How he will continue his business is a concern.

Freja is looking for a way to supply the army with her pastries. She is sure that it will help the boys, as she calls them, to train harder and fight better. If anyone can manage to do this, it would be her.

I am in a quandary. What can I contribute to the war effort? Oskar says we do not know how long the war will last, maybe months, possibly years. He advised me to stay in school. It sounds reasonable, but I am agitated and feel like I should do something. I just don't know what!

Nora ignores all the turmoil and talk of war. She says if the world is still at war once she finishes college and medical school, she will do her part. Until then, she doesn't want to hear about it.

I remember talking to Mr. Mitchell about the war in Europe. I was right about that, but this attack in the Pacific was totally unexpected, at least by me. I have been so busy with my studies that I have not read a newspaper in weeks.

There was a considerable antiwar sentiment on campus when I first came, and it is still going strong. We have many students of Japanese descent. What will happen to them, I wonder. A few of them have already stopped coming to class. They are Americans, and I assume they are afraid because of their ancestry. I have heard some wild rumors, but won't voice them. What a world we are living in.

For now, I am continuing my daily life. I'm sure I will be packaging lots of pastries and Danish cookies in the coming weeks. As Freja said, there is a Navy yard in Bremerton and an army camp just outside of Tacoma full of young men who need "feeding up, doncha know." She is sure the war cannot be won without her baking.

Please write and let me know if everyone is okay. I know that Firy is often afraid of the future and things that are not yet, but might be. I shall write her in the next few days.

I miss you and my Alaska.

Franella

PS: If Mr. Mitchell is not too busy keeping the citizens of Sitka informed of local and world events, please ask him to write to me. I am very interested in his take on the hostilities. How does he figure Alaska will play into the war with Japan? Just looking at the map makes me think Alaska is strategically placed.

TWENTY-SIX
Late Spring 1945

Franella Feddersen raced down the gangway and embraced Miss Ruth. The salty sea air was more bracing and tinged with a chill than Seattle's Puget Sound had ever been. She glanced up Lincoln Street and said, "Everything looks the same, except for all the soldiers and sailors."

Miss Ruth laughed, "Several seem to be looking at you, and they like what they see."

Franella blushed, "No time for that."

"How was your trip?" Miss Ruth asked.

"It was difficult getting a ticket. With the war, there are so many travel restrictions, but I'm here now."

Miss Ruth looped her arm through Franella's. "And I hope you will be here for a long time. Although I'm glad you stayed an extra year and worked with Professor Good to get that additional degree."

Franella frowned, "I have to decide what my life will be now that I am finished with school."

"Are you finished, dear one?"

Franella grabbed her large suitcase, and Miss Ruth picked up the smaller one. "What do you mean?" Franella asked.

Miss Ruth looked fondly at the young woman who seemed to have gained a measure of confidence and some social graces over the last few years. "I thought you might go on to graduate school, perhaps at Yale or Harvard."

Franella dropped her suitcase and turned to Miss Ruth. "What are you saying?"

"Here we are at the Sitka Café," Miss Ruth said. She saw a teenage boy on a bicycle across the street and called, "Sven, can you take these suitcases to my cabin? Franella and I are in need of Agrafena's French crullers."

"Sure, Miss Ruth. I just have to drop these letters at the post office for my ma."

"We'll keep an eye on your bike. Thanks, Sven."

The two women entered the café and sat near the street-side windows. Franella wanted to see everyone passing by. "How are Firy and Johnny, the Bear Boy?"

"Firy has a beau, although I think Anna Marie is the one who truly loves him. He's a soldier, a good guy, and a great baseball player. His unit was transferred to Germany some months ago. Anna Marie is miserable. But you know, Firy, she holds everything inside."

"She does do that, but I can't believe she has a boyfriend." Franella shook her head and picked up a cruller. "I want to see Mr. Conner soon to thank him for sponsoring my education. And I want to talk to Mr. Mitchell about the war. Everyone is so war-weary. It must end soon."

"There's time for all of that," Miss Ruth signaled Agrafena for more coffee.

"Tell me about Yale and Harvard. It sounds impossible to me," Franella said.

"The University of Washington also sounded impossible to you. Remember, with Bozhe, all things are possible."

Franella nodded and reached into her pocketbook. "Here is a check from Oskar. Just as he predicted, the land outside of Ballard had increased in value."

Miss Ruth pocketed the check without looking at it. "Good old Oskar, we will put this toward furthering your education. Which do you prefer, Yale or Harvard?"

"I don't know anything about either one."

"Perhaps you can write to Professor Good and ask what he would recommend. I have course catalogs and application forms from both schools at the cabin."

As they finished the crullers and Miss Ruth reached for the receipt, Franella said, "You never told me how Johnny, the Bear Boy, is doing."

Miss Ruth fished the money out of her pocketbook and then looked out the window.

"Miss Ruth?" Franella's voice quivered.

"I'm afraid Johnny is no longer in Sitka."

"Is he okay? Where is he?" Franella bit the end of her finger.

"That summer I took you to Seattle to visit the university was not a good one for you or Johnny."

"I remember."

"Johnny was beaten by a group of high school boys. Several times."

Franella gasped. "I'm sure it was Lester. Wait until I see him."

Miss Ruth reached across the table and took Franella's hands. "This all happened several years ago. It's over."

"That doesn't matter. It's still not right."

"Lester enlisted in the Marines right after Pearl Harbor. He was killed during the battle of Iwo Jima."

Franella slumped, nearly falling from the chair. She grabbed the edge of the table. Both her knuckles and her face were white with tension. Tears swam in her eyes, but she refused to let them spill over. "Why didn't you write me any of this?"

"My dear, what good would it have done except make you miserable and distract you from your studies?"

"Where is Johnny now?" Franella asked in a small voice.

"His mother's clan was from Kake. Petrov Bravebird and Ade Bunderson took him there, and Petrov spoke to the elders. They welcomed Johnny for the sake of his mother and promised to care for him."

"I'd like to see him soon."

"We'll talk to Ade. I'm sure we can make it happen."

So Franella Feddersen, a graduate from the University of Washington with degrees in philosophy, world history, and American literature, came back to Sitka but still felt as if she did not belong.

"It seems as if the townspeople have forgotten the circumstances of my departure," Franella said, grateful that it was so.

"It was only some who gossiped and judged. Once the war started, the state of the world and their loved ones on the battlefield took all of their attention, that, and how to live with the strict rationing. Government regulations regarding hunting and fishing are a burden, and many find ways to ignore or circumvent them."

"That's Alaska," Franella laughed.

"Petrov Bravebird takes his grandsons into the woods, and they forage. Many housewives in Sitka are happy to buy the produce when they go door to door, at least those who know something about Native cuisine."

Franella remembered her foraging excursions with Johnny, the

Bear Boy. "Everyone is so busy. Do you think Mr. Bravebird and Father Alexi would resume tutoring me? My Russian and especially my Tlingit are getting rusty. I also need to find some kind of job."

"You can ask them about tutoring, and I think I can help with your employment."

"What do you have in mind?"

"I thought you could help Sophie at the orphanage part-time."

"All those little kids!" Franella made a face.

"It's not the kids you are afraid of. It's the memories!! You need to lay them to rest."

"You wouldn't ask Oliver Twist to go back to the orphanage, would you?" Franella muttered.

"Miss Drake has spoken to me about you. The library's budget is small, but you could work there a couple of days a week."

"I'd love that. I'm more comfortable with books than kids."

Miss Ruth chuckled, "The library has a copy of Dale Carnegie's book. Maybe you need to read it again."

Franella laughed and linked her arm with Miss Ruth's as they headed to Akervik's general store and then the post office. "You know, all I have to do is picture the word or phrase, and then I can see the whole page in my mind. I never have to read a book twice."

"I sometimes forget how your mind works."

"It comes in handy when all the professors want you to do is vomit back everything they've made you swallow. I much preferred Professor Good. He made you think! You didn't even have to agree with him as long as you could prove your thesis with decent research. I'm going to miss him!"

"I don't know how we are going to keep your mind occupied before you continue the next phase of your education."

Franella stopped on the sidewalk and gulped in Sitka's salty air. "To tell you the truth, Miss Ruth, I'm weary. I could do with a long rest."

"You rest as long as you wish, but I don't think it will be long. You love learning too much."

"I shipped a steamer trunk full of books recommended by my professors. It should arrive soon, and when I become restless, I will just open the trunk."

"Clever girl."

TWENTY-SEVEN

"It's not fair! It's just not fair, Miss Ruth."

"Sit down, my dear," Miss Ruth signaled Agrafena.

The café's owner brought coffee and a menu to the agitated young woman. "More bad news?" she asked.

Franella nodded and jerked the letter out of its envelope, her eyes scrolling down the page. "Listen... 'expecting many military veterans to enroll—saving space for young men returning from war'—it's not fair!"

"It sounds the same as the letter you received from Yale a few days ago," Agrafena said.

"It's almost word for word. It's like all those mucky-muck Ivy League colleges got together and decided they preferred veterans. Easy money. I suppose—the GI bill."

Miss Ruth sipped her coffee and patted Franella's hand, "I have learned Bozhe usually has another plan when the current way is blocked."

"Maybe He wants me to stay here and let my mind rot," Franella fumed.

Agrafena and Miss Ruth exchanged a look and tried not to smile. "Drink your coffee," Agrafena said, refilling the cup. "Do not be a child."

Franella had the grace to blush.

"We will pray on it," Miss Ruth said as Agrafena headed back to the kitchen. Franella bit her tongue. Praying! Miss Ruth seemed to think that solved all of life's problems. She knew for a fact it didn't. Praying hadn't brought her parents back. Praying hadn't stopped Major Bernice from tormenting her. Praying hadn't stopped Blanche's hateful bullying. It hadn't stopped the vile rumors about her purity. It hadn't kept Johnny, the Bear Boy, safe. Praying might work for Miss Ruth, but it hadn't worked for Franella. As these thoughts swirled through her mind as she sighed and reached for her coffee.

Several days later, Miss Ruth came into the library and found Franella reshelving books. "Bozhe has put an idea into my mind. How do you feel about leaving the country?"

"What?"

"America is not the only country that has prestigious universities."

Franella let the books fall back on the cart. "We'd better sit down."

Miss Ruth signaled to Miss Drake, "Do you have any books about Oxford?"

Miss Drake crossed the room to the card catalog and thumbed through the 'O' drawer. She brought two books to the table. "Are you thinking what I think you're thinking?" she asked.

"I am," Miss Ruth answered.

"I can't go to England. London is in shambles. The country is a mess. The economy is in ruins. There is still strict rationing, and it's too expensive."

"Precisely," Miss Ruth said.

"Exactly," Miss Drake echoed.

Much to Franella's amazement, the two older women were enthused and excited. Miss Ruth wrote to the university for admission forms. She researched how to apply for a passport and visa to England. Miss Drake found out about climate, dress codes, food, and fashions. They also decided that when the time came, they would send a steamer trunk of non-perishable foods and then send regular parcels. There was no need for Franella to go hungry amid England's extreme rationing, still in effect.

"What about all the British soldiers returning? Won't they take all the university spots?"

"Oh dear, I hadn't thought about that," Miss Drake said, scribbling on her notepad, "I'll add that to my list of things to find out."

Miss Ruth remained her serene self. "I'm sure we will overcome all obstacles. Bozhe wouldn't have told us to pursue this if He wasn't going to go before us and lead the way. He will show us how to proceed."

"If it happens, it's not going to be quick, is it?" Franella asked. "Overseas mail is so slow."

"We'll aim for January, dear one. That's probably the soonest you can be enrolled."

The three women aimed for January but missed. Franella Feddersen was not on her way across the lower forty-eight until the fall of 1946.

Bob Nels flew her and Miss Ruth to Seattle in his small plane.

The older woman accompanied her to the train station, lecturing her the entire way. Freja and Oskar came to say goodbye. Nora was, of course, in her room, studying. Freja blew her nose twice and hugged Franella three times. "Why you must go so far away, I don't understand. So many boys have come back from over there. You could find a lovely husband and settle down."

Finally, Franella put her hand up. She laughed and said, "No husband for me, not when there are so many books left in the world."

"You are just like Nora. Is too, too bad."

Franella patted the older woman, "It will be all right." She turned to Miss Ruth, "You've made me check my tickets, passport, and money at least four times. You've looked in my lunch tote twice. You've warned me about talking to strangers. I will be fine."

"Are you sure, Dear One?" Miss Ruth hugged her and slipped a small parcel into the girl's coat pocket. "I've never been to Europe. I'm still pretty spry."

The train whistle blew, and as the conductor urged her aboard, Franella said, "Too late now." She hugged Miss Ruth and waved to Freja and Oskar. "I'll be fine," she said again, but her lip trembled.

"Trust the redcaps when you have to change trains." Miss Ruth waved her handkerchief until the train was out of the station, then she used it to blow her nose. "Go with her, Bozhe. She is going to need you."

Freja linked arms with Miss Ruth, and Oskar followed them out of the station.

TWENTY-EIGHT

Franella's book lay open on her lap as she gazed out of the window. The train had chugged east for a day and a night, and she had not read more than a few pages. Even during the night hours, when the soft clatter of the tracks should have lulled her to sleep, she pressed her face against the window and stared at the passing countryside. Moonbeams and starlight gave an ethereal light to the terrain. Mile after mile, she was enthralled. When passing a lone farmhouse, she pictured a family gathered around the dinner table. It should have been a homey, comforting image. Instead, it made her acutely aware of her aloneness.

How big this country was! She knew of its vastness from her geography and history classes, but to experience it for herself was intimidating—the purple mountains' majesty and amber waves of grain had her humming the song, which brought a warmth to her heart that was comforting yet overawed her. She gnawed on her lower lip and clutched her stomach. What kind of intense longing was she feeling?

The Cascades and Rockies were rugged and incredibly majestic, but they couldn't compare to the mountains of Alaska. The high desert, the prairies, and the plains were endless. Those wide-open spaces made her feel small, insignificant, less than. Familiar feelings, but usually for different reasons.

As the train reached the twin cities of St. Paul and Minneapolis, Franella remained in her seat, gazing out of the window. Where did all those city dwellers come from? Could they fill all the towering buildings? How could they all live in such a tightly packed space? Didn't they get on each other's nerves? How could they breathe? She shrank back in her seat and didn't realize she had voiced her thoughts aloud until the woman across the aisle laughed and said, "This is nothing. Wait until the train arrives in Chicago! Union Station is chaotic. Everyone's in a hurry. So many trains are coming and going in every direction. It's madness. And that's just the depot; the city itself is worse." The woman clutched her hat and coat, picked up her small suitcase, and left.

Franella turned back to the window and shuddered. She opened her book and forced herself to read. She wouldn't look again until the train was well away from those imposing twin cities.

Many hours later, Franella agreed with the woman who had left the train in St. Paul. As the locomotive approached the outskirts of Chicago, she saw tall buildings in the distance that rivaled the trees near her home in Port Alexander. The closer they came to the city center, the more Franella stared. Block after block of buildings almost leaning into each other. When the train pulled into Chicago's Union Station, she saw many passenger and freight trains chugging along in every direction. The multiple tracks resembled a spider's web of wood and steel. Brakes screeched. Whistles blew. Creosote from the railroad ties and diesel fumes assaulted everyone. Conductors urged their passengers to depart quickly if they were continuing to another city and had to make connections.

Along with everyone else, Franella hurried to comply. A pocketbook and an overnight case in one hand and a large, heavy suitcase in the other impeded her progress. Its weight pulled on her shoulder as she made her way to the lobby. Why had she packed so many things?

Once she reached the cavernous main lobby, she sank to a bench, ignoring the smell of floor cleaner as janitors swished their mops close to her. She wrinkled her nose and pulled her ticket out of her pocketbook. She sighed when she saw it was a six o'clock departure. She had about eleven and a half hours to fill. What was she going to do all day?

She waved to a redcap and asked if there was a coffee shop nearby. He pointed to the far end of the lobby as he hurried by. It took some time to make her way there. She finally began pushing the heavy suitcase with her foot. The little diner was crowded, and there was no room for her luggage at the counter or under the small booths. She sat on it outside the entrance and waited. Every time the door opened, her hunger increased as the clinking of crockery and silverware and the smell of hot dogs and hamburgers wafted through the air. When an older woman and a teenage girl were about to enter, Franella said, "Excuse me, if I give you some money, could you bring me a cup of coffee and some toast or a donut? I can't leave my luggage."

The mother smiled, "We'd be happy to. You can pay us when we bring your breakfast."

"I have the money right here," Franella said.

"I'm going to assume you are from a small town where you know everybody." At Franella's nod, the woman continued, "This is Chicago. Don't ever give your money to strangers. You don't know who's trustworthy."

After the girl delivered her coffee and donut, Franella found a bench close by. She didn't want to have to drag her suitcase any farther than necessary. She knew she would have to find another kind stranger at lunchtime.

Franella read for several hours but kept nodding off, so she decided to make up stories about the people passing by. That amused her for some time. It was a long, tiring day, especially since she hadn't slept much on the train. Now it was time to make her way to Track Twenty-Two. To her dismay, there seemed to be multiple platforms, and the platform numbers were not sequential. How inefficient!

She held her ticket in her hand and searched the overhead signs. Metal screeched on metal as the engineers applied the brakes, whistles blew, steam belched out of the smokestacks, and people pushed past her. Fathers yelled at their families to hurry. Children fretted, and mothers tried to comfort them while encouraging them not to dawdle. Businessmen complained that their trains were late and asked the redcaps what they were going to do about it as if the luggage carriers had the power to change things.

The sights and sounds of this alien environment caught Franella unprepared. True, Seattle's depot had been busy and chaotic. But Miss Ruth had paved the way and acted as a buffer against all the mayhem.

Exhausted, she sat on her suitcase and thought. She could do this. Where was Track Twenty-Two? Had she missed it? Was it on another level? Had she passed it? Miss Ruth said to trust the redcaps. There appeared to be a lot of them rushing here and there, directing passengers and toting luggage. She held her ticket high, and after a few minutes, a young redcap stopped, looked at it, and pointed her in the right direction. Tired as she was, she told herself she was an Alaska girl, independent and self-reliant. She could take care of herself and her luggage.

She didn't need a porter to tote her suitcase. Up the stairs, down the hallway, through the overpass, and down the stairs to the platform at track twenty-two, Franella distained her independence and wished she had paid the young redcap to help her. Lifting that suitcase up the stairs pulled at her upper arm and neck muscles. Sliding it down was tricky. Gravity wanted to help, but she couldn't let go of the case lest she injure those in front of her.

Finally, she was on the correct platform. Where were all the passengers? A distant whistle blew, and she saw the end of a train leaving the depot. She looked at her ticket. This was the right track and the correct train, wasn't it?

Another train pulled in, and people bustled down the staircase, eager to meet those deboarding. She sat on her suitcase, cupped her hands in her chin, and a single tear rolled down her cheek.

A tall, thin redcap rushed past her and motioned to another porter. He handed him a sheaf of ticket stubs, issued instructions, and then retraced his steps. "Pardon, miss, yo's okay?"

She shook her head and held out her ticket. He took off his glasses, squinted, and held the ticket close to his eyes. He noted the gate number, the ticket number, and the track number. "Yep. Yep. Dat's right. Everything as it should be, 'cept yo be missin' de train."

"But I'm early," Franella cried.

He took off his cap and scratched behind his ear, then looked at the ticket again, "Not meanin' to contradicts, but yo's late."

Franella snatched the ticket, pointed, and said, "Look here, six o'clock. I'm forty-five minutes early. How could the train have come and gone when I'm so early!"

He scratched his other ear, "Miss, yo's 'bout eleven hours late!"

The color drained out of Franella's face. "I couldn't have misread the time. I'm smart."

"Yes, miss." The redcap nodded. "Yo gots friends or family in Chicago?"

She shook her head, and another tear fell.

"Where you goin'?"

"Oxford."

"Dat up in Vermont?"

Franella looked at him and mumbled, "Across the ocean, in England." Lines of exhaustion creased her face, and her shoulders sagged.

The redcap scratched both ears and said, "Maybe yo should go backs home."

"Alaska?"

"Somewhere in Canada?"

"Next door."

The redcap looked around, hoping to see his supervisor. He scratched his ear again and felt as helpless as the young woman sitting on her suitcase, trying not to cry.

Franella jerked and fell as she was shoved off her suitcase. Her head smacked the marble floor. She jumped up, arms flailing, almost knocking over the redcap. "Stop! He's got my bag!"

The redcap ran after the scrawny teenage boy who had snagged the pocketbook and overnight case that lay beside Franella's suitcase.

"He's a thief! Stop!" Her head hurt, and her vision blurred as she yelled and raced past the elderly redcap.

He slowed his steps and returned to the young lady's large suitcase. If left unattended, it would undoubtedly disappear. As he retraced his steps, he pulled a tin whistle from his pocket and blew until his cheeks puffed out. Other redcaps and porters looked in his direction. He pointed toward the east exit, "That way! Thief!" They gave chase.

A few minutes later, a frustrated Franella trudged back and stood before the redcap, "Thanks for guarding my suitcase, Mr...?"

"Folk calls me Hard Workin' Willie. I sees yo didn't catch him."

Franella held out her empty hands, "We ran as fast as we could, but it was like nailing jelly to a wall. No footprints."

"Footprints? Not on dis marble floor."

"Johnny, the Bear Boy, taught me to track. I could nab that blasted thief if we were in the woods."

Hard Workin' Willie mumbled something unintelligible under his breath, then said, "First thing, I takes yo to de ticket master. He change yo ticket to de next train goin' to Grand Central."

"My passport was in my pocketbook. I can't cross the ocean without it. Is Grand Central Station bigger than this one?"

Hard Workin' Willie grinned, "Yes, miss. It shore is."

"Then I'd rather be stuck here than in New York City."

Willie shrugged, "De ticket master can put de date in later."

Franella looked in the direction the thief had taken and sighed, "I hope that dirty, rotten thief is proud of himself." She chewed on the end of her thumb.

"Yo money?"

"Gone." No need to tell him she had a few dollars tucked into her shoes. "My steamship ticket to England is gone as well. Everything is gone!" Her voice rose as her anger increased. "I'm stuck!" Think, Franella, she told herself as she pounded her fists on her head, which aggravated the pain. She felt a large lump forming on her forehead. She made a face and then growled, "Is there a Salvation Army around here? Someplace I can stay until I figure out how to get another passport."

"Yo don'ts wants de army. Dey's in de worst part of town."

Franella picked up her suitcase. "Thank you, Mister Willie. You've been kind." She took two more steps and looked around; her eyes were full of tears.

Hard Workin' Willie pulled on both ears until they felt hot. "Lawd, I already regrets dis," he mumbled to himself. He took the suitcase from her and picked his way through the crowd as he said, "Follow me."

She stood, uncertain, then quickly followed. As she matched her step to his, he said, "Pardon, miss. Best if yo follows a step behind."

"Why?"

"It's de way we does it. If yo know where's yo goin', yo walks in de front."

"Since I am totally lost, I will stay right behind you." Franella saw his eyes dart in every direction, and he kept looking over his shoulder as he walked swiftly through the width of the cavernous room. He led her through an alcove and down several flights of stairs into the bowels of the station, rounding corners and descending into long, dingy passages, twisting and turning until they came to a large steel door. He glanced around before slowly opening it. "Don't say nothin'. Best yo closes yo ears, too."

The dingy, smoke-filled room in the bowels of the Chicago train station was filled with men of various ages, all of them black. Some were on cots, sleeping or reading. Others sat around a large round table, playing poker, smoking, and discussing the events of the day. One bent over a small hot plate, cooking a mess of greens.

Franella let herself smile, picturing the men of the Sitka Café at their big round table.

The men's eyes grew large, and their mouths fell open as they saw the young white woman with a large lump on her forehead follow Hard Workin' Willie into the room.

"This be our break room. She can't be here." One man removed the cigarette from his mouth, blew the smoke upwards, and looked at Franella, "Meanin' no disrespect."

Franella nodded and put her hand to the lump.

"Folks sees yo and her and dat lump, dey think yo does it, Willie."

"She gots knocked over. Not by me."

"Dat don't matter. Yo gots trouble now, Willie." another said.

Hard Workin' Willie scratched his ear, "She aint got no money and nobody in Chicago."

The head porter, Lou, chewed on his cigar. "I feels for de girl, but dere be trouble if she found here."

"Why?" Franella asked.

Unbelieving, they stared at her. Finally, Lou whispered, "Yo's white. We not."

"Like dogs and Indians." Franella nodded as understanding filled her eyes. Theirs were questioning. "Back home, we don't have any colored people, just Indians—Natives of Alaska. Some stores have signs that say, NO INDIANS OR DOGS ALLOWED. It's nasty."

The men around the table nodded, and some hung their heads. "Dis be trouble," Lou said.

"You mean I'm trouble," Franella said, thinking about the difficulties she had created for Johnny the Bear Boy. She picked up her suitcase. "It's okay. I'll go."

"We gots some figurin' to do." Hard Workin' Willie motioned for her to put the suitcase down. Franella sat on it and tried not to listen, which was not difficult since the pounding in her head had increased.

All betting on the poker game was suspended as the men debated the best course of action. All but Lou laid their cards face down on the table. He put his in his shirt pocket. "She can't sits in de station overnight. No accounts come out in de wee hours," he said.

"Thieves and thugs."

"True. But she can'ts be here."

Hard Workin' Willie pulled on his ears and said, "She mentioned de Salvation Army."

The men shook their heads. "De YMCA don't takes women."

"You sure you gots nobody?" Hard Workin' Willie asked.

"Why can't we puts her on de next train to somewhere?"

"I'd rather be alone in Chicago than in New York City. I'm not sure what to do or where to go, but I'll figure it out," she said with more confidence than she felt.

Lou looked at his watch. "We gots 'til shift change. Give her coffee and crackers. I'll thinks on it." After a few minutes, Lou shrugged his shoulders. "We makes dis our problem; it come back on us, guaranteed. What was yo thinking, Willie?"

"Wants to help is all."

"You always wantin' to help."

"Nothin' but trouble," A voice came from the cot in the corner. The young colored man stood, stretched, and said, "I wants no part of dis." He slipped on his red jacket and buttoned it up to his throat. He edged past Franella without looking at her, turned at the door, and said, "Yo smart, yo does the same."

196

"Keep yo head downs and stay out of trouble, I says," another said as he picked up his cards and threw them down in disgust. "I's had a winning hand."

Franella tried not to listen, but the words painted pictures in her mind. Pictures of these men facing unfortunate consequences. She shuddered and closed her eyes.

"Maybe we should prays on it. Dat's what my wife do."

The men grumbled, but chairs were pushed back. Those reading on the cots placed their books over their faces and pretended to sleep. The rest circled themselves and sank to their knees. Franella couldn't imagine the men in the Sitka Cafe ever doing such a thing. As these colored men closed their eyes and prayed, she picked up her suitcase and tiptoed out of the room.

The corridor was a rabbit warren of dark hallways. Many of the lights had broken bulbs. She passed doorways labeled supplies, maintenance, and furnace. Many doors were locked and had no signage.

A stocky but muscular redcap turned the corner and came toward her.

"Pardon me, can you..."

"Whats you doin' here?" he growled, "No tellin' what happen to white womans in de dark." His yellow teeth glowed in the dim light.

"I just want to find the lobby."

"De lobby be far away." He stepped closer and leered at her.

Franella waved her arms, jumped around, and screamed at him in Russian, Danish, and Tlingit. She thought of Hamlet. That's it! If she acted crazy, it might scare him, and it did. He ran down the corridor, muttering, "Crazy white woman. Nothin' but troubles."

Heart pounding and breathing heavily, Franella dragged her suitcase as fast as she could and eventually found a sign that pointed to the main lobby. This vast station was as alien to her as the wilds of Alaska would be to the redcaps and porters rushing to and fro. She found an unobtrusive corner and set her suitcase behind a massive pillar and scanned the alcove. This out-of-the-way area had few people and even fewer benches. There was a small one halfway across the room, and she hefted her suitcase onto it. Exhausted and with a massive headache, she finally fell into a fitful sleep with her arms around her luggage.

Franella tossed and turned on the uncomfortable wooden bench. Her suitcase was a miserable pillow, and her shoulder ached, disturbing her sleep. She dreamt Chicago's Union Station rose high in the air, traveled across the country, and settled itself in the Tongass Forest. Jimmy the Raven squawked and flew overhead, dropping trinkets from his beak. He cawed and shrieked as he swooped down to retrieve them. Johnny, the Bear Boy ran after him, offering the bird Agrafena's French crullers. Blanche and Ruby yelled and threw rocks at Johnny as Miss Ruth knelt on the big round table in the Sitka Café and led the redcaps in prayer. Mike poured coffee but refused to share his secret ingredient. The Sitka Café was closed to whites, and they stood outside the locked doors, complaining. Trains filled with King salmon and herring roe rumbled down Lincoln Street.

Franella felt a slight tug and then a firm tap. Anxiety and confusion followed her as she left the dream behind and slapped at the intruder. "Stop! Thief!"

"It be me, Miss," Hard Workin' Willie said, "You shore is hards to find. When I gots home, my Phanie Lu send me rights back to fetch you. Why yo runs away?"

"What?" She rubbed the sleep from her eyes and felt the bump on her forehead. It was slightly smaller, although it still hurt. She stared at the tall, thin black man.

"He said you doesn't mind."

Franella, still half asleep, asked, "Who said I wouldn't mind what?"

"The Good Lawd." Hard Workin' Willie mumbled something else and held his black arm next to her white one.

"Oh, good grief. Of course, I don't mind. But why would your wife want you to fetch me?"

"My Phanie Lu love everybody."

TWENTY-NINE

Hard Workin' Willie insisted on carrying Franella's suitcase once more and instructed her to walk two steps ahead of him as they headed for the L.

Walk behind him in the station; walk ahead of him now. Why couldn't she just walk beside him? "Is that the city transit?" Franella asked, seeing the elevated track and a short train speeding by.

Hard Workin' Willie nodded and spoke over his shoulder, "We takes the Green Line straights to Bronzeville, de colored part of Chicago."

"Like Indiantown in Sitka. That's where most of the Natives live. It's stupid to section people like that."

"Don't be talkin' like dat on de L, sides, most peoples likes to be with der own. We gots Greektown, Little Italy, Polish Downtown." He scratched his ear and grinned, "Lots of Poles, some Mexicans, and a few Irish. But coloreds mostly. Like goes to like, I says."

"If it was up to me, we'd be all mixed up. We could learn a lot from each other if we just got along."

"Yes, Miss, but don't talks like dat on de train."

It was just a five-minute walk from the stop at East 35th Street. They passed large, dilapidated apartment buildings that were overcrowded and unsafe. Hard Workin' Willie turned his head away when Franella questioned him. He talked about dirty, low-down, money-grubbing landlords and greedy, corrupt politicians who caused these apartment dwellers so much misery.

His own neighborhood, established before the influx of colored people who had migrated from the South in search of employment, consisted of modest, unpainted houses on roads filled with potholes and no streetlights. It was considered the ritzy part of Bronzeville. Franella tried to ignore the stares of the children playing stickball on the road. They fell in line behind her and Hard Workin' Willie.

The little parade continued to the end of the street. Willie turned and yelled, "Scat, lest I tells your mamas you gots bad manners."

All but one boy ran for home. He was older than the others and not as apt to take orders from the redcap. "You bringin' a white woman home, Mr. Willie? What Miss Phanie gonna thinks?"

Franella, annoyed at the boy's smirk, bent to look him in the eye, "I'm just passing..." His eyes rounded, he gave her a knowing look, winked at Willie, and ran toward home, "...through." Franella finished her sentence and asked, "What's so funny?"

Hard Workin' Willie was doubled over, holding his stomach. His enormous belly laughs were a little unnerving. "Soon, all Bronzeville gonna think yo a colored who passes white." He scratched his ear. "Probably better dat way. Don't tells dem different, 'specially Lucilla."

"Isn't that the same as lying? I'm not a liar."

Phanie Lu witnessed the conversation from the front step, "Yo has de truth waiting. Dey ask, you tells, but they don't ask. I saved yo dinner, Mr. Willie. Plenty for this po' thing."

Franella bit her lip and looked at the tiny house, "If you're sure you have room for me."

"We gots room fo' whoever de Lawd send."

When they entered the house, Franella saw that it was no larger than the girls' room at the Salvation Army Orphanage in Sitka. Next to the back door, a stove, a sink, and floor-to-ceiling cupboards made out of packing crates filled the entire wall. A large wooden table with four unmatched chairs anchored the center of the room, and a gingham curtain partitioned the opposite end. An old sofa with sagging cushions was set in front of the curtain. The only other furniture in the room was a sideboard next to the front door. "Are you sure I won't be any trouble?"

"Oh, yo be trouble, alright," Phanie Lu laughed, "But I likes a bit a trouble now and den. I leans on de Good Lawd just a little bit more. Mr. Willie done told me de whole story fore I sent him to fetch yo. Now eat. Yo needs feeding up, girl."

Franella sat at the place Phanie Lu indicated and looked in wonder at the plate set before her. The unrecognizable greens reminded her of foraging with Johnny, the Bear Boy. She picked up the fork and thought about how she had eaten food from Sitka's woods and waters. Surely, she could eat food from Chicago.

"The only thing I recognize on this plate is the bit of bacon. It all smells good, though," Franella said, taking a bite.

"Collard greens and okra rolled in cornmeal and fried in bacon grease."

"Dat okra gonna smack in yo mouth like popcorn," Hard Workin' Willie said.

After trying it, Franella agreed and added, "These collard greens tastes better than seaweed."

"Yo eats seaweed?" Phanie Lu asked.

"It's mostly the Natives that eat it," Franella mumbled with her mouth full.

Phanie Lu boiled water on the stove and poured it into the sink. After helping with the dishes, Franella stifled a yawn. Phanie Lu handed her a kerosene lamp and said, "Time to sleep, and tomorrow, we lets the Good Lawd tell us whats to do. Mr. Willie and me sleeps behind dat curtain. De room upstairs is de attic. De space behind the quilt I hungs, belong to our granddaughter, Rosetta Samara. She work for white folk during de week but come home Saturday night and go back Sunday. De rest of de room belong to my grandboys. You can takes any de boys' bed."

At Franella's alarmed look, Phanie Lu smiled and said, "Dey in France, helping de army clean up de mess." She sighed as she pointed to the photograph on the sideboard, two young men in uniform. "Dey said French folk be goods to them, even give one boy a medal."

Franella picked up the photo, "Handsome."

Phanie Lu laughed, "All my babies handsome."

Franella glanced over the sideboard crowded with framed photographs. "Are all these pictures of your children?"

Phanie Lu nodded.

Franella shuddered, "But there must be over fifteen photographs. They can't all be yours!"

Phanie Lu wiped her hands on her apron. "I gots two boys from Mr. Willie. Rosetta Samara come when her mama disappear."

"What?"

"When our mama and papa die I tries to raise my sister good but she wild. She gots in de family way when she fourteen. She leave de baby wit' me. I never seen her since." Phanie Lou dusted the photos with her dish towel. "I fears poor Rosetta Samara be like her mama."

Franella didn't know what to say, so she said nothing. Phanie Lu continued, "After dat, when a baby be orphaned or abandoned, I takes 'em." She led Franella to the narrow staircase at the end of the room. "Sleeps as long as you likes. Mr. Willie be gone 'fore yo wakes. I gets up early to pray. Yo come down when yo smells de coffee. First thing we gots to do is kink up yo hair."

"What?"

"If yo be a colored woman, passin white we gots to kink up yo hair, then smooths it so folk thinks yo tryin to get rid of de kinks. Yo skin is light, so yo is high-yellow, a real mulatto."

"What?"

"Never minds." Phanie Lu clucked her tongue and sighed, 'Dem blue eyes looks too white."

"I am white," Franella laughed.

"In Bronzeville yo's colored, passing white. Anybody wants to know, yo great-great grandmama's massah got blue eyes."

"I'm not a liar, and it feels like I'd be living a lie."

"Some coloreds just as hateful as whites, safer to pretend, at least while yo here."

In the attic, Franella chose the narrow bed closest to the window. The sounds of the L rumbling past just a few blocks away shook the house. Other city noises kept her awake longer than she wanted. She shivered and pulled the faded patchwork quilt up to her chin. Sometime in the night, she pulled the quilt off the other bed. Moonlight streamed through the uncurtained window, the same moon that shone down on Miss Ruth. *What do you think,*

Miss Ruth? Here I am, halfway across the country in the poorest part of Chicago, being taken care of by kind colored people, strangers, but I feel a comfortable kinship with them. Strange. I'm pretending to be someone I'm not! Somehow, I think you would laugh and insist that Bozhe put Mr. Willie and Phanie Lu here just for me.

She smiled, rolled over, and promptly fell asleep.

Her first thought in the morning was of her missing passport and steamship ticket. Her recently obtained National Registration Card had also been in her pocketbook. How was she going to replace that? Most of her money was gone as well. The only documents in her suitcase were a letter of acceptance to Somerville College and a line of credit to the Royal Bank of England. She also had a few letters of introduction—nothing that would do her any good in Chicago.

Franella took several deep breaths and stilled her racing mind. She was nothing but a small-town girl from America's Last Frontier, and that's where she should have stayed. Tears threatened again, and her stomach burned. The hours of peaceful sleep faded, and she felt her anxiety rise. Franella forced herself to slow her breathing and relax. Instead, she moaned, "Oh, Miss Ruth, tell me what to do."

When the smell of coffee reached the attic, Franella dressed quickly and tiptoed down the stairs. When she realized Phanie Lou was not alone, she crouched next to the sideboard and watched a stream of women parade through the kitchen. Phanie Lu encouraged some, advised others, admonished a few, and prayed with all. Franella marveled at the women's wise kitchen table counseling.

One woman lagged behind. She was dressed in a wildly ruffled floral dress. "What about de woman passing white what Mr. Willie brung?"

Phanie Lu rolled her eyes and stood, "We hads a good visit, Lucilla. Here's de elixir to purge yo innards. Come back next week." Phanie Lu handed the woman a Mason jar filled with a nasty-looking liquid and escorted her to the door.

"Now, Phanie, I's yo best friend. yo can tells who she be."

"She be sent to me."

"Who gonna send you a high yellow like dat? There be trouble comin' to dis house." She shuffled to the door, shaking her head.

"De Lawd send her." Phanie Lu practically forced Lucilla out the door. Once the curious Lucilla was gone, Phanie Lu poured herself a cup of coffee.

"Yo can come to de table now," she said to Franella, "I loves Lucilla dearly, but she de biggest gossip in Bronzeville. Have some coffee while I warms up de grits."

"Grits?"

"Like mush. Yo eats now. We gots work to do."

"I'll help however I can, but please don't ask me to cook. I'm terrible."

Phanie Lu's laugh started deep in her belly. She was as short and round as her husband was tall and narrow. "I means we gots to get yo life sorted." She refilled their coffee cups, pulled the Bible toward her, and said, "Best we starts."

With many cups of coffee and a sweet tone, Phanie Lu was able to draw Franella's history out into the open.

"I'm at home in the forest or on the water. I even became comfortable in the ivory tower of academia at the University of Washington. But here, surrounded by thousands of people, buildings as tall as trees, buses, trains, the noisy, smelly L, along with streetcars and automobiles. Everyone coming and going, hurrying this way and that." Franella took a deep breath, let it out slowly, and raised her eyes to Phanie Lu. "I'm lost, Miss Phanie."

"Come to de stoop," They stood together in the doorway, and Phanie Lu said, "We call de tiny stoops a porch. No one gots a real porch; no one gots a car. De houses be tiny and dem tall buildings be in de city center, way over der. And de thousands of peoples? Why, chile, you and I be de only ones here. Just looks at what be here, not over der."

A small child ran up to them, saying, "Miss Phanie, Mama say Marvella's baby comin'. Can I have a cookie? It comin' now."

Phanie Lu nodded, reached into the highest packing crate for a bag of doctoring supplies, and told Franella, "I don't knows when I be back." She turned to the child. "Lulu stays with Miss Franella 'case she need somethin'. Yo hear me, girl?"

The little girl nodded.

"And Lulu, one cookie."

As soon as Phanie Lu raced out the door, Lulu had a cookie in each hand. Franella sighed and finished her coffee. "Who is Marvella?"

"My sister what gots married last year when her fella gots back from de war. I'm eight. How old is you? You don't looks colored."

Franella nearly choked on her coffee.

"Yo like passin' white? Wants to walk? Yo ever see a baby borned?"

"Once a mama seal had her baby on our boat."

Lulu stared at her, "I don't believes yo. Der no seals round here."

Franella opened her mouth to say she was not a liar and realized it would be a false claim. She rubbed the nape of her neck and said, "Lulu, I'm from very far away. Would you like me to tell you about it?"

The little girl nodded and said, "De whites don't 'llow us at der hospitals. We don't gots money for de colored one on East 51st Street."

Franella took the girl by the hand and said, "I'll tell you all about baby seals as we walk." But she wondered if the child would stop talking long enough to hear the story. No matter. Her incessant chatter was a good distraction. Lulu talked all day, asking Franella a myriad of questions, but didn't pause long enough to hear the answers. She never learned a thing about baby seals or Alaska. Franella, however, knew more than she wanted about life in the poor black section of Chicago.

At the end of the day, Marvella had a baby boy, Franella had a headache, and little Lulu had eaten all of the cookies.

THIRTY

The following morning, after she finished the breakfast dishes, Phanie Lu layered a brown wool coat over her only Sunday-go-to-meeting dress. She perched a large green felt hat with a black brocade brim and pheasant feathers atop the kinky hair she tied at the nape of her neck. Franella thought it a bit much but didn't say anything. *Miss Ruth would commend me for not blurting out that Phanie Lu looked like a colored Friar Tuck wearing Robin Hood's hat.*

Franella scrambled to the attic bedroom and pulled her best dress out of her suitcase. It was a bit crumpled. She shook it and hoped it would be fine. Much to her dismay, Phanie Lu said, "Dat dress has mo' wrinkles den my face. Best iron it. De dress, not my face," she chuckled as she shed her coat and pulled the ironing board from behind the couch. "Only takes a minute for de irons to heat up," she said as she placed two of them on the stovetop. She lifted the burner of the cast iron stove and added more coal to speed the process, then handed Franella a worn bathrobe. "Be quick, now."

After changing, Franella attacked the wrinkles as if going to war. Phanie Lu watched her for a moment, then took the iron from her. "My great-grandmama irons her whole life fo' de massah. She be turnin' in her grave to see yo smacking her irons like dat. You gots to glides across da wrinkles."

"My mama could do it faster and better herself. She never had the patience to teach me."

Hands on her hips, Phanie Lu arched a single eyebrow. Franella bit her lip and said, "To be fair, I didn't want to learn."

"Uh huh, dat sound right." Phanie Lu pulled the dress from the ironing board and handed it to Franella, who dressed quickly. Phanie Lu plopped a red pillbox hat on Franella's head as the girl buttoned her coat. She stepped back and said, "Even with dat veil across half yo face, dem eye's too blue. Here Mr. Willie's reading glasses to hide 'em." Once Franella passed Phanie Lu's inspection, the only wrinkles in sight were the ones on the colored woman's face.

They took the L into downtown Chicago. The elevated train was noisy and crowded, but Franella snagged a window seat and motioned for the other woman to sit. Phanie Lu shook her head and shuffled through the crowd to the back of the rail car. There were no seats left, so she grabbed the hand strap hanging from the ceiling. Franella followed her and said, "Why didn't you sit?"

"Dem's white seats."

"That's stupid!"

"Keeps yo voice down. We don't wants trouble."

Franella looked around; the whites in the front of the car and the coloreds in the back were eyeing her; most with disgust on their faces. She lowered her gaze and stared at her shoes. Sometimes, she wished she could wear horse blinders and ear muffs to filter out all of the world's sights and sounds. She slowed her breathing and counted to twenty in English, Russian, Danish, Norwegian, and Tlingit. It took several minutes of counting before she felt her body relax. She missed most of Phanie Lu's description of the city.

"Mr. Willie's cousin de elevator operator fo' de gov'ment. He tell us where to go," Phanie Lu said as they exited the L and walked several blocks to the large office building on the corner. She reached into her large pocketbook and pulled out a rat-tail comb. "Yo hair look good. Straight, but wid some kink," she said as she fluffed the hair around Franella's face.

Franella snorted and felt like a fraud. Her distorted vision was already giving her a headache. Nevertheless, she followed Phanie Lu into the building. The large lobby was busy with men in 3-piece suits, looking intent and carrying bulging briefcases. They bustled to and fro, avoiding eye contact with everyone. The reception desk, located near the entrance, spanned the width of the lobby. Three middle-aged women, also dressed in suits, answered the phones and directed people to the appropriate government office.

"May I help you?" the one in the center asked.

Franella was reading the directory behind the woman and didn't answer, so Phanie Lu said, "We wants the passport office."

The woman bristled and addressed Franella, "Please tell your maid I wasn't talking to her. She needs to keep her place. Passports are on the eleventh floor. The elevator is around the corner, miss. Your colored can take the stairs."

Franella felt the heat crawl up her face. She took a deep breath and leaned over the counter. She squinted through Mr. Willie's glasses. Her words came out with military precision, "She is not my colored or my maid. She is a nice woman with much better manners than you!"

The receptionist took a long look at Franella, especially the kinky hair curling around the edge of Franella's hat. "I see now. You can both take the stairs." She frowned and rolled her eyes at the other receptionists and whispered a remark about no accounts who didn't know their place. The other receptionists nodded.

Phanie Lu took Franella by the arm and pulled her around the corner to the bank of elevators. "You needs to mind yo place."

"What are you talking about? What place?"

"When we's out in public, people needs to thinks yo de lady and me de servant. I miscalculated. I should makes you colored after we gets de passport."

"People are stupid, and I don't mind telling them so."

Phanie Lu shook her head and sighed, "We wants de people in Bronzeville to think yo colored, nots de people in Chicago. Oh, Lawd, I should a waited to kink yo hair. Don't tell nobody nuthin' no more today."

Franella felt her hair, then took off the glasses and rubbed her eyes. She knew she was going to mess this up. The elevator bell dinged, and the doors slid open. People exited, but Phanie Lu didn't move, although she did nod her head to the elevator operator, who slightly inclined his. After a couple of businessmen entered the elevator, Franella took a step forward, but the colored woman held her back.

"What?" Franella said.

"We waits."

Franella raised her eyebrows at Phanie Lu, who sighed and said, "You don't sees like a colored person. Dem two white man look at us like something dey scrape off der shoe. Sides, we 'posed to take the stairs."

Franella shook her head and growled, "The nerve! I'd like to tell them a thing or two! And we are not climbing to the eleventh floor!"

Phanie Lu laughed, "Yo right, but yo knows nuthin' bout bein' colored."

212

The next time the bell dinged, the doors did not open. The adjacent elevator bell sounded, and the people waiting disappeared into it. After a moment, the first elevator's doors slid apart, and the operator poked his head out, looked both ways, and hissed, "Hurry yo up."

"We's goin' to da eleventh floor." Phanie Lu said. She discussed Franella's dilemma and then chatted with the elderly operator about his family.

Franella held her breath and kept her eyes forward. Her heart pounded, and she tried to remain calm. This was her first elevator ride, and she didn't like it. She didn't want to seem like a backward girl from the wilderness of Alaska. *After all, I am a college graduate. I'm smart. I know things.* But she didn't know her way around Chicago or this large government building. Franella jammed her white-knuckled fists into her coat pocket. *I don't know how to navigate these unwritten segregation rules.* She thought about her years at the university and couldn't remember any colored students in her classes. There were several Asians and one Indian, but they kept to themselves. Back in Sitka, there was a de facto segregation, but it wasn't solid or rigid. It seemed like the people who wanted to look down on others did. Why couldn't people just be people?

Three hours later, a deflated Phanie Lu and an angry Franella stood across from the bank of elevators. People passed them as if they were invisible.

Several minutes later, the elevator bell dinged, and the doors slid open. The only occupant was Mr. Willie's cousin. "You gots dat passport?" he asked.

Franella stepped into the elevator, breathing hard, her cheeks puffed out, and she snapped, "That miserable small-minded, ignorant, condescending clerk called me an uppity ni..." she slammed her fist into the elevator wall, "I can't even say the word. I'd like to march right up to his face and give him what-for."

Charlie and Phanie Lu exchanged a look. "What you say Miss Phanie?"

"Charlie, I's fixin to spit."

He pointed to his engraved metal name tag, pinned to his lapel—Charles Emerson, III.

"Don't gets high-falutin' on me, 'cause you takes white folks up and down." Phanie Lu said, "Franella gots no papers sayin' who she be. So they don't give her a passport."

Charlie pushed the button for the ground floor. He stroked his chin and said, "You needs a vip."

"What dat?" the colored woman asked.

"De white folks make de rules, and if dey be important enough folk, dey can breaks 'em. Only vips or dere friends can do dat. You needs a vip." At the consternation on both the women's faces Charles Emerson III rubbed his thumb across his nametag and said, "In dis elevator I be de vip—very important person. Dat's what you needs, alright."

"I don't know any important people in Chicago or anywhere else," Franella cried.

"Sorry, Miss," Charlie wished them good luck as they stepped out of the elevator and left the building.

"Now what?" Franella asked as they walked toward the L.

"We prays more, and we waits."

Phanie Lu's calm voice and demeanor did nothing to encourage Franella.

On Saturday, Franella helped Phanie Lu clean the house and visited with her in the kitchen while the older woman cooked and baked. "Rosetta Samara, be here soon. I misses dat chile somethin' fierce."

Franella wondered what Rosetta Samara would think about finding a stranger in her home. She gnawed on her thumb and refused to voice it. "Do you want me to take some of that soup to Marvella?"

Phanie Lu filled a Mason jar and slipped a dozen biscuits into a battered wicker basket. "Don't dawdle. My Rosie be here 'fore long."

Franella nodded but intended to stretch this errand into at least a semi-dawdle. She was followed through the neighborhood by several children. Lulu led the procession.

"You be Miss Phanie's family, Miss Franella?"

"Course she be. Why else she come?" A small black boy named Rodney picked up a rock and put it in his pocket.

"Dem eyes blue as da sky. My mama says no colored gots dem eyes."

"You shut up, Darla. Miss Phanie say der be a blue-eye massah way back."

"Well, I feels bad fo' her." Darla kicked a tin can into the road. "Nothin' but trouble when you gots dem eyes."

"I likes her. She pretty," Rodney fingered the rock and wondered what or who he could use as a target.

"She talk white, too." Darla said. "My mama say dat uppity. She believe Miss Franella colored on Miss Phanie's say so."

"Dat right," Lulu said, "Everybody know Miss Phanie tell de truth."

Franella bit the inside of her cheek and stared straight ahead. If these young children only knew! She held the basket to her churning stomach and felt like the liar she was.

The basket was gratefully received, and Franella was escorted on the return trip by the same little entourage. This time, the conversation centered around the topic of murder.

"It murder, e'body know dat," Darla said.

"Murder is peoples, not bugs," Rodney said as he lined up another fuzzy caterpillar near his bare foot. He stepped on one end of the bug and laughed when green goo squirted out the other end.

"Murder! Murder!" Darla yelled and shoved Rodney. "I gonna tells yo mama yo kills things. Yo gonna git whupped."

He took the rock from his pocket, threw it at her, and ran off.

"Missed me!" Darla stomped her foot, shook her fist, and yelled, "Miserable little pickaninny."

Lulu rolled her eyes and grabbed Franella's hand. "My mama say most kids in Bronzeville be little hell'ons. Dey needs cibilazising, cibilizationing."

"Civilizing," Franella said.

"Dat be it. Look, Rosetta Samara 'bouts to go in de house." Lulu called to the fashionably dressed young woman in high heels and a green boiled-wool coat with a thick fur collar. Rosetta turned and greeted the little girl.

"Miss Phanie make you wipe that paint off yo face," Darla smirked.

Rosetta Samara sniffed. "You watch yo mouth and minds yo business. I's a workin' woman now." She gave Franella a long look.

"This be Miss Franella. She livin' in yo house," Lulu said.

Rosetta's eyebrows arched to the brim of her hat. "Yo better stop tellin' tales, chile."

216

"She passin' white. See dem blue eyes." Darla added.

"What Lulu says is true. I'm staying with your grandparents for a while. They've been kind to me and I'm so grateful." Franella held out her hand, but Rosetta Samara turned and stomped into the house.

"Big Mama!" she yelled, "Why you gots some uppity high yellow, passin' white, in yo house?"

Franella hung her head and walked away from the house with Lulu and Darla following. She sniffed a couple of times, patted her pockets, looked for a handkerchief, and then wiped her nose with her sleeve.

Lulu reached for her hand, "Rosetta, be jealous, is all. She de uppity one."

"Watch yo mouth," Darla put her hand on her hip and imitated Rosetta's smirk and tone.

"Marvella say Rosetta goes to de Blue Note Nightclub and de Sunset Café, 'stead a church," Lulu said.

"How Marvella know?" Darla asked.

"Marvella hear Rosie tellin' some boys she like de music and de spirit in de club. Make her want to laugh and dance. I say Rosetta be nasty," Darla said.

"She go to de devil for certain sure," Lulu shook her head, "Church be lively 'nuff for me."

"I think I be nasty and wears high heels and make-up likes her."

"Yo mama skin you alive!"

Darla's eyes flashed and she shook her fist at Lulu. "I does what I wants jus' like Rosetta Samara."

Lulu turned away and said, "I s'pose Rosetta be done yellin' at Miss Phanie 'bout now. You best pray, Darla, dat de Lord keep yo from de nasties."

Supper around Phanie Lu's kitchen table was eaten in silence. Finally, Hard Workin' Willie pushed his plate away and reached for Phanie Lu's Bible. He had quit school to work after third grade, and his reading showed it. He stumbled through the larger words and read without expression. Phanie Lu encouraged him with her eyes. Franella struggled to pay attention, and Rosetta Samara threw her napkin on the table.

"Dat new jazz musician, Louie Armstrong, be up from N'Orleans, and I's goin' to hear him."

"Please, Rosie. Dem jazz clubs be filled with de devil's music."

"It gots more spirit than any church I's ever been in."

"De devil spirit," Hard Workin Willie's eyes were sad, but his voice was gentle, "Stays with dem dat love you, girl."

Rosie grabbed her coat and purse and called from the doorway. "I mights be out all night!"

Phanie Lu used her napkin as a handkerchief as she looked in horror at Hard Workin' Willie. He reached across the table for her hand.

"I'm sorry," Franella said, "I shouldn't have come."

Phanie Lu shook her head. "De Lawd sent yo. My sweet Rosetta Samara be makin' bad choices, been doin' it awhile now."

"De Lawd won'ts let her go," Willie squeezed his wife's hand.

"I knows," Phanie Lu blew her nose again, "I just aches for de hurt gonna come her way 'til she git right wit' Him. We jus' gots to pray."

Franella sat at the table while Rosetta's grandparents sank to their knees and began to pray. After a few minutes, she found herself on her knees next to them, echoing their prayers. When they asked the Lord to give their beloved granddaughter wisdom and direction, Franella added an "amen" and hoped the prayer would also apply to her.

"We's gonna be late fo' church," Hard Workin' Willie adjusted his bowtie, "I gots to git to work after."

Phanie Lu wiped her hands on her apron and said, "Rosetta Samara not home. I waits."

"Would you like me to wait with you?" Franella asked.

"You goes to church with Willie. I wants you to feel de Spirit." Phanie Lu hugged Franella, "Says a prayer for my poor granchile. She be runnin' from somethin' bad."

"She runnin' to somethin' bad," Willie frowned and adjusted his bowtie again. He pulled it off and stood in front of Phanie Lu.

She tied it into a perfect bow and kissed him on the cheek. "We's got to show her de Lawd's love. She cain't feels it."

Hard Workin' Willie and Franella left the small house and began walking to the church. Most of the neighbors were going in the same direction. They were dressed in their Sunday best. If truth be told, their wardrobes reminded Franella of what she found in the donation box at Sitka's orphanage. However, these clothes had been scrubbed, ironed, and patched by the enterprising and resourceful women of Bronzeville. Bits of rick-rack and ribbon adorned the women's dresses, hiding the worn places. Men's suit jackets, although frayed and out of style, had elbow patches in contrasting fabric. Some of their shirts resembled the patchwork quilts that adorned their beds. Nevertheless, they all walked together, forming a casual neighborly parade at the edge of the dusty, unpaved road. Some sang and others chatted.

Heads turned, and voices faded as Rosetta Samara slowly stumbled down the middle of the road. She held the heel of one of her shoes as she limped along. Since there were no vehicles on the road, there was no danger of her being hit by oncoming traffic.

Her make-up was smeared, her eyes unfocused, and Franella watched the unsteady girl concentrate on putting one foot in front of the other. Rosetta seemed unaware of the looks from the families she passed. The women shook their heads and hissed at their children to mind their manners and not stare. The men averted their eyes.

"Looks at you, Rosetta Samara. What yo Big Mama gonna think? Yo is a wild, wicked chile!" Lucilla stepped onto the road and blocked Rosetta's way.

Rosetta tried to step around her, but Lucilla wasn't having it. "Yo is a disgrace to yo family and everybody at de African Union Methodist Protestant Church know it. Wicked, wicked girl!" Lucilla's shrill voice cut through the crowd, and they stopped to watch.

Hard Workin' Willie approached, took Rosetta by the hand and walked her around Lucilla. "I walks you home, Rosie."

"I don't needs nobody." She poked him in the chest with the high heel.

"Franella, yo takes her other arm. We walks her home, then we goes to the church."

Franella risked a glance at Hard Workin' Willie and then wished she hadn't. The man's face had crumpled, and his eyes were wet. Rosetta knocked his hand away, seemingly unaware of the heartbreak on her grandfather's face.

Franella swallowed and wished she had a grandfather—someone like this man—someone whose gentle compassion oozed from his pores, someone whose love streamed from his eyes in the form of salty tears. She took a step nearer and silently slipped her hand into his.

Franella marveled at the emotions rising within her. These feelings must be friendship—the aching she felt for his pain and the comfort he seemed to find in her hand.

"The house be close by. I guess she makes it alright," Hard Workin' Willie sighed.

They stood hand in hand and watched Rosetta stumble toward the house, then continued to the church. Before they entered the building, Franella asked, "Will Phanie Lu be okay?"

Hard Workin' Willie squeezed her hand and smiled, although the pain did not leave his face. "I gonna tells the congregation to pray, but I 'spect Miss Phanie's heart get broke again by dat girl."

THIRTY-ONE

Hard Workin' Willie's prophecy proved true. Phanie Lu's heart did break when she looked out the window and saw Rosetta Samara teeter at the edge of the small dirt yard. Phanie sucked in her breath and pictured herself rushing out to envelop the girl in a fierce hug, but knew it would not be welcomed. Instead, she set the old tin coffee pot on the stove and added fresh grounds.

"Big Mama? I's here." Rosie stumbled to the kitchen table. She hung her head and wouldn't meet her grandmother's eyes. "I don't wants a talkin' to."

"Grits be ready," Phanie Lu said, pouring a cup of coffee for the girl.

"I means it Big Mama, I don't needs no talkin' to."

"I loves yo. That's all I's gonna say. You eats and gives me your clothes. I washes 'em while you have a nice nap. They be clean and pressed afo' yo goes back to work."

"I's fine. My clothes be fine."

"De white folk don't want yo in der house smellin' of cigarettes and cheap liquor."

"I told you I's fine." Rosetta smelled her sleeve and the hem of her dress, and nearly gagged, "All right, wash 'em but don't say I burns in hell."

"I loves yo and de Lawd do, too. Now, give me yo clothes, and takes yo nap."

"Don't talk to me like I's five-year-old." Rosetta snapped but obeyed her grandmother.

Hard Workin' Wille and Franella Feddersen sat in the last row of the balcony. She kept her focus on him, he kept his on the choir when they sang and the pastor when he preached. She didn't clap her hands and sway to the music like the choir. She didn't shout *amen—preach it, brother—yes, Lawd,* or *dat's right*—like the deacons and elders in the first row did. She didn't pass notes like the snickering teenagers in the back. She didn't shush the babies and give them the evil eye like Lucilla. She didn't carry on a whispered conversation during the entire service like the young couple in the third row. She didn't slip small pieces of candy to the children like the old usher leading them to their seats did.

Instead, Franella sat quietly next to Hard Workin' Willie on the hard wooden pew. She stood when he did. Knelt when he did. Sat when he sat. Opened the hymnal when he did. Put a dollar in the collection plate when he did. Bowed her head and folded her hands when he did, although she did not close her eyes.

Franella's attention was pulled to and fro by all the motion and emotion in the small building. Her heart pounded, her eyes teared and she felt a pull toward—something.

As they left the church after the invigorating church service, Franella stood to the side and watched as the parishioners crowded around HardWorkin' Willie. Many patted him on the back, shook his hand, or said they would pray.

Lucilla bustled through the crowd and declared, "I's coming

tomorrow to console poor Phanie Lu fo' raising' such a sinful granddaughter."

Franella gasped and bit her tongue. She wanted to tell Lucilla to mind her business. The pastor rolled his eyes and motioned to his wife. She took Lucilla by the arm and led her away.

"I's just sayin' dat girl wild like her mama. She bring shame to poor miserable Phanie Lu." Lucilla's shrill voice carried throughout the congregation. A few nodded in agreement, most turned away from the ugly comment.

Franella bristled, but Willie shook his head and whispered as they left. "She be a wicked gossip. Phanie Lu gonna give her what fo' 'iffen she hear Miss Lucilla talkin' 'bout Rosetta like dat."

Franella held his hand again. The feel of his warm fingers clasping hers was reassuring. He looked down at her with a slight smile and deliberately changed the subject, "Say, why you not be speakin' to de folk?"

Franella grinned and said in what she thought was the Bronzeville way, "Mr. Willies, yo knows I talks white. Caint let de folk think I's uppity."

Hard Workin' Willie laughed, and they walked the rest of the way in an agreeable silence, although both were uneasy with their thoughts.

As they approached the tiny house, Hard Workin' Willie said, "I don't knows what we find when we's open de door."

"It's not really my business. Would you rather I wait out here?"

"No chile, the walls be thin. If there be yellin' yo hears it anyways."

Rosetta sat at the kitchen table filing her long red nails while Phanie Lu ironed her dress. "Don't put no scorch marks on my dress 'cause yo mads."

Phanie Lu set the iron on the stove to reheat and sat across from her granddaughter. "I never do dat. I loves you."

"Did Big Mama talk to yo?" Willie asked as he hung his coat on the peg next to the door.

Phanie Lu's head jerked around, eyes wide, and she shook her head. Rosetta jumped up, nearly knocking over her coffee. "It my life! I don't needs nobody talkin' 'bout it." She pulled the half-ironed dress from the board and stomped out of the room. Franella hugged the wall as Rosetta pushed past her.

The three people in the tiny kitchen stood with their mouths open, unable to speak. Before they knew it, the angry young woman was back wearing the half-ironed dress. She pushed her feet into her high heels and swore under her breath as she shoved the broken heel into her pocket. She grabbed her purse and coat, all the while angry words burst from her. "I makes my choices. I lives my own life."

"Of course yo does, Rosie, honey," Phanie Lu tried to hug the girl.

"Can we prays, fo' yo go?" Hard Workin' Willie asked.

"I don' need no prayers." Rosetta shrugged into her coat, "And look like yo don't needs me since you gots...this...uppity ni...she even talk like dat Professor yo work fo' back yonder." She gave Phanie Lu a hard look, "I don't cares to come home no mo' since she be here." Rosetta Samara, breathing hard, her chest rising and falling in rhythm with her angry words, turned to Franella and snarled, "Yo took Big Mama away from me. I hates yo fo' sure."

She slammed the door behind her.

THIRTY-TWO

"I don't likes leavin' yo alone, Phanie Lu, but I gots to git to work." Hard Workin' Willie hugged his wife.

"Franella be here."

"We's got to be trustin' dat's all." He grabbed his napkin from the table and blew his nose.

Phanie Lu would not meet his eyes, "I fails that girl, just like I fails her mama. Why dey be so wild?"

"Yo knows everybody gotta choose de Lawd fo' der own self. Yo's not failed."

"Thank yo Mr. Willie." She wiped her eyes with the edge of her apron. "Yo goes to work now and when yo thinks of our girl, yo prays." Phanie Lu handed him a paper sack filled with yesterday's leftovers. "Yo eats, even if you don't be hungry. It be easier to prays with a full belly." Phanie Lu reached for her coat. "I walks yo to the L. We prays as we go."

Franella sat on the front step and watched the elderly couple walk down the street. The love they extended to each other, as well as everyone in the community enveloped her, but she wondered how could they continue to love Rosetta Samara when she acted so ugly and wicked? How could they be kind to Lucilla with her rampaging gossiping tongue? Where did such a love come from? She knew Miss Ruth would say it was Bozhe's love. Mr. Willie would say it was de Good Lawd's love. Franella gnawed on her thumb. The

226

thing is, they didn't keep that love to themselves, they gave it away. How did that work exactly, the receiving and the giving?

In their poverty, they had opened their home to her and were trusting God to provide them with the solution to her problems. Franella shook her head in amazement as an unfamiliar longing spread through her.

When Phanie Lu returned she said, "We don't talk 'bout my Rosie no more. She in de Lawd's hands now. I feels better now dat Mr. Willie prays all de way to de L and I prays all de way back." She bustled about the kitchen after hanging up her coat. "Rosie give me an idea. We's gonna see de professor tomorrow."

"I don't have much of an appetite after all the commotion," Franella said as Phanie Lu put more coal into the stove.

"I dasn't neither, but we gots to eat or at least we drinks some coffee and has some bread. I gots to think about the professor. He de only vip I knows."

THIRTY-THREE

As they approached Professor Albright's house. Phanie Lu said, "Don't be fooled by his look. He be a mousey little man. But he smarts. Dem gray eyes can sees what yo thinkin' I 'spose. He know just about everthin' I guesses."

Franella barely glanced at the man sitting behind the massive desk. She feasted her eyes on his floor-to-ceiling bookcase, which she thought might be made of teak because of its rich golden-brown color and its leather-like smell. If she closed her eyes and took a deep breath, she could imagine she was on Ade Bunderson's fancy new fishing vessel.

She longed to pull out and inspect each book, to read the table of contents, and riffle the pages. Breathing in the smell of the aged leather-bound volumes felt like a homecoming. Books were stacked on either side of the professor's desk and on the wide window sill. Franella measured the study with her eyes; it was large enough to house Sitka's tiny library. She noticed Phanie Lu was talking, so tried to pay attention.

"Professor, we's come on important business. We hopes you be a vip for us," Phanie Lu said.

Professor Albright leaned across his desk and frowned, "Have you forgotten how to speak, Miss Phanie?"

Phanie Lu sat up straight and stilled her nervous laughter. "It's been so long since I've seen you, Professor.

Franella's mouth fell open, "Why, Miss Phanie, yo's talkin' like white folk."

"When I'm around my people, I speak as they speak. The professor taught me proper English so I can go anywhere and fit in—except for my blackness," she laughed.

It's not funny!" Franella snapped, "You should be able to go anywhere and do anything."

"When the kingdom comes, dear one," Phanie Lu smiled and folded her hands in her lap.

"It's not a problem we'll be able to fix anytime soon, I'm afraid." The professor turned to Franella and said, "And you, my dear, although your dialect is good, did not grow up in Bronzeville or any place like it. Am I right?'

Franella blushed, "I usually have a good ear for languages. In fact, I speak several and without much of an accent. There's just something about the Bronzeville parlance I can't quite duplicate."

"I thought you sounded just like us," Phanie Lu said.

"It's subtle," The professor said, "But I'm sure that's not why you came to see me."

Between Phanie Lu and Franella, the professor received the whole story. "I think I have the gist of it. Do you have any kind of paperwork, Miss Franella?"

As the Professor and Franella began to talk, Phanie Lu excused herself to visit the kitchen. "I hope the woman I trained is feeding you well, Professor?"

He nodded, "She's doing an excellent job, but no one is a better cook than you, Miss Phanie."

"I'm too old to stand on my feet all day, but if you ever have a fancy party or large dinner, I will come and cook for you."

"Then I'll do that soon."

Although they were nothing alike in looks, Professor Albright reminded Franella of Professor Good from Seattle, practical and pragmatic. She pulled the papers from her purse and laid them on his desk. He perched a pair of reading glasses on the end of his nose and picked up the papers one by one. "Some of these envelopes are sealed. Do you mind?"

Franella chewed on her lip as the professor read each paper and set it aside. "Well, my dear. I assume you haven't read the sealed papers."

"Just the acceptance from Oxford, which wasn't sealed."

"Very impressive, but you've missed the beginning of the term."

"It won't be hard to catch up. That is if you can help me get a passport soon."

"There is no birth certificate among your papers. Isn't that a requirement?"

"Yes, the clerk was nasty about it. It's not my fault I don't have one. I was born on my parent's fishing boat—no doctor, no midwife, just my mother and father. I assume they didn't think about it once they were back on shore."

"But you had a passport?"

Franella laughed, "I did, but no birth certificate."

At the professor's questioning look, Franella added, "Alaska's a big place, but the towns are small. Everybody knows everybody. I didn't have to prove I was me."

"That's the problem. We will need to verify that you exist and that you are who you claim to be. Let me think." Professor Albright leaned back in his chair and closed his eyes. After a few moments, he shuffled the papers on his desk. He held up the Letter of Credit,

"Do you know what you have here?"

"I think it's the funds to pay for my education," Franella said.

"Hmmm. It also includes information regarding shares in a gold mine in Alaska."

"What?" Franella took the papers. "I don't believe it. Sean Conner, you wonderful old sourdough." Franella explained about the man who financed her education. "I suppose I can't access the gold to buy a ticket to England."

"It doesn't really work that way." The professor polished his glasses and put them in their case.

"Then I'm going to need to get some kind of a job, preferably away from people."

At the professor's arched eyebrow, Franella added. "I'm often nervous in social situations, and I absolutely abhor small talk."

Phanie Lu's footsteps pattered down the polished wood floor outside of the Professor's study. "Is everything settled, Professor? Can you be our very important person?"

"I'm afraid I don't know anyone in government." When he saw the disappointment on their faces, he hastened to add, "That doesn't mean I'm giving up, but the fact that Miss Franella's birth was never registered is problematic."

"But Professor, you've always said every problem has a solution."

He rubbed his chin and said, "At the moment, I can't think of a thing."

Phanie Lu smiled and said, "The Lord told me to come to you and that you would help. I will pray He gives you wisdom. You are a smart man, but it's the Lord who knows everything."

Professor Albright's eyebrows shot up, and he said, "You better pray with all your might because I'm at a loss."

Phanie Lu opened her pocketbook and took out a scrap of paper. "The barber shop Mr. Willie's second cousin's nephew owns has a telephone. This is the number. When you receive that wisdom, you call and they will get a message to us to call you back."

Professor Albright took the paper and placed it under the glass paperweight on the corner of his desk. As they said their goodbyes, Franella couldn't tell if the Professor believed he was going to receive any divine wisdom.

THIRTY-FOUR

Several days passed, and Franella's appetite sank.

"Eat up. Yo gots to keep yo strength up. De professor be callin' any day now," Phanie Lou said.

"It's been almost a week," Franella groused.

Phanie Lu picked up the worn Bible that lay open on the kitchen table and flipped through the pages. She read the verse that said the Lord counted time differently: a thousand years was like a day and a day like a thousand years.

"Well, I certainly can't wait a thousand years, and I don't want to wait a thousand days."

Phanie Lu laughed, "De Lawd's time is de best time. Has faith, Miss Franella. Dat's all; has faith."

Franella took the Bible from Phanie Lu and read the verse for herself. It didn't make any more sense to her than when Phanie said it.

"I'm getting antsy," Franella said.

"Yo's can walk down to the barbershop and reminds dem dat de professor not a wrong number."

Four days later Rodney banged on the door. "Miss Phanie, dat professor man done call. He give dis number fo' Miss Franella to calls back."

Franella raced several blocks to the barbershop with Rodney trotting along behind. He panted and increased his pace. Grabbing her hand, he said, "I takes yo, Miss Franella. I tells everybody a professor call yo. Yo be important."

Franella's eyes were focused on the shop's barber pole. Its helix of red, white, and blue stripes and downward-moving spiral pulled her attention to the windows. She saw three barber chairs inside, all occupied by colored men. One chair was tilted back as the barber washed his customer's hair. The next chair had a half tilt and the man's face was enveloped in a hot, damp towel. The third chair was upright. The barber swept the man's back and shoulders with a little whisk broom, pulled the white cape from the gentleman's shoulders, and called for his next customer.

All conversation stopped when Franella was pulled into the shop by Rodney, who announced, "Dis be de womans de professor want."

Above the four occupied straight-backed waiting chairs was a long shelf filled with various kinds of smokes and shoe polish. The handmade sign said—Smoke while you shine. Three men in the waiting chairs followed Franella with their eyes as she crossed the room. The fourth pair was glued to an upraised newspaper. Apparently, the news of the day was more interesting than the white woman in a barbershop in colored Bronzeville.

The head barber pointed his scissors to the corner. "De phone be on de back wall, next to my papa's picture. He be a barber afore me."

Franella moved carefully through the small shop, aware of all the eyes on her. Not hostile or unfriendly, just curious.

"Yo be's gentlemen now. We gots a lady in here," the head barber ordered.

"Dat mean no cussin' or such like," Rodney said.

"Hush boy or we sends yo home," the man behind the newspaper growled.

Franella dialed the number, knowing everyone in the barbershop would hear her side of the conversation and guess at the professor's. This little neighborhood in Bronzeville was much the same as small towns in Alaska. She turned to the men, smiled, and held the phone six inches from her ear. "Speak up, Professor Albright. I'm all ears."

"Da's lots of ears. Even lil' Rodney,'s ears be open," the head barber laughed.

"I've been thinking a lot, Miss Franella, and this is what I have come up with. Nothing about your passport, I'm afraid, but I might be able to get you a job. My gentlemen's club, mostly academics and wealthy alumni of the university, has a dining room in need of another waitress. No small talk from the wait staff is a requirement."

Franella wondered if it was dishonest not to mention how she often blurted things without thinking.

"What do you think?"

"I do need to make enough money to buy my tickets to England. I'm not sure how long that will take."

"I assume you can take their orders accurately," he continued.

"I have an eidetic memory." Several of the men looked confused, and Rodney whistled and scratched his head.

"Dat's big word," he said loudly. The barber shushed him.

Franella turned her back on her audience, held the phone close to her ear, and whispered, "I also have a highly superior autobiographical memory. I'm not lying or bragging. I remember everything about my life, down to the smallest details. I constantly see pictures in my head. But I'm often nervous around people, Professor Albright. I won't lie and say that I'm not."

"We are stuffy old men who like to eat and discuss the affairs of the day. You might enjoy overhearing the conversations at the various tables."

"Thank you for thinking of me." Franella pictured the men of the Sitka Café. They were from a different social stratum and economic level, as well as a different geographic location, but they also liked to eat and discuss the affairs of the day. She smiled as she imagined the professor eating black bear bacon at the Sitka Café or Ivan Mishkin holding court at a gentlemen's club in Chicago.

"Perfect. I'll make the arrangements," he said.

"I'm worried about my passport."

"There are several men at the club who have connections with government agencies. I'll let it be known you own a gold mine."

"Just a few shares in a gold mine. And it won't help me get a passport," she turned her back again and held the phone close to her ear as she whispered.

"Gold mine!" Rodney hollered. "Holy moly! She gots a gold mine!"

"What gold mine?" The head barber's scissors jabbed his customer, who yelled, "Don't be stabbing me!"

The man behind the newspaper looked over the top of it and said, "She say what?"

The head barber shushed him, and all the men leaned closer. The conversation had just become more interesting.

"Can you repeat that, professor? I didn't hear you." Franella glared at Rodney, who was pulling on her sweater and jabbering about gold and wondering if there were diamonds in the mine also.

"Money talks, my dear, and gold talks loudest of all," the professor said.

THIRTY-FIVE

Dear Miss Ruth,

As you can see by the Chicago postmark, I am not in England, but don't worry, I'm fine. I have sent a telegram to the college telling them of my misfortune and asking them to hold my place and store the two steamer trunks we sent. I have not yet received a reply, but I intend to sail for England in a few short weeks. I'm sure if I study hard, I will be able to catch up.

As you know, I had to change trains in Chicago. Unfortunately, I was robbed. I repeat, I am fine. You were right to tell me to trust the redcaps. Hard Workin' Willie and his wife, Phanie Lu, are the kindest people I have ever met, besides you, I mean. They live in the poorest section of Chicago called Bronzeville. There is no electricity or hot water, and no indoor bathrooms. I suspect the rest of Chicago has all those conveniences. Most of the colored people live in Bronzeville. They are tight-knit like the Tlingits, but their lives are centered around the churches rather than the clan houses.

Mr. Willie's house is tiny, but he and Phanie Lu welcomed me like the good Christian people they are. Phanie Lu used to cook for Professor Albright, and through his contacts, I was able to secure a job. You would be so proud of me; I am working in the dining room of an exclusive gentlemen's club in downtown Chicago. I take their orders for dinner and serve them with a smile.

I don't have to talk much, although sometimes I have to bite the insides of my cheeks to keep from blurting out how inane they sound. I tell you, Miss Ruth, the hardworking and under-educated men of the Sitka Café often have more common sense than some of these academics and urbane businessmen.

Without a birth certificate, it seems impossible to secure a passport. As far as I know, my parents never thought to register my birth. The professor is still looking for a solution. It was so easy in Sitka when we went to the mayor's office and asked for the passport application. Nobody had to prove who they were.

Tell that sneaky old sourdough, Sean Conner, that I was altogether gob-smacked to find out he had given me some shares of his gold mine. I still can't believe it! Thank him for me, please.

I can't tell you how much I miss all of you and my Alaska.

Franella

THIRTY-SIX

The Windy City Gentlemen's Club was housed in one of Chicago's elite 19th-century mansions. Its ivy-covered brick exterior reminded Franella of several buildings at the University of Washington. While a college student, she thought Seattle was a large and bustling city, but Chicago, so much larger, had an intense and fast-paced style that intimidated her even more.

Employees and service personnel were instructed to use the side door and were only allowed in the rooms where they performed their duties.

The rich mahogany trim, thick carpets, and dark leather furniture gave the smoking room, billiard room, library, and reading rooms a calm and quiet atmosphere, focused and studious. The dining room, with its mahogany wainscoting and forest green embossed wallpaper, crisp damask tablecloths, and low ambient light, projected an understated elegance. Professor Albright allowed Franella a peek into each of the rooms before taking her to the kitchen and introducing her to the dining room manager, who explained her duties.

"I'm not sure about this, Professor Albright," the manager said, handing Franella a pair of black slacks and a matching vest, a white long-sleeved shirt, and a black bowtie. "We've never had a, er, female person on our wait staff." He looked down his long nose at Franella, which was difficult since she was half a foot taller than he was. "You may have to alter these to fit. I assume you can handle a thread and needle?"

Franella raised her chin and mimicked his disdainful look.

He turned away, "I hope you know what you're doing, Professor."

"She'll be fine," he said.

"I don't think he likes me," Franella said as they left.

"He doesn't have to, and you don't have to like him."

That evening, as she left the building after her shift, she saw Professor Albright, hands in his pockets, leaning against the street light.

"Are you checking up on me?" she asked.

"More like checking in. How did it go?"

"The menu was easy to memorize, and the specials simple to explain. I didn't make any mistakes with the orders." Her brow furrowed, and her eyes darkened.

"I can see by the look on your face that there is a 'but' coming."

Franella hung her head. He patted her shoulder, "It can't be that bad. I'll drive you to Bronzeville, and you can tell me all about it."

The journey was almost half over before Franella spoke, "I don't agree with Jean-Paul Sartre."

"I assume you joined a conversation."

"I should have warned you I was a blurter," Franella whispered, "I tried so hard to keep quiet, but I am enthralled with philosophical anthropology and phenomenological psychology and how it relates to the imagination. It's the images in my head, I suppose."

Professor Albright sighed and tried to hide his smile. "I can see it would be difficult to refrain from giving your opinion."

"It's not my opinion; it's a fact. Sartre lets his Marxist leanings taint his thinking. I thought those who were having the discussion should know that. I gave them several examples, but they did not appreciate it."

"It is just your opinion, my dear, and you are free to share it when appropriate. Unfortunately, this was not your conversation."

Franella bit her lip. "But Professor Albright, they didn't know what they were talking about."

"Again, that's your opinion. A lot of people agree with Sartre and with Marx, for that matter."

"Well, they shouldn't."

Professor Albright laughed. "I do love your mind, but people are different, and they think differently. Very few have a mind like yours, Franella. You need to give others some grace."

"They didn't give me any," she huffed.

"Why? What happened?"

"They called the manager over, and he reprimanded me right there in front of them," Franella sniffed and pulled her handkerchief out of her pocketbook.

"He should have done that privately."

"I'm nervous about going back there, Professor. Everyone will look at me."

"Most people are too busy thinking about themselves, and those who don't will have forgotten the incident. Tomorrow is a new day, my dear."

Franella ignored the remarks from the other waiters while they set the tables and prepared for that evening's diners. While serving, she tried not to listen to the conversations at the various tables. Most of the talk centered around history, literature, or philosophy, which interested her, and local and national politics, which did not. There was a bit of mudslinging and much one-upmanship among the academics and successful alumni.

While at dinner one evening, Professor Albright called her over to his table. "Let me introduce you to my colleagues," he said. "At this table, Professor Stanton—science, Professor Johnston—English and American literature, Federal Judge—Wainwright, and North Western Railway President—Josiah Hamilton. All are successful in their fields."

Franella stood with a coffee pot in hand, smiling slightly. Once the introductions were made, she said, "Pleased to meet you," and turned to go.

But Professor Albright said, "Wait, my dear, tell these gentlemen what you think of Einstein's letter to the United Nations advocating for a one-world government."

"It seems to me..." Franella began hesitantly but became flustered when she was cut off.

"Forget that. What do you think of his theory of relativity?" Professor Stanton asked.

"Albright says you're from a small town. What do you think of *The Heart Is a Lonely Hunter*? Did Carson McCullers get it right?" Professor Johnston lifted his eyebrow and smirked, "I assume you've read it?"

Franella's stomach began to churn. "Yes, I..." Franella's eyes darted between the men at the table and Professor Albright.

"Do you think Einstein's right that atomic power can be used peacefully? Perhaps to run my trains?" Mr. Hamilton stared at her. His elbows rested on the edge of the table, and he clutched a cigar in his right hand.

"I want to know if you think Rosie the Riveter should go back to the kitchen and let the man be the breadwinner?" Judge Wainwright demanded.

"Just a minute, gentlemen..." Professor Albright tried to intervene, but the questions continued to come fast and furious, leaving no time for Franella to answer. The tone and demeanor of the questioners seemed somewhat hostile. She couldn't identify their attitudes, but she felt the acid rise in her stomach and the color drain from her face.

"Speak up, girl. Show us how smart you are," the judge ordered as he waved his cigar.

"Maybe she's not," Professor Stanton didn't bother to lower his voice as he added, "The few women taking my courses think they're smarter than most. They're not." He reached for another dinner roll. "She's just like them."

"What did you tell them about me?" Franella demanded, glaring at Professor Albright.

He had the grace to blush, "I just wanted to show how intelligent you are, extraordinary, really."

"For a waitress, you mean," Mr. Hamilton, sitting next to Professor Albright, snorted.

"For a woman," Judge Wainwright laughed.

Franella glared and slammed the coffee pot down, splashing dark liquid on the pristine cloth. "My father was a fisherman. When fishing was bad, my mother took in laundry and worked in a bakery. Their intelligence was not measured by their work or their gender. Mine isn't either."

"Of course, you are right, Franella. I'm sorry," The professor's face was a mottled red, and he felt the heat of it.

"I'm not a monkey on a string you can parade before your esteemed colleagues, Professor. It's nasty!" Franella's strident voice carried throughout the tranquil dining room.

All conversation had ceased, eyes widened, and heads turned in her direction. As a child in Port Alexander, when she didn't know what to do, Franella had run to the safety and comfort of the meadows and forests. In Sitka, when life overwhelmed her, she ran to Miss Ruth or Johnny, the Bear Boy. She looked around like a frightened bear cub or fawn might, took a deep breath, and bolted!

Professor Albright rose to follow the girl, but Judge Wainwright said, "Sit down. You can never reason with a hysterical woman!"

"Come now, Albright. You know you didn't mean any harm," Professor Stanton shook his head, "Women!"

"Gentlemen, your questions seemed patronizing. I never thought you were snobs. I can see I'm going to have to revise my opinions."

Professor Johnston picked up the abandoned pot and poured himself another cup of coffee. "It was just a bit of fun."

"Typical woman, can't take a joke." Mr. Hamilton stubbed out his cigar after the manager glared at him. "I'm going to the smoking room."

Professor Stanton dabbed his lips with his napkin and laid it back in his lap. He shrugged, "It doesn't matter how smart they are; their emotions always get the best of them."

Professor Johnston nodded, "Temperamental, every one of them."

Professor Albright had lost his appetite and all desire to participate in the conversation. He made his excuses, left the dining room, and wandered into the adjacent reading room. He settled into a plush leather chair and wondered how he could make peace with Franella. None of his students had ever confronted him like that. He asked himself if any had wanted to over the years. As he made his way home, his mind reviewed several ways he could make it up to her. His courage failed him, and instead of arranging to see her, he took his finest stationery and favorite fountain pen from his desk.

Dear Miss Franella,

I am horrified by my actions earlier at the club. It was inexcusable to put you on display like that and with no warning. I had been bragging about you to my colleagues, who had difficulty believing me when I told them of your superior intellectual ability, which I learned from our discussions in my library.

They refused to look past your status as a waitress or your gender. It irritated me, and I wanted to prove to them that I was right.

I failed to see the situation from your point of view or the depth of their condescending attitudes, and I am genuinely sorry.

I am enclosing two of my favorite books from last year's best-seller list: Animal Farm and Hiroshima. They can in no way atone for my actions, but I want you to have them. I would be interested in your thoughts once you have read them. There would be no audience, just you and me and several cups of tea or coffee, if you prefer.

Once again, I beg you to accept my sincere apology.

Yours,

Professor Albright

Franella crumpled the letter and threw it in the trash. She fished it out a moment later. How could the professor have treated her like that? "I thought he was trustworthy," she said.

"He is. He just made a mistake," Miss Phanie said.

"He had no right!"

"Come over here and kneads this dough. Get yo mad over so yo can forgives him."

"He doesn't deserve forgiveness."

"Nobody does. But de Good Lawd forgive us."

"That's different." Franella punched the dough several times.

"It be different but it be de same. Yo gots to learn dat."

"It's easier to stay mad."

"De mad eat yo up. De professor is yo friend."

Franella sniffed, "I don't want to talk about it."

Phanie Lu patted her shoulder, "Dat be okay. I prays for de Lawd to work His forgiveness."

Franella shivered. Things happened when Phanie Lu prayed. Not always right away, and not always the way you expected, but things happened.

It took several days for Franella's anger to begin to dissipate and another for her to think she could forgive the professor. It wasn't until he invited her to come to his house as often as she liked to borrow any of his books that she felt able to forgive him.

She wondered if she was motivated by her lust for his library or if she had really forgiven him. *I should ask Phanie Lu to help me figure that out, but I know what she'll say. I'll just read his books and not think about the issue of forgiveness. What is it anyway?*

Of course, whenever she had to serve the men who had humiliated her, she was mad at the professor all over again. When she remembered how horribly they had treated her, she pictured herself pouring hot coffee on their heads. She bit the inside of her cheek to keep from grinning at the thought. They eyed her warily but did not speak.

THIRY-SEVEN

The morning sun drifted through the window of Phanie Lu's kitchen. Its rays sparkled off the little glass bowl of peach jelly.

"Yo can stays with us, Miss Franella. Yo's gots a job. Yo likes us and we loves yo," Mr. Willie said.

"Yo fills de empty place in dis house," Phanie Lu added, "but I 'spect de Lawd has bigger things for yo den a little life in Bronzeville."

Franella had to smile. There were no empty places in this tiny house, but she knew Phanie Lu was saying there was room for Franella in her heart.

"Nuthin' wrong with a little life in Bronzeville," Hard Workin' Willie reached for more grits and butter.

Franella let the conversation wash over her as she thought about the weeks she had sojourned in this place. The anxiety about traveling solo after the drama in Chicago's Union Station needed to be shared. She bit her lip and took another bite of grits, which she had come to love, especially smothered in butter.

"What de trouble, chile? I sees it on yo face." Phanie Lu said.

Franella took a deep breath. "Grand Central Station is so big..."

Hard Workin' Willie grinned, reached across the table, and took her hand. "I gots a nephew at dat station. He know New York and gets you to de steamship."

Franella sighed, "Really? He can take me all the way to the

ship's terminal?"

"Phanie Lu writes him soon as youcomes to us. It be two mile to de docks. Yo can walks, gets a taxi, or take de subway. My nephew, Booker, goes whichever which way yo says. He help yo find de boat."

"I certainly don't want to carry my suitcase for two miles," Franella laughed.

"Booker carries yo case," Phanie Lu said, "Yo carries a big basket of food I packs."

Franella sniffed and rubbed her chest. The warmth she felt from this poor colored couple who refused payment of any kind actually caused her heart to hurt. The intense reaction to their kindness confused her. She rubbed her chest harder to soothe away the pain and said, "Excuse me, I need some fresh air."

She stumbled out of the house and down the road, not knowing where she was going. Head down, eyes blurred, she continued for several minutes.

Hard Workin' Willie rose to follow her. "Let her go, Mr. Willie. She thinkin' 'bout things."

"What things?"

"She don't know love. She want it, crave it, she desperate fo' it."

He scratched his head, "We loves her."

Phanie Lu cut another piece of cornbread. "We gives it, she don't takes it."

"Don't make no sense." He smeared butter on his cornbread.

"She like our Rosie girl," Phanie Lu pulled a hankie from her apron pocket.

"She nothin' like dat wild chile!"

Phanie Lu patted his hand, "Franella not wild, I knows dat, but she only know 'bout de Lawd. She don't knows Him. Till dat fixed, love hurt her in de heart. She fight agin it like our Rosie do."

Franella found herself in front of the African Union Methodist Protestant Church. Its peeling paint and cracked foundation told of its age and poverty, but the door was unlocked. The bouquet on the altar drooped, and the fresh flower scent had dissipated. Instead, Franella's nose was assaulted by the pungent odors of floor cleaner and furniture polish.

She sat in the front pew. The pain in her chest had not subsided, and she wanted to push it away. It had inhabited her past and was now affecting her present. All she could see were the faces: her parents disappearing underwater; she gasped as Mr. Willie and Phanie Lu's faces superimposed over her parents. What did that mean? Would she lose them, too? Franella breathed rapidly, and her heart beat erratically. She told herself to slow down, but she couldn't. Finally, she grabbed her pocketbook, opened it, and breathed into it. That didn't help. She let it fall to the floor, spilling the contents. Franella cupped her hands, pretended they were a paper bag, and breathed as slowly as possible. It was several minutes before she could breathe normally.

She leaned back in the pew and saw the scattered contents of her purse. As she bent to pick up the contents, she asked herself how this colored couple had come to mean so much to her in such a short time. It wasn't logical or probable, but it had happened.

She forced her mind away from that menacing image and saw Miss Drake giving her new clothes, Johnny, the Bear Boy, feeding

249

her, Oskar and Freja providing a place, Mr. Willie rescuing her, and Phanie Lu welcoming her. And over all of it, there was no-nonsense Miss Ruth. These memories kaleidoscoped through her mind for some time.

Moaning, Franella clutched her stomach and rocked back and forth. The pain increased as she focused on each face. She pressed her palms against her temples, squeezed her eyes tight, and prayed the images would dissipate. Time stretched as they slowly faded, and then she noticed the sun's slanting rays through the stained glass. She wasn't sure how long she had sat on the hard wooden pew, but it was time to go home. *Home? Since when do I think of Mr. Willie and Phanie Lu's place as home?* Her heart started to ache again, and she quickly pushed the feeling away. *I have no home. I need to find out what my life is about. I can't get tangled up in this emotional turmoil.*

Franella stood in the open doorway of the church, looking back into the sanctuary. There was a reason it was called a sanctuary. The gold candlesticks on the altar gleamed. The sunlight shining through the stained-glass depiction of the crucifixion made her shiver. She turned away from its agony. There was no sanctuary for her. *I will find the answer at Oxford. I just wish I could articulate the question.*

THIRTY-EIGHT

Dear Miss Ruth,

Professor Albright has written me an affidavit testifying to who I am. He's not sure how much weight it will carry since he hasn't known me long. His bank manager will also come and flash my Letter of Credit and talk about my shares in Sean Conner's mine. They say money talks. I hope so.

Phanie Lu says we are little Davids who need five smooth stones to fling at the government's bureaucratic Goliath. The largest and smoothest stone is prayer, the second is the affidavit from Professor Albright, the third is the bank manager, and the fourth is Mr. Willie's cousin Charlie's recommendation that we go late on a Friday afternoon when the workers are anxious to leave and might shove our application through just to get rid of us. The fifth, well, I don't know what the fifth is...

It's not just traveling to Grand Central Station and across New York to the docks that concern me; it's also leaving Mr. Willie and Phanie Lu. It's strange, but I know I will miss them almost as much as I miss you and my Alaska.

Franella

There was no need to share with Miss Ruth the agony and confusion of her emotional state, Franella thought as she posted her letter. Rodney and Lulu accompanied her to the post box, three

251

blocks away. They peppered her for stories about Alaska which was a good distraction but left her feeling homesick. When they reached the stoop she said goodbye, and told them Phanie Lu didn't have any cookies. She went inside and closed the door firmly in their faces.

"Miss Phanie always gots cookies," Rodney said, "She let us in de house whenever we wants." He shook his head and rubbed his toes in the dirt. "Miss Franella, be a liar."

She talk so white. How can dat be lies?" Lulu asked.

Apparently, four smooth stones were not enough. The clerk at the passport office did not care about Oxford or the gold, although she added copies of all of the documents to Franella's file. She refused to process the application until Franella provided definitive proof of her identity. Hard Workin' Willie was ready to take the day off and tell those government clerks how unrighteous they were. Phanie Lu shooed him out of the door and told him to have a nice day at work and not to worry. She alone seemed unperturbed. She continued to believe and pray.

"I'm so mad, Phanie Lu. Why didn't your prayers work?"

Phanie Lu finished dusting the photographs on the sideboard, saying a prayer for each person pictured. "I'll pour the coffee. Yo takes two big sugar cookies out o' de jar."

After lifting the lid, Franella said, "It's empty."

"I bet little Lulu snuck in while I's hangin' out de wash." She laughed and said, "We's can have de leftover cornbread with some honey. Dat be good."

Franella wasn't hungry but cut the cornbread and set the honey pot on the table. Once the coffee was poured and they were settled at the table, the older colored woman looked at Franella for a long moment.

Franella squirmed and looked everywhere but at Phanie Lu.

"What yo thinks prayer is?" the older woman asked.

"I guess you tell God what you want, and sometimes He gives it to you."

Phanie Lu laughed and wiped the crumbs from the corner of her mouth, "Chile, when I prays, I knows I's talkin' to King Jesus, de boss of de universe. I don't tells Him what I wants like He a genie in a lamp. I comes with thank-yos for who He be, and what He done. Den I tells Him my troubles and ask what He think about dat, and what He gonna do? Den I asks what He want me to do."

"But we prayed and prayed, and He didn't do anything!" Franella added too much honey to her coffee and nearly gagged on the sweetness. "I still don't have my passport."

"You don't haves it—yet. So, we keeps on."

"That seems illogical. Doesn't He care? Doesn't He know? Wasn't He listening?" Franella gnawed on the end of her thumb.

"He listenin' all de time, and He know afore we says it."

"Then what's the point?" Franella's stomach churned, and she felt the beginnings of a headache forming behind her eyes. She closed them briefly.

"He want to see iffen we keeps askin', keeps trustin', keeps believin' and we does." Phanie Lu lifted the last piece of cornbread from the pan and split it in half. Franella shook her head, and said, "I haven't even eaten this one. Best save it for Mr. Willie."

Phanie put both halves on her own plate. "De Lawd be building' our faith. I builds Mr. Willie more cornbread tonight."

Not my faith, Franella thought, but didn't voice it.

Phanie Lu put the dishes in the sink and said, "Now we prays again, and we listen. Dat's important. We gots to listen."

The following morning, Rodney knocked on the door, then burst through, jabbering the whole time, "De professor call and say he be coming in his car. You best be ready, he say."

"Did he say where we're going?" Franella asked.

"He just say be ready." Rodney turned to Phanie Lu and said, "I shore do like de smell of dem cookies, Miss Phanie." He smacked his lips and widened his eyes, "Yo gots de best cookie smell in all Bronzeville."

"Fresh out of the oven, chile."

He left with a cookie in each hand.

Professor Albright's car stopped in front of the house thirty-five minutes later. He jogged to the front door, which Phanie Lu opened before the man had a chance to knock.

"I've got it," he said, grinning broadly, looking past Phanie Lu to Franella. "I know how to prove who you are—Oxford!"

Franella and Phanie Lu looked at each other. Confusion swept across their faces. "My acceptance letter didn't prove anything. They said so," Franella's voice sounded shrill in her own ears.

"Right." He laughed.

254

"Pardon, but yo's confusin' me," Phanie Lu said, "How's de college way over in England gonna helps?"

"When you sent in your application, you had to include a photograph, right?"

"Yes, the Photo Shop in Sitka made two copies. One for my passport application and one for Oxford."

"We are going to telegraph Somerville College and have them send a radiophoto transmission to the passport office along with your application, declaring that you are Franella Feddersen. When the passport clerk sees that, I'm sure she'll believe you are who you say you are."

"That would be faster than writing to Miss Ruth and asking her to have the Photo Shop make another print. The mail in Alaska can be erratic." Franella scratched behind her ear, "How did you think of that, Professor?"

"I woke up at three o'clock in the morning, and I just knew," Professor Albright said. "Get your coat; we're going to the telegraph office. We'll ask the Dean of Somerville to request the passport process be expedited."

Franella ran upstairs to get her coat, and Phanie Lu said, "De Lawd give yo dat wisdom."

The professor shook his head. "Maybe, Miss Phanie. I don't know."

"I knows. He wake me up at three in de morning and tells me to pray fo' yo so I knows." Her smile nearly split her face in two.

"Let's go, Professor." Franella hugged Phanie Lu. "This has got to work, Miss Phanie. It just has to."

"Not to worry, chile. Just have faith."

THIRTY-NINE

Just after midnight, the ship reached the point of no return. That is, it was now equidistant between North America and Britain. The occasional fin slapping and the splash of whales breaching pierced the inky black waters of the North Atlantic. Moonlight shimmered over the ripples with a silvery gleam. The glistening waters were serene and tranquil, reminding Franella of the waters of Southeast Alaska's Inside Passage. She wondered if the storms of the North Atlantic were similar to those in the Gulf of Alaska.

She left the ship's rail where she had been standing mesmerized for almost an hour and crossed the deck to a teak lounge chair and covered herself with a blanket. She could see her breath and shivered frequently, but that did not induce her to seek the warmth of her cabin. A deckhand on night duty, uneasy at seeing this sole passenger who had not retired for the night, passed by regularly. Every time he asked if she needed anything, every time she shook her head. But whenever he passed, he brought her a little something: a thermos of hot chocolate, a small plate of cookies, and an extra blanket. She nodded her thanks and wished he would busy himself elsewhere. She eventually drank the chocolate and ate the cookies, but right now, contemplating the night sky consumed her. The expansive tapestry of stars reflected off the water as if the North Atlantic was a vast mirror.

She lay back in the chair, snuggled into her blankets, and gazed upward. *Little Franella Feddersen from Port Alexander's tiny village on the tip of Baranof Island, Territory of Alaska, America, sailing distant seas.* The stars seemed near, and she gazed in wonder. *Papa, what are stars made of? I remember I was six years old when I asked you that.*

FORTY

"Get your boots, Franella. We're going fishing."

"Mama doesn't like me on the boat when she's not there."

"Mama's needed at the bakery today. Come, we fish. The weather is good. No storms coming."

"She won't be mad?"

"You are six years old. Time for you to learn to be a fisherman, eh?"

"I will be a fishergirl, Papa."

"That is good. I promised your mama we would stay in the calm waters between Port Alexnder and Port Protection."

"I want to go far out on the ocean."

"When you are older," he lit his pipe and blew the smoke toward the ceiling. "The inside waters are calm. When you are older, we will fish the ocean, and your mama will not worry."

It was a long day for a young girl, eighteen hours of sunlight. Franella leaned over and dipped her hand in the water as the summer sun finally dropped into the sea.

"Careful," her father said as he clamped his pipe between his teeth, "I don't want to have to pull you out of the water. Your mama would not be pleased."

"Papa, what are stars made of?" Franella lay back on the deck and peered at the sky as it darkened and the stars became increasingly visible.

He steered the boat into a sheltered cove and killed the engine, poured himself a cup of coffee from the thermos, gave Franella a sip, and laughed at the face she made. "Daughter, the heavens are full of angels, flying to and fro, doing the Great King's bidding. When they finish, they must journey back to His throne room. When darkness comes, they see the candles."

"The stars?"

He nodded and sat on the deck next to her. "He sets every star in its proper place."

"How do the angels know the way?"

"They are homing angels. Like pigeons, they always find their way home. Like candles, the stars are beacons. Do you know what a beacon is?"

Franella shook her head.

"A beacon is something that shows the way."

"So many star candles, Papa?"

He pulled her onto his lap and tugged on her braids. "His kingdom stretches from one end of the universe to the other. He has lots of angels and doesn't want them to get lost."

"Have you ever seen an angel, Papa?"

He drew deeply of the aromatic tobacco and looked into the night sky, "I have been in many storms and did not perish. I think invisible angels helped me."

"What did they do? How did they help? Are they always invisible? How can you tell they are there? Did they talk to you?"

"I don't remember them talking, but once I felt their wings flutter next to my ear."

"Really, Papa? What did it feel like? What did you do? What did they do?"

He ran his hand over the stubble on his cheek and sighed, "Too many questions. Save them for your Sunday School teacher."

"But Papa, you know everything." Franella tapped her fingers on the deck and waited.

"I will say something to you that you must remember."

"About the angels and the stars?"

"About you. You are not like other children, other people. You think in a different way." He tapped the ashes of his pipe against the boat's edge. "Sometimes it is difficult."

Franella hung her head and choked back tears. She clutched her stomach and wondered what kind of different she was. Poor Papa. She saw the look on his face, the disappointment in his eyes. "What do you mean, Papa? How am I different?" she whispered, but her father had turned his attention to his fishing lines.

FORTY-ONE

The splendor of the Milky Way and the stars scattered across it reminded Franella of an article she read about a primitive tribe that couldn't understand why the anthropology team that came to study them couldn't hear the stars. How she wished she could have been part of that group. She would have asked so many questions.

What do the stars sound like? What do they say? How were you taught to listen? Could anyone learn? Franella had twice heard the Lady Aurora sing as she splashed great waves of green and violet across the Alaskan sky, but as hard as she strained her ears, she had never heard the stars speak. Franella shivered again in the dark night as she surveyed the faraway sky. *Distant stars. Distant seas. Distant Alaska.*

Franella, though lonely, smiled through her shivers, pleased she could recall that fishing trip with her father without grief overwhelming her. It was bittersweet. Looking back, she realized the look in her father's eyes was sadness for her, not disappointment in her. He must have sensed the difficulties she faced and how they would increase as she grew older. That kind-hearted man may not have comprehended the intricacies of her mind, but she now knew how much he loved her. She pulled the blankets tighter around her shoulders. *I miss you, Papa. Are you talking to the angels now? And the stars, do they shine for you, speak to you? You said the angels know the way home—to the Great King's palace. Oh, Papa, where's my home? Where do I belong?*

She had been utterly bereft as she said goodbye to the people of Bronzeville. Mr. Willie made sure she had a good seat on the train and gave her precise instructions about where to meet Booker. As he left the train car, she heard him tell the conductor she was a very important person and he must watch over her.

Booker, the New York redcap, was a younger version of Mr. Willie. He had the same outgoing, genial attitude and pleasant face, the same lanky frame and big heart. Booker grinned from ear to ear when she gave him the flour sack filled with sugar cookies as large as your hand. "Miss Phanie doesn't forgets me."

He called for a taxi and rode with her to the ship's terminal. He did not leave her side until she was walking up the gangplank. "I promise Miss Phanie I's not lettin' yo outta my sight 'till yo on de ship." He tipped his cap. "Goodbye Miss Franella."

That melancholy aloneness stayed with her during the voyage. She couldn't shake it, even as she entered the dining salon. A small orchestra played in the far corner of the room. Those at the Captain's Table were elegantly dressed. The rest of the passengers were seated according to the price of their tickets. First and Second Class close to the Captain's Table and the music. Those less fortunate were sitting close to the galley, where the clatter and clank of silverware and pots and pans could be heard. The lower-class ticket holders had their own cafeteria on a lower deck.

Franella sighed as she watched the waiters move silently

through the room, doing their duties efficiently with a smile and a nod. That is what the Windy City manager demanded of her and exactly what she could not deliver. She had received several reprimands and write-ups in her file. And he told her to never ask for a reference. She turned her attention back to her meal. The food was exquisite, but she would rather sit with Mr. Willie and Phanie Lu, eating grits and collard greens. *I guess it's not always about where you are but who you are with.*

Franella had not spoken to the other passengers at dinner or afterward in the lounge or when she strolled along the deck. She had spent most of her time the past few days in the ship's library, but the books were insipid romances, and they bored her.

Franella stretched and took a deep breath, trying to ease her melancholia, but she couldn't shake it. She looked again at the stars.

Still unsettled, she threw back the blankets and went to her cabin. She crawled into bed but did not sleep. Her mind raced as the moonlight spilled in through the tiny porthole.

Why won't the stars talk to me? Where's my candle? She punched the pillow and turned over. Her racing mind and disturbing thoughts kept her awake for hours. *I'll think about how diligent I'll need to be in order to catch up academically. No time for introspection. The ship is docking tomorrow in Southampton, and I will have to find the way to Somerville College, somewhere in the middle of Oxford.*

The journey consisted of a short taxi ride to Southampton Central Station and then a sixty-mile train trip to Oxford. And she did it without a redcap!

FORTY-TWO

Somerville Women's College
Oxford, England 1947

Dear Miss Ruth,

You will be happy to know that crossing the Atlantic was uneventful, and I am presently ensconced in my rooms at Somerville Hall. I have met with my advisors, and tomorrow will attend my first lecture. I'm sure I will settle in quickly and catch up with the coursework.

Everyone says this is the coldest winter England has ever experienced, and I can believe it. Colder than the panhandle of Alaska, for sure. Even though the war has been over for some time, there are still many shortages and strict rationing. I'm so glad we sent those two steamer trunks full of nonperishable food, although the registrar's office is having difficulty locating them. I hope they will turn up soon. Ah, well, I won't starve, although I must say beans on toast do not appeal. Freja and Phanie Lu were both excellent cooks, even though each had very different cuisines. I did love both. I shall try to keep an open mind about the food provided to the students here. I still have several small packets of smoked salmon I've been saving. I had to air out my clothes when I arrived. The odor lingers in the lining of my suitcase. I don't mind. It reminds me of my Alaska.

Franella

Franella Feddersen made her way across the Commons of Somerville Women's College to attend her first lecture after missing the first nine weeks of term. She looked around the medieval buildings of Oxford with their spired domes, tall towers, and pointed arches. Ribbed vaults, flying buttresses, tall windows, and steep gabled roofs surrounded her. Franella thanked God the German Luftwaffe had not destroyed them. *If you could see me now, Miss Ruth, you would be proud. I'm here in the midst of all this Gothic architecture, with no forests, mountains, or water in sight, and I'm fine.* She took a few more steps, looked at the incoming clouds, and admonished herself to be honest, at least in her thoughts. *Actually, my stomach is churning, and I am breathing rapidly. I know you'd tell me to stand up straight and look everyone in the eye, but I'm keeping my eyes on my shoes and not looking at any of the other students on the way to their various lectures. To those who murmur a greeting, I merely nod. My mouth has gone dry, but I am determined to enter the lecture hall calmly and serenely. Oh, Miss Ruth, I don't want anyone to know that experiences make me feel alone, isolated, and anxious.*

Franella took a deep breath and exhaled slowly. The clouds released their moisture in a frozen frenzy. She believed the reports that this was the worst winter the British people had ever experienced. Shivering, she dashed into the hall ahead of the rapidly falling rain, bumping into a short, stocky girl with a face full of freckles.

"I say that rain would make Noah proud. Our Irish mist is soft and warm, not like this freezing wetness."

"Don't worry. It will soon turn to snow," Franella said, sniffing the air.

"How do you know that?" the Irish girl asked.

"Personal experience," Franella mumbled, but too low for the Irish girl to hear.

"I'm Kay, short for Kathleen. I'm just across from Ireland. You?"

"Franella, Territory of Alaska."

"What?" The upturned nose in the midst of those freckles wrinkled. "Never heard of it. Is it one of those tiny islands off the north coast of Scotland?"

Franella shook her head.

"You don't sound Scottish. Never mind, the lecture is about to start." She took Franella by the arm and plowed into the crowded auditorium. "Make way! The Irish lass and Not-a-Scot are coming through!"

Eyes rolled, and laughter followed the Irish lass and the Not-a-Scot as Kay dragged her to the front of the large room. Franella kept her eyes on Kay's back and sighed when she motioned to the center seat in the front row. "Here we are." She bowed to the rest of the class and turned toward the professor. "Professor Abney, may I present Miss Franella," Kay turned and asked, "What's your surname?"

Franella mumbled.

Kay leaned closer, "Again, please—thank you. This is Franella Feddersen, Not-a-Scot."

Professor Abney arched a single eyebrow and fingered the pearls at her neck.

"She says she's from Alaska. Uh, it's not part of Scotland."

"I should say not. Just where did you study geography, Miss O'Malley?" The Professor peered over the half-moon glasses perched on the tip of her nose. The frames hid the smile lines at the corner of her eyes.

Kay laughed, "I think I was off with the fairies or looking for the pot of gold when my teachers reached for the globe. If it's not Ireland, I have difficulty believing it's relevant."

"So I've heard. However, you had better consider this class relevant," Professor Abney rustled the papers on her lectern and said with a smile, "Remember last term?"

The Irish girl's face became almost as red as her hair, and her freckles popped. "Yes, Professor. I shall do my utmost. I will give your lectures my intense Irish attention."

Professor Abney shook her head. "Do you carry the Blarney Stone around with you, Miss O'Malley? You are certainly full of it."

"We keep it in the castle at Cork. I've kissed it often." The young women filling the lecture hall giggled, Kay most of all. Professor Abney shook her head, welcomed Franella, and brought the class to attention.

As the mature, smooth-skinned professor began her lecture, Franella realized that the butterflies and churning in her stomach had disappeared. Was it because her attention had been focused on the Irish girl and not herself? Franella was amazed that she felt calm and relaxed in the large lecture hall full of strangers. A feeling that had eluded her at the University of Washington.

Kay leaned over and said, "We are going to be great chums."

FORTY-THREE

As she walked throughout the city during her off-time, Franella marveled at the old structures. Once again, she was thankful the Germans had not bombed the city. Some said Hitler had a fondness for Oxford and had elaborate plans for it after the war. She shuddered as she thought of this grand place in his evil hands.

Somerville Hall, one of only five colleges for women in the midst of the medieval city of Oxford with its scores of academic institutions and a multitude of ancient architectural styles with spires reaching to the sky, was far away and as different from Franella's homeland as one could imagine. Today was misty, and a lacey fog swirled among the towers and "dreaming spires of Oxford," as they were called. Franella turned up her jacket collar, pulled her knit cap over her ears, and squinted as she looked up. She tied her scarf tighter around her neck and was grateful Miss Ruth had gifted her a pair of mukluks as a bon voyage present. They might look out of place in this medieval British city, but they kept her feet warm.

She imagined the stately spires as the majestic forests of home. She wondered how everyone was faring back in Alaska. Although Miss Ruth and Miss Drake promised to send regular newsy letters, she knew it wouldn't be enough. The smell of the forests and the sea couldn't be sealed in an envelope. Alaska remained etched on her heart. As she neared the post office, silver rain fell in piercing sheets, another reminder of the Northwest. She purchased several stamps and posted her letters. Freja, bless her heart, had sent a package of Danish cookies that the post office had held for her. They were mere crumbs but would be enthusiastically consumed.

I really must write more often and let everyone know the details of my life. Miss Ruth and Miss Drake want to know everything. They can keep the people in Sitka informed of my adventures. Freja and Oskar asked me to correspond regularly, and of course, Phanie Lu and Mr. Willie made me promise to write; who has the time? She thought about how many people Miss Ruth correspondence with even though she was extremely busy. Franella vowed she would make the time to stay in touch.

The tutorial instruction at Oxford was very different from the lecture method at the University of Washington. She studied every evening at the UW but heard that Oxford students had about forty hours of homework per week.

Just this week, she was required to write a two-thousand-word essay for her History of Literature class after completing the assigned reading and doing her research. Comparative Philosophy required two essays per week. She had to formulate and describe her theories and support her assumptions, citing her sources. She must know her material so well that when she met with her tutor, Constance Penrose, she could defend her evaluation of the material and her perspective of it.

After hearing her tutor's response and notating her ideas, Franella would write the final draft of her work, incorporating her tutor's ideas or refuting them with additional research.

She thought about her first meeting with the middle-aged, slightly graying Constance Penrose. The rooms her tutor occupied at Somerville Hall were filled with dark leather furniture and heavy mahogany bookcases that overflowed with a myriad of volumes. Stacks of books filled every nook and cranny of the crowded office and sitting room. Dead and dying houseplants topped the stacks of books, giving the room an atmosphere of gentle disarray.

Miss Penrose had stood behind a massive desk and said, "You can sit across from me in that dark leather chair, or we can go to the window nook where I have two chintz-covered chairs and a tea table."

Franella chose the window nook that overlooked the Commons. "Good choice. It's more friendly this way," Miss Penrose said as she removed the sleeping tabby from his favorite spot and sat. The cat stretched, gave her a disgruntled look, and tip-toed to the open hearth in front of the small fireplace in the corner.

"How is sitting near a window friendlier than at a desk?"

Miss Penrose laughed and patted the flowered chintz chair, "Ask Mr. Darcy. This chair or the wide windowsill are his favorite places to be." The cat meowed in agreement, then closed his eyes. A quiet purr filled the room.

Halfway through their tutoring session, Miss Penrose frowned silently. At Franella's quizzical look, she said, "Miss Feddersen, you are apparently not used to the tutorial method. May I share some insights with you that you might not like but need to hear?"

Franella bit the inside of her cheek and nodded.

"I find you extremely intelligent. In fact, you are probably eligible for a newly formed group here called Mensa." She shook her head as if to wipe the thought away. "We'll talk about that later. I sense that you are a person with little patience, for what shall I say," she tapped her temple with her forefinger and sighed, "for what you perceive is a lack of intelligence in others?"

Franella shifted in her chair and gnawed on her lower lip. Her eyes questioned the tutor. Constance continued, "At Oxford, learning requires an exchange of ideas. Ideas that you may disagree with, and perspectives different from your own. You seem to be a typical brash American, eager to talk and reluctant to listen, assuming your thinking is true and your opinions are facts."

Franella opened her mouth to respond but, at Miss Penrose's upheld hand, chewed on the inside of her cheek again. Seeing the struggle on Franella's face, the tutor smiled and said, "I commend your restraint."

Again, Franella nodded.

"We are going to have many rigorous academic discussions during our weekly sessions, and you will have ample opportunity to defend your ideas. I challenge all of my students to first listen, process, and finally, speak. You must also learn to accept constructive criticism whether it comes from me or your peers."

Franella hung her head and wondered if she had any actual peers but said, "Yes, ma'am."

Constance Penrose picked up the Brown Betty—ceramic teapot—and asked, "Tea?"

Franella nodded.

"We won't always agree, and that is acceptable, even laudable." She held up the sugar bowl, and Franella shook her head. "I haven't made you afraid to speak, have I?" Miss Penrose asked.

"Yes, ma'am. No, ma'am. That is, I often blurt things without thinking, especially if I'm nervous or anxious." Franella wrung her hands. "I'm trying to rid myself of that compulsion."

The middle-aged tutor nodded, "I hope you will become comfortable with me. I expect you to listen, and I will offer you the same courtesy. It's about respecting the other person."

Franella scrunched up her face, gnawed on the end of her thumb, and said, "Freja told me I shouldn't blurt things or correct people. They don't like it."

"You seem younger than your years, Miss Feddersen. There are times when people must be corrected, but with gentleness and respect. Other times it will not be your place to do the correcting. I believe as you mature, you will learn to discern which is which."

"If I learn this discernment thing, do you think people will like me better?" Franella tried not to sound so insecure and childish.

"Has that been an area of concern?"

"I've been an outcast most of my life. I attended a regular school for a few weeks when I was young, but most of my education was through correspondence. When I was sent to Sitka, they put me in the high school although I had already finished my correspondence classes through grade twelve. I didn't last very long. I wasn't used to being around other kids. At the University of Washington, the classes were large, and I was alone in the crowd. I don't know how to have friends." Franella leaned against the soft chintz and closed her eyes. She heard her heart thump in the midst of the thick silence and wondered if her tutor sensed her fear. Mr. Darcy jumped into her lap. Absently, she began to scratch his ears. Franella's face burned, and she whispered, "I don't know why I told you all of that."

Constance Penrose drank her tea thoughtfully, "You will be in a study group with two others. Perhaps if you focus on listening to them, defending your own opinions without aggression or insisting theirs are incorrect, they can become your friends."

"Maybe," Franella didn't sound too sure.

"I'm arranging those groups now. Hmm. I will put you in a group with a student who is extremely outgoing and friendly, Miss Kay O'Malley."

Franella brightened, "I've met her, and she said we'd be friends. I thought it was the blarney. Professor Abney said she was full of it."

Miss Penrose arched her eyebrows and ignored the comment. "Excellent. The other member of your study group will be, oh dear..." Miss Penrose took a sip of tea and consulted her list again, "Well, it can't be helped."

"That doesn't sound good," Franella said.

"Georgine Alexander-Wessex."

"That's a fancy name."

Miss Penrose leaned forward and whispered, "An ancient British noble family. Georgine has had the finest boarding school education and a year at a finishing school in Switzerland."

"I don't know what finishing school is."

"It's a private school that teaches the social graces and deportment to young women."

"Didn't she already know that?"

"I don't want to prejudice you against Georgine in any way. She has had every advantage, but I don't think it has made her a happy person. Anyway, the three of you will meet in the Hall two evenings a week to discuss the assigned reading and work on your projects and papers. The other three nights will be filled with seminars, lectures, and guest speakers."

"Thank you, Miss Penrose."

Crossing the pristine gardens and manicured lawn of the quad on the way to Kay's room for her first study session, Franella felt a surge of gratitude for Miss Ruth, who made Somerville a possibility. However, she knew Miss Ruth would insist on giving all the credit to Bozhe.

Franella breathed deeply of the chilly winter air and decided to spend some time in the chapel when her study session ended. She longed for the serene atmosphere of the chapel, which was usually empty and always free from commotion.

She was grateful she had already met Kay. Georgine sounded like a high society girl, popular and sure of herself. What if she was like Blanche, the sovereign of Sitka High School? Franella dreaded meeting her.

"Welcome Franella. Did you get all of your reading done? I was up most of the night. Have you met Georgine yet? Some of the other girls say she's snooty, but we'll give her a chance, right? My Irish grandmother always said may good and faithful friends be yours wherever you may roam. You've roamed a long way, Franella. Me, not so far, but I'm all for having as many friends as I can get. Now, where is Georgine?"

Franella shrugged, emptied her book bag of all her study materials, and looked over her notes while Kay kept up a lively chatter in her musical Irish brogue. Georgine strolled in half an hour later.

"You're late," Franella said.

"Are you taking attendance? I wasn't aware that was required." Georgine said as she sat at the table and sniffed, "What is that ghastly smell? Is there a dead fish in here?"

Franella grinned and reached into her bookbag. She held out a dried, brown object to the blond girl, "Baleek. Old Russian recipe. Acquired taste."

Georgine held a handkerchief to her nose. "I—I—think I'm going to be sick." She stumbled from the room.

Franella looked at Kay and said, "Well! What do you think of that?"

"I can't decide if you did that on purpose." Kay grinned and took a bite of the dried, smoked fish. "It is an acquired taste, but my Da fishes often, I am from County Cork, you know. We have smoked fish quite often. Not as strong as this, though. I can see why Georgine's refined stomach couldn't take it."

"I'm really upset my steamer trunks cannot be located. Miss Ruth and Miss Drake made sure they were full of such good food. Dried berries of all kinds, pilot bread, bear and moose jerky, canned fish, and low-bush cranberries. I'm hungry just thinking about it. I'll check with the post office again tomorrow."

Kay put another piece of the fish in her mouth and talked around it. "I hate to tell you this, Franella, but I think your trunks are gone forever. They were probably inspected at the Southampton Customs House and then stolen. People are hungry and have been all through the war years. We were lucky back home in Ireland. We had a bit of land, some chickens, a pig or two, and, of course, Maeve. That sweet Jersey cow kept the hunger pangs away. City people did not fare as well."

Franella sighed, "I could write Miss Ruth and tell her it's all gone. I know she would move heaven and earth to take care of me. But I don't want to do that. I'm an adult."

"You can do what I do."

"What's that?"

"I got a job at a pub. The pay is terrible, but a meal is included. I start next week. I'll let you know if they need another waitress."

Franella nodded, "It's a good idea for later. I still have a bit of studying to do to catch up, but I have references from some of the patrons of the Windy City Gentlemen's Club in Chicago. The dining manager didn't think much of me, but Professor Albright had several of the regulars write glowing letters about my performance. He said it was the least he could do." Franella felt it wise not to mention how she slammed the coffee pot down, ruined the tablecloth, and ran out of the dining room. She thought the professor probably cajoled or even forced the glowing references to be written.

At the end of the week, Georgine returned to the study session. No mention was made of the offending fish. She pulled a nail file from her small alligator purse. Her boredom was evident, and she refused to make eye contact with either girl.

"Where are your study materials?" Franella tried to keep her voice calm but it sounded sharper than she intended.

Georgine shrugged, and Kay said, "It's all right. I've lots of extra paper and pencils, a dictionary, and notes from all this week's lectures."

Georgine pointed her nail file at Kay, "That's clever of you. May I have a copy of your notes?"

Franella snorted, "It's hardly fair to take advantage of Kay's hard work."

"I don't mind, Franella. We're all in this together." She turned to the other girl. "I only have one copy, but here's some blank paper, and I've just sharpened these pencils."

Georgine looked over the notes, "These are difficult to decipher. Perhaps next time, you could type your notes and use a carbon. It would be very helpful."

Kay looked a bit startled and said, "That's a great idea, Georgine, but I don't have a typewriter."

"It's not a problem, my dear. I will give you mine. I never use it."

Kay shrugged and looked to Franella, who said, "Taking notes during the lectures and seminars and then copying or typing them later helps cement the information into one's brain."

"My brain doesn't need any help from you, thank you very much." Georgine's spine straightened, and she looked down her nose at Franella, frost in her tone and eyes.

Franella was ready to respond with a sarcastic remark, but she remembered her conversation with Miss Penrose. She bit the inside of her cheek and remained silent.

Kay reached under her bed and pulled out a cardboard box. "Here is a loaf of Irish soda bread and a small crock of sweet cream butter. It just came from Maeve. I miss her."

"Who is Maeve?" Franella asked.

"My Jersey cow. She has enormous brown eyes and gives the sweetest milk. She follows me around like a puppy. I'm lonely without her."

"One can hardly bring cattle to Oxford." Georgine's nail file stopped in mid-air, and her eyebrows rose. "How can you have a cow in Dublin?"

"There's more to Ireland than Dublin," Kay laughed. "I'm from County Cork in the province of Munster, a small village no one has ever heard of."

"And you miss your cow? Incredible!" Georgine stared at Kay

and repeated, "A cow?" She shook her head and bent over her nails.

Kay wiped a tear from the corner of her eye, "Yes, I do," she muttered, trying to ignore Georgine's condescending tone. "Maeve's milk is helping pay for my education, along with several scholarships. What about you?" Kay sliced the bread, smeared it with the butter, placed it on cloth napkins, and slid one across the table to each girl.

"Me?" Georgine said, "I'm here because my great-aunt insists."

"Is she paying?" Franella asked, then wondered if it was rude to ask.

"Either her or my parents." Georgine shrugged, "I just know that if I graduate from Somerville, I will inherit her estate, which is considerable. If not, she'll leave it to my cousin, Thackery. She doesn't like him much."

"Why not?"

"It's more she doesn't like his father. He, shall we say, arranged for Thackery to sit out the war in some made-up civil service job in London."

Franella frowned as Kay said, "How could your uncle do that? What did Thackery think? Did he go along with it? Is he a coward? What did his friends say? Is that even legal?"

Georgine put her hands up to stop the barrage of questions, "All I know is, I'm assured of her fortune if I graduate." Georgine ignored the bread and butter and continued to file her nails. "Thackery is, well, there are no words to describe him. If you are lucky, you will never meet him."

Kay shrugged and turned her attention to Franella, "What about you? How did you arrive here all the way from Alaska?" Kay asked around a mouthful of bread, several crumbs collecting in the corner of her mouth.

"While all this talk of cows and Alaska is absolutely riveting, I must go. I can't spend all my time studying."

"You haven't studied at all," Franella muttered.

Georgine paused at the door. "I do have a social life, you know." She directed her gaze toward Kay, "Miss O'Malley, I will have my typewriter sent to you with a supply of paper and carbons."

Georgine missed the next three study sessions. When she finally returned, Kay thanked her for the typewriter. "It's been helpful to type my notes. I've made copies of everything for you." She pulled a stack of papers from her book bag.

"You wouldn't have made two copies of your essays, would you? It would be so helpful if I could read them."

Franella muttered, "Or put your name on them!"

Georgine's head snapped up, and she glared at Franella, who stared right back. Kay's gaze bounced from one girl to the other, and she rushed to say, "Remember our first session when I told you all about Maeve? You told us about Thackery, and I asked about Franella's journey here?"

Both girls nodded while still eyeing each other.

"Franella's answer was a fairy godmother and a cigar box full of gold nuggets," Kay said, "What do you think of that?"

"What?" Georgine said.

"It was a great story. Tell her, Franella."

"I'm sure she doesn't care about me."

"It sounds like a good story." For once, Georgine's tone was soft and sounded genuine. Her face lost its snooty arrogance. "My nanny used to tell me stories every night."

Franella shook her head, "We're supposed to talk about our essays and work through any problems we might have. You know this time is for discussion and debate. Professor Abney is waiting for our latest project on Languages, Culture, and Communication."

"They sent my nanny away when I was ten," Georgine's sad eyes looked into the past. She sniffed and shrugged, then whispered, "I suppose we're all too old for stories."

Now, it was Franella who had a faraway look in her eyes. After a moment or two of silence, she said, "The clouds darkened the waters off the coast of Baranof Island, and Ade Bunderson saw a wall of green water rise before him. His boat nearly floundered during the storm. When the gale was over, I was sent to an orphanage run by the worst ogre ever." Franella paused.

Kay slathered more butter on her ever-present loaves of soda bread. Georgine leaned forward and said, "Where's Baranof Island? Who is Ade Bunderson? How did you become an orphan? What do you mean, ogre? What happened next?" Absently, she nibbled on the buttered bread.

"I was rescued by Johnny, the Bear Boy, and it ruined his life." Franella frowned and reached for another slice of bread. She picked at the crust instead of eating.

"What about your fairy godmother? Did she help this Johnny person?"

"She took him away."

"People you love are always taken away," Georgine said with a catch in her throat. She sniffed, gathering her gloves and purse. "I have to go."

"But you haven't heard the rest of the story," Kay protested.

"I have to go." Georgine dipped her head and angled her face away from the girls. She hurried out of the door without seeing that it latched. Her sharp footsteps struck the hard surface of the tile floor. The staccato rhythm of each frantic step echoed Georgine's eagerness to get away.

"I guess she didn't like my story." Franella scowled, "She's rude."

Kay went to the window, leaned over the barely warm radiator, and watched Georgine cross Woodstock Street. "I feel sorry for her."

"She's only been here a few minutes and didn't open her books. She hasn't done one thing to help our little study group. She takes it for granted that her education is paid for, not to mention all the extras she seems to be able to buy despite the rationing."

"Didn't you hear what she said?"

"So, they sent her nanny away," Franella saw the old image of her drowning parents hovering at the entrance to her mind. She forced it away.

Kay let the curtain fall over the window. She crossed to the table in the corner and plugged in the electric teakettle. Cups, saucers, and Franella's small jar of fireweed honey were added to the tray. And, of course, a small jug of Maeve's sweet cream. The kettle whistled, but before Kay prepared the tea, she took a small pot from an equally small cupboard and banged on the radiator. The result was a dented pot and no heat. "I thought these steam radiators were supposed to warm our rooms efficiently."

"Not since they started turning off the electricity at night to save power," Franella said.

"At least at night, we can burrow under the covers. Now that they started to turn it off randomly during the day, I'm freezing."

"Doesn't your Irish grandmother have a saying for that?"

Kay laughed, put on another sweater, and said, "The building's handyman said he bought a small supply of coal yesterday, on the black market, I think. I'll go to the basement and make a trade. You clean the grate." Kay took the last of Maeve's sweet cream and butter with her. "It's a good thing he likes Irish butter and cream."

"Try to get a whole bucket of coal. It's the smallest fireplace in the world and doesn't give much heat."

Kay returned with the handyman in tow. He had a pail filled with live coals. He knelt before the grate, and soon, a weak warmth began to slowly fill the room.

"I'm sorry I could only give you a little. Rationing is still in effect, and it's hard to come by, even on the black market."

"You would think the government would see that the schools and universities had an adequate supply of coal and electricity," Franella said.

"And enough food for their students," Kay added.

"They can't give what they don't have," the handyman said.

"I can't ever remember a colder winter," Kay said, "I'm wearing all the sweaters I own."

"It's the coldest winter since 1881, according to the London Times. Too many winter storms. Regular blizzards, they are. Sorry, miss." He tipped his cap and left.

Franella rubbed her hands together, hung a blanket over the window, then folded a towel and pressed it against the bottom of the door jam. "That should keep some of the cold air out."

They wrapped themselves in blankets and sat near the fire.

Kay returned to their previous conversation. "My Irish grandmother was a nanny here in England before the Great War. It broke her heart. The family was like Georgine's, really top drawer."

"Top drawer?"

"You know, the higher-ups. The rich, the gentry, the bluebloods, surely you have them in America."

"We have rich people who think they are better than anyone else, and then there's the filthy-rich," Franella said, "the muckymucks, the swells, the well-off."

"Those are the ones. My granny always said we should live like we had one foot in heaven. Anyway, the father was a minor aristocrat but high up in the government. When he wasn't working, he was in the country hunting foxes or shooting pheasants. The mother had her luncheons, clubs, and committees, as well as the opera, theatre, and the latest art exhibitions. They spent their lives being seen if you know what I mean."

Franella wasn't sure but nodded anyway.

Kay continued, "Weeks would go by without the parents seeing their little girl. My granny was everything to that wee thing, and when the little girl was around ten or eleven, just like Georgine's nanny, my grandmother was sent away. She said it was like a death. She never took another job as a nanny."

"Like a death, but not a real one," Franella sniffed and looked away.

"To my grandmother, it was. She loved that little girl like a daughter, and the child thought of my grandmother as a mother, not a nanny. I think it was the same for Georgine. Can't you spare a little mercy for her, a bit of understanding? What if such a thing happened to you?"

Franella pulled a large white handkerchief from her skirt pocket. It was one of several Miss Ruth had given her before she left Sitka. She blew her nose and said, "It did."

Kay was relentless until Franella shared every detail of her childhood. They cried together, and Kay offered to pray for her.

"You sound like Miss Ruth. She prays all the time." Franella shrugged. "You can pray if you want."

As Kay's prayer droned on, Franella tried to pay attention but failed. She pulled back the blanket and tracked the clouds journeying across the gray sky.

"And thank you for bringing this Not-a-Scot here to be my friend. Amen," Kay said. She jumped up and gathered Franella into a suffocating hug.

Franella felt her heart accelerate and tried not to let her body stiffen. After a few seconds, she carefully maneuvered herself out of the embrace. "I'll disappoint you. I haven't had much experience being a friend."

"Don't worry. I will overlook your broken fences," Kay laughed.

"Huh?"

"My Irish grandmother always said a friend overlooks your broken fence and admires the flowers in your garden."

"I don't have a garden, much less flowers."

"My dear Franella, your soul is full of Alaska's beautiful wild-flowers. I imagine they sprout up along trails, in mountain meadows, beneath mossy trees and fallen logs, under huge forest ferns. I think your mind keeps building fences and walls. I'm determined to break them down. And if I can't, with God's help, I will climb over them to get to those blossoms."

Franella shook her head. "I wish you luck."

"I have found two four-leaf clovers in my life."

284

What does that mean?"

"It means, despite your doubt, we are going to be pals—with Georgine, too." Kay's freckles popped as a delightful grin spread over her face and filled her mischievous green eyes.

FORTY-FOUR

Georgine avoided the study group for several weeks, although the other girls often saw her around campus or in the back of the lecture hall. When she finally returned, Kay welcomed her in her friendly, chatty way.

"Georgine, are you ever going to write your papers?" Franella asked.

"It's all so boring. I can't seem to force myself."

"What are you interested in?" Kay asked.

"Not any of my classes, that's for sure."

Franella folded her hands across her chest and looked at the society girl. "What do you talk about with your friends?" That will tell you where your interests lie."

Georgine sat up straighter, smoothed the creases from her skirt, and twirled the pearl ring on her finger. "Now that the war's over, I'm hoping the fashion houses in Paris will become more productive. It was so grim throughout the war, with everyone who volunteered for the war effort wearing ugly military styles. Some of my friends had uniforms made, complete with epaulets. Hideous! Nylons were impossible to get," Georgine moaned.

"Unless you knew an American soldier," Kay grinned.

"And did you?" Georgine looked at the other girl with interest.

"She runs to the post office after class every day. Haven't you seen all the letters with a Wisconsin postmark? Oh, that's right, you're never here or you would have noticed," Franella said.

"The subject under discussion is how to get Georgine to relate her interests to her classes, not my love life," Although Kay's tone was light, her face was as bright as a berry.

"There's a lot of cows in Wisconsin. I bet Maeve would love it there," Franella teased.

Georgine took pity on the still blushing Kay and quickly said, "I really need a couple of serious shopping trips. My wardrobe is a mess."

"But Georgine, I've never seen you wear the same outfit twice. You have so many lovely clothes," Kay said.

"When you are part of society, it is important how you look. It shows who you are."

Kay wrinkled her nose, "The only thing my Irish grandmother said about clothes was it's comforting to be warmly clad in winter. My mama made over Granny's tweed coat to fit me."

"That's hardly what I meant," Georgine sniffed.

Franella had been grinning wildly. Now she burst out laughing. She pressed her arms against her sides. Tears rolled down her cheeks. The roaring laughter gave her the hiccups. Both girls looked at her in amazement.

Kay joined in the laughter but said, "I don't know why I'm laughing."

Georgine frowned, "Are you laughing at me?"

Franella shook her head as she tried to control herself. Between hiccups and a few more chuckles, she said, "I was picturing you in front of the donation closet." At Georgine's questioning look, Franella explained, "The good people of Sitka donated their cast-off clothing to the orphanage. Most were worn and patched, some smelly and stained, and none too clean. Major Bernice was no seamstress and wasn't too concerned about a proper fit."

Georgine shuddered, "I don't think I could wear anyone else's clothes. They're...they're..." She shuddered again.

"I could. As long as it's clean. I'm a whizz with needle and thread just like my Irish..."

"Grandmother!" the other two girls finished the sentence for her.

Franella's laughter faded as she remembered the rejection and jeers from the kids in Sitka. Their taunts still had the power to hurt. Her ill-fitting attire was either a source of amusement or derision. The adults usually looked at her with pity, if they looked at her at all. She bent her head over her paper and tried to push the images and the feelings away.

Georgine, tall, slim, blond, and lovely, was always elegantly clothed. She moved graciously and spoke in modulated cultured tones. Franella bit the inside of her cheek and pushed down the prickle of envy. Georgine seemed perfect when she wasn't being the pretentious, high-society-bored debutante. She was intelligent and could do the work if she chose to. Franella gnawed on her bottom lip and said, "I had a thought, Georgine. Why don't you write your paper on the influence clothes have on society for our Language, Culture, and Communications course?"

"On individuals, too," Kay said.

Georgine's eyes sparked, "What do you mean?"

"You said that many women took to wearing military-type fashion during the war. Why would they do that? What were they trying to say? How did it make them feel? Did they start issuing orders? Talk like soldiers?"

"I wouldn't wear a ball gown to muck out Maeve's stall," Kay said. "I wear a ragged pair of my brother's trousers and my Da's old Fair Isle sweater."

"And I wouldn't wear that outfit to a ball. It would make me feel out of place and extremely uncomfortable. They would probably deny me entrance."

"My Irish grandmother always said, if you put silk on a goat, it's still a goat," Kay said.

"Not in the world I live in. At least that's what Aunt Eleanor thinks."

"What do you mean?" Franella asked.

"She says society is full of old goats and shrewish women, but nobody looks beyond their elegant and fashionable clothes. I'm telling you, if you dress the part, that's all people see."

It's a good thing our Lord looks at the heart," Kay said.

"I can attest to that," Franella admitted, although she was not talking about the Lord looking at her heart, "Miss Ruth and Miss Drake bought me some clothes from the Monkey Wards catalog, new ones. It made me feel less like an outcast."

"Monkey Wards? Catalog?" Georgine swallowed and averted her eyes, "Yes, well, very nice."

"It was!" Franella remembered the impromptu fashion show she had given the two spinster ladies.

Georgine rubbed her hands. "I think I might be able to come up with a thesis. Will you girls help me when it's time to prove it?"

"Sure, we will," Kay answered for herself and Franella. Neither one suspected what that would entail.

FORTY-FIVE

The study sessions fell into a routine of sorts; Georgine's attendance was sporadic, and she seldom participated in group studies, except to ask for help with her own projects. Kay was happy to oblige, but Franella fumed that Georgine wasn't doing her share yet expected help whenever she asked.

"But you promised." Georgine said, "It will be fun."

"I didn't promise, and it won't be fun," Franella sighed.

I said we'd help her, remember? You didn't disagree," Kay said.

"If you don't come, it's like you're going back on your word," Georgine snapped.

"I'm not a liar!" Franella fumed, wondering how she could avoid the whole situation. "Take Kay. That will be enough to prove your thesis."

"We'll have to work on your accent. You sound positively provincial," Georgine said to the Irish girl.

Kay stretched to her full height, raised her chin, and looked down her nose at the other two girls, "I assure you, I can sound as posh and blue-blooded as the best of them."

Georgine laughed and said, "I don't sound like that!"

Franella rolled her eyes, clamped her lips together, and didn't say anything.

"Can you do an American accent?" Georgine wanted to know.

Kay proved that she could. Georgine clapped her hands and

said, "That's wonderful! You'll both be Americans. That way, people will make allowances when you use the wrong fork or spoon."

"Just what do you have planned, and why would we use the wrong utensil?" Franella's eyes flashed.

"We are going to a Thanksgiving dinner at the American Embassy, and since it's a six-course dinner there will be at least fifteen pieces of silverware at each place setting."

"Fifteen?" Franella exclaimed, "I'm not going!"

"Turkey, mashed potatoes and gravy, and cornbread stuffing, whatever that is," Georgine said, "Where else are you going to find a real American Thanksgiving dinner in England."

"Please, Franella. We said we'd help her," Kay said.

"And I will help you," Georgine promised, "We'll go to my home this weekend. I'm sure I can find something in my closet for both of you. If not, we'll go shopping."

"You forget, Georgine, that Kay and I are on very tight budgets."

Georgine blushed, surprise crawling across her face, "I'm sorry. Didn't I make it clear? This is my treat. You can borrow my ball gowns if they fit. I'll buy high heels for each of you, and my Auntie will supply jewelry and mink stoles."

"Does your Auntie know that we are not," Kay bit her lip, "upper class?"

"She was a suffragette and is the least class-conscious of anyone you will ever know. She is delighted that you girls are going to dress up and fool all the diplomats, aristocrats, and others who think they are God's gift to England. Kay, can you keep up your American accent for a whole evening?"

"Sure. I'm more worried about which fork to use."

"Remember to start from the outside in or just watch me.

You'll be fine," Georgine said, "I hope this will prove my thesis that the clothes you wear impact how others perceive you. Most of the time, they don't look beyond to see the person within."

"Shades of Pygmalion!" Franella exclaimed.

FORTY-SIX

The limousine picked up the three college students on Friday afternoon after classes. After trying on ball gowns, which delighted Kay and made Franella uncomfortable, they left the large manor house. The chauffeur drove them across the valley. They arrived at Georgine's Great-aunt Eleanor's in time for tea.

"I still can't believe we left all your clothes strewn across your bedroom," Kay said.

Georgine shrugged, "The maid will take care of it."

"My mama would have my hide," Kay said.

Georgine's voice was flat and she looked out the window as she spoke, "As you noticed, neither of my parents were there. They never are."

Kay patted the girl's hand. Franella surprised herself by wondering if Georgine was lonely. She saw herself in that vast mansion, surrounded by servants but no parents. She shuddered and almost felt sorry for the society girl.

Franella's isolated island life had not prepared her for such luxuries. She was used to oil slickers and rubber boots, not ball gowns and limousines. Life was easier when she lived in her books. She chewed on the end of her thumb and wished the weekend was over.

A man-servant opened the door, took their luggage, and sent them to the drawing room.

"This is just like the movies," Kay said as her neck arched and she stared at the ornate chandelier and gold-framed family portraits.

"It's more like a mausoleum if you ask me," said the stylish older woman as she pushed a tea trolley into the room.

"Auntie," Georgine said, "You have a maid to serve tea!"

"I'm perfectly capable of pushing a tea trolley into the room. Besides, Molly is helping cook. We are having a six-course dinner tonight. Practice, you know." She smiled and said, "Introduce me to your friends."

"The short, freckled one is Kay."

"The Irish girl with the cow?" Aunt Eleanor offered her hand.

"Yes, ma'am," Kay resisted the urge to curtsy.

"And you must be Franella, the wild Alaska girl," Aunt Eleanor said.

Franella glared at Georgine. "Yes, Lady Eleanor."

"I meant it as a compliment, so don't disparage Georgine with that look. In fact, that is one of the things we are going to practice this weekend."

"What's that, Lady Eleanor?" Kay asked, "Glaring? Franella is really good at that, and it usually comes with a barb."

Franella glared. Kay grinned and pointed. Before the Alaska girl could say anything, Lady Eleanor took each one's elbow and led them to the brocade settee. "All of you girls can call me Auntie. We are going to have a great time. But first, we have a lot of work to do."

Eleanor served the tea and made polite small talk as the girls sampled the delicate pastries and cucumber sandwiches. When they had finished, Aunt Eleanor asked, "Did any of you notice anything?"

Kay shook her head. Georgine remained quiet with her hands folded in her lap. Franella looked from one girl to the other and, before she could stop herself, blurted, "The food was good, but the conversation was inane."

"Exactly. Did you notice, my dear, that every time you tried to say anything interesting or significant, I deflected and led the conversation back to banal and insipid subjects?"

"Why did you do that? I was so frustrated," Franella bit the words off and spit them out one by one.

"Because that is exactly the type of conversation you are going to have at the embassy dinner. We don't want to speak of anything that people may have strong opinions about: how the war was managed, the severe rationing still in place, the troubles the veterans faced when they returned, how to rebuild, and so forth. Everyone wants to have a pleasant time. I suspect it's going to be difficult for you." She turned to Kay, "What about you, Miss Ireland?"

Kay laughed, and her eyes sparkled, "It's going to be great fun. I can talk about nothing for hours if I put my mind to it. I'll be an actress in a play. The Best Thanksgiving Dinner Ever. How's that for a title?" Georgine and Aunt Eleanor smiled, but Franella glowered.

"It sounds deceitful and arduous. I feel like a liar already. I don't think I can do it," Franella said.

Georgine poured another cup of tea and gulped the entire cup, "Of course, you can, you promised." She held out the dainty cup, and her aunt poured more of the fragrant amber liquid.

"My dear niece, you have brought some excitement into this old lady's life. As I said, we have a lot to do, my dears. Let's get to it."

FORTY-SEVEN

Dear Miss Ruth,

It wasn't the best Thanksgiving ever! It was a disaster! For me, at least. Kay was the Belle of the Ball and had a wonderful time. She really could be an actress! She looked like a debutante but convinced everyone she was the daughter of the largest and richest rancher in West Texas. She described rodeos, cattle drives, and bar-b-ques. She even had some ridiculous stories about cow punching, as if anyone would punch a cow. It was amazing to watch.

Georgine and I were farther down the table. Aunt Eleanor sat across from us. She asked me question after question. I knew she was trying to draw me out. Georgine glared at me and whispered through clenched teeth that I wasn't holding up my end of the bargain. She even pinched my thigh. When I yelped and everyone looked in our direction, she smiled sweetly and patted my hand. It was horrible!

You know how I shut down or run when I'm overwhelmed. I stared at the silverware, unable to speak. I had memorized the order of the courses and which fork to use. That was not the issue. It was Georgine and the curious glances and stares from those at the table. After the appetizer, I was ready to run out of the room, and I suspect Lady Eleanor knew it.

She motioned for a waiter to come over and whispered to him. He approached the ambassador at the head of the table, who raised his eyebrows, looked our way, and gave a slight nod. The waiter then escorted us to a private sitting room. I am writing our conversation exactly as it happened:

"Why are we here? Don't misunderstand; I'm more comfortable here than in that huge dining room," I said.

"That's precisely why, my dear. We should never have put you in this position. I blame myself."

I reached across the table and took Lady Eleanor's hand. "Please don't blame yourself. I shouldn't have let myself be talked into it. I knew I couldn't handle it, but tell me, what did you whisper to the waiter?"

"I told him I felt faint and asked him to make my excuses to the ambassador. I asked for a room where my companion and I could enjoy our meal as soon as I recovered myself."

Of course, there was nothing wrong with her; she was kind enough to rescue me. We waited for twenty minutes, then she peeked out of the door, saw a passing servant, and instructed him to set up a table and serve us. He stammered and stalled, but she just looked at him with the expectation that she would be obeyed. To tell the truth, I've often seen that look on your face as well. It's very effective.

"The ambassador said we were to have our dinner here, and so we shall." Lady Eleanor said, closing the door.

As we ate our dinner, she asked so many questions about my life that I felt like she could write my biography. She said I've inspired her to journey to Alaska, one more adventure before she dies. Perhaps you will meet her one day.

I miss you and everyone and especially my Alaska.

Franella

Constance Penrose had a cozy fire in the small fireplace that warmed the room. The tea was hot and fragrant, as usual. Franella looked forward to the English tea during their weekly tutoring sessions.

"What flavor?" she asked.

"Your favorite, Earl Grey."

Mr. Darcy, who purred in front of the grate, jumped up when he heard Franella's voice. Soon, he was settled in her lap, enjoying the absent-minded petting she gave him.

"Before we discuss your studies, let's talk about your weekend at the American Embassy," Miss Penrose said, pouring tea into the delicate bone china cup and placing two tiny shortbread cookies on the saucer.

"I'm sure you heard all about it. Georgine has spread her version of events throughout Somerville Hall."

"Has she been malicious or incorrect?" She said, handing the tea to Franella.

Franella almost blurted out a vehement yes, but she was not a liar. She put her head in her hands for a moment and then looked up at Miss Penrose. "I stepped on her hem as we entered, causing her to stumble. She fell into the side of the ambassador from Luxembourg, causing him to spill his drink. She was mortified. A few moments later, I felt something irritating in my eye. I forgot I was wearing those fancy elbow-length gloves. After rubbing my eyes, there was mascara smeared on my face and the gloves. Georgine drug me to the nearest powder room and tried to repair the damage, lecturing me all the while. Things went downhill after that."

"Oh, dear." Miss Penrose set her teacup on its saucer and took Franella's hand. "I'm so sorry."

"Aside from all my embarrassing mishaps, I didn't do anything to help her prove her thesis. But I don't think that was a bad thing. The thesis was flawed, and I had told her that."

Miss Penrose sipped her tea thoughtfully, "How so?"

"Georgine thinks clothes make the woman, but that's not true, as my lack of success proved. I told her it's the woman inside the clothes that counts."

"Perhaps it's a combination of the two," Miss Penrose said, re-filling her cup. She nodded toward Franella's empty cup.

Franella shook her head and continued, "Both Kay and I were dressed like the upper classes. We had lessons in deportment and etiquette. Kay pulled it off beautifully. Everyone was enthralled with this so-called cowboy princess. She was accepted and admired. I was another story." Franella shook her head and smiled sadly, "Professor Higgins would have thrown me back into the gutter."

Constance Penrose drew her brows together and chose her words carefully. "Georgine is devastated. I tried to help her modify her thesis, but she is too angry to think right now. In fact, she insists that I put her in a different study group."

"She hasn't spoken to me since Thanksgiving, and I don't think she will ever forgive me for not meeting her expectations, although, in my defense, I told her I was not a liar and couldn't pull it off."

"Ordinarily, I would not consider Georgine's request, but her parents are generous benefactors and have donated thousands of pounds to the school."

"They can't make you give in to her demands."

"Unfortunately, they can." Miss Penrose set her teacup on

the table and picked up her notepad. "That's just the way the world works."

"Miss Penrose, may I confess something to you?" Franella gnawed on the end of her thumb. At her tutor's nod, Franella stuffed her hand behind her and took a deep breath. "I knew the intellectual challenges here in Oxford would be great, but I knew I could handle them. It's the cultural distinctions I miscalculated. I don't mean the general differences between America and Britain, but the unspoken rules. There seems to be some kind of social code among students like Georgine."

"I'll brew another pot of tea as you try to explain what you mean."

Franella absorbed the comfort of the tutor's room. The British décor was nothing like Miss Ruth's cabin, homespun and cozy, amid towering trees on the edge of Sitka, but it had the same comforting atmosphere. If it wasn't the architecture or the furnishings, it must be the women themselves. *I wish you were here, Miss Ruth. I think you and Constance Penrose are kindred spirits. I feel comfortable, almost at home, with both of you.*

"Everything is so foreign to me. There are too many expectations, and most of them are unsaid. That's not really fair," Franella said.

Miss Penrose nodded and poured more tea. "I have noticed that most of the scholarship girls seem to have trouble adapting. They keep to themselves."

Franella accepted another cup of tea. Her mouth had gone dry, and she gulped it down, nearly scalding the inside of her mouth.

Miss Penrose tilted her head and quietly asked, "What about Kay?"

Franella laughed, "She seems to be the exception to the rule. She truly doesn't seem to recognize class distinctions or even the various groups or cliques. She just plows ahead, assuming everyone will like her, and they do. I wish I had her confidence."

"Oxford must seem like another planet to you. Not only have you traveled halfway around the world, but you have also come from an isolated small town to an ancient and very large city."

"If it weren't for Kay, I would bury myself in my studies and ignore everyone and everything else."

Miss Penrose, serene in her tweed suit and a simple strand of pearls, smiled, "Precisely. Now, where are you on this week's assignment?"

Franella changed the subject every time Kay brought up the embassy dinner or Georgine's abandonment. Finally, the Irish girl plopped a whole bag of lemon drops on the table and said, "Eat up. I'm going to have my say. You are my friend, and Georgine is my friend. She refuses to be anywhere near you, and that breaks my heart. I won't let her speak ill of you in my presence. I will remain friends with both of you, although I hate that I have to see you separately."

Franella started to speak, but Kay said, "I'm not finished. It's been two weeks, and you have got to stop hiding."

"I'm not."

"You come into lectures a few minutes after they begin, sit in the back row, and leave right before they end. You don't attend any of the optional lectures or concerts. I'm grateful that you still come to our study sessions, but you've lost your enthusiasm. Your studies don't bring you joy anymore. You're miserable."

Franella couldn't meet Kay's eyes.

"I'm your friend, Franella, and I won't give up on you. I know it's hard, and you think everyone believes Georgine and is judging you."

"Georgine is right. I let her down. Ruined her thesis. I failed."

"You tried to tell her several times you couldn't pull off pretending to be someone you're not. You told both of us. It's us who let you down, Franella. I hope you can forgive us."

Franella shook her head. She had not thought of it like that.

"And I hope you can forgive Georgine for not making peace with you. You'll feel better if you do."

"She hasn't asked, and I don't think she ever will."

"That doesn't matter. Do it for your own inner peace. And another thing: you can't hide in your room forever. My shift at the Eagle and Child is starting soon. The other waitress is ill, and they are desperate for someone to fill in."

"I don't feel up to it."

"My Irish grandmother always said a good laugh and a long sleep are the two best cures. I suspect you've been sleeping a lot?"

Franella reluctantly said she had.

"All right then, time for a laugh. It's Tuesday; the Inklings will be there for lunch."

"Who?"

"Several literature professors and a few others. I've heard they meet in Professor Lewis's room at Magdalen on Thursdays and read passages of their writings aloud. They continue their discussions at the Bird and Baby during Tuesday lunch. It's quite interesting. That is, if you like myth, fantasy, and such, which I don't," Kay laughed as she shrugged into her coat.

"But I…"

"Those discussions sometimes become animated, especially when Lewis and Tolkien go at it. Put your coat on; it's only three-tenths of a mile, American. We'll be refreshed by a nice brisk walk in the cold, my dear, Not-a-Scot."

FORTY-EIGHT

Kay introduced Franella to the harried manager, Phineas Brumley, and told him Franella had worked at an exclusive gentlemen's club in Chicago, America.

"I'll not pay extra for that," he chewed on his mustache.

"She doesn't expect you to," Kay said while Franella stood mute beside her.

"Fine. Fine. Get her kitted out. I have no time." He rushed past them with the silverware cart.

Kay took the reluctant Franella to the staff room and handed her a uniform. As she scrambled into it, Franella said, "The age of these old buildings just amazes me. You said it was built in the 16th century and has been a pub ever since. Fantastic."

Kay nodded. "I'll take the main room. The lunch crowd is usually university students, rude and rowdy. You can take the backroom. It's usually just the Inklings, although sometimes a few others like to eat there. The Inklings will be so busy talking, they won't notice if you are slow or inaccurate with their orders."

"Is there a menu I can look at?"

"It's written above the bar. Let's go."

The dark wainscoting and dim lighting of the back room created an Irish pub atmosphere in the place. At least, that's what Kay said. Franella thought it was dark and rather gloomy. She took the men's lunch orders and served them silently. This group of literary men refrained from engaging in gossip, politics, or discussing current events. The conversation was nothing like what she had heard in the Sitka Café or the Windy City Gentleman's Club. Franella marveled at the snippets of conversations these grown men were having about fairies and dragons, enchanted forests and castles, heroes and villains, good and evil. They spoke as if everything was real. She tried to circle back to their table without being noticed. The way these academics interacted with myth and fantasy was new to her.

Some of what she heard reminded her of the stories Johnny the Bear Boy shared. Franella wondered if these British academics were familiar with Tlingit and Yupik legends.

Tuesdays at the Eagle and Child became her favorite part of the week. These men could vehemently disagree with each other, criticize each other's literary efforts, and still raise a glass as friends and colleagues.

As the two girls walked back to Somerville Hall, Franella asked, "Do you think Mr. Brumley will hire me permanently? I only want to work when the Inklings are there."

Kay laughed, "You find those old academics interesting, do you?"

Franella nodded. "I haven't sorted them all out yet. The one with the long face and a pipe permanently clamped between his teeth—."

"That would be Professor Tolkien."

"He's having an intense discussion with the one who is rather portly and always looks rumpled—."

"Professor Lewis."

"Thanks for naming them. Anyway, Professor Lewis seems to be a former atheist, and the others are trying to convince him of the veracity of Christianity."

"Hmm."

"He can accept a deity but said he doesn't get the whole sacrifice thing, which is foundational to the religion, but the others talked about all the sacrifices for the good of others in the Icelandic and Norse myths, even some Germanic ones, I think."

"Hmm." Kay stopped to look into a shop window. "Cute shoes."

"Kay! This is important! Pay attention!"

Kay smiled and took her friend's arm, and they continued on their way. "I'm listening."

"I missed a lot of the conversation. I can only refill their teacups so many times. I heard the long-faced one, Tolkien, say that Professor Lewis should think of myth as truth, and so they discussed the merits of that. Professor Lewis said he could possibly accept that the Christian myth was a true myth, one that really happened."

"My Irish grandmother always said all true is God's truth, no matter where you find it."

"They aren't finished with the conversation, and I need to be there to hear the rest."

"You want to be a mouse in their pocket?"

Franella stopped and questioned her friend, "Don't tell me your Irish grandmother said that. What does it mean?"

"Aye, she did. It means if you really want to understand someone, you should be as close and as quiet as a mouse in their pocket.

Watch and learn."

"That's exactly what I'm going to do if Mr. Brumley cooperates and gives me a permanent part-time job."

"I'm sure he will. I heard that Darcie, the other waitress, is quite ill," Kay said.

"And I'm going to read all the Norse myths I find in Somerville's library. I also want to explore the meaning of the word 'myth'. The Inklings are fascinated with it and seem to think it has a deeper meaning, something other-worldly. Intriguing, don't you think?"

"If I had time to read for fun, I'd pick a good romance every time."

Mr. Brumley cooperated and hired Franella when Darcie returned home mid-term to recover from her illness. Franella offered to always serve the Inklings, and since she never made a mistake on the orders, he agreed.

Several weeks later, as the two girls were studying, Franella said, "I'm going to do it, Kay." She sucked on a lemon drop.

"My dear Not-a-Scot, these men are brilliant academics and authors. I don't think it's wise to do anything that makes them notice you." She shivered and reached for the bright yellow candy. "Mr. Brumley likes you because you are efficient and don't talk to the customers."

Franella laughed and said, "I learned the hard way at the Windy City Gentleman's Club. I'll tell you all about it, but not today."

"Tonight then, after our tutoring sessions. I can't wait."

"Can I borrow Georgine's typewriter to transcribe a story about Raven and Eagle? I'm sure the Inklings would be interested. I'll casually place it on the table before they arrive next Tuesday. Better yet, you set the papers there."

"Me?"

"That way, if they ask me if I put them there, I can shake my head."

"You are becoming quite devious, even if you're not a liar," Kay laughed, "But if you are determined to do this, be strategic."

"What do you mean?"

"Michaelmas is almost over, and the next term, Hilary, won't start for several weeks. The college closes down over the break. If you want the Inklings to consider your stories seriously, it's best you wait until after Christmas."

Dear Franella,

I am pleased your Irish friend has invited you home for the Christmas holidays. I pray you will relax and let the joy of the season flow over you. It is a wonderful thing to celebrate the dear Savior's birth, and I look forward to hearing all about it.

Your letters are always interesting and full of delightful descriptions of where you are and what you are experiencing. I sense the Lord is doing a work in you, even if you can't see it.

I must confess that Sam Mitchell has often asked after you, and I let him see portions of your letters. That's all Sam needed. He published several articles about your adventures, and the people of Sitka are enthralled.

Because of Sam's articles, they now see you as Sitka's one and only genius. And of course, the men of the Sitka Café are taking the credit. Ivan thinks it was his idea to send you to England, not so much to be educated, but to straighten out the British. He says you should stop in Washington, DC, on your way back to Alaska. There is a lot to be straightened out there, he says.

Ade Bunderson takes full credit for making you a resident of Sitka since he brought you here so many years ago. No mention is made of Major Bernice or the troubles and gossip you experienced. The staff at Sitka High School says it was their educational instruction that brought out your intelligence. Sean Conner and I just keep our lips together, but we're laughing inside. He envies your Christmas in Ireland. He dearly loved his time there so many years ago.

People have such distorted opinions of themselves and of the past. All that to say is, the people of Sitka now claim you as one of their own. They now delight in what they call your smart, brilliant quirkiness. I can imagine your snorting as you read this!

Everyone wonders when you are coming home and what you will do with your life. Of course, they all have different ideas.

Sam says he's going to write and offer you a job as his overseas correspondent. You can write anything you want, and he will publish it! I hope you take him up on the offer. I told him to include a list of possible subjects, just to get you started.

Bob Nelles has bought another small plane and hired a pilot. His name is Jacob, a nice young man from somewhere in the Midwest. He's tall. I rarely meet anyone I have to look up to, so it's nice. If the weather cooperates, he'll fly me to the Pribilofs. I'll spend Christmas with Heaven Ray and her family. I'm planning to convince Jacob to stay and celebrate with us since he has no family here in Alaska.

Merry Christmas, my dear. I look forward to the day you graduate and come home. I don't know what your future holds, but I have a sense it will be here in Alaska.

Much love,

Miss Ruth

"Thank you for coming to tea, Georgine. I've missed you." Kay nudged the teapot across the table. "You pour while I cut the soda bread." Kay glanced toward the other girl as she carefully sliced and buttered the bread. "I'm excited to spend Christmas with my family. I'd like you to come."

"Is she going to be there?"

Kay looked away and gnawed on her bottom lip. Franella had quickly accepted her invitation, saying it was impossible for her to return to Alaska for Christmas.

"I'll come, Kay, but only if Franella doesn't." Georgine's cup rattled in the saucer as she set it down more firmly than she intended.

"I've invited her, and she has accepted. Can't you forgive her, Georgine? She's sorry she let you down." Kay pleaded.

Georgine stuffed her nail file back into her purse. "I think she planned it. She's never liked me. I know she wanted to spoil my project. She never believed in my thesis."

"I'm sorry you feel that way," Kay said. "Can you put aside your anger over Christmas? My family would love to have both of you visit." That wasn't entirely true. The letter Kay had recently received from her mother had expressed concerns about having a rich society girl in their humble home. They had no reservations about a poor village girl from the wilds of Alaska. Nevertheless, Kay was determined to bring the two young women together. "Don't you want to meet Maeve? I'll teach you to milk her," Kay said.

Georgine shuddered. "I've had offers to go skiing in San Moritz or vacationing on the coast of Mallorca."

"What about your family?"

"My parents are touring Australia. Aunt Eleanor always has Christmas in Scotland with her dead husband's relatives." Georgine sniffed, straightened her shoulders, and attempted a smile.

Kay blinked rapidly, then smiled, "Christmas with my family is the most fun you will ever have, Georgine. I promise."

"It won't be fun if Franella is there." Georgine's eyes grew hard. "That's all I have to say about it."

Kay felt like stomping her foot. Instead, she took a deep breath and said, "My Irish grandmother always said—may you never forget what is worth remembering, or remember what is best forgotten."

"What's that supposed to mean?"

"You'll have to come to Ireland to find out."

"The train is approaching Paddington station. We'll have to change trains to connect to Holyhead in Wales. After that, it's a ferry across the sea to Dublin.'

"I've missed the smell of the sea; thank you, Kay, for taking pity on this lost Alaska girl," Franella said.

"The train ride is over nine or ten hours, so you see both the English and Welsh countryside. The ferry takes approximately five hours. I'm afraid you won't see much. We'll reach Dublin after midnight."

"I've spent many a dark night on a boat. I love the sea."

Kay led the way to the next train. The conductor punched their tickets and directed them to their car.

"In America, the train cars have a door at each end, and the seats are arranged in rows like a bus. I much prefer the English style with outside doors to each small compartment. No crowds, no vying for the best seats, no fuss."

Kay laid her suitcase on the seat and said, "I'm just going to pick up your Christmas present and a few snacks. I won't be long."

Franella held up a canvas carry-all. "But Mr. Brumley packed meat pies and apples."

"Train travel makes me hungry."

Kay bought a package of biscuits, some crisps, and a small Paddington bear, Franella's gift.

"There you are, Kay. I looked for you everywhere. Have you got my ticket?"

Kay turned and saw Georgine's two suitcases, overnight case, and fancy hatbox. The elegant young woman wore a fur coat and high heels. Kay pulled the ticket out of her coat pocket and handed it to Georgine, who looked at the ticket and said, said, "We had better hurry; we only have six minutes to board."

"You have time to buy a snack; the track is close by."

"Are you sure?"

Kay nodded, and Georgine bought a tin of Turkish Delight as a shrill whistle blew.

"That's our train. Let's go!" Kay picked up one of Georgine's suitcases and her overnight case and ran.

"Wait!" Georgine yelled. "I thought we had time. You said the track was close."

"Not that close. Hurry!" Kay did not slow her pace or turn around.

Georgine's high heels clacked, and she sputtered as she ran after Kay. "Wait! My luggage is too heavy. Where's a porter? My feet hurt. I can't run in heels."

Georgine, panting, was several yards behind when Kay pulled open the door to the compartment and climbed in, partially hampered by the heavy suitcase. Franella saw her grab the doorframe and lean out as the train chugged and slowly began moving. The whistle shrieked.

"Wait! Don't leave me!" Georgine yelled.

"Hurry!"

The wheels spun, the train moved faster, and Georgine, eyes wide, forced herself to give one last spurt.

"Hang on to me, Franella. I need to lean farther!" Kay grabbed Georgine's suitcase and pushed it behind her. Then held out her hand for the girl herself.

Georgine, out of breath, stumbled into the compartment and dropped her hatbox. She plopped into the seat and kicked off her heels. She rubbed her feet for a moment, then stood, took off her coat, and threw it on the opposite seat. "You! What are you doing here?"

Franella picked up the coat, which had landed in her lap, and handed it to the distraught girl. "I'm going to Ireland for Christmas. Same as you." Franella kept her voice calm, although the acid in her stomach began to rise.

Georgine turned angry eyes to Kay. "I thought she—never mind!" Georgine's chest rose and fell rapidly as she tried to calm herself. "I told you I wanted nothing to do with her!"

Franella had several angry retorts ready, one for Georgine and two for Kay, but when she looked at Kay, who couldn't mask the hurt in her eyes, she remained quiet.

"You'll have a wonderful time in Ireland, Georgine. I promise. Please don't be mad." Kay wrung her hands.

"How soon will we arrive in Holyhead? I intend to turn right around and head back to London."

"It will take all day and into the evening before we arrive," Kay said.

"You'll just have to make the best of it," Franella said.

"I'm not talking to you," Georgine said, opening her tin of Turkish Delight and pulling several fashion magazines from her chic, vellum hatbox. She didn't say another word until the train pulled into Holyhead Station.

Georgine gathered her things and stormed off of the train without speaking. She stood on the platform, looking for the ticket office.

"There's our Kay!"

"I see her!"

The two cheerful young men were neither tall nor short. Neither thin nor stout, but both were pleasant looking, even handsome in a redheaded, Irish sort of way. They surrounded Kay.

"Put me down, Finn," she demanded.

"As soon as I put you down, little sister, Paddy is sure to pick you up. Isn't that right, brother?"

"Aye, it is, although these two pretty colleens look like they want to be picked up and hugged. What say, brother?"

"Certainly not!" Franella's face was bright red, and she backed up a step. Georgine, on the other hand, stepped forward and smiled, "Is that a typical Gaelic welcome?"

"Aye, it is," Paddy laughed. He picked up Georgine and twirled her around twice before setting her down. "Welcome to Ireland. We won't hold it against you that you're British."

"What are you boys doing here?" Kay demanded.

"Da didn't want you driving across Ireland without a man."

"I thought you'd meet us at the Dublin terminal."

"We love you enough to spend over five hours crossing the sea and then another five back again."

Kay turned to her friends, "I love them to death even though they haven't got the sense of a toad."

"We brought a deck of cards and a sack of dominoes."

"Forget that. I want to hear the pipes," Kay said, looking at the bag near Paddy's feet.

"Bagpipes? I love bagpipes," Franella clapped her hands.

Paddy put his hands on his hips and stared at Franella, although he directed his remarks to Kay. "Have you taught this American nothing, sister dear? Bagpipes, indeed."

Kay laughed and punched her brother on the arm. "Leave my friends alone, you big oaf." She explained to Franella that Irish bag-pipes are called Uilleann pipes.

"Sweeter and softer than those offensive Scottish things," Finn said, "We will entertain you all the way across the Irish Sea like the lovely lads we are."

"Finn sings as well as Paddy plays."

Paddy laid his hand over his heart, "I'm grieved, dear sister."

"Are you alright?" Georgine opened her purse. "I have some headache powder and ginger pills for stomach upsets."

Finn laughed, "It's just his feelings that area hurt. Kay knows Paddy doesn't sing as well as I do."

"But you can't play the pipes and sing at the same time," Georgine said.

"I can, and I do, my charming English lass. You'll see." Paddy doffed his hat and bowed, "I thank you for your concern about my well-being."

"The Irish pipes are fueled by bellows under your elbow, so you're free to sing." Kay grabbed each brother by the arm, "Lead on, boys."

"And deprive myself of escorting these lovely ladies like the true Gaelic gentleman I am? I don't think so," Paddy disengaged himself from Kay and took each girl by the arm. "Allow me, ladies."

That one has kissed the Blarney Stone too many times, Franella thought, but allowed herself to be pulled along.

Crossing the Irish Sea was like visiting a pub. The melodic Irish pipes were played, and the boys sang the entire way. At one point, Kay snatched Finn's hat and placed it on the floor. By the time the ferry docked, the hat was full of coins.

FORTY-NINE

"Where's the ticket office? I need to return to England," Georgine said.

"That was the last ferry. The office is closed until morning. Why would you want to leave us when you've just arrived?" Paddy asked.

"She doesn't want to look at your granna face," Finn laughed.

"You're the granna one, brother," Paddy said.

"Now, boys, neither one of you is ugly, as we all can see. Behave yourselves."

Paddy led Georgine to a nearby bench. "Seriously, my dear, I wouldn't feel right leaving you alone all night in the ferry terminal. You're too tempting a creature for anyone who sees you."

Georgine sat up a little straighter and couldn't keep the smile from her eyes. Nevertheless, she said, "I really must return."

"You shall come home with us, and if you're not happy, I'll bring you back myself."

Georgine let herself be persuaded as Paddy pulled her to her feet and led them to the parking lot.

"That's our mode of transportation? There's not enough room for everyone." Georgine squeaked.

"I admit Da's old truck has seen better days," Kay said.

Finn opened the passenger door, "Paddy will drive. You two girls will ride with him. Kay and I will be cozy under blankets in the back of the truck."

"I threw in a couple of bales of hay before we left home. They'll be fine," Paddy assured Georgine.

Georgine fell asleep with her head resting on Paddy's shoulder. He put an arm around her to keep her from sliding forward and drove with one arm. He winked at Franella and whispered, "Shall I entertain you with Irish lore, or will it disturb your friend?"

"If you keep your voice low, I would love to hear whatever you know about Irish history."

The nearly four-hour drive to County Cork passed quickly for Franella. Paddy was a good storyteller, although for each story he told, he would demand that she answer a question about herself or Georgine. Franella's answers about herself were precise and as short as possible. When discussing Georgine, she tried to be as fair as possible. There was no need to tell Paddy about the disdain Georgine felt toward her.

It was near dawn when the truck pulled into the O'Malley farm. Kay and Finn had slept the entire journey, so after Mam had hugged everyone, she issued instructions like a military officer.

"Finn, you can do the milking. Kay, you can help. Maeve has been missing you." Kay didn't need any urging. She was anxious to see her brown-eyed Jersey friend. Finn grabbed an apple from the sideboard and sauntered after her. Mam told Paddy to take himself off to the barn as well and go to sleep.

"Mrs. O'Malley, you want your son to sleep in the barn?' Georgine asked.

"Worried about me, my sweet colleen?" Paddy winked.

Georgine's face warmed, and she bit her lips. Franella almost felt sorry for her.

"Pay him no mind. He only acts the fool when he really likes someone."

Georgine's blush deepened, and Franella rushed in to fill the awkward silence. "Thank you for allowing us to share your Christmas, Mrs. O'Malley."

"Call me Mam. Paddy and Finn have been sleeping in the barn ever since Kay came into her woman-time. The house only has two bedrooms, and Christmas was made to be shared."

"It is a lovely Irish cottage, Mrs. O'...er, Mam," Franella said.

The Irish woman nodded, "My mam always said there's no hearth like your own hearth."

"Kay's always talking about her Irish grandmother. I can't wait to meet her," Georgine said

Mrs. O'Malley smiled, "My mam died long before Kay was born."

"But she talks as if she knows her," Georgine stammered.

"Aye, she knows her." Mam bustled around the kitchen, setting the breakfast table.

"I apologize, Mrs. O'Malley. I seem to have put my foot in it."

"My mam always said when you slide down the banister of life, may the splinters never point the wrong way. Now, sit yourself down and eat. Then you'll have a good sleep. This one," she pointed to Franella, "seems half asleep already."

Franella nodded, "I didn't nap on the way. In fact, if you don't mind. I think I'd rather sleep now."

"Mr. O'Malley, turn yourself around and take this child up the stairs."

"I've just come down." He saw Franella sway and grab the back of her chair. "But I see she's nearly asleep on her feet. Where's her suitcase?"

"The boys ran them up."

"Come along, my dear," He took Franella's elbow and gently led her to the stairs.

Dinnertime was at noon. After the meal, Georgine asked Paddy if he had a ferry schedule.

"Are you unhappy then?" he asked.

"Not exactly. Your parents are lovely; it's just that—I can't stay."

"I said I'd take you to the ferry if you were unhappy. Let's save that four-hour drive to Dublin until tomorrow. If you're truly unhappy, I'll take you then," Paddy promised.

"Four hours? I didn't realize it was so far."

"How could you? You slept most of the way. I'm assuming it's because my shoulder made a wonderful pillow." Paddy winked, "No need to be embarrassed. It was my pleasure."

Georgine had a sarcastic reply and haughty look ready but realized she rather liked this brash Irish young man. She smiled widely, executed an exaggerated curtsey, and said, "I thank you for your gallantry, Sir Patrick."

"We are going to get along fine, my beautiful colleen," Paddy laughed.

Each evening during supper, Paddy asked Georgine what made her happy that day. Her answers were full of the ordinary: seeing the young calves and lambs dancing in the green pastures, watching Mam O'Malley weaving or doing rush work, learning to make soda bread, listening to Finn sing while Paddy played the pipes."

"What about my singing?" Paddy couldn't keep the laughter from his voice.

"You sing quite nicely, but Finn is a true Irish tenor."

Finn punched Paddy on the arm. "Hear that, brother? You sing quite nicely."

Georgine rushed in to finish her list amidst everyone's laughter, "...visiting the centuries-old local church, I even liked the cold, rainy bike rides around County Cork with all of you. I've always ridden horses, not bicycles."

Every evening, Paddy shared his plans for the next day, which were designed to keep Georgine from becoming unhappy.

"Christmas is three days away, and I still haven't done any shopping. I want to buy gifts for your family," Georgine said.

"We're happy to have you here. That's gift enough," Kay said.

Georgine glared.

Kay laughed and said, "For a minute, that glare looked just like Franella's."

"Humph!"

Mrs. O'Malley came into the small living room, drying her hands on a tea towel. "As soon as the morning milking is done tomorrow, the boys will take you to County Cork's Christmas Market."

"What about Franella?" Georgine asked, "Where is she anyway?"

"She's mucking out the barn with the boys. I know she already has her gifts, but it would be rude not to invite her," Kay said.

"If she already has her gifts, there's no need for her to go." Georgine fingered the pearls around her neck.

Kay sighed and asked her mother to put the kettle on. Once she left the room, Kay said, "I don't think anyone has noticed, but you haven't said one word to Franella directly since we boarded the train."

"And I don't intend to," Georgine frowned, "I don't want to talk about it."

"But Georgine, the one you're hurting the most is yourself."

"I don't want to talk about it!"

That evening at tea, which Franella called supper, Finn announced, "We'll leave early in the morning. I'm taking Franella up to Belleek. She wants to tour the pottery factory and buy something to take to friends when she returns to Alaska."

"You'll drop us at the market on your way?" Kay asked.

"Of course. I don't know when we will return, so you can catch a ride home with one of the neighbors."

Georgine smiled and said to Franella in a sugary voice, "I'm sure you'll have a wonderful time."

Franella looked startled but replied evenly, "I'm looking forward to seeing the scenery between here and there."

Later, when Franella had gone to help the boys with the evening milking, Kay said, "It was nice of you to speak to Franella."

Georgine frowned and said, "I forgot I was mad at her. I won't do it again."

Kay hugged the girl. "I'm proud of you, and I'm going to pray that you do forget again."

Georgine hung her head and turned away, but Kay saw a small smile trying to escape.

"Your brother is a happy-go-lucky fellow, isn't he?" Franella asked Finn after they dropped him and the girls off at the Christmas Market.

"He's very Irish."

"What do you mean?" Franella kept one eye on Finn, even though the lush green fields and craggy mountains vied for her attention as they traveled north.

"When Paddy is happy, he is very, very happy. When he's not, he can be melancholy, as heartbreakingly sad as the Irish ballads he sings."

"You Irish!" Franella chewed on her thumb and glanced sideways at Finn. She wondered if she had offended him. "I mean, your family isn't afraid of showing their feelings." She took a shuddering breath and asked, "Should I have said that?"

"Why not?" he laughed, "It's true."

"I've never been too sure what to say and not say."

"An intelligent woman like you? I've heard some of the conversations you've had with Da. Way above my head."

"Your Da is extremely well-read, and his mind is so agile."

"He and Paddy are the smart ones," Finn sighed.

"Shall I tell you what I think, Finn? Remember, I'm not comfortable with conversations of a personal nature, especially with people my own age."

"As my Irish grandmother always said, if God sends you down a stony path, may he give you strong shoes."

"Huh? What does that mean?"

He kept his eyes on the road and his hands on the wheel. "It means, dear girl, say what you need to say."

Franella took a deep breath. "It's true; you're not as smart as your father or brother." She saw his face redden, his mouth tighten, and his knuckles whitened as he gripped the steering wheel tightly. She hurried on, "Not as savvy when it comes to books, history, or even current events. But you are much brighter when it comes to determining what is wrong when your cows and sheep are feeling poorly. I'm amazed how you run your hands over an ailing animal, look into its eyes, almost as if you can communicate with them. Paddy runs to his veterinary books, but when he comes back, you've already figured out the proper diagnosis and treatment. I've seen you tinker with this old truck and get it running again while Paddy stands by and scratches his head. You have shown me all of the native plants growing in the hedges and what they are good for."

Finn sat a little straighter, "You can talk like that all day long. I won't tire of it."

"You are a comfortable sort of person, Finn. Easy to be with."

"You sound surprised."

"I'm surprised at myself. I can sit in silence or engage in conversation without becoming nervous or fretful."

"Ireland is working its magic on you, my sweet colleen," he grinned.

Franella laughed, "And I thought Paddy was the only one that kissed the Blarney Stone."

The Christmas Market was crowded and cold, but the morning fog had lifted, and the vendors shouted to catch the attention of the bundled-up passersby.

"I believe our Christmas Market rivals the ones in Dublin. We have live music and strolling carolers. The pubs keep their doors open even though it's cold. You can hear the festive laughter. It draws people in," Kay said.

Paddy laughed, "I think it's more the hot whiskey and Irish coffee that draws them in."

Georgine spun around, looking everywhere at once. "The stalls with all the handcrafts, the smell of the mince pies and hot scones, and all of the decorations—it's like a Christmas fairyland! I want to buy everything! My mother always sent her personal maid to do our shopping." She fingered a lovely Irish tartan. "The workmanship is extraordinary. Every stall is better than the last."

"Don't go overboard, Georgine," Kay said.

"What do you mean?" Georgine looked genuinely perplexed.

"Mam and I have made simple homemade gifts. We can't compete, and we don't want to."

"Kay, let me escort Georgine around the market. I'm sure you'll find some school chums to chatter away the morning. We'll meet for lunch at Sullivan's pub."

Kay saw a girlfriend across the square, wished Georgine luck, and told Paddy to behave himself.

"Now that I have you to myself, let's enjoy the market. We'll take a look around at all the stalls, have some hot cider or mulled wine, and listen to some of the live music."

"Everything is so lovely; I won't have any trouble spending money."

"I've no doubt. But that's not the essence of gift-giving. The idea is to choose a gift that will be meaningful to the person receiving it."

"I will. I'm just saying the cost is unimportant. I have money."

"To folk who count their pennies, money is significant. Sometimes, receiving an expensive gift makes one feel," Paddy took off his cap and scratched his head, "less than."

"Less than what? I don't understand." Georgine looked around the market.

Paddy took her elbow and guided her through the crowded stalls. "You will figure it out. Let's take our time and enjoy ourselves."

Georgine stopped at a stall exhibiting leather goods. "These boots are exquisite. How about these for your Da and Finn?" She imagined Paddy's legs encased in the knee-high, soft leather boots.

"They wouldn't be comfortable accepting them," Paddy said. "It's very generous, but these leather belts will be just as nice."

"Are you sure? It doesn't seem like much."

"Trust me."

Georgine took his arm and surprised them both by saying, "I do trust you, Paddy."

He smiled and began to hum a romantic Irish ballad, glad that Georgine wouldn't know the words. He felt her relax against him. He leaned toward her and breathed in the delicate perfume she wore.

The next stall sold Irish tatting, a variety of lace shawls, and head coverings. Georgine fingered the soft material. "These shawls would be perfect for your mother and sister."

Paddy shook his head no.

"I'll take three," she told the stall keeper., "I suppose I'll give one to Franella, although she is not the lacy shawl type."

Paddy handed the frowning vender two inexpensive but pretty head coverings and said, "These will do." He turned to Georgine. "Mam and Kay can wear them to church. You're right. Franella's not the lacy type."

Georgine looked longingly at the shawls as she paid for the scarves, and they continued through the market.

"I want to buy a special ornament for your family's Christmas tree and one for myself to remember my visit."

"Ah, my lovely colleen, I'll not let you forget your time with the O'Malleys, especially not this O'Malley." He squeezed her hand and steered her toward the Sullivan's pub. "If Kay's not there, and she probably won't be, we'll start without her."

Georgine smiled, "I'm sure she'll enjoy visiting with her friends."

FIFTY

The three girls, clad in pajamas, sat on the big double bed in the upstairs room.

"I can't believe it's Christmas tomorrow," Kay said.

"I can't believe how late it is. I've never been to a church service at midnight," Georgine yawned.

"Tell me what your holidays were like," Kay said.

"They were just that, holidays," Georgine frowned. "We always went somewhere sunny and warm. There were gifts and a quiet dinner at an exclusive restaurant, but it never felt like a family Christmas."

Franella remembered the holidays in Port Alexander, where her mother wanted everything just so, and Franella could not please her. Christmas at the orphanage in Sitka was something she preferred not to remember. The only festive holidays were the ones spent with Miss Ruth. "Your family has such fun together, Kay. It's loud, chaotic, and energetic. I envy you."

"It's happy," Georgine whispered.

Kay hugged a pillow. "I guess I never thought about it. My brothers drive me bonkers, but I can't imagine life without them. Mam and Da are pretty special."

Georgine burst into tears. "I'm so jealous of you, and I hate myself for it. I'd trade all the money in the world to have a family like yours—parents who care and siblings who are crazy about you. You don't know how lucky you are."

Franella pressed her hands to her stomach. She looked at Georgine and whispered, "I feel the same way. I've been alone since I was eight years old and lonely before that."

Kay's eyes filled and spilled over, and she hugged both girls. "I declare you two are my sisters. You are officially O'Malley's."

Georgine sniffed and then smiled slyly, "I don't think I want to be Paddy O'Malley's sister."

Franella's mouth hung open, and Kay shrieked, "Georgine, what are you saying?"

"I don't know. I've never met anyone like him. He quotes Yeats, for heaven's sake."

"I'm not a fan of Yeats," Franella frowned.

Kay tossed a stuffed lamb in Franella's direction. "That's a topic for another day. I want to know more about what Georgine thinks of my Paddy."

"I know he's taking college business courses. He's learning everything about animal husbandry and farming. He's an expert on Irish history and politics." Georgine grabbed Kay's pillow and hugged it. "When he plays the pipes and sings, my heart aches, but not in a negative way. I don't know. I feel some kind of connection to him. Makes me yearn." Tears formed in her eyes, and she let them fall. "Am I mad?"

"You couldn't do better," Kay said.

"He'll never be rich," Georgine frowned, "or have a high social standing. I can't picture him at an embassy dinner."

"Is that important?" Franella asked, remembering the Thanksgiving fiasco at the American embassy.

"My mother thinks so, but I believe Aunt Eleanor would love him, even in his farm clothes. It doesn't really matter what he wears," Georgine said.

"Well, there goes your thesis," Franella said.

Georgine chuckled, "That doesn't matter anymore." She plucked at the bedspread, then raised her eyes to the two girls. "It's early days yet; promise me you won't say a thing to Paddy. He doesn't know I exist, not in that way, I mean."

Franella had seen the way the young Irishman stole glances at Georgine when no one was looking. "Georgine, he probably thinks he's not in your class. He may not say anything even if he's interested."

Kay pulled her pillow away from Georgine, fluffed it, laid it at the head of the bed, and crawled under the covers. "Merry Christmas to all of us. It's time to sleep. We get up early on Christmas morning. And Georgine, if you want Paddy to know you're interested, ask him to teach you to milk the cows."

Georgine's face lost all color, and Franella hid her smile.

Christmas morning was everything a family Christmas should be. Mam O'Malley had prepared a lavish breakfast, including Irish soda bread, rashers, potatoes, eggs, and Black and White pudding.

"Why are these things called Black and White Pudding? They look like meat patties," Franella said.

"You don't want to know," Finn said.

Mam O'Malley flicked her tea towel at him. "Mind yourself," she said. She set a large bowl of oatmeal on the table as she answered Franella, "The black is made with blood, and the white is pork fat and oats. It's a little bit like haggis, only better."

"But why do they call it pudding?" Franella asked. "In America, a pudding is a custard-like dessert."

"And in England, it can mean any dessert," Georgine added.

"It's an old Latin or Norman word that means sausage."

Franella nodded, knowing she was going to study the origin and meaning of the word. She tried a bite of each. "They are both good; the black is stronger, more earthy." She noticed Georgine limited herself to the eggs and rashers.

The gifts exchanged after breakfast were thoughtful and mostly homemade. Finn had written a song dedicated to his parents, and Paddy created the melody. He and Paddy sang while Paddy played the pipes, and then they gave their mother a framed copy of the lyrics. They gave their father a new tobacco pouch. Mam had knit gloves for everyone, and Kay had made matching hats.

"Oh, Da, it's beautiful," Kay exclaimed as she unwrapped a small oak box with a Celtic cross carved on the top. Franella and Georgine expressed awe at his workmanship when they received identical boxes. Georgine had purchased leather belts with Irish knotwork for the men of the house and lace headscarves for Kay and Mam.

"Merry Christmas, Franella," Georgine said and handed her a package.

It felt heavier than a bit of lace, and Franella wondered what it could be. She turned it over several times without opening it.

"Paddy said, that is, I thought you would like this better than a headscarf." Georgine sucked on her bottom lip.

"Have no doubt, Georgine. Franella will love it," Paddy called from across the room.

Franella tore off the paper and saw a two-volume set of Irish history. "Paddy is absolutely right. This is the perfect gift for me.

Thank you." Franella wondered if Georgine had forgiven her. She was certainly acting like it. "Now, it's my turn to give gifts." Franella silently thanked Miss Ruth for insisting she stuff a dozen or so gift items in her luggage. Scrimshaw earrings for the ladies and bilikens for the men.

Finn held up the two-inch figure and said, "It doesn't look like a leprechaun."

"That's because it's an Alaskan leprechaun," Paddy laughed. "Is it ivory?"

"Yes. It's called a Billiken. It's supposed to bring you luck."

"What about a pot of gold?" Paddy laughed.

Franella rolled her eyes and bit the inside of her cheek to keep from blurting that she had shares in a gold mine!

They donned their coats, hats, and gloves and took a long walk. Mam said they needed to work up an appetite for dinner.

Franella marveled at the bond this Irish family shared. They seemed to enjoy each other without judgment or undue expectations. She saw how Georgine was soaking in the softness and aligning herself with each family member. It was changing the girl, and Franella sensed a shift in herself as well. She sighed deeply and stored the ambiance in her soul.

You could put the O'Malleys in the middle of Bronzeville or bring Hard Workin' Willie and Phanie Lu to the Emerald Isle, and they would each feel at home. Their family values were the same. She would ponder all of this later. Right now, she wanted to be like Georgine and take it all in.

"The boys will drive us to Dublin right after Little Christmas," Kay said.

"What's that?" Franella asked.

Mrs. O'Malley set a large bowl of potatoes on the table and sat down. "It's also called Women's Christmas. The men do all the cooking and cleaning. The women meet at the pub or the local tea room, and hopefully, when we get home, the Christmas decorations have been taken down and stored away."

"That sounds like a great tradition," Franella said. "When does it happen?"

"January sixth, the same day as Epiphany," Kay said. "Then it's back to our studies."

Georgine and Paddy shared a long look, and he reached for her hand under the table. "Don't worry, my beautiful colleen, this is not the end, it's the beginning. Remember what Yeats said when two souls fall in love."

Georgine's face flamed, and she felt everyone's eyes on her. But she leaned close to him and whispered, "Tell me again."

"It's not one I memorized, but I believe he said souls do not have calendars or clocks, and they don't understand time or distance."

"The distance is too great, and the time is too long," she sighed.

He squeezed her hand, seemingly unaware that they were still at the table and that everyone had turned their attention toward them. "The end of the poem assures us that being apart is only temporary. I will memorize the entire poem and recite it to you when we meet again."

Georgine smiled and used her napkin to wipe her eyes. Franella swallowed with difficulty and wondered if she would ever feel that way about someone. She shook the thought away; it seemed improbable.

Kay jumped up, circled the table, hugged her brother, and then hugged Georgine. Finn began to sing a love ballad. Mr. O'Malley rose, tugged his wife out of her chair, and danced her around the kitchen. Paddy and Georgine joined them. Finn raised an eyebrow at Franella, who said, "I never learned. You keep singing, and I'll clear the table."

FIFTY-ONE

The ferry crossed the Irish Sea with fair weather and calm waters. The train rattled across Wales and England with Georgine sighing and asking the other two girls if they thought she had a future with Paddy. Kay entered into the conversation with gusto. Franella looked out of the train's window and tried to close her ears.

Franella relished the regular college routine, although her mind often drifted to Kay's family in County Cork.

"I'm glad you come to all our study sessions now," Kay said to Georgine.

"I think she does it to hear your mother's chatty letters and to ask you questions about Paddy," Franella said. "Although she waves her letters from him in our faces, she doesn't let us see what's in them."

Georgine laughed, "You are not going to irritate me, Franella. But yes, that's exactly why I came. My studies mean even less to me now."

"You should switch to business and marketing. If you and Paddy get together, that would be helpful," Kay said.

"Paddy has a keen mind as far as the business side of the farm goes. He doesn't need me," Georgine moaned.

"You could help the women of the county. I think you could find markets for their knitting, basketry, and tatting, even their Irish tartans and Fair Isle sweaters. They are highly skilled, but they don't earn a lot of money. It would keep you from getting bored if you become a farmer's wife."

Georgine glowed, "Do you think I'll become his wife?"

"No, I don't. You are worlds apart," Franella said. "He'll soon tire of you."

Georgine's shoulders slumped, she turned away, took a deep breath or two, then sniffed and turned back to Franella. "Paddy says you are the most honest person he knows."

"I'm not a liar."

"You say exactly what you're thinking without regard to the listener's feelings," Georgine said. "Paddy doesn't mind, but the rest of us do."

"What are you talking about?" Franella growled.

Georgine folded her hands and gazed at Franella without anger. "Paddy says every sunrise is an invitation to live in God's grace. I will not allow you to pull me away from that. Your words will not hurt me."

"I have no idea what you are talking about."

Kay took both of Franella's hands in her own and said quietly, "Dear Franella, it would be wise if you could speak more gently or diplomatically, at least some of the time." You can get your point across without hurting anyone's feelings if you're not too blunt."

"I've learned a little bit of softness never hurts," Georgine whispered.

"I am not a liar," Franella said, shaking off Kay's hands.

"True, but as my Irish grandmother always said, a good word never broke a tooth."

"What's that supposed to mean?"

Kay laughed, "You're a smart girl. You'll figure it out."

Georgine scanned the pages of her latest letter. She sniffed and reached for her handkerchief, then looked up. "Has Paddy said anything to you about not wanting to marry me? Tell me."

Franella stood and reached for her coat. "I need some air." She left Georgine crying, and Kay consoling her. Franella wandered down Woodstock Road and through several alleys, backtracked, and finally made her way to the Eagle and Child on St. Giles Street. She wasn't scheduled to work today, but she spent some time sitting and watching the people, listening to their conversations, and observing their facial expressions and tones. *I may never be naturally soft or tender. It's not my nature, but I can learn to tame my tongue. I will!*

FIFTY-TWO

The following week, Franella hurried through her studies and made her way to the Eagle and Child. She arrived after the breakfast rush was over and the lunch crowd had not yet arrived.

"You're early," Mr. Brumley said. "I'll not pay extra for that."

"That's okay. I just want to tidy the back room a little," Franella said.

"I'll not pay extra," he licked his lips and repeated, "I'll not pay extra."

"I know. I just want to take my time and do a good job, and you don't have to pay extra for that." Franella gathered the cleaning materials and ignored Mr. Brumley's mumbled comments about sassy young things.

Truth be told, the back room of the pub was always tidy and dust-free. Somewhat of a miracle, Franella thought, given the building was hundreds of years old. She wandered through the dim room, gathering her courage. She had promised herself it would be done today. According to the large clock on the mantle, it must be done within the next five minutes. The clatter of silverware as Kay set the tables in the main dining area echoed her actions. Franella folded each napkin precisely, set the cups and saucers at the exact angle to the silverware, and looked around.

The soft lights and patina on the centuries-old paneling gave the room a serene feel. She felt anything but serene—her heart raced, there was a mustache of sweat on her upper lip, and her hands were clammy. The ornate clock had ticked away several minutes. Mr. Brumley would soon amble in to light the fire. If she was going to do it, it must be now. She took the paper from her apron pocket, folded it, and called Kay, who slipped it under the napkin at the head of the table where he usually sat.

They hurried out of the room. Franella knew if she stayed, the paper would find its way back to the safety of her pocket.

The Inklings entered as a group, deep in conversation, as they did every week. Their standing order was the Ploughman's lunch, which she always served promptly. They thanked her absentmindedly as she set the steaming plates before them.

Professor Lewis leaned and sniffed the savory dish, then picked up his napkin and shook it. The paper fell to the floor. Charles Williams retrieved it. "Jack, you dropped this."

Jack Lewis took the paper and stuffed it into his pocket without looking. Franella bit her lip and wondered if the brilliant man would remember it was there.

He did. After lunch, while they were drinking their tea and lager, Jack pulled the paper out, read it, raised his eyebrows, and passed it to Tolkien. Franella's heart raced as Professor Tolkien sucked on the pipe he clamped firmly between his teeth. Without comment, he passed the paper along. Charles Williams chuckled several times as he read.

Kay tapped her on the shoulder, and Franella jumped. "Why are you hovering in the doorway?" Kay whispered, "Hiding?"

Franella pointed to the gentleman reading her story.

"I can't believe you talked me into slipping that story under Mr. Lewis's napkin. Who's reading it now?" Kay asked.

"That's Warren Lewis, Professor Lewis's brother."

When the paper circled back to Jack, he asked the men what they thought. The next thirty minutes were spent discussing the possible links between ravens in Norse and Icelandic mythology and wondering how the lore could have reached the Native Americans of Alaska—no one thought to ask where the paper had come from.

After their shift was over, Franella and Kay walked back to Somerville Hall. "That was certainly anticlimactic," Franella said.

"What did you expect?"

"I don't know. They totally missed the point that it was an anonymous mystery paper and just focused on the content." Franella jammed her hands into her coat pocket.

"You could have told them you were the author."

"I couldn't. I'm a nobody."

Kay threw her arm around Franella's shoulder. "You are not a nobody, but we'll save that discussion for another day. It seems to me they were fascinated by what you wrote."

The following week, the scenario repeated. Kay tucked another of Franella's stories under Jack's napkin. When Jack shook it and laid it across his lap, the paper fluttered to the floor. Once again, Charles Williams retrieved it. His eyebrows rose as he handed it to Jack. The story was as well-received as the last one, and the discussion was just as lively.

After their meal, the men refilled their pipes, and soon a hazy cloud rested above them. Franella refilled the men's teacups, and Professor Lewis motioned her to his side. He held up the story. "Do you know anything about this?"

"That's the wrong question," Franella said, gripping the suddenly too-heavy teapot.

"I beg your pardon," Jack Lewis said.

Franella swallowed and then swallowed again. He was supposed to ask who put it there. She glanced around the table, sucked on her lower lip, and said, "I didn't put it there."

"But you know who did." Charles Williams stared at her as he tamped tobacco into his pipe.

Her face felt hot; she backed up a step and remained silent.

"You do know. Tell us," he commanded.

"Leave the girl alone, Williams. Can't you see the look on her face? She doesn't want to say." Warnie Lewis turned to Franella and spoke with a soft voice, "Tell whoever wrote this that they have aroused our curiosity once again. This story is even more intriguing. We shall study it thoroughly at our next meeting at Magdalen."

Franella swallowed, nodded, and made her escape.

"You two have been absolutely worthless these past few weeks," Kay said, "Although I dearly love you both."

Georgine glanced up from the letter she was writing to Paddy. "What do you mean?"

Kay laughed, "All you do is write to Paddy or reread his letters." She turned to Franella and said, "And all you do is write more of those mythical raven stories. It seems I'm the only one who's paying attention to the professors and tutors of Oxford."

Franella finished writing the last sentence of her story. "I've worked ahead and finished all my projects for this semester so that I can devote my time to these stories."

"When are you going to let them know it's you?" Georgine

asked as she sealed and stamped her envelope.

"In their eyes, I'm just a waitress. I put my stories under the napkin and received a written response a week later. It works."

"Maybe you judge them too harshly. I think they would treat you the same whether you are a waitress, an Oxford student, or a member of Mensa, that new club for geniuses."

"I told you I don't have time for that Mensa nonsense," Franella said.

"It was an honor they invited you," Kay said.

"Bunch of smarty-pants trying to outdo each other," Franella mumbled.

"Paddy likes your stories. I sent him a copy of the first two." Georgine sighed, "I can't wait until the spring holidays. Ireland here I come."

Kay and Franella looked at each other over Georgine's head. Kay arched her brows, and Franella rolled her eyes.

"I have the day off, so you'll have to walk to the Eagle by yourself," Kay said.

Georgine stuffed her letter into her purse. "I'll walk with you partway. I want to mail this to Paddy."

"You write each other every day. I can't imagine what there is left to say," Franella said as she shrugged on her coat.

Georgine smiled and said, "There is always more to say."

Franella arrived at the Bird and Baby, as the pub was affectionately known. She hung up her coat and tied an apron around her waist. The Inklings had not yet arrived. Franella clutched her story in one hand and lifted Jack's napkin with the other.

"It is you!"

Franella yelped and spun around. The napkin dropped to the table. "Professor Lewis! You're not supposed to be here for another six minutes."

"I've been watching you for the past several months, and I suspected you were the author."

"I'm sorry." Franella chewed on the end of her thumb. "I'll stop."

"I don't want you to stop. I want you to take my literature courses, and I'd like to become one of your tutors."

Franella forced her thumb away from her mouth. "Is that even possible?" she squeaked. "Magdalen doesn't admit women."

"You can't be officially admitted, of course, but I'll do everything I can to make sure you hear my lectures." He took the story from her. "Shall I introduce you as our mystery author?"

Franella's face reddened, and she cupped her cheeks. "Please, no," she whispered.

"Your secret is safe with me. But your stories are fascinating."

"An old Tlingit told me those stories."

"Tlingit?" Jack pulled a smoldering pipe from his jacket pocket.

"Johnny, the Bear Boy. From Alaska. He was kind to me when many weren't."

Jack, unsure of himself, opened his mouth but closed it when Franella took a step back and turned her head away. He paused then repeated, "Your secret is safe."

"Thank you, Professor Lewis."

"Call me, Jack."

"I can't."

"Of course you can."

Franella shook her head. The words wouldn't form in her mouth. He was the esteemed Professor Lewis. Just having a simple conversation with him made her stutter and shake.

"The others are coming." He folded the paper and put it under his napkin.

True to his word, Jack kept her secret, although before too many months had passed, Professor Tolkien suspected the truth. He agreed to keep her secret as well. The rest of the Inklings never learned the source of the mysterious stories under Jack's napkin.

FIFTY-THREE

Professor Lewis found a way to allow Franella to audit his classes. She never asked how he accomplished this, and he never volunteered the information.

The following months at Oxford were profitable, and Franella was grateful that CS Lewis became one of her tutors, although unofficial. The books and papers he recommended broadened her education, and the way he asked questions pulled ideas out of her mind she didn't know were there. He occasionally winked at her during lunch at the Eagle, and she nodded slightly in reply, feeling as if she were a part of something. Of what, she didn't know.

"I just want to fit in," Franella said.

"You fit in with my family during our Christmas vacations, and last summer, we had a great time exploring Ireland."

"I didn't fit, not really."

"My dear, Not-a-Scot, what do you mean?" Kay asked as she linked her arm with Franella's. "We've got a few blocks before we reach the Bird and Baby, so you've got time to explain yourself."

"I envy you, Kay. You fit in everywhere. It doesn't matter if we're in a large lecture hall, an embassy dinner, or a study group. Whatever student activity we attend, you fit right in."

"So do you."

"It may look like it, but inside, I'm trying to guard my tongue and not blurt anything harsh or inappropriate. I often fail, and everybody looks at me as if I'm a clod from an uncivilized region."

"We are a few short weeks from graduation, and I can truthfully say you've come a long way. When you first arrived at Somerville, I don't think you realized words have power."

Franella nodded and chewed on the end of her thumb. "I say what I think."

Kay laughed, "Sometimes it's best to think first, and then decide if you want to speak or keep quiet."

"You have a lot of empathy and affection for people. I'm trying to develop some of that. It's difficult. I don't know how you do it."

"It's easy when you realize we're all the same. We all have disappointments and losses. I don't want what I say or do to add to anyone's pain."

"It seems to be second nature to you," Franella sighed.

"It's not. I've practiced for years, and over time, I realized I actually like people."

"I guess that makes it easier. People don't like me. I feel like I'm on the outside looking in."

"Outside of what?"

"Everything. I don't belong."

Kay stopped and pulled Franella to a bench on the sidewalk. She took Franella's hands and looked intently into her eyes. "Be grateful for the way God made you and the life He has given you. If you can do that, you won't worry about fitting in."

Franella shook her head and pulled her hands away.

"And my dear Not-a-Scot, you must begin to like yourself."

"We better hurry. We'll be late."

By the time Tollers had settled Franella at the Inklings' table in the back room of the Eagle and Child, she had gone quiet. The tears had been wiped away, and the crying ceased. It unsettled him that he couldn't engage her in conversation, and he prayed Jack would arrive soon. Her tea had grown cold, so Tollers signaled the waiter for a fresh cup. The pimple-faced young fellow nodded and hurried to do the esteemed man's bidding.

Jack arrived several minutes later, yet Franella remained frozen. The two middle-aged professors exchanged a glance, looking confused.

"What are we going to do with her?" Tollers asked.

"I don't know anything about women. You're the one that's married."

"Precisely, that's why you're going to take her home."

"Me? I couldn't possibly." Jack said, pulling his smoldering pipe out of his pocket.

"Think about it, Jack. I can't bring a beautiful young woman home to my wife and say she's staying with us until she figures out, well, life, so to speak." Tollers tried to sound stern, but his eyes twinkled.

Lewis sighed, "I don't appreciate the glee you are feeling at my expense."

They sat at the table, but Franella didn't seem to notice as she huddled over the tea, refusing to drink and refusing to speak. Tollers took her hands. "They're ice cold, Jack. We have to do something."

Jack shook his head and lit his pipe. "I don't understand it."

"It's the humiliation in front of her peers and professors, don't you think?" Tollers whispered.

"I shouldn't have insisted she give the speech," Jack said.

"She could have stumbled through. It's running out of the room that she's ashamed of. She feels like a failure—like she'll never make anything of herself."

"She said that?"

"From the phrases I collected while she wept, that's what I gathered. It took a while to calm her down, but now—she's too calm."

"Poor child," Jack muttered, "What's to become of her?"

"She'll find peace at the Kilns. Warnie can mother her a bit, and perhaps she'll open up," Professor Tolkien said.

"That's a great idea. I'll pack her necessities," a voice behind them said.

"With that red hair and those freckles, you must be the Irish lass. Franella told me you were study partners," Lewis said, turning toward the voice and offering his hand.

She shook it vigorously and said, "More than that, we're friends, although she doesn't often realize it. I overheard Professor Tolkien mention the Bird and Baby, so I knew he was bringing Franella here. I couldn't afford a taxi. My Irish grandmother always said legs were made for walking, and my Irish legs are strong." Kay said, eyeing Franella while talking to the two men. "Our rooms at Somerville Hall aren't far from here. Do you have a car, Mr. Lewis? Taxi? Whatever your mode of transportation is, stop by the Hall on your way to the Kilns." She wrapped her arms around Franella's shoulders and whispered in her ear, "It's going to be all right, my dear—Not a Scot."

"Not a Scot?" Tolkien raised an eyebrow. Kay stood and explained the origin of the phrase, then stooped and whispered in Franella's other ear. "You think you humiliated yourself; push that thought away. My Irish grandmother always said gladness waits everywhere. You will surely find it."

Franella's eyes flickered just a little as Kay kissed her cheek. "The luck 'o the Irish to you, my dear friend." Kay set a small bag of lemon drops on the table as she prepared to leave. "Tea won't do it for this American. She needs a strong cup of coffee. A friend in the States keeps her supplied. I'll include a tin or two in her overnight case."

"What's this?" Jack picked up the bag.

Kay winked, and her freckles popped as her face exploded in an impish Irish grin. "My Irish grandmother swears what's in that bag will cure whatever ails you, but only if you take it with a wee bit of faith and a big bucket of prayer," Kay called over her shoulder.

The two professors bundled Franella into the back of a taxi. Jack bid Tollers goodnight and said he'd telephone the next day. Franella stared out the window, unaware of the passing English countryside. When the heartsick girl and the man who desperately wanted to help her arrived at the Kilns, the setting sun threw a golden glow over the gardens.

Jack led her into the rambling red-brick house and wondered what he and Warnie could do for her. Was she in shock? Should he have taken her to a hospital? Need they call a doctor? He must have said the words aloud because Warnie answered, "From what I can see, she looks despondent, almost in a stupor, as if she doesn't want to think or feel. She's the waitress from the Eagle and Child, isn't she? We'll let her sleep as long as she likes. What room shall I put her in?

Jack ran his hand through his thinning hair, then slumped into his favorite leather armchair. "It's been a long day, brother. Put her wherever you like."

"There are several boxes stored in the room overlooking the garden. I'll move them and put her in there. Your supper is in the oven. Dried out, I'm sure. I'll put the young lady to bed, then make you a scramble."

"Thanks, Warnie." Jack leaned back and closed his eyes.

Warnie took Franella by the elbow and led her to the staircase. He turned to Jack and said, "I'll want a detailed explanation. We often open our home to guests, but we've never had one in this condition."

Franella slept for twenty-two hours. When she awoke, she pictured herself running out of her graduation amid the stares and astonishment of everyone attending. How could she have crumpled her speech and thrown it on the floor? What a coward! She was a failure, a nothing. She pulled the covers over her head and refused to get up. However, sleep eluded her, and she knew she had to face the day. She threw back the covers and sat up. She found her bathrobe at the end of the bed and her overnight case on a bench in front of the mulled window. It was not a feminine room, sparsely furnished with no bric-a-brac. There were, however, two overcrowded bookcases and several stacks of books piled next to them.

Franella promised herself she would examine all the books later, but where was she?

Although her shoes had been removed, she had slept in her clothes, which were now rumpled and wrinkled. Moonlight streamed through the open window, and the scent of roses filled the room. There was a note atop her overnight case that said she was at the Kilns.

She crept down the stairs and into a gathering room of sorts, which was filled with overstuffed, old-fashioned, and very masculine furniture. She paused in what appeared to be a study. Her eyes devoured the floor-to-ceiling bookcases, which were also over-stuffed. She followed the low hum of male voices into the kitchen and saw Professor Lewis and his brother, Warnie, who was also an Inkling. They enjoyed their afternoon tea at a sturdy wooden table that had aged to a golden patina.

"I'm confused, Mr. Lewis. Why am I here?" She stretched her arms wide, yawned, and then hiccupped. "Sorry—uncouth American."

The men grinned and ignored her statement, the yawn, and the hiccup.

"You need to eat, my dear, and then we'll talk."

While Jack was speaking, Warnie fixed Franella a plate of currant scones and clotted cream, as well as crustless cucumber sandwiches cut into triangles. He set the electric percolator to brew some of the American coffee Kay had packed. Franella looked from one brother to the other. The concern and kindness on their faces melted her. She choked back tears.

Warnie patted her arm. "We are just two old men, but we've lived a bit of life." The ever-practical Warnie added, "You feel lost, empty."

"I never admit that," Franella's blue eyes filled again. "How did you know?"

"Warnie knows things, deep things. You might not be aware, but he was one of the founding members of the Inklings, and he's written several books on French history."

"Now, Jack, French history isn't going to help the girl."

"I just wanted her to know you are an intelligent and worthy man, Warnie. Well known for your work."

Warnie laughed, "You're the famous one in the family, and that's the way I like it." He turned to Franella and said, "You are going to stay here just as long as you like."

"Why are you bothering about me? I'm nobody."

"That is a lie from the pit of hell. You are a marvelous somebody, and we will keep you here until you believe it. What say you, Jack?"

"Franella is one of the most intelligent creatures I know, but she doesn't realize her worth." Jack pointed his pipe at Franella, "You must see yourself as God does."

Franella shivered and inhaled the sweet aroma from Jack's pipe, swirling over her head. The man and his pipe would always be entwined in her memories. She couldn't think of one without the other.

"My dear?" Jack poured a cup of coffee and set it before her.

How could she explain the vast valleys of darkness within her? She dipped her spoon into the small crock of clotted cream and plopped a healthy dollop onto a scone. She refused to look at the two men. Warnie pushed a jar of strawberry preserves toward her.

"This endeavor will be painful. Are you ready?"

Franella, mouth full of the scone, shivered and shook her head, "I can't."

Jack took her hand, "You are at a crossroads, my dear. Are you going to wander, lost forever?"

"Please make the right decision, dear one," Warnie pleaded.

'Your life depends on it," Jack said.

"I'm tired. I need to go back to bed." She hurried out of the room.

The next day, she knocked on Jack's study door. After asking if he had a moment to talk, she said, "I'm not stupid. I know my extensive education has changed my life, but it didn't give me a life, not a transformed one."

Jack sucked on his pipe and then observed the swirls of smoke enveloping him, "It's not what you know, my dear. It's who."

"I've recently read *Mere Christianity*. Twice. I know who you're referring to." Franella gnawed on her thumb, then thrust her hands behind her back and struggled to choke out the words, "There's a chasm I can't cross, a mountain I can't scale, a darkness I can't penetrate. I'm always learning and never knowing. Not like you, Mr. Lewis."

"I've told you to call me Jack."

Franella nodded but knew she would always think of him as Mr. Lewis, even if she someday summoned the courage to call him by the name he preferred. She couldn't look at him. Instead, she gazed past the numerous bookcases and out of the window. Warnie strolled in the garden, then sat on a wooden bench beneath the rose trellis. He looked content as he opened his book. If only she could find such peace. She turned to face Jack, "You know the secret of the universe, the mystery of the human soul."

"You think so?"

"It's in your books, Professor Lewis. I know what you've written, I even believe it, but it doesn't make a difference."

"The demons know and believe." He spoke gently and thrust his lit pipe into his tweed jacket's pocket. "It's not enough."

Franella saw that the pocket had been patched several times and wondered if the pipe still smoldered. She closed her eyes for a moment and pulled her attention back to her inner agony. "Is there no hope for me then?" *My soul is a graveyard. I'm dead in the shadows.*

"Believing the facts is a start, but you must move past them. Find the Person."

"I don't know how." Franella cried and punched her head with her fists. "I'm telling you, I don't know how!"

He pulled her hands away and rubbed his thumbs over her knuckles. "If you truly want to be found, He will pursue you to the ends of the earth."

Franella lowered her eyes and stared at their entwined hands—hers were young and smooth, his older and tobacco-stained. She took a deep breath. *Do I want to be found?* She whispered, "What if it's the end of me?"

"It will be," Jack chuckled, "but then you'll live. You will be surprised by joy."

"Promise?"

Jack nodded and waited for Franella's response. She pulled her hands away and fisted them, then shook them as if they were numb. She stood, twisted this way and that, then abruptly sat down and held her head in her hands. "I feel chained to myself and can't move. I don't know which way to go."

Jack nodded. "You're at the lamppost. Just follow the faun."

Franella's head jerked up, and she stammered, "A baby deer?"

"Not that kind of faun. He'll introduce you to the beavers."

354

"Are you feeling okay, Mr. Lewis? You sound a little crazy." She pressed her hands against her hot cheeks. "Sorry, did I say that out loud?"

"Pay attention to the beavers. They know."

"Beavers? Fauns? Are you sure you're all right?"

Jack laughed and reached into the bottom drawer of his small wooden desk. "This is a copy of my children's story. As you know, every good story for children can and should be enjoyed by those who are no longer young."

Franella didn't know that but nodded and glanced at the manuscript—*The Lion, the Witch, and the Wardrobe.* "Forgive me for saying so, Professor Lewis, but a lion and a witch in a closet aren't going to help me."

Jack grinned. "It will be published later this year. The Inklings are familiar with it, but no one else has read it."

"I'm honored, of course, but…"

Warnie stood just inside the doorway to Jack's study. "At mealtimes, I will set a tray outside of your door. Jack will supply you with any writing materials you require. When you are ready to talk, we'll listen. Jack has given you the best counsel he could."

Franella held the manuscript to her chest and stood. "If you think it will make a difference, I'll read it. But a child's story, a fairy tale?"

Warnie patted her shoulder, "Don't let Jack get started on the value of fairy stories, or we'll be up half the night."

Lewis laughed, "I think this tale will reveal the secret of the universe and the mystery of the human soul that you are searching for."

Franella Feddersen did not come out of her room that day or the next. The trays Warnie set outside of the guest room were left untouched. Jack leaned his ear on the door but could hear nothing.

"The door is too thick. Do what I do." Warnie said, "Stand underneath the window. She opens it every morning."

"What have you heard?"

"I couldn't make out the words, but there was much weeping and laughter. Rants and raves. Pleading and prayers. She's doing the work, Jack."

"Hmm."

Franella wrenched the door open and shouted to the startled men, "I'm not who I thought I was!"

"Who are you then?" Warnie asked.

Franella grinned, "Who He says I am, but you already knew that, didn't you?" She kissed the middle-aged bachelor on the cheek.

"Come to the table, I'll make tea, er, coffee. There are lemon curd and scones just waiting for you," the pleased but embarrassed Warnie said.

"Good. All I've had for sustenance the past two days was the lemon drops."

"Tell us everything," Jack demanded.

"Oh, Mr. Lewis, I was consumed by loss and disappointment. Hate for those who hurt me and guilt about those I hurt. The only emotions I could feel when I let myself feel anything were anger and rage. He removed all of it and filled me with—with—Himself. My season of longing is over, and I didn't even know what I was longing for." She laughed and twirled around the room. "I'm filled and clean. I'm not an orphan anymore!"

Warnie set the tea tray on the table but wasn't able to sit because Franella grabbed him and danced around the room. "Warnie, I met the Lion, and I know His name!" *I have no words for His kindness and mercy. I'm no longer outside looking in. I can't describe how His light shattered the shadows and filled every crevice of my soul. Freedom! Joy! There are no words!*

"And He knows yours." Warnie beamed, stumbled, and fell into the chair. Franella continued dancing without him. Jack enjoyed seeing his rather sensitive and gentle brother led around the room by an exuberant Franella. He poured Warnie a much-needed cup of tea and turned to Franella.

"I'm delighted, my dear. Your journey with the great roaring Lion, who is also the loving Lamb, has begun."

"You were right, Professor. It's not enough to know about Him or believe He is who He says He is. You also have to trust Him and everything He's done. That's real faith."

"That's right, my dear," Jack smiled.

"Welcome to God's family," Warnie said.

Franella nodded and took her place at the table. "All of a sudden, I'm starving."

"What now? What does the Lion have for you?" he asked.

"I'm going home."

"Alaska?" Jack asked.

She nodded. "I don't know what awaits me there."

"Are you sure you're not running away?" Warnie asked, concern clouding his eyes.

"He told me to go! And He's going with me!" She laughed until tears ran down her face, and she pressed her palms against her sides. She couldn't stop.

Warnie joined her, although he couldn't say why. Jack watched the pair of them for a long moment, laid his pipe in the ashtray, and clapped his hands. When the laughter dissipated, he said, "What makes you so mirthful, my dear?"

"Do you know what He said to me?"

Jack and Warnie shook their heads, waiting expectantly.

She stared at each man in turn, eyes sparkling, lips upturned. She couldn't help herself; she laughed again. She wiped her eyes, blew her nose, and giggled until Jack demanded, "Tell us!'

"Two words—FINALLY, FRANELLA!"

EPILOGUE
Sitka, Alaska 1956

Dear Kay,

This letter may ramble a bit. I have some heartfelt things to share with you, and as you well know, it's difficult for me. These are things I should have told you in person, but it's so much easier in a letter.

I remember the day we met. You dragged me into the lecture hall and declared we would be great friends. I didn't believe you, but that didn't deter you in the least. You showed me what friendship is, and I am grateful.

Looking back, I can see that the holidays and summers I spent in Ireland with you and your family were such a time of growth for me. I want to have a family as precious and loving as the O'Malleys of County Cork, Ireland.

I'm so glad we have corresponded regularly and you have followed my romance from the beginning. Your analysis and advice have truly helped me to accept the love my Jacob has for me. I still sometimes struggle with feeling worthy of his love. I wonder what your Irish grandmother would say about that.

He's such a great guy. He loves to fly into the remotest areas of the interior of Alaska. He brings books and newspapers to those living in the remotest areas. He buys them with his own mon-

ey. He doesn't buy the Native children candy or sweets since he's seen the harm it does to their dental health. He doesn't forget them, though. He buys crayons and coloring books, and little toys. They love him!

Mr. and Mrs. Paddy O'Malley fell in love with him last year. Georgine's Aunt Elenor was so generous in gifting them that extended honeymoon. I was excited they chose to travel across the United States and then north to Alaska. It's sad that her parents haven't spoken to her since she married Paddy! But she will blossom with all the love your parents rain on her.

Georgine took so many photographs, not just of the glorious landscapes, but of Jacob and me. And I'm sure she's told you how handsome he is. Tall and strong, yet kind and gentle. It's his gray-green eyes that look beyond the surface that make my heart flutter!

I was heartened by your last letter telling me how she has folded into your family and let go of all her upper-class trappings. Shocking! It's hard to picture her as a farmer's wife. I'm sure she will bring her own style to it!

Please tell Georgine I understand she can't travel since she will be giving birth soon. Your mama is going to be the best grandma ever, and you will be the best auntie.

Enclosed you will find a money order for your trip. No argument. What's the fun of having a gold mine, or a few shares anyway, if you can't spend it on those you love? I couldn't get married without you! My maid of honor and best friend—Kay O'Malley!

We are going to have so much fun, and you are going to love my Jacob.

Come as soon as you can arrange it, so that we will have some time together before the wedding.

Love,

Franella

Dear Mr. Willie and Phanie Lu,

Some years ago, Miss Ruth told me to trust the redcaps, and I did. I will always be grateful for the day I looked up and saw Hard Workin' Willie coming my way. He was sent by the Lord to rescue me. You also rescued me, Miss Phanie, and I love you for it. You showed me your heart and welcomed me into it.

The weeks I spent living with you before traveling to Oxford and the extended visit after I graduated were some of the most precious times I've ever had. And now, I would like to share my world with you as you shared yours.

My friends Oskar and Freja have a fishing boat and are coming to Alaska next month. They would be happy to have you as passengers. I have enclosed train tickets from Chicago to Seattle. Mr. Willie's ticket master can fill in the dates.

At the end of your stay, you can come to my wedding! Sit down, Miss Phanie. I can see you dancing around the kitchen and hollering—Praise de Lawd!

My Jacob is looking forward to meeting you and showing you our Alaska from the windows of a very small airplane. I know Mr. Willie says he plans to keep his feet on solid ground, which is why you are coming to me via land and sea. I do hope Jacob can persuade him to soar. I know he would love it!

I do have a huge favor to ask. Will you be the host and hostess at the reception afterward? It won't be fancy, but it will be nice. The event will be held at the Sitka Café, and the entire town is invited.

And, Mr. Willie, I have tears in my eyes as I write the following—will you do me the high honor of walking me down the aisle?

Love,

Franella

Dear Professor Lewis (I still can't call you Jack) and dear, dear Warnie,

I am writing to tell you that I am getting married in two months. I am giddy with happiness.

This is not an invitation since I know Joy is ill and you won't want to leave her. And Warnie won't want to leave you, but I know you both wish me all the best.

His name is Jacob Prince, and he is a prince. At least, I think of him that way. He is not college-educated, but I can't mention an author, idea, philosophy, or historical incident that he doesn't know about. I think he has read more books than all of the Inklings combined. And he can discuss all these topics with anyone, no matter their intellectual capacity. He doesn't come across as a know-it-all but meets people where they are. Besides that, he's kind and funny and the life of the party.

Can you imagine me with the life of the party? Honestly, he watches out for me. When the social atmosphere begins to overwhelm me, he is right there to take care of me.

Not to be forward or awkward, but I know you will want to send a gift. Would you please autograph a copy of Mere Christianity for him? It was instrumental in his salvation. And Warnie, if you could figure out a way to send a bucket of Devonshire clotted cream, I would love you forever!

With much love for you both, and prayers for Joy.

Franella

MY MAMA'S MAMA: BOOK 7

ALL THAT GLITTERS

A MISS RUTH NOVEL

ALL THAT GLITTERS
Sitka, Alaska, 1962

Cold rain plastered itself to the windows of the Sitka Sentinel. Gray clouds hung low and miserable over the town, reflecting the editor's mood. Sam Mitchell, Jr., threw his dead cigar into the overloaded wastebasket next to his equally overflowing desk. Papers scattered as he pushed through the piles. Where were the notes from his interview with Ivan Mishkin?

The notes were as fragmented as the conversation he'd had with the aged Russian. Ensconced in the Pioneer's Home and confined to his bed, Ivan was not doing well. His concentration had become erratic, and he had fallen into a listlessness that Sam couldn't penetrate. He left unsatisfied.

Thoughts of what Ivan might know filled Sam's mind, and he had difficulty concentrating on the Sentinel's business. Coffee, cigars, and grousing at Margaret Mary didn't help. He swung his chair around and stared out the window until the shrill ring of the telephone cut through his foul mood. "Yes. Yes. I'll be right there."

Sam found the small notepad containing his scribbles in his shirt pocket. He swore as he tried to decipher what he had written just a few hours ago, and then remembered the doctor said Ivan could slip into a coma at any time. Sam swore again and grabbed his hat. "Margaret Mary, I'm off to the Pioneer's home."

"That old Russian?"

"Yes. He's awake. They don't know for how long." Sam shoved his fedora over his bald spot and grabbed his jacket. "That last interview was confusing. I couldn't make sense of what he was saying, but I knew it was important."

"Leave your notes. You know I can interpret your writing better than you can yourself."

"Thanks, MM, you're the best." He tossed the notepad. It landed three feet in front of her, and the door slammed behind him.

"Don't I know it?" she spoke to the closed door as she picked up the pad. "What will you do when I retire, Sam? I'm not getting any younger."

She frowned as she looked at his writing, then shrugged into her own coat. She'd deal with the impossible script when the post office. It had been six months since Miss Ruth's funeral, and she didn't expect many more letters to the editor about the woman, not after the scores they had received in the weeks following her obituary. But there would be the newspaper's usual mail to deal with.

The Pioneer's home had that medicinal smell that Sam hated. He sprinted down the wide hallway to Ivan's room. The self-proclaimed Russian seemed aware, but his eyes had an unholy glitter, and the pallor of his skin was worse. Ivan gasped for breath when he saw Sam. He lifted claw-like hands and whispered, "She had to—"

Sam took the cold, bony hands in his own. "It's okay, Ivan. I know she had to."

Ivan fell back against the pillows. His breathing labored, "Not—her—fault."

368

"What, Ivan, what wasn't her fault?"

"She not guilty," he gasped.

"Whatever she did, I'm sure she had a good reason."

"I not mean to tell."

"You haven't told me anything. I don't know what you're talking about."

"Is good."

"You know I'm trying to find out everything I can about Miss Ruth. I want to understand why everybody loved her."

Ivan winced, coughed, and said, "Not everybody."

"I'm going to write a book about how she influenced and shaped Alaska. It's important, Ivan. Surely, you can agree."

Ivan raised himself and reached for the water pitcher, but groaned and slumped against the pillows. Sam poured a glass and held it to the old man's lips. Ivan smiled his thanks and said, "She think not important."

"Nevertheless, it is. But that doesn't mean everything I learn will make it into the book. You can trust me."

"I think she tell Father Alexi—confession. After they be friends. Not friend to begin." Exhausted, he closed his eyes.

"Ivan? Ivan?" Sam didn't know what he felt, and wished Alice, a nurse at the Pioneer's home, was working today. All the old pioneers loved her. He was sure Mishkin did, too.

Ivan Mishkin's eyes flew open, and he stared at Sam. "To the grave—I promise." The old man shuddered, his body quivered, and the death rattled sounded deep in his throat. The light faded from his eyes, and he breathed his last.

"The mail is on your desk, Sam. How was Mishkin?"

He tossed his hat toward the rack in the corner and ignored it when he missed and it fell to the floor. Sam shook his head. He wasn't ready to talk about the death he had just witnessed. "What did you learn from my notes?"

"Your handwriting is so bad, you could have been a doctor," Margaret Mary said.

Sam didn't respond to her weak joke. Instead, he rolled a clean sheet of paper into his 1942 Remington typewriter.

"When are you going to get an electric typewriter?"

Sam patted his old Remington. "This baby's been good to me for the last twenty years and will be for many more. I'll not abandon her."

Margaret Mary shrugged. "Fine, live in the past."

Sam unwrapped the cellophane from a fresh cigar. "One of my favorite places. Now, your translation of my notes?"

The Sentinel's aged linotype operator and general dogsbody frowned and dragged herself to Sam's desk, lowering herself into the chair opposite him. She really needed to retire, she thought as she rubbed her swollen ankles. "Sam, do you think Miss Ruth was capable of murder?"

The freshly lit cigar fell from Sam's mouth as he gaped and screeched, "What?"

Margaret Mary looked at the notes again, "As far as I can tell, Ivan witnessed an incident that resulted in a man's death. Apparently, Miss Ruth had a secret loop inside her cowboy boot where she kept a derringer."

Sam scratched his head, "I don't remember writing that? Are you sure?"

Margaret Mary pointed to the sentence. Sam shook his head, puffed on his cigar, and blew smoke toward the ceiling. "I do remember Mishkin talking about gold fields and scallywags, saying Miss Ruth felt guilty."

"Look here, Sam." Margaret Mary pointed to a line, "See, it says—couldn't t be helped—deserved to die."

"That doesn't mean she killed someone," Sam said.

Margaret Mary flipped through several pages in the small notebook. "Here, Mishkin says justified—she had to." She flipped through several more pages. "And here it says—thank God for the gun."

Sam rubbed his forehead and dropped his cigar into the ashtray, where it smoldered, adding its foul odor to the musty smell of newsprint and ink. Margaret Mary quietly reached across the desk, picked up the offensive cigar, and stubbed it out.

Sam typed several sentences, ripped the paper from the machine, wadded it into a ball, and threw it in the trash. "There's not enough here to tell the story."

"Maybe we weren't meant to know."

Sam glared at his long-time employee, the woman who had mothered him for years. "You know me better than that. I will find out."

Margaret Mary sighed and flipped to the last of Sam's scribbles. "Apparently, the last thing Mishkin said was—to the grave, at least, that is what you wrote."

"He said that to me just a few minutes ago." Sam scowled. Ivan had kept his promise and taken Miss Ruth's secret to the grave.

The clatter of silverware and crockery was as comforting to Sam as the culinary aromas coming from the kitchen when he entered the Sitka Café.

"Where's Ade?" he said as he approached the round table and waited.

"You sit," Bill Wall said, imitating Ivan's accent, then added, "Fishing."

"You look troubled, Sam. What's up?" shoreboat pilot Jake Steiner asked.

"Miss Ruth." Sam stirred too much sugar into his coffee and nearly choked when he took a sip. He pushed the offending brew away and signaled Mick to bring him a new cup.

"Your mother has done well. I never thought you'd give up sugar, except for Ma's French crullers, of course," Mick said.

The others at the table laughed. Sam winced; he was a grown man, well into middle age. Everyone in town was aware of Sam's reluctant battle with sugar. His mother had been well-liked by the people of Sitka, and even after her death, she had her allies. The grocer would refused to sell Sam candy bars or soda pop. He was not allowed in the bakery, although the baker grumbled that his income was down severely since losing Sam as a regular. Agrefena was the only person in town who looked the other way. Whenever Sam was in the Café, she set a plate of crullers near him and walked away. What happened when her back was turned was out of her control.

Sam sighed and looked around the Café. Agrefena was in the kitchen, and there were no crullers anywhere. He reached for the sugar once more, but Bill Wall grabbed it and placed it out of reach.

Sam sighed again and said, "About Miss Ruth? I don't want

any of you to get riled up, but do you think she was capable of killing anyone?"

The uproar from everyone in the Café was just what Sam expected. It was several minutes before the men were calm enough for them to ask Sam what he meant. He shared what he had learned from Ivan Mishkin, which wasn't much.

Jake slammed his coffee cup on the saucer, and it rattled, sloshing the hot liquid over the rim.

"I can imagine Ivan saying—Miss Ruth good woman. Almost Russian," Bill said.

"Are we talking murder or self-defense?" Jake asked, "Hypothetically, I mean."

This caused another row. Sam bit the inside of his lip and waited as Agrefena set heaping lunch platters before the men. "The question isn't could she, it's, would she? Back in the day, things were wild and lawless, especially up north." How Agrefena kept tabs on all the conversations in the Café, even while closeted in the kitchen, was a mystery.

It was an awkward and uneasy situation. Miss Ruth had influenced many lives and helped many people. Some thought her a tad too interfering, but all believed her motives were pure.

"I don't care what the situation was, Miss Ruth would not take another person's life," Bill declared.

"What are you talking about?" Ade Bunderson asked as he neared the table.

Heads swirled, and Jake said in Ivan's voice, "You fish."

"I would if there were."

Sam repeated his question about Miss Ruth.

Ade rubbed the stubble on his chin. "I can't say. I really can't say."

Sam's fingers twitched. "You mean you won't say." He patted his pocket, then remembered he had thrown his notepad at Margaret Mary. "C'mon, Ade, give me a fact or two, a clue, something. I know there is a story here."

"Why do you want to go messing around in other people's lives, maybe ruin their good name?" Stormy Durand said as he swung his chair toward the round table. The men shuffled to make room for him. "I believe Alaska has more unsolved murders than all the rest of the states combined."

The others at the table leaned forward. Miss Ruth was a paragon, even more so now that she was no longer among them. What was Stormy hinting at?

Jake reached into his pocket for some change, threw it on the table, and stalked out. "I don't want to hear anything bad about Miss Ruth. Leave it alone, Sam." He growled over his shoulder.

Sam sighed, "Maybe Jake's right. See you later, guys." He gave Stormy a look and jerked his head toward the door. Stormy gave a slight nod and, after a few moments, left the Café. His aging mastiff followed him.

"Anything you want to tell me, Stormy?"

"Anything I might know is pure speculation. Hearsay. Wouldn't stand up in a court of law."

"Just tell me."

Bull, the retired lawman's faithful canine, growled. Stormy spit into the gutter. "Hearsay, Sam. I deal in facts."

Sam scowled and then told Stormy that Ivan Mishkin had passed away. "Word will get around town soon enough. I just didn't want to be the one to tell. You know how it's going to affect the guys."

"Don't blame you, Sam. I'll just mosey over to the Pioneer's home. Mishkin left me in charge of his affairs."

Sam made his way back to his office; he stuffed thoughts about Miss Ruth into his back pocket. He had a paper to get out, but he knew this wasn't over.

It was nearly three months later when Franella Prince burst into the Sentinel's office, "Remember me, Mr. Mitchell?"

"Franella Feddersen, how could I forget?"

"Sounds like you forgot I was married right here in Sitka a few years ago," she grinned.

Sam chewed on his cigar. "Franella Prince doesn't roll off the tongue quite as easy. What can I do for you, and who is your friend?" Sam looked carefully at the short, squat Native of indeterminate age who stood behind the young woman.

"This is Joe Suskin. You wouldn't be able to pronounce his Native name."

Sam held out his hand and indicated the chairs across from his desk. "What can I do for you, Joe?"

"It's what we are going to do for you, Sam. We heard about your conversations with Ivan Mishkin before he died and the ruckus you caused at the Sitka Café when you wondered if Miss Ruth murdered someone."

"Now, Franella, I never said murder."

"The rumors have spawned like the herring. I remember how small towns operate. Joe was born in the interior but started boarding school here in Sitka when he was five. He was taken back to visit his family when he was ten. It was the law at the time."

Sam nodded, "And?"

Joe squirmed in his seat and looked at Franella. She patted the old man's hand.

"My Jacob flew supplies into his village last week, and I went with him. We brought Joe back to Sitka for a medical procedure at Mt. Edgecomb Hospital. When his grandchildren came to say goodbye, he pulled a handful of lemon drops from his pocket." She paused and looked expectantly at Sam, who raised an eyebrow. Franella shook her head and said, "Lemon drops? Miss Ruth?"

Sam slapped his forehead, did some mathematical calculations, and addressed the Native, "She must have taken you home when you were a child."

Franella answered for him. "Joe said it was some time after gold was discovered in Nome. Lots of sourdoughs had left the Klondike and were either sailing down the Yukon or trekking across the Territory. A lawless time."

Sam pushed through several stacks of paper on his desk until he found a blank sheet. He ignored the pages that slid to the floor. His search for a pencil proved fruitless until Franella said, "Tucked behind your ear, Sam."

Sam pulled the pencil from his ear and held it poised above the paper. He turned to the silent Native. "Tell me about it."

The Native looked at Sam without speaking.

"Miss Ruth took Joe and half a dozen other children north. Things did not go as planned," Franella said, and then added, "My Jacob is flying him back to his village this afternoon. Joe is a man of few words, but after I told him what Miss Ruth meant to me and how she helped me find myself, he was willing to talk." Franella reached into her bag and pulled out a sheaf of papers. "He doesn't remember the year nor some of the place names, but the school should have records of dates and routes. Joe says it all became confusing after their guide abandoned them. He remembers being lost in the bush, rogue miners, and a shooting. It's jumbled in his mind, but I wrote it all down."

Sam scratched the back of his neck and sighed. He wished Joe were more forthcoming.

"Joe says Ivan Mishkin was there."

"What?" Sam rubbed his hand over his thinning hair. "I have so many questions."

Franella lowered her voice. "Joe's procedure did not go well. He is going home to die surrounded by his family. He has said all he is going to say."

"But he didn't say a word." Sam shook his head in disgust. "Typical Native."

"Be nice, Sam! You know, they like to speak when they have something important to say. It's their way."

Sam sighed, "I do know that." He glanced at the Native.

Joe responded with a slight nod and said, "Miss Ruth, good woman." He crossed his arms, leaned against the back of the chair, and closed his eyes.

Franella laughed, "Everywhere I go, the Natives like me. Joe says it's because I talk a lot, and they don't have to." Her eyes twinkled, then turned serious. "I tried to think like you, Sam, and asked Joe everything I could think of."

Franella signaled Margaret Mary and asked her to take Joe to the Sitka Café and order him coffee and a cruller. Joe patted Franella's shoulder and shuffled after the linotype operator.

"What time is Jacob taking off? I'm going to scour your notes and give you a list of questions. Do you think you can get Joe to answer them?"

"I'll do my best, but right now his mind is focused on walking into the forest."

Sam shook his head, then asked, "How long will you and Jacob be in Sitka?"

"After taking Joe home, my Jacob will be flying out of Kotzebue for a couple of weeks. I'll stay here with Miss Drake." She pulled a tissue from her jacket pocket. "So many of the old pioneers are passing away. First Miss Ruth, then Mr. Conner, and now Ivan Mishkin."

Sam glanced at Connor's wooden leg propped against his file cabinet and remembered the old man's legacy. He scratched his head and glanced at Franella's notes. "What were Joe's exact words about the murder?"

Franella gasped, "Murder?"

Sam looked chagrined. "Some newspaperman I am. Actually, the word he used was killing."

"He was only ten and said he had been knocked out by an evil man, but he saw everything." She shrugged her shoulders. "It's all so confusing. I'm not sure he's remembering what really happened."

The hairs on the back of Sam's neck stood on end, his face heated, and his hands tingled. There was a story up north, and with Franella's help, he was going to get it.

I would very much like to connect with you here.

Cheryle Coapstick

✉ chercoaps@gmail.com

ⓐ amazon.com/author/cherylecoapstick

🅕 facebook.com/cherylecoapstickauthor

www.ingramcontent.com/pod-product-compliance
Lightning Source LLC
Chambersburg PA
CBHW020016120726
47903CB00004B/1313